A CEREMONY OF DESIRE . . .

"We've got to stop. Darling? Please. Let me go. Let me go, Luis."

She tried to move his hands away, but he grabbed her, holding her wrists with one hand as he moved to kiss her . . . until she moaned beneath him.

He released her hands, but his legs still held her pinned to the mattress. He tore his shirt off, loosened his belt, and pulled at his trousers.

Afraid again, she cried, "You can't. I'm going to marry Andres."

He looked like his Aztec ancestors now with his strong angry masculine face, his piercing eagle-like eyes, his lips pulled back showing the strong white teeth.

"Perhaps you will marry him," he snarled. "But by all that's holy I'll have you first."

The Moon-Kissed

BARBARA FAITH

PUBLISHED BY POCKET BOOKS NEW YORK

A POCKET BOOKS/RICHARD GALLEN *Original*
publication.

POCKET BOOKS, a Simon & Schuster division of
GULF & WESTERN CORPORATION
1230 Avenue of the Americas, New York, N.Y. 10020

ISBN: 0-671-83331-6

First Pocket Books printing January, 1980

10 9 8 7 6 5 4 3 2 1

Trademarks registered in the United States and other countries.

Printed in the U.S.A.

This book is dedicated, with love, to my husband, Alfonso Covarrubias. And to my mother.

—*Barbara Faith de Covarrubias*

Chapter 1

The clang of the trolleys grew fainter when the coachman turned the carriage with the high-stepping horses into the park and started up the steep hill overlooking the city. As they climbed higher they could see the length of the Paseo de la Reforma below them. And it seemed to Sarah Finch that all the lights of Mexico City shone especially for her in honor of her eighteenth birthday.

She loved everything about this city: the tree-lined boulevards, the fountains that sparkled in the sunlight, the fashionable shops, the faces of the people, and the parties.

There'd been parties the whole month of this August of 1910. Days and nights were filled with a procession of gaiety because President Porfirio Diaz wanted to celebrate the achievements of his government. The National Palace, the Opera House, the Cathedral, all of the big public buildings shown in a blaze of lights. Foreign guests were invited to visit Mexico, all expenses paid. The Indians, the peasants, all who showed their poverty, were forbidden the central thoroughfares.

But Sarah saw only the beauty that was Mexico City. And her only thoughts were of her eighteenth birthday and that she would see Andres again.

The thought of him brought a faint smile. She'd been sixteen when she'd last seen him. A tall, gangly, unsure-of-herself sixteen, with a voluminous skirt and a

3

too-wide middy blouse. Twenty-one-year-old Andres had taken one look at her and shuddered. Visibly!

She'd wanted to tear his heart out. Punch him squarely on his aquiline nose. Blacken both his velvety eyes. Pluck out his winged brows. But oh Lord, he was so handsome! She'd have fought anybody who touched one curly hair on his perfect head.

She hugged her father's arm, and when he saw the flush on her face he laughed and said, "I believe you really are excited."

"Excited! I could jump out of the carriage and race the horses up the hill!"

"In that dress?"

"Do you like it?"

"It's beautiful, Sarah. And you're beautiful. So beautiful it makes me a little sad."

"Why, Dad?"

"Because I look at you and I know you're not a little girl any longer. With your hair piled up on your head that way you remind me of your mother, and that makes me proud as hell, but just a little sad. I wish she could see you tonight, see what kind of a young lady you've become."

"It's been four years since she died. You still miss her, don't you?"

"I'll always miss her."

"So will I." She kissed his cheek. "Let me stay in Mexico with you. I've had enough of school."

He shook his head. "You're going back the end of the month. I've seen the way some of these men look at you. I'll be glad when you're safely back in Texas." He chuckled. "But when you are I'll probably worry about those Texas boys. I tell you, Sarah, having a daughter turn eighteen is a worrisome thing for a father."

Her laugh was gay. "This is going to be the best birthday I've ever had. Do you think President Diaz will dance with me?"

"There'll be over three hundred guests tonight. But since you'll be the best-looking woman there, and

4

since I hear that even at eighty the President has an eye for beauty, I'd say your chances were pretty good. But I didn't think it was the President you wanted to impress tonight."

"Didn't you?" Her green eyes crinkled with laughter. "I wonder why I think I can hide things from you, Charlie Finch. You always seem to know what I'm going to do before I do it. When I was a little girl I thought you had eyes in the back of your head. I'd reach for a forbidden object, you'd have your back to me, and suddenly you'd say, 'No, no, Sarah.' That's always been a puzzlement."

"Good! Parents should be a puzzlement to their offspring."

And as the horses struggled to the top of the hill and stopped in front of the magnificent Chapultepec Castle, the castle that had once been the home of the doomed Maximilian and his equally doomed Carlotta, two young men stood in the foyer arguing.

"You promised," Andres Ortiz said.

"No, I didn't. I said I *might* waltz her around the floor once or twice. But I'm not going to be stuck with your Senorita Finch. Your family invited her—not mine."

"Please, I beg you. Take her off my hands, Luis."

Luis Vega. He looked older than his twenty-three years. He was taller than Andres by a good four inches. And while Andres had the pale skin of his Spanish-French ancestors, Vega's coloring and features bore the stamp of rich mixtures of blood. He had the strong masculine face and the piercing eagle-like eyes of his Aztec ancestors. Skin tones, like the matte finish of a Renaissance painting, showed the blend of the Spaniard and the Mexican Indian. His lean body had a look of controlled savagery that the tailor-made clothes and fine Spanish boots didn't quite disguise.

He should never have agreed to help Andres. They hadn't seen each other during the two years Andres had been in France, and he had been in Colorado. Now, as they made their way into the ballroom, Andres said, "There's the President now. Just coming in. He still has the look of a king, doesn't he?"

"And he acts like one," Luis growled. "It's time he stepped down. Time we had an honest election."

"He'll stop being president the day he dies," Andres said. "He'll run for re-election in October."

"And be elected! The same thing for the last thirty years."

"It's been a good thirty years. Look what he's done for Mexico. The new Post Office Building with the most magnificent tiles in the world. Railroads that run the length of Mexico. Electric lights. The new Palace of Fine Arts, made of Italian marble. The glass curtain from Tiffany's cost almost three million pesos."

Luis turned on him furiously. "Three million pesos for a glass curtain—and the people are starving!"

"You sound like one of those revolutionaries. You'd better watch yourself or . . ." He stopped. "Father is signalling us. I think Senor Finch and his tall ugly daughter are about to make an entrance." He took Luis by the arm. "Please, *amigo,* I'll dance with her once, walk her back to her father, and then you take over. Do me this favor and I'll owe you a big one. I've got my eye on the little Gonzales girl and . . . Holy Mother!" he said softly.

Luis followed his gaze to the girl descending the wide marble staircase at the side of an older man. Her skin is as white as the marble, he thought. But as she came closer he knew that wasn't quite true because marble was cold and pale, and this girl was not. The color was high in her cheeks. Even her bare shoulders had a slightly rosy glow to them. Her face held a look of barely suppressed excitement, the full red lips parted, the wide green eyes shining. Her pink lace dress hugged her small waist and fell just to the tip of her pink satin slippers. Small pink blossoms nestled in her copper-penny hair.

6

Beside him Andres whispered, "Forget the favor, Luis. I've decided I'm up to the sacrifice. I'll leave the Gonzales girl to you." He put out his hand and said, "Senor Finch, what a pleasure it is to see you. And Sarah. How nice that you were able to come with your father. Allow me to present my friend, Luis Vega. Mr. Charles Finch and his daughter Sarah."

"Sir." Luis shook the older man's hand. And then he turned to her and saw her extend her pale white hand, and for just the fraction of a second he hesitated.

She saw the hesitation. Then his hand was on hers, hard and firm and male, and she looked up and met his eyes.

"Good evening, señorita," he said. "It is a pleasure to meet you. I hope you and your father will have a pleasant evening."

"Buenas noches, señor. Y gracias. Es un placer conocerle."

"Your Spanish is excellent, señorita," Vega said.

"Thank you. I spoke Spanish before I spoke English."

She looked around her. Dozens of couples were already dancing, the ladies lovely and elegant in their ballgowns and jewels, their hair coifed in the latest Paris style, the men polished and handsome. "Isn't it beautiful?" she continued in Spanish. "This castle, the people, everything."

Andres took her arm. "Come say hello to father. I know he's eager to see both of you. He wants to know how things are farther north, Señor Finch. Are Villa and his boys really stirring up trouble along the border?"

"We hear rumbles," Charlie Finch answered. "More and more peasants going off to join him. A few skirmishes. Last month he held up a train. Took it over and made the passengers get out and walk. Sarah's going back to Texas the end of this month and I have to admit that I'm worried."

"Then let me stay here," she said with a smile.

7

"You're going back to school, young lady. And that's final."

"And if I'm carried off by Pancho Villa?"

"Heaven help him!"

Introductions were made. Old acquaintances renewed. Señor Rafael Ortiz and his thin prim wife, two elderly aunts, Alberto Vega, Luis' father, a tall gray-haired man with the most gentle face Sarah had ever seen. Señor and Señora Gonzales and their daughter Adela, a small shy girl who blushed painfully and looked terrified when Andres said, "Adela, my sweet, Luis wants to dance with you but he's much too shy to ask."

"That poor girl," Sarah said as Andres led her out to the floor. "Why does she look so terrified?"

"She's led a sheltered life. Mexican girls are more protected than you Northamericans. And that is as it should be, *cherie*."

"Cherie?" She smiled. "And how *was* Paris, Andres?"

"Exciting."

"The Sorbonne?"

"Educational."

"The Seine?"

"Wet."

"Notre Dame?"

"Damp."

"Shame on you! Two whole years in Paris and that's all you've got to say?"

"I'd rather talk about you. You've changed, Sarita."

"Have I?"

"You're . . . quite lovely."

He was just as handsome as she remembered. More so, if anything. Quite a man of the world now. Elegant. Foppish. The word came to her suddenly and unexpectedly. She thrust it out of her mind. After all, he'd occupied her thoughts for two whole years. She couldn't dismiss him because a silly word like foppish had popped into her head.

"Has the President arrived?" she said.

"Yes, there he is, dancing with the fat lady with the chins and diamonds."

President Porfirio Diaz. Handsome at eighty with a full head of white hair, a superb moustache, and a broad chest covered with medals.

"He's magnificent," Sarah said, unaware she was staring as Andres danced her closer to the President. And suddenly the old man saw her. He nodded and beamed, and before she realized what she was doing she smiled back and waved. And when Andres whirled her away she laughed and said, "What a charming old man. How can people not love him?"

"Most of them do. Not Luis perhaps, but most of them. But I don't want to talk about Don Porfirio, *querida*, I want to talk about you. I wish you could stay in Mexico. I wish you didn't have to go back to school."

"So do I, Andres, but Father's right. And when I finish he may let me study in Paris."

"Paris! Girls don't study in Paris!"

"European girls do. And some Americans."

"Well, they shouldn't. And neither should you. It's time you found a husband and settled down."

"Settled down! I'm only eighteen!"

"Most Mexican women are married at that age and starting their second baby."

"But I'm not a Mexican woman." Her voice was tart.

But the small flash of anger passed and she gave herself up to the sheer pleasure of the music, and to the hum of life swirling around her. Women sparkling with beauty and jewels. Handsomely dressed men, some in uniform, strong arms leading their ladies in a whirling kaleidoscope of color under the crystal chandeliers. There was a sensuous pleasure in the feel of her own ballgown whirling around as she moved in time to the waltz and the pressure of Andres' gloved fingers against her back. She closed her eyes, savoring the feel of motion around her, and when she opened them she saw Luis Vega.

9

His hand restrained Andres. "The Señorita Gonzales is tired of my clumsiness. She thinks it is time we changed partners."

Poor Adela Gonzales with her sad serious face, turning to Andres with such a look of humility and worship that Sarah wanted to shake her. But she forgot about Adela Gonzales when Luis Vega put his arm around her and swept her away, one hand firm against her back, the other hand holding hers.

Except for one quick glance, she kept her eyes level with his shoulder. She was more aware of his body than any man she'd ever danced with.

"Where do you go back to in Texas?" he said.

"Denton. A college for women."

"Have you been in Mexico City all summer?"

"No, I've been in Torreon. Father's an engineer with the Penoches Mining Company. Andres—his family, rather—invited us to come to Mexico City for the ball."

"And are you enjoying it?"

"Yes, oh yes!" She raised her face, and for the first time since they had started dancing, she looked directly at him. "Today is my birthday," she said.

"And how old are you, Señorita Sarah Finch?"

"Eighteen."

"Eighteen." He reached out and tucked a loose strand of hair behind her ear. The tips of his fingers lingered, traced the shell-pink lobe, and moved lightly to the back of her neck to test the soft tendrils of curls that had escaped. When he said, "Your hair is the color of copper in the sun," his voice sounded strange.

And when his hand moved to capture hers she trembled. "My hair is too long," she said, trying to keep her voice steady. "A lot of the girls at school are getting their hair bobbed. It's quite fashionable and . . ."

"And you must never do it. Never cut your hair."

"But all the girls . . ."

"Ah, but you are not 'all the girls.' You are . . ." His piercing eagle eyes met hers. Held hers.

10

She felt her breath catch in her throat. His eyes did not waver.

"Are you in love with Andres?"

And when she didn't answer, his eyes narrowed. His hand tightened on hers. "Well, are you?"

"That's none of your concern, Senor Vega," she managed to say.

"Good. You're not. Are you staying with his family while you're here?"

"No, we're staying with company friends. The Gaston Solorzanos."

"I think I know them. They live in San Angel, don't they?"

"Yes."

"As I recall, the Solorzanos have a garden."

"Yes they do, but . . ."

"I will meet you there tonight after the ball."

She stopped dancing and stared at him. "What did you say?"

"I will wait for you in the garden. Now dance, people are watching us." And without waiting for a reply he pulled her to him.

She felt a sharp ping of excitement. A small scratch of fear. She knew he was not like the Texas boys she had known. Boys she could flirt with and tease. "A smart girl can handle any boy walking," she often told her friends. And believed what she said. Until now.

She looked quickly up at him, met his look, and lowered her glance. She leaned her body ever so slightly into his and felt the movement of his fingers against her bare shoulders.

"Meet me," he said.

She laughed up at him, more sure of herself now. "Why should I?"

She felt his body tighten. "Don't flutter your eyelashes at me, señorita, or I'll . . ."

"Here is the little pink rose," a voice beside them roared. "The prettiest girl at the ball."

They stopped dancing and she turned to see the President of Mexico and an aide smiling at her.

11

"It is my birthday," he said. "Will you humor an old man by giving him the honor of this dance?"

"It's my birthday too, and I'd be delighted, sir." Her smile was a twinkle of delight as she stepped into his arms. *"Adios,* Senor Vega," she said softly. *"Hasta luego."*

The President was still a strong man, and he moved with strength and grace. The bright medals and ribbons glinted against the bright blue jacket on his broad chest. His shock of white hair and large white moustache were startling against his dark Indian skin.

She felt her hair escaping down her neck as he whirled her around the ballroom floor, turning again and again, faster and yet faster to the music of a polka.

Thoughts ran round and round her head in time with the music. I'm eighteen and I'm dancing with the President of Mexico. And the most exciting man I've ever met is watching me. Faces flashed before her; Andres and Adela, Andres' prim proper mother, frowning disapproval, men who smiled, women who looked envious. And Luis. Luis.

She laughed with pleasure. "I don't know about you, sir," she said to the President, "but this is the best birthday I've ever had."

The house was quiet. Outside, in the patio, she could hear the water running in the green frog fountain. The scent of wisteria and roses, calla lilies and jasmine filled the night, so quiet now after the noisy festivity of the ball. She didn't want morning to come, she wanted this night to go on forever. She wanted to be eighteen forever.

She took a white shawl from the chair and put it over her shoulders. When she stepped outside and found herself alone, she felt a small stab of disappointment. Stepping closer to the fountain, she dipped her slender fingers into the water, feeling the coolness, the wetness, the life of it. And when her eyes became

12

accustomed to the darkness she looked around her, and there, at the edge of the garden, she saw him.

She gathered the shawl closer around her shoulders and moved toward him, her head high to tell herself that she wasn't afraid, that the pulse beating in her throat was nothing, that the sudden prickling on her arms was from the cold.

And when she was close to him, she said, "I came to tell you . . ."

"Be still," he said. He pulled her into his arms and held her quietly. Held her until the pulse beating in her throat quieted, until the chill was replaced by warmth. He kissed her, almost angrily at first. But when she gave a small sound of protest his lips softened and warmed. She answered the warmth, feeling a strangely pleasurable excitement building inside her.

She felt the thud of his heart against her breast, the hardness of his long legs pressing against hers. The hand against her back urged her closer. His other hand was on the back of her head, his fingers searching, finding the pins that restrained her hair, until finally her hair was free, falling loose and soft over her bare shoulders.

He twined his fingers around the copper curls, pressing her face even closer to his. She was caught in so tender a grasp that she could barely move. His lips left hers, traveled to her cheek, down to her slender throat, to her white shoulders, returned to her waiting lips, responded with a sharp intake of breath to her small moan of delight.

When his hand cupped her breast she tried to pull away, but his arm held her while his other hand caressed her, the hot fingers searching, reaching inside the material of her dress to touch her skin, the small peak of nipple. His mouth crushed hers, searching, demanding, and she answered with an aching eagerness.

Abruptly he held her away from him. "Go in the house," he whispered, his voice hoarse with feeling.

13

She looked at him, bottom lip caught between her even white teeth, her green eyes searching his.

"Go in the house!" he said again.

When he reached down and picked up the white shawl and placed it around her shoulders, she saw that his hands were trembling.

"Luis . . . ?" His name was a question on her lips.

"I'll see you after tomorrow. We'll talk then."

"But . . ."

He held her away from him. "I didn't say 'Happy Birthday,' did I?" He leaned down and kissed her on the cheek. "Happy birthday, my dear Señorita Finch. My very dear Señorita Finch."

Then he turned her around and gently gave her a little shove toward the house.

Chapter 2

A half smile touched her lips all the next day. Bemused, she thought, that's what I am. Bemused, beguiled, bewitched. Dazed, delighted, delirious. Surely no other girl—woman—has ever felt quite what I feel. For surely no other man is quite as wonderful as Luis.

She thought again of the way he had kissed her, of the touch of his fingers against her breasts. And suddenly, from out of the past, she remembered Mrs. Zambeck and Mrs. Baumgartner and that last summer before her mother died, the summer that she turned fourteen. The two ladies had come to visit her mother, and Sarah had thought to surprise them with lemonade. As she silently approached the wide front porch she heard Mrs. Zambeck sigh and say, "Well, it's Saturday, and I guess you know what that means."

Another sigh. Was it Mrs. Zambeck or Mrs. Baumgartner?

"I steel myself all day Saturday, just worrying about what the night will bring."

"It's your duty, my dear," Mrs. Baumgartner said.

Sarah's mother cleared her throat and said, "Ah . . . ladies . . ."

"Do you know that when we were first married Arthur tried to put his hand on my breast whenever we had . . ." Mrs. Baumgartner's voice was hushed so low that Sarah had to strain to hear the word . . . *"relations.* But I soon set him straight. I told him that no decent woman allowed a man to touch her there.

15

And besides, Mama always told me that's how women get cancer."

"The thing to do," Mrs. Zambeck said, "is to try to think of other things while it's happening. I recite Bible verses in my head, or plan the next day's menu—anything to take my mind off it."

Sarah had quietly withdrawn to the kitchen, where she thoughtfully drank all three glasses of lemonade.

Poor Mrs. Zambeck, poor Mrs. Baumgartner, she thought now. Had they never felt the way she had felt last night?

At breakfast the next morning her father said, "Was the party everything you expected?"

"More than I expected. I had a lovely time."

"And was Andres?"

"Was Andres what?"

"All that you expected."

"I'm not sure I know what you mean," she said carefully. He looked stern and she couldn't imagine why. If he'd seen her go down to the garden last night . . . But what did Andres have to do with it?

"You've mooned over him for two years. I've got to admit he's a good-looking fellow, but . . ." He shook his head. "It's not up to me, of course, but I have to tell you that I'm not all that crazy about him." He put his coffee cup down carefully. "Damn it all, I suppose what I want to know is whether or not you think you're in love with him."

"Oh. Well, no, I don't think I'm in love with him."

His sigh was audible. "All right. We won't talk about it, then." He pushed his chair back from the table. "The Vegas have invited us to a fiesta at their ranch tomorrow. That all right with you?"

She looked down at her plate, barely able to suppress a smile.

"I liked the old gentleman. Didn't think there were any more of his caliber around. He has two sons, you know. Luis, and a younger boy, a seminary student. Luis has had an offer of a job in El Paso. Working for a mining company. Be going back about the same time

16

you are. Might even ask him to accompany you as far as the border if it's all right with you."

"It would be all right with me if . . . if you'd feel better about it." She came over and kissed the top of his head. "Is it all right if I ask the Señora Solorzano to go shopping with me? I'd like to buy something new for the fiesta."

"Want to impress Andres, I suppose?" His look was dour.

"Not especially." She started for the stairs. "Dad, whatever happened to Mrs. Zambeck and Mrs. Baumgartner?"

"Mrs. Zambeck and Mrs. . . . . Good Lord, what made you think of them?"

"I don't know. I just suddenly thought of them last night."

"Couple of old harridans. Your mother couldn't stand them and neither could I. Old John Zambeck finally ran off with a widow from Dallas. Al Baumgartner blew his brains out. Guess each of them escaped the best way he could." His look was puzzled. "Can't imagine what made you think of them."

"Neither can I," she said. "Neither can I."

The hacienda of the Alberto Vega family was a two-hour drive from Mexico City on the Pachuca road. Sarah sat in the back seat of the Reo touring car with Señora Solorzano and Señora Ortiz. Andres sat on the jump seat facing them, talking about Paris, the students, and which student came from which wealthy European or Mexican family.

"I miss Paris," he said, "but Mexico City is pleasant too. We have our aristocracy just as Europe does. It's going to be an exciting winter, Sarita. The elections are in October. There will be celebration balls. I'd love to escort you to them. I wish you'd stay. I wish you wouldn't go back to Texas."

Charlie Finch turned from his seat next to the driver and glared at the back of Andres' neck.

"I am sure Señor Finch knows what is best for his daughter," Andres' slim prim mother said. "You have your military career to think of. You must pay more attention to it and less to parties." She turned her face to Sarah. "Andres has entered the Colegio Militar, you know, and he has already received a lieutenant's commission."

"Really?" Sarah murmured. "How nice."

It was eleven o'clock when they finally turned off the main road. On either side, beyond tall poplar trees, the corn was ready-for-picking high. And beyond the corn were golden fields of wheat ready for harvest.

Sarah smoothed the skirt of the pale green muslin dress, and noticed with a touch of surprise that her hands were shaking.

As they approached the wide entrance gates they could hear the music of the *mariachis*. They had scarcely alighted from the car when Don Alberto Vega and his wife, Doña Maria, rushed to meet them, crying, *"Bienvenidos, bienvenidos a su casa,* welcome to your house."

Sarah had heard this warm Mexican greeting many times. No matter how humble or how grand the dwelling might be, the guest was always greeted by these words.

Señora Vega had not attended the President's Ball, and now, when Sarah was introduced, she knew where Luis had gotten his strong face. The señora was a handsome woman in her early fifties. Her bearing was proud, but she greeted Sarah and the others with a warmth that belied the first appearance of austerity.

"Luis and Carlos are with the other guests," she told them. And to Sarah she said, "You have not met my other son. He is a student in the seminary in Monterrey. We wanted our firstborn, Luis, to become a priest, but alas, he did not have the calling."

Alas indeed, Sarah thought to herself.

Inside, the house was cool. The rooms were large and light and beautifully furnished in warm earth

18

tones. The floor tiles shone from the morning's scrubbing. Bowls of orange sunflowers added splashes of color. It was a house made comfortable by loving hands. This is where he lives, Sarah thought. This is where Luis lives.

When she was in the bedroom that Maria Vega had shown the ladies to, she splashed cold water on her face and when the others weren't looking, pinched her cheeks until they were rosy. She brushed her copper hair until it shone, and re-tied it with the wide green ribbon. And finally she went with the others to join the fiesta.

Colored paper was hung all across the wide patio, with lights and lanterns everywhere so that the fiesta could continue far into the night. A group of *mariachis* played, a few couples danced, others chatted in groups of three or four. The smell of barbecuing beef and pork filled the air.

Andres appeared beside her and put his arm around her waist. She tried to ease away from him, her eyes searching the guests. And then she saw him. A small dark girl had hold of his arm, talking with great animation, smiling up at him. And suddenly, as though he knew Sarah was watching him, he turned and saw her. Their eyes met and held. She barely heard Andres when he said, "You must meet Carlos," and led her to a young man dressed in Franciscan robes. "Carlos, my dear boy, how are you? Allow me to present Señorita Sarah Finch."

"I am happy to meet you, señorita." He was a little older than she was, twenty perhaps, with the same gentle face as his father. "It is a pleasure for my family to have you visit us here."

"And for me to be here."

"We hope you will come often. But I understand you will be leaving for Texas soon?"

"In two weeks."

"Ah." His face was thoughtful. "I believe Luis will be going to Texas then also. It would be nice if you

19

could make the trip together." His eyes were merry.

"I hardly think Sarah's father would approve of her traveling with Luis," Andres said.

"I don't think father would object, Andres," she put in sweetly. "However, I wouldn't think of inconveniencing Luis."

He detached himself from the small dark girl and moved across the patio in their direction, looking handsome in his *traje corto,* the tight corded pants, short jacket, and white ruffled shirt.

"Andres, would you be an angel and get me a glass of wine?" Sarah said.

"Of course, my dear."

And as he turned away Carlos lowered his voice and said, "A neat move, señorita."

She smiled prettily. "Why, whatever do you mean?"

"I too will disappear," he said. "But if you need help with that brother of mine I am in shouting distance."

"I heard that," Luis said. "What makes you think the señorita will be in need of help?"

"I saw the way you looked at her from across the room."

"Dear brother, unless you take to your heels in this second, I will throttle you."

Carlos laughed. "I'm going. I'm going. I will see you later, señorita. And remember, I am here if you need me."

"Go!" Luis said, his face mock serious.

And when they were alone he said, *"Buenas tardes,* señorita."

"Buenas tardes, señor."

He bowed formally, took her hand and said, "Welcome to your house." He lowered his voice. "I did not sleep last night. All I could think about was that today I would see you. You know what's happening to us, don't you?"

Her eyes met his. "Is it all right if I'm just the least little bit frightened?"

His face softened. But before he could answer

20

Andres was beside him. And with him was the small dark girl. "You were going to dance with me," she said to Luis. "Instead here you are with someone else. I know you must welcome your . . ." She hesitated just a fraction of a second before she said . . . "foreign guests, Luis, but . . ."

He scowled at the girl and said, "Rosa, this is Señorita Finch from Texas."

"Ah yes, she is with Andres, isn't she?"

"I am with my father," Sarah answered. "And if you will excuse me I must go find him."

She danced with Andres, and with other young men whose names were Raoul and Manolo and José and Manuel and Roberto and Pepe and Paco and Ignacio. She laughed at their jokes, listened to their lies, and lied in return. And all the while she thought Luis . . . Luis . . . Luis.

It was just after lunch when the trouble started. They had been served the rich cinnamon-flavored coffee when someone said, "So Andres, you are going to join the Federal Army."

"I have already joined," he said. "There's a great future in the military if you have the right connections. And of course I believe in what I'm doing. President Diaz is the greatest president we've ever had, greater even than Juarez."

"Don't be a fool, Andres," Luis said. "He's a barbarian."

"But a great barbarian, my friend. He keeps our country at peace. Heads of state visit us. We are once again on friendly terms with the United States. Every country in the world looks up to Diaz."

"And why shouldn't they?" Luis voice was bitter. "He's given away one-fifth of Mexico to foreign investors. And as if that wasn't enough he opened the remaining Indian lands and gave them to land sharks for seizure and settlement. When the Mayas and the Yaquis objected, the army and Rurales put them down, took them prisoners, and sold thousands of them into slave gangs in Yucatan."

"That's exactly what he should have done. Those Indians are animals, *mano*. What right had they to speak out against a man like Diaz? The President needed foreign investors. Without them we probably couldn't have opened the old Spanish mines. You talk as though Diaz was a despot. And he isn't. There's the legislature. They . . ."

"And do you know what people call them?" Vega's face was white. " *'Mi caballada,'* my herd of tame horses. You know damn well the elections are a farce. All of the offices are filled with his men. The election this October won't be any different."

"Luis, *por favor*, remember Andres is our guest." His father's voice, like his face, was gentle.

"I am sorry, father, but these things must be said. I don't know how long any of us can continue to turn our backs on the truth. How long must we stand by and see children go hungry, and their fathers thrown into prison when they speak up or ask for better wages? The Belen Penitentiary is filled with such men, and with writers, speakers, anyone who disagrees with Diaz."

"Some unfortunate things always take place when there is progress," Andres said smoothly. "On the good side, Luis, you must admit that Mexico City has been cleaned up and modernized. We have electric lights, streetcars, and buildings to rival the finest in Europe. Railroads cross the length of the country."

"Railroads! I would rather see food in hungry bellies than all the railroads in the world."

Andres leaned back in his chair. "This is strange talk from you, *amigo*. You and your family live like kings on this hacienda." He chuckled. "And you prefer to spend most of your time in the United States."

Luis flushed and bit his lip.

"If you think as you say, you would be off with that crazy peon, Emiliano Zapata, or that bandit Villa," Andres said.

"Zapata tries only to restore the land to the Indians. I don't know about Villa, perhaps he is a bandit. But

22

perhaps, just perhaps, he and Zapata are true patriots.''

Andres' face went white with anger. "Be careful what you say. I am a Federal officer and I do not like to hear these things." His smile was thin, his voice soft. "If you keep this up I may one day have to kill you."

"Kill me?" Luis laughed. "A blue-nosed popinjay like you? And who would furnish you with the courage?"

"Luis!" His father's voice was firm. "Andres is your friend and our guest. I will not have you speak like this. Apologize to Andres. And then perhaps you'd be so kind as to show Señorita Sarah around the hacienda."

"Of course, father." He offered his hand to Andres. "I am sorry," he said. "I should not have spoken so—at this time."

When they were out of earshot Sarah said, somewhat cautiously, "Why did you get so angry? Andres was partly right. Don Porfirio has done wonderful things for Mexico."

"If you tell me that he brought trolley cars to Mexico I'll shake you."

"No, I'm not going to tell you that." She suppressed a smile. "But I am going to tell you that friends shouldn't quarrel over politics."

"This is more than politics, Sarah. People really are starving. Land has been stolen. Children are denied education and medical care."

"I know, Luis, but . . ."

"No, you don't, Sarah. Carlos told me that this summer over five hundred babies died of dehydration in Monterrey. Hundreds more died of malnutrition. And that's just in Monterrey. And Andres talks of electric lights and railroads. But he was right about one thing—I'm not doing anything about it. I live on the other side of the border."

"El Paso?"

"Yes. I'm an engineer for a mining company. I'll

23

work there two years and then I'll be transferred to the Valenciana mine in Guanajuato. You're where? In Denton?"

She nodded. "I think father is going to ask a favor of you."

"What kind of favor?"

"He's going to ask you if you'll escort me to the border. I think he's afraid Villa will make off with me."

"And so I am to protect you from Villa?"

"Something like that."

"And who is to protect you from me?"

"I don't think he's thought about that."

"Have you?"

"Yes."

"And what did you think?"

"That I wasn't sure I wanted to be protected."

"Be careful, Señorita Finch," his voice mocked. "Be careful of what you say." He touched her hair briefly. "Come," he said, "let me show you the bulls."

Twilight had settled in to soften the heat of the day as they wandered slowly down the tree-lined path. They crested a small hill and then she saw them, big and black and beautiful and dangerous.

"Our brave bulls," Luis said. "We raise them for bullrings in Mexico and South America. My father loves them. He's proud of their blood. Last year when we needed money Andres' father offered him a fortune for the bulls, but he refused. He said we'd manage, and we did of course. His bulls, his family, his home, these are my father's life."

"He's such a gentle-looking man."

"He is as he looks. And so is Carlos."

"But you are not."

"No, I am not."

She could feel the strange excitement building in her as they turned away from the fences surrounding the pastures. He took her hand and led her under the cottonwood trees.

"You said this morning that you were afraid. Are you still?"

She could feel the thudding of her heart. "No," she lied, "I'm not afraid."

He reached out and untied the ribbon that held her hair back from her face. He put his hands on her hair, running his fingers through the thickness of it. When he looked at her his fingers tightened, forcing her face to his, and he kissed her with deliberate slowness. His lips parted and moved on hers, drawing a response that was as hungry, as eager as his own.

She stood on tiptoe, leaning her body into his, loving the feel of the whole hard length of him against her slender body.

When at last she felt the grip of his hands on her waist, and felt herself being pulled away from him, her lips felt bruised and tingling with life.

"Perhaps we should go back," he said.

A part of her was relieved, a part disappointed. She felt a strange sad yearning, a trembling on the edge of some unknown wonder. How could she feel these extraordinary new emotions with this man she'd just met? How was it that he only need look at her, as he was doing now, to start the quiver of feeling deep within her? It was all too new, and she was afraid because she didn't understand what was happening to her.

"I don't want to do anything to hurt you," he said. "You're so young, so . . ." And then his arms were around her again, pressing her close to him. One hand reaching, loosening the bow at the front of the green dress, searching against the coolness of her flesh.

Her hand, raised in a brief struggle, tried not too hard to pull his hand away. Surrendered and was lost, beyond thinking, only feeling, feeling. His mouth on hers, his hands on her breasts, hip touching hip, closer and still closer, melting into warmth.

He held her away from him, the breath coming fast in his throat, his eyes narrowed, his hands hurting her shoulders. "You are a guest in my father's house,"

25

he said at last. "You and your father. I know what I must not do, what I cannot do. I am the man, it is my responsibility." His fingers marked the delicate white flesh of her shoulders. "But you must help me, Sarah. You must not look at me with those great green eyes of yours."

He released her, turned abruptly, and started back toward the hacienda.

When it grew dark, torches and lanterns were lighted and the party became even more festive. Bright Mexican skirts swirled away from shapely legs, and dark-eyed señoritas, their long silver earrings catching fire from the torches, their hair shining black, spun round and round the patio in the arms of their escorts. And the parents, their eagle-eyes dulled by the wine, watched from tables surrounding the patio.

Sarah was a popular partner, but with Luis cutting in each time she danced with someone else, the other men left them alone.

Unlike the President's Ball, where the music was all European, tonight it was pure Mexican. The rhythm was gay, fast, exciting, like the country itself.

She looked up at Luis, at his face, bronzed by the glow of the torches. I'm falling in love with him, she thought. And it's more than wanting him to touch me. It's as though I'm complete now. The me that is me all comes together when I'm with him. I don't know what will happen between us, but I don't believe I will ever find this feeling of belonging with any other man that I have when I am with him.

She looked up and met his eyes.

"What were you thinking just then?" he asked.

She felt a small catch in her throat. Felt her lips tremble when she tried to speak.

"Tell me," he said again.

"I thought . . . that I have never felt this . . . this sense of belonging that I know with you."

She saw the slow jump of muscle in his cheek, felt the sudden pressure of his arms. Then he took her hand and led her away from the dance floor.

26

"My mother is going to invite you and your father to be our guests next weekend," he said when they were safely behind one of the arches of the terrace. "Will you come?"

"Of course."

"And you will allow me to call on you this week?"

"Yes."

"We should get back to the others now."

"I know." She ached to touch him.

"Sarah . . ." With a groan he pulled her into his arms. "Sarah," he said again as she raised her lips for his kiss.

Suddenly she was thrust away from him, shoved roughly against the stone arch. In the shock of the moment she saw Luis, blood streaming from his mouth, while Andres circled him.

"You son-of-a-bitch!" Andres spat. "Sneaking behind my back. Stealing my girl."

"She's not your girl, Andres." Luis' voice was deadly calm. "She never was your girl."

"Bastard!" He struck out again, but this time Luis was ready for him. He side-stepped and hit a glancing blow to Andres' chin. "I don't want to fight you," he said.

"Coward! Coward and traitor." This time his fist landed on the side of Luis' head.

"Stop!" Sarah cried. "Please stop!"

Andres circled him, and then they were locked together, raining blows on each other. Blood came from Andres' nose. The cut on Luis' mouth was open. And at last Luis pushed Andres away, planted his feet firmly on the ground, and came up with a blow that sent Andres sprawling.

A woman screamed. Someone said, "My God, what's going on?"

Luis' father, his face concerned and angry, put a restraining hand on Luis. Carlos rushed forward to say, "_¿Qué pasó, mano?_"

Andres got to his feet, his face white and drawn with rage. When he lunged at Luis, Carlos stepped

27

between them. "Easy," he said, "easy, This is no way for friends to act."

"Friends!" Andres spat the word.

"I'm sorry about this," Luis said. "But what is between Sarah and me has nothing to do with you, Andres. Or with our friendship."

"Our friendship! Be assured, Luis, there is no friendship. It's a good thing you're going back to Texas. It would be dangerous for you here. Go soon, Luis, but before you go be careful where you walk. And when you return be careful." His lips curled. "Or perhaps you should not return. You express words of treason, and I'm a Federal officer. As you said, the Belen Penitentiary is filled with men—men who, like you, express traitorous thoughts." His voice dropped to a hiss. "Be cautious, Luis. I warn you, be cautious."

Chapter 3

The next morning her father confronted her. "I don't like what happened last night," he said. "Two men scrapping over you. You've led Andres on, let him believe you cared for him, and then you sneak off with Luis."

"I haven't led Andres on," she protested. "You've been with me both times I've seen him."

"Have I?" His voice was ironic.

"Of course you have. The night of the ball and yesterday . . ."

"And what about after the ball when you met him in the garden?"

She tried to keep her voice light. "So you really do have eyes in the back of your head."

"This is no time to joke, Sarah. I don't like any of this. Playing two friends against each other and clasping your hands in girlish glee while they try to pound each other senseless."

"Listen to me," she said, her hands on her hips facing him. "Just listen for a minute. It wasn't Andres in the garden the other night. It was Luis. I'm sorry you're upset, but after all, I'm eighteen. I could hardly go to you and ask permission to go outside." She paused for breath. "And last night at the party . . ." Her face flushed. "I'm sorry there was such a commotion. But Luis and I . . ."

"Luis and you what?"

"We're . . . very drawn to each other. I know you're

29

going to say it's foolish, that I've only known him a few days, but I think I'm in love with him."

He stared at her, swallowed painfully, and sat down.

"You're too young," he said at last.

"A year younger than mother was when you married her."

He bit his lip. She looked so young, so vulnerable. And damn it, she knew so little of life. And part of that was his fault. He should never have sent her to live with Clara after her mother died. Sarah had cried and pleaded to be allowed to stay with him in Mexico. She hated the coldness, the austerity of her aunt's house. She was chilled by the waspish spinster lady after the warmth and love of her mother. But he'd sent her away, sure at the time he was doing what was best for her.

The three years she'd spent in San Antonio were lonely years for both of them, but he stood firm in his decision that she live with Clara until she entered college.

He looked at her now. standing before him, her copper hair spilling over her shoulders, looking exactly the way her mother, his dear Ann, had looked at eighteen. "I'm in love," she had said. He remembered the way he'd felt, the wonderful-terrible hungers that Ann had stirred in him. Now here was Ann's daughter. His daughter. And he was afraid.

Luis came that afternoon. They were having tea with the Solorzanos when their maid announced, "Señor Luis Vega is here."

Sarah pushed her chair back and got to her feet.

"No, señorita," the maid said. "It is your father he has come to see."

So she sat, trying to drink her tea, trying to chat with the Solorzanos while her father went to speak to Luis. And finally the maid returned and said, "Your father would like you to join him in the library."

Their faces were serious. *"Buenos días,"* Luis said, his voice formal.

30

"Buenos días, Luis."

Her father cleared his throat. "Luis has explained about last night. And he has apologized."

She darted a glance at Luis. He did not look at her.

"He has also spoken to me about his feelings for you."

Her mouth went dry. Her heart skipped six beats.

"He realizes that you're too young to consider marriage. He also realizes there's a difference in your two cultures that could create a problem."

"But . . ."

"I haven't finished, Sarah. I have serious misgivings about a marriage between two people of different nationalities. I won't give my permission for any such alliance without a lot of thought. I have nothing personal against Luis, but my first concern is for you. Luis may visit you at school and at Clara's, but I won't countenance any talk of marriage now. Is that clear?"

"It's clear that you're treating me like a child," she said angrily. "I'm old enough to make my own decisions."

"No, you're not!" His face was stern. "If you and Luis do feel deeply about each other, it will keep. We'll talk about this next summer and if you still feel the same I'll give you my blessings." He turned to Luis and extended his hand. "Is that agreeable?"

"Perfectly agreeable, sir," Luis said, shaking Charlie Finch's hand.

They looked at each other for a long moment when her father left the room. "Do you mind that I spoke to him?" Luis said. "If you do not want . . ."

"Of course I want. But he's wrong about there being any 'cultural differences.' I've lived in Latin countries most of my life. And besides, if two people love . . ." She stopped. Color pinked her cheeks.

"Two people love." He took her in his arms. "Two people love, my little Sarita."

*　　*　　*

31

She and her father spent the next weekend with the Vega family. And because it was the first time Luis had ever brought a young lady to the hacienda, they suspected he might be serious about her. If they had misgivings, they did not express them. His mother and father were kind, but reserved. His brother was obviously delighted.

The following weekend Charlie Finch took Sarah and Luis to the train, and tried to keep his face cheerful when he helped Sarah aboard and shook hands with Luis.

"Perhaps you'll be able to join us in San Antonio for Christmas," he said.

"I'd like that."

"There hasn't been any trouble with the railroads in a month or so. I reckon Villa and his boys are busy somewhere else. But you never know. I'm glad you're with Sarah."

"What do you think of Villa, Señor Finch? Do you think he's a traitor?"

"A bandit perhaps. But no, I don't think he's a traitor. I listened to you and Andres the other day and I agreed with you. Long past time for Don Porfirio to step down and let somebody else run things. Time for an honest election. My sympathies are with both Zapata and Villa. If I were a younger man I might even join 'em."

" 'Board!"

Luis put his hand out. "It's always a temptation for a man, isn't it?"

"A temptation, not a reality. You'd better get aboard. You take care of my girl, you hear?"

"I will, sir."

"And Sarah, write as soon as you get to school."

"I will, Dad." She blew a kiss down to him.

It was strange to be alone with Luis. Alone, but not alone. Side by side on the green plush seats, watching the miles go by. It would be a long trip to Laredo, three days and two nights. Plenty of time to talk, to make plans.

32

"What were you planning to do after you finish school?" he asked her.

"I wanted to teach. But I know I won't be able to when we're married. I know how most men feel about their wives working." She smiled at him. "Especially Mexican men."

His face was thoughtful. "I think whether or not you teach will be up to you, Sarah. The children in my country need thousands of teachers. If you decide to teach I would not stop you because I know you are needed. Over half the population can't read or write. I see a boy tending sheep and I think, what chance will he have? And I know what the answer is. He has no chance at all. He will do nothing more with his life when he is forty than he is doing at this moment. That is the injustice, Sarah, that is the sadness and the waste of Mexico under Diaz."

By noon it was so hot in the car that they had to open the windows. And when they did, cinders from the track, ashes from the boiler, and clouds of dust blew in on them. They ate part of the lunch that Luis' mother had prepared for them. "Don't eat those barbaric things they sell in the stations," she warned. "Heaven knows what they're made of." She'd prepared enough food to last them until they reached Texas.

The air cooled when the sun went down and they closed the window. When darkness came and the gas lamps were turned lower and the other passengers prepared to sleep, they drew closer. Her head was on Luis' shoulder, his arm around her, their hands clasped.

"I wish this night would last a long time," he said.

"So do I." It seemed impossible that she had known him only two weeks, that her life could have changed so drastically in that short time. I know where I'm going, she thought. My life has a plan. In two years I'll be through school and then, no matter what anyone says, we'll be married. I'll teach for a while and then I'll have three children: Luis, named after him; Charlie, after father; and Ann Maria, after both mothers. She smiled in the near dark.

When the train stopped the next morning they were able to have a breakfast of eggs and hot coffee in the station restaurant. They were more at ease with each other this morning. They talked with the other passengers, tried to ignore the man in front of them who drank too much, and the whispered pleas of his wife. When a tired-looking woman on the other side of the aisle tried to control a noisy three-year-old and care for a baby at the same time, Luis called to the little boy to join them, and spent an hour or two amusing the child.

In the late afternoon they saw the riders. "Cowboys," Sarah said. "They look like they're in a terrible hurry."

"Too much of a hurry," Luis said.

"Then what . . . ?" But the shrill blast of the train whistle drowned out her words.

The horsemen drew closer. More than a hundred of them.

"Get down!" Luis ordered.

"But what is it?"

The first shot broke the window in front of them as he shoved her roughly to the floor.

The blast of the train whistle was drowned out by the screaming passengers, the ping of bullets, the shouts, the muttered oaths, the cries of children. Across the aisle Sarah saw the three-year-old clinging to his mother in terror, almost tearing the baby from her arms as he tried frantically to climb onto her lap.

Sarah got to her knees and reached across the aisle. "Give me the baby," she cried.

The woman, her face white with fear, managed to hold her terrified son while she handed the baby to Sarah. "What's happening? What's happening?"

"I don't know. Get down. Make the boy stay down."

The men inside the train were shooting now. And
34

Sarah, clutching the crying baby to her, was shocked to see Luis pull a revolver from his waistband and shoot through the broken window.

It's Villa, she thought. It has to be him. She pressed the infant to her shoulder, and dared a glance when it seemed as though the noise of the horses' hoofs were inside the car. She was terrified to see some of the bandits swinging themselves onto the platform at the rear of the car. She heard the squeal of brakes as the train screeched to a jarring stop.

The cries grew louder. She hugged the baby to her, whispering, "Shhh, shhh, don't cry. Please don't cry."

The shooting stopped. Men shouted. Slowly she raised herself to her seat, to see Luis, white-faced beside her, putting his gun away. The door at the head of the car opened and men poured through it. "Stay where you are," they threatened. "If you move you are dead."

They started slowly up the aisle. "Your wallets," a fat man shouted. "Pull them out slowly. You move too fast and we take them out of your pockets ourselves as we speed you to hell. And you ladies, if you will be so kind, we are collecting jewelry. Old jewelry, new jewelry. We will be happy with whatever you have. And do not be sad, it is all for a good cause."

A large man with a round stomach, a Texas hat, and a bushy moustache shoved his way to the front of the men making their way down the aisle. "As my man told you," he said, "your money and your jewels will be put to a good use. We do not fight for ourselves, we fight for you—all of you."

"It's that son-of-a-bitch Villa," the man ahead of them muttered.

His wife put her hand on his arm. "Shhh," she whispered.

"Evil bastard," he snarled, shoving her hand away. "Time somebody . . ." He reached inside his coat, his arm came up. Sarah heard him say, "Say your prayers, you son-of-a . . ."

Luis jumped forward and knocked the man's arm up just as the gun exploded.

Villa had not moved. He slowly raised his hand and took his hat off. He looked at the bullet hole, put his finger through it, whistled softly, and replaced the hat. Then, in three strides he came up the aisle, grabbed the man by his neck, and hurled him to his own men. "Take care of this *cabrón*," he ordered.

He turned to Luis, looked him up and down and said, "What is your name?"

"Vega. Luis Vega."

Villa put his hand out. "Thank you, Luis Vega. That *pendejo* would have killed me. If you had not stopped him I would be wearing a hole in my forehead instead of in my hat. But why did you stop him, señor? Do you believe in the revolution?"

"I'm not sure. I suppose I do, Señor Villa, or I would have let him shoot you."

Villa laughed and scratched his broad belly. "When you are sure, señor, I will be glad to have you join me. My army grows every day and I need brave young men like you. Where are you going now?"

"To Texas, señor."

"And this is your wife and child?"

Luis shook his head. "The child belongs to the woman across the aisle. I am escorting this young lady back to school in Texas."

"This is a schoolgirl?" His belly shook with his laughter. "Do you not have eyes in your head, *hombre?* This is no schoolgirl. This is a ripe peach ready to be picked."

Sarah's indrawn breath sounded a soft protest. Luis cautioned her with his hand.

"If you decide to join me," Villa continued, "you will find me in Chihuahua City. You tell somebody you are the man from the train and that I said they were to take you to me. You have saved my life and I thank you. I do not forget such things." His smile flicked to Sarah. "And you, young lady, you may come with him. We can always use *soldaderas,* women soldiers. If you decide . . ."

"Don't hold your breath until I do," she said, her voice as cold as ice.

"Ay, Vega, be cautious. This girl will lead you a merry chase. She is angry now, and she will be angrier still when I tell you that I must ask all of you to get off the train. It is being confiscated by the Army of the Revolution."

The muttered protests were ignored as the men, women, and children quickly gathered their luggage and made their way down the aisle. Luis carried his suitcase, Sarah's large carpetbag, and the basket of food. She carried the baby and a smaller bag.

When they were all off the train she glanced to the front and saw the engineer, pale and frightened, a gun to his head, and heard him quaver, " 'Board!" Then the train moved and the grinning members of Villa's army waved to them. This time from inside the train.

Chapter 4

The grumbling stopped after the first hour, and the passengers saved their energies for walking. Men who wore suit jackets shed them. A few fortunate women who carried parasols opened them and were shaded from the hot afternoon sun. Younger boys walked the railroad tracks or skipped ahead on the ties. Husbands swore under their breaths and growled, "I told you not to pack so much." Farmers, both men and women, hefted sacks over their shoulders and walked on in stolid acceptance.

"We'll get to a village before too long," the conductor said. "All we have to do is follow the railroad track until help comes. Please do not worry, the railroad will take care of us."

"Take care of us!" someone said. "You call this taking care of us?"

The wife of the man who had been taken away by Villa's men cried for a long time. But after a while she stopped crying and said to Sarah, "Let me carry the baby."

When Sarah handed the baby over, she set her bag down and rested for a moment. "I can take the food now," she said to Luis.

She'd had little to say to him since they'd left the train. His exchange with Villa puzzled and frightened her. Pancho Villa, the legendary bandit who rustled, burned, plundered, robbed, and raped, had asked Luis to join him.

He'd been preoccupied ever since they'd left the train, his mouth drawn into a thin line, his brows together, silent and uncommunicative. And that frightened her because he'd closed himself into a tight little world that, for the moment at least, she couldn't enter. She remembered his disagreement with Andres the day of the fiesta, the angry words he'd spoken in defense of the revolution. And she remembered the expression on his face when Andres said, "If you think as you say, you would be off with that bandit Villa."

She wanted to reach out to him, to turn his thoughts away from Villa. She put her hand on his arm, holding him back. "Luis . . ."

"What?" His eyebrows came together in a frown. Then, as he looked at her, his face softened and he said, "Are you tired?"

"No, I'm all right. You've been so quiet since we left the train that I . . ." She searched his face. "It's Villa, isn't it?"

"Perhaps." He tried to smile. "Are you sorry I didn't let that man shoot him?"

She shook her head. "No, but . . . I think it's just as well you're going back to El Paso." She tried to smile. "I'm afraid you're getting some silly romantic notion . . ."

The expression on his face stopped her. A small knot of fear tightened as his eyes met hers and looked away.

"We gotta rest," a man said. "The women can't go on like this and neither can we."

For as far as they could see there were endless miles of tracks, telegraph poles, cactus and mesquite. Purple-shadowed mountains huddled in the background, but there was no sign of a town or a village.

"We'll stop soon," the conductor said, "and make camp for the night."

"Out here?" a woman cried. "On the desert?"

"I'm afraid we have no choice, señora. But don't worry, help is sure to come by morning. When the

39

train does not arrive at Monterrey the company will send a rescue party."

"But all night?" another woman wailed.

"How come that bastard had to steal the damn train right out from under us?" a grizzled Texan said. "Rode them damn horses right onto the train. What the hell they want with a train anyway?"

"Sometimes they live in them," Luis said. "They make a livable as well as movable home, for them and their women."

"Their whores, you mean," another man said.

"No, señor, I mean women. Most of them are their wives. Some are sweethearts, but most are wives."

"Some trees up yonder," the Texan said.

"Just the spot for us to camp for the night." The conductor's voice was cheerful. "We'll have a fire going in no time and if a rescue train is looking for us they'll see the fire."

"And what are we supposed to do for food?" a man asked.

"We have some," Sarah said. "Probably others do too. It we all share what we have there'll be enough for everybody."

"Hell, yes," the Texan said. "And I got a couple of bottles of tequila. My contribution to the dinner. Couple sips and you all won't care what you eat."

Someone laughed and said, "You are right, *hombre*. A taste of tequila first and what food we have will taste better."

Little by little the grumbling ceased as the men busied themselves with the fire and the women and children put down their suitcases and rested under the trees. By the time the fire was going and the tequila had been passed around, spirits rose. As the night grew cold they drew close to the fire, children with their heads in their mothers' laps, women drawing closer to their husbands.

"Do you have a jacket in your bag?" Luis asked. "It's getting colder."

"Yes. I even have a serape that I was taking for Aunt Clara."

"Then let's move back a bit and try to sleep."

He led her away from the others, a little behind the trees. He put two jackets from his own suitcase on the ground and said, "These will help against the cold."

Sarah's teeth began to chatter when they lay on the ground, side by side, not touching. She wasn't sure if it was from the cold, from being in an almost-bed with a man for the first time in her life, or from being afraid of what her father would think if he knew.

"Come here," he said, "let me warm you." And he pulled her close and folded his arms around her. "Are you cold, or frightened?"

"Both."

"Don't be frightened, Sarita. If I kiss you it is only to keep you from getting pneumonia."

She coughed delicately. And heard him chuckle.

"Very well, but only for your own good." His lips were on hers, moving with his laughter at first. But the laughter gave way to urgency and he pulled her closer, the whole length of him pressing against the soft curve of her body. Her response, as it had the first time he'd kissed her, surprised him. This was not a girl who would hold back from the man she loved, a girl who would grow into a woman who went to her husband's bed out of a sense of duty. No, this girl's hungers were as deep as his. And once she was properly awakened . . .

His body ached with desire as his mouth crushed down upon hers, searching, searching, tasting the honey of her lips, her mouth. His arm slipped down to her buttocks and pressed her closer against him, feeling her quiver as he urged her closer, as she felt the pressure of his loins. With his other hand he fumbled with the front of her jacket, felt quick anger when her hand came up as though to push his hand away, but stayed instead to undo the buttons. And felt a

41

sudden swift joy because he knew that she felt as he did. A soft moan escaped her lips when his hand touched the sweetly rounded breasts. The sound of her pleasure excited him even more. He had to have her. He had to . . .

Suddenly he thrust her away from him and sat up.

"Luis . . ." She put a tentative hand toward him. Her mouth looked bruised and swollen with desire.

"We can't do this." His voice was hoarse with feeling. "I told your father I would take you safely to Texas. I told him we would wait. I could not look at him again if we do this now."

"I don't *care* what you told my father." Her eyes were stormy. "The two of you decided that we'd wait, you didn't consult me, you didn't even ask how *I* felt about it. Well, I'll tell you how I feel—I don't want to wait!"

"Sarah, please."

She put her arms around his neck. "And I don't want to stop now."

"Sarah." His voice was a low groan of desire. He took a deep breath. Then he reached up and took her arms from around his neck. "What is between us is special, *querida*. We must handle it with care because it is something that will last. This is difficult for us now because we want . . . we want so much. But we have all of our lives ahead of us. You have your school and I . . ." He stopped. And looked away from her.

Her eyes were suddenly frightened. "What? What do you mean, Luis? You have your job. Is that what you mean?"

"I don't know. I'm not sure that's enough. Not now." He turned away from her abruptly. "We'd better try to sleep," he said. "Let's move closer to the fire."

And before she could answer he helped her to her feet, picked up the blanket and jackets, and moved swiftly to the side of the fire.

*   *   *

The rescue train came for them the next morning, and by dawn of the following day they reached Laredo. The other passengers were jubilant. Now that they were all right what had happened was an adventure, something to tell their children and grandchildren. "I was on a train that was held up by Pancho Villa," they would say for years to come.

Luis and Sarah did not join in the talk around them. Her mind was a jumble of frightened thoughts, and the only clear words she could put together were, I don't want him to leave me. *I don't want him to leave me.* They raced around and around in her brain until she thought he must surely hear them. But when she looked at him she knew that he was a million miles away.

When they got to Laredo he borrowed a car from a friend and drove her to San Antonio. Her quiet fright had given way to nervous chatter. "Aunt Clara's going to be surprised," she said. "She's expecting me, but not you. Don't be put off by her, Luis. You won't know whether she likes you or doesn't like you, approves or disapproves, because she wears a constant look of disapproval."

But when they stopped in front of the plain gray two-story house her chatter gave way to sadness. She leaned back against the car seat. "I hate to go in," she said. "I've never been happy there. I've never felt any sense of belonging."

"You'll be going back to school soon."

"I don't want to go back to school either. I want to be with you."

And when he didn't answer she said, "El Paso's not too far, Luis. Will you come to visit me soon?"

He looked at her for a long moment. Then he reached out and touched her hair, smoothing it back from her face. "I'm not going to El Paso," he said.

Fear gripped her. Held her. "But your job . . ."

"I'm not going back to my job."

She looked into his eyes, and suddenly she knew.

43

"Villa," she said at last. "You're going to join Villa."

"I have to."

"You *don't* have to!" Her words were a cry of anguish.

"There's a wind sweeping Mexico, Sarah. A clean fresh wind that will bring changes to the country. I want to be a part of those changes. I have to be a part of them."

"And what about us?"

"We agreed to wait."

"You and my father agreed to wait." Her voice was bitter.

"We've already seen how difficult that's going to be." He tried to smile. "Perhaps the revolution will take my mind off you."

"Luis, let's run away. Let's drive away from here and find a justice of the peace and . . ."

"I can't do that, Sarah. I promised your father."

"Remember how we felt last night, Luis? I didn't know two people could feel like that." She felt the color creep up to her cheeks, but made herself go on. "I thought wives let their husbands do . . . make love to them because it was their *duty* to make love. I didn't know that a woman could feel the way . . . the way I felt last night."

"Sarah." He put his finger underneath her chin and forced her to look at him. *"Mi preciosa.* It will be such a joy to teach you the many ways of love."

"Teach me now," she said softly.

"I can't. Try to understand. This is something I have to do."

"But I don't want you to do it. I don't want you to fight. I don't want to worry about you every day and every night. I couldn't stand that, Luis. If you leave me now . . ." She tried to control her panic. She remembered the first sudden awareness that she was falling in love with him, the sense of belonging she'd had, the feeling of coming home at last.

She wanted to tell him how much she needed him.

44

But panic froze her voice to coldness and she said again, "If you leave me now . . ."

"Don't threaten me, Sarah."

"It isn't a threat, it's a promise," she said in her strangely frozen voice. "If you leave me now you don't ever need to come back to me."

His brows drew together. His eagle eyes pierced hers. "We belong together," he said at last. "And when this is over we'll be together."

When he pulled her to him she tried to pull away. Balling her hands into fists, she struck out at him. And when her lips were cold and unresponsive under his he shook her angrily. "You're mine," he said, glaring at her.

He kissed her again, almost savagely this time, not caring that they were in front of her aunt's house, not caring about anything except the softness of her lips, the feel of her body against his. And finally her lips parted and warmed and clung.

When he released her he said again, "You're mine, Sarah, and you always will be."

"Then marry me!" Her voice was a soft wail of anguish.

"Sarah . . ." He shook her gently. "I can't. Not now."

"Then I'll find someone who will!" She grabbed the handle of the door, got out, and slammed it. She was sick with humiliation. She had begged him to marry her, and he had refused.

"You're behaving like a child. I won't be forced into something I know is wrong at this particular time."

"Could you bring my bags, please?" Her voice was like ice.

He stared at her straight stiff back. He got out of the car, took her suitcases out and carried them to the wide front porch.

She didn't turn to look at him when he passed her and got back into the car. She didn't even turn when she heard him start the car. Or when he drove away.

45

Part II

MEXICO CITY,
February 1913

LUIS

Chapter 5

Sunday morning, the ninth of February. The air was cool and crisp and sparkling clear. The sun shone as the people hurried along the streets to early mass.

Francisco Madero had been president since 1911. In 1910, after Porfirio Diaz was ousted, Madero had been hailed as the "new savior of the country." But two years had brought disillusionment and disappointment. Behind Madero were self-serving politicians headed by members of his own family. Some even said that the real power was his brother, Gustavo. Gustavo, who, like Porfirio Diaz, organized a small army of gangsters to silence anyone who dared to raise a voice against the new government. There had been talk of restoring lands to the Indian villages. But the talk was never acted upon. Zapata resumed the burning of the haciendas and the murder of the men who owned them.

In the North, Orozco pronounced against Madero, and Madero gave the job of hunting him down to a murderous drunkard by the name of General Victoriano Huerta.

And Pancho Villa, whom Madero had once hailed as his greatest friend, had been imprisoned at the orders of this same Huerta. But Villa had escaped and was living in exile in Texas waiting until the time was right.

And the time was right.

Arms were secretly imported into the country, transported to Mexico City, and the Diaz party, led

49

by Porfirio's nephew, Felix, gained strength. The word was out; the country was once again ripe for revolution.

Sarah had not heard the rumbles and rumors of discontent. And even if she had, she would have paid no attention. She had been graduated from college in January, and while she felt satisfaction in her achievement, the last two and a half years had not been happy ones. Especially the first year. She'd been impatient with her friends and teachers, waiting for weekends when she could be free to roam the quiet country roads alone, to find a spot where she could read or think and not have to listen to the chatter of her friends.

They seemed so young. They talked about boys: "You should have seen that Frank Logan trying to sneak his arm around my shoulder. Why honey, I slapped his hand away 'fore you could say 'Sam Houston.' What makes boys act that way?" Or clothes: "Isn't this the most daring dress you've ever seen? It's cut almost to mid-calf! Mama had a fit when I chose it. She said, 'Cissy Lou, I absolutely will not have you wearing a dress like that to the Spring Ball.' But I said, 'Mama, I will die, really die, if I can't have this precious thing.'"

They arranged dates for Sarah. At the Spring Ball she dated Cissy Lou's cousin from Fort Worth, gritting her teeth while she danced with him, trying not to look at his pimples and bad teeth. Margaret Hastings' brother was her escort at the June picnic. He looked presentable at least, but when they'd teamed to play a game that required their hiding behind the trees, he'd tried to kiss her and she'd hit him a terrible blow on his rather nice nose.

She had not seen Luis. He wrote twice, but when she didn't answer, he stopped writing. She heard from her father, who had seen Luis' father, that Luis had joined Villa's Northern Army and that he was fighting somewhere in the state of Chihuahua.

Because of the fighting she did not return to Mexico until Christmas of the following year. And it was then that she had seen Andres. On Christmas Eve she and her father went to the Palace of Fine Arts to hear Mary Garden. She'd seen Andres at the intermission. Or rather, he'd seen her. He was with his mother and father, and when he insisted Sarah and her father join the traditional Christmas Eve family dinner after the performance, his parents had seconded the invitation.

After the first awkward moments, Sarah found that she rather enjoyed Andres. He was older than the boys she'd met, and handsome in his blue military uniform. As the evening went on, the laughter, the food, and the wine, they grew more comfortable with each other. And when he asked her to his regiment's New Year's Eve Ball, she accepted.

He loved his military career and had risen to the rank of captain. It was obvious, even to Sarah's untutored eyes, that he would go far. His fellow officers seemed to respect him, and he was pleased and flattered that they found Sarah attractive. Sarah, dressed in a blue velvet gown, was almost surprised to find that for the first time in a long time she was enjoying herself. The young men, older and more sure of themselves than the boys she'd dated at school, cut in often, until finally a not-displeased Andres had threatened to have them shipped to the Yucatan if they didn't leave Sarah alone.

When they were returning to her hotel in the carriage after the dance he brought up the subject of Luis. "I was angry for a long time," he said. "I couldn't forgive either of you. I'd assumed, Sarah, that when I returned from Paris we would take up where we'd left off two years before."

You assumed no such thing, she thought. I remember your look of mild distaste when your mother made you dance with me at my sixteenth birthday party. But she smiled at him and held her tongue.

He took her hand. "I was deeply hurt that day at the Vega ranch when I found you and Luis together. But I've thought about it, Sarah, and I know that it was his fault."

51

"But . . ." she started to say.

"And my fault," he continued. "He's always had a terrible reputation with women. But I didn't think he would be that way with you, not when he called himself my best friend. So it was a blow, Sarah, finding the two of you like that. But I shouldn't have blamed you."

"Have you seen Luis since that afternoon?"

"No! And I have no desire to see him except on the field of battle."

"Really, Andres. Don't be so pompous. You and Luis have been friends for years. Surely . . ."

"It's not just you, my dear. Luis is my enemy now. As far as I am concerned he's as much a brigand as Villa. And for as long as he fights for the revolution that's what he will be."

"What about his family? How do they feel about his fighting with Villa?"

His laugh was scornful. "Like son, like father, in this case. The old man has always been a bit of a renegade."

"I can't believe that! He has a face like a saint."

"And that's what he pretends to be. He's a wealthy man. He lives in a fine hacienda on some of the choicest land in the state of Hidalgo. My God, Sarah, I'd give my life to own such land. And what is he doing? He's talking of dividing the land and giving parcels of it to his peons! He's as much of a revolutionary as his son is. And the younger brother, Carlos, has started a school for them. That's a dangerous thing to do. You give an ignorant peon a finger and he'll take your arm. Carlos should spend more time in his church and less meddling in family affairs. My family no longer associates with the Vegas. They are politically unhealthy."

But when she tried to question him further, he said, "No, we will think of Sarah and Andres now. We will forget the past."

Forget. She'd tried to. Once when she'd visited her Aunt Clara in San Antonio she'd followed a man for five blocks because from the back he looked like Luis. And she'd cried like a child when it wasn't him after all. Yes, it was time to put the past away. Time to stop weeping for a man who didn't want her.

She and Andres corresponded, and the following spring he was her escort at the Spring Dance.

Three of her friends were engaged and planned to be married as soon as they graduated. They talked incessantly of how many bridesmaids they would have, what kind of flowers they would carry, how much money their families were spending on the reception. And how nervous they would be on their wedding night. "I'm going to wear the filmiest floatiest chiffon I can find. Blue, I think, just to be different," said Margaret Hastings.

"Just to be honest, you mean, don't you?" Cissy Lou said, because everyone knew that Margaret and her fiancé had been making love ever since last summer when they'd been together at his parents' cottage on Padre Island.

"You'd better be careful at the dance," Shirley warned. "If Miss Thatcher catches you sneaking off she'll have you expelled."

Cissy Lou turned to Sarah and said, "I don't suppose you have a date for the dance yet, honey?"

"I was thinking of asking someone," Sarah said.

"Oh?" Cissy Lou's china-blue eyes opened wide. "Anyone we know?"

"I doubt it, dear. He's a captain in the Mexican Army, on President Madero's personal staff." She felt a moment of satisfaction at the expression on the other girl's face. "The only thing is, he travels a lot. He was in Paris last month, and next week he'll be in Washington. But I know he'll come if he can possibly arrange his schedule." She smiled sweetly at their startled faces.

And that night she wrote Andres and invited him to the dance.

* * *

He looked dashing in his uniform, but even so, she held him at arm's length until she saw Cissy Lou cuddle close to him as they danced and heard her say, "I just love a man in uniform. But a man with a moustache *and* a uniform is enough to drive a poor little ole girl like me wild."

Later, when they were alone, Sarah smiled at him and said, "I do declare, Andres, I just love a man in uniform." She touched his moustache, widened her eyes, and with a theatrical sigh said, "But a man with a moustache *and* a uniform . . . is enough to drive poor little ole me wild."

He chuckled as he pulled her to him. "Let's see, Sarita. Let's see if I drive you wild."

His kiss was passionate as he pressed his mouth against hers, his arms tightening, his fingers caressing her back. His lips moved to her cheek, her ear, to her throat, returned to her mouth where his tongue explored its warmth.

She pulled away from him, trying to hide her disappointment, her mild distaste.

It will come in time, she told herself later. He's everything a girl could possibly want. And the following August, when he asked her to marry him, she said yes.

When her father objected, she agreed to wait until she graduated. Now she was finished with school, and next week she would become Señora Sarah de Ortiz.

She had the teaching certificate she'd worked so hard for, but very likely she'd never have the opportunity to teach. Andres and his family had frowned when she suggested it.

"My dear," his mother said, wincing delicately, "an Ortiz woman doesn't go out in the world. She doesn't do common things."

"I don't consider the teaching profession common," Sarah said somewhat tartly. "Mexico needs teachers. There are thousands of children who can't read or write. Children of peons who . . ."

"Children of peons couldn't learn anyway, Sarah.

They are meant to be just what they are. They wouldn't have the mental capacity to learn. They're irresponsible and lazy. It's better for them to work in the fields. That's all they're capable of doing. You mustn't worry your head about such things. It's not seemly. You'll have enough to do being the wife of an officer. Pretty little things like arranging teas and giving dinner parties." She patted Sarah's hand. "And having babies, of course."

Of course.

Except for goodnight kisses, Sarah had not permitted Andres to touch her. "There will be time after we're married," she told him over and over again. And wondered, sometimes with anger, if after all she was going to be like Mrs. Zambeck and Mrs. Baumgartner. She hated Luis for awakening all the terrible hungers that she knew deep inside her would never be filled by Andres.

It was just as well. It was better for a woman not to feel that kind of need. That kind of pain. It was better to make a nice sensible marriage and raise nice sensible children.

As she approached the Zocolo she saw that the giant square was filled with people, many of them on their way to the Cathedral to attend mass. As she was. She usually went to mass with Andres and his family, but he had been away from home all week and his parents preferred a church near their home. She was glad to have this time alone. She didn't have many days left to be Miss Sarah Finch, and she felt a glad sense of freedom on this bright Sunday morning.

As she started across the Zocolo she became aware of a slowly mounting sound of feet marching to the "tum tum, tum tum" sound of drums. She looked at the people around her, saw their startled faces, heard their whispered questions.

There was a commotion in front of the National Palace. Guards beckoned, soldiers suddenly appeared to set up gun placements. More soldiers gathered on the roof.

Suddenly a dark surging mass of people came into sight and those around her began to run, pushing each other out of the way. Some of them were eager to see what was happening, but most were frightened, wanting to get out of the wide open space of this giant square.

The dark mass surged into the Zocolo shouting, "Viva General Reyes. Viva Felix Diaz." When they reached the doors of the War Ministry they paused, as though gathering strength, then charged forward, eight or ten abreast, guns glinting in the February sun.

And as they exploded into the Zocolo the roof of the National Palace began to crackle with rifle fire. The attackers screamed and broke formation, trying to seek cover, firing at the soldiers as they ran.

Sarah began to run toward the Cathedral. She was pushed, knocked aside, carried along in the crush of people trying to escape the bullets.

The pounding feet of the rioters drew closer.

"Please," she cried, "let me through."

But her voice was lost in the terrible volley of shots that came from the National Palace.

"The bastards are shooting at *us*," someone shouted.

Machine-gun fire sprayed the ground. A grenade exploded. Through horrified eyes she saw people fall. Screams split the air as men, women, and even children sprawled in the street. Blood streamed from wounded bodies. The people went wild in their frantic need to escape, shoving, clawing, falling over fallen bodies.

She was caught up in the terrible human tide, swept along with the mass of hysteria as the sharp ping of bullets and the staccato bite of machine-gun fire filled the square. She heard the thud of bullets as they struck walls and people.

The screams were deafening. People fell and were trampled. Sarah's hat and purse were lost, her coat torn, her face scratched. She tried to break away from the mob, but she was caught and swept along with the others away from Zocolo, crushed as hundreds of them squeezed into a narrow side street. She cried out in pain and in terror, not of the bullets now, but of the mob. She felt as though she couldn't breathe, was suffocated by the smell of terror as bodies pressed against her. Saw the wide terrified eyes of a fat woman just as the woman put a hand on her chest and shoved her against an old man who bleated like a goat and cried, "Save me! Save me!" She stumbled, grabbed at an arm to save herself from falling, and was struck on the side of her head.

Nothing would penetrate this frenzy of fear. There was no air; she couldn't breathe. She felt her knees grow weak, and knew that if she fell she would be trampled. No one would help her. No one . . . And then, through the press of people, she saw his face. And she cried out, "Luis! Luis!"

He saw her, mouthed her name, looked around him, trying to see how he could get to her. People pushed in front of him and he disappeared from her view. When she saw him again his face was white and set with the effort to force his way to her.

She managed to raise an arm, trying to reach out to him. She called his name. A man swore at her and tried to push her aside, but she stood her ground, trying to fight her way to Luis. He was closer now. An arm reached out, was knocked aside. He pushed forward. Their hands reached out, touched, and clasped.

Chapter 6

He was beside her, one arm strong around her shoulders, his other arm extended, pushing against the crowd, trying to find an opening, a way to the side of the street. A man struck him, a woman cursed him, but he refused to stop. Inch by tortured inch he propelled them to the edge of the street, up to the sidewalk, close to the buildings. There were a few stores along here, some offices, a few apartments. Suddenly his arm tightened and he thrust her through the mob into a passageway. He pulled her along after him as the passageway widened into a patio.

She was gasping for breath, almost fainting, as he leaned against the wall of the building and pulled her to him. His body shook with the reaction of being away from the crush of the mob. She trembled so that she would have fallen if he hadn't held her.

After several minutes he held her away from him. "Let me look at you," he said. "Are you all right? Your face is bleeding."

"My God," she moaned. "Oh, my God, Luis, what happened? All those people. I saw them on the ground. Children, children on their way to church. What in God's name . . . ?"

"Not in God's name, Sarah. In General Huerta's name. He's in charge of the Palace troops. He must be behind this."

"And the men who rushed into the Zocolo? Who were they?"

58

"General Reyes' men, I think."

"But he's in prison."

"He *was* in prison. I'd heard early this morning that the garrison troops of Tacabaya marched to the prison and released him. He's probably joined forces with Felix Diaz."

"But why did the men in the Palace fire into the Zocolo?"

"Huerta's been waiting for a chance like this. He . . ." He listened for a minute. "The shooting's stopped. Stay here and let me . . ."

"No! Luis, no, please don't leave me."

"All right." He saw that she was still almost hysterical. "Come and sit on the stairs for a minute. This patio is a little too exposed." He led her to the stairs. He took a handkerchief out of his pocket and wiped the blood from her cheek. "It's only a scratch," he said.

She looked up at him. She reached out and touched the hand that lay against her cheek. "When I saw your face . . . when I saw your face I thought I must be imagining that it was you because I needed you so much."

"Sarah . . ." He touched her hand. And saw the ring.

"Whose is it?" His face looked frozen and still.

"Andres'." Her voice was a whisper.

A muscle jumped in the side of his face. He let go of her hand.

Suddenly, above them, they heard people running, the loud crash of doors, and they looked up to see men and women slamming doors of the apartments on the second floor and rush for the stairs. "Hurry," they called to each other. "If it starts again we'll never get out." They carried suitcases, baskets, bundles, babies.

Luis pulled Sarah away from the steps to make room for the tenants that rushed past them.

"I want to see the soldiers," a small boy roared.

"Be quiet," his mother ordered, yanking him along

after her. "Those idiots are going to start shooting again any minute."

"Do you want to make a run for it too?" Luis asked.

"No. Not with all those people out there. I couldn't do that again. That mob . . . that was worse than the bullets. I didn't know people could behave that way." Her voice was trembling. She clutched the stair railing, as though afraid that he would pull her away, make her go out onto the street again.

He knew they should leave while they had a chance, but she looked so white and frightened. "It's all right," he said, "we'll wait a bit. Just rest for a few . . ."

An explosion rocked the building. And then a second as a grenade hit the entrance hall, spattering the walls and bringing down an avalanche of brick and plaster dust.

"Upstairs," he shouted above the noise. He shoved her ahead of him, taking the stairs two at a time as the street exploded in a barrage of machine-gun fire, grenades, and cannon shot. They were exposed by the open balcony on the second floor too. He tried a door and when he saw that it was locked rammed it open with his shoulder. A bullet shattered a window of the apartment just as they entered. He grabbed Sarah and pulled her to the floor.

The noise was deafening. They lay on the floor behind a worn-out blue-green sofa, unable to talk in the cacophony of nerve-wracking sound, his arm around her, her face pressed to his shoulder.

When the shooting became more sporadic he let her go and eased away from her. "It's quieting down," he said. "But we'd better stay here for a while."

The apartment was small; living room, kitchen, a windowless bedroom, and a bath. There were beans on the stove and warm bread sliced and ready to eat.

"I'm hungry," Luis said. "What about you?"

"I'm too frightened to eat." But when he handed her a plate of beans and a slice of the homemade

60

bread, she managed to smile and say, "That looks good. Thank you."

And after she'd eaten she went into the bathroom, washed her hands and face, and found some alcohol to put on her scratched face. There was a clean comb on the back of the sink. She'd put her hair up this morning, but the pins had come loose and her hair was half up and half down. Now she took out the few remaining pins and combed her hair. She pulled out the blue velvet ribbon that ran through the eyelet lace at the neck of her shirtwaist and tied it around her hair.

Resting her hands against the cool porcelain sink, she whispered his name to the reflection in the mirror, "Luis." How many times had she daydreamed of meeting him? She would be calm and cool, but friendly, and so beautifully elegant that he would gnash his teeth and curse himself for being fool enough to leave her. She looked at her scratched face and torn shirtwaist. So much for daydreams.

He looked older. His face was leaner, harder, more masculine. And still . . . so dearly familiar.

When she returned to the living room he had taken the mattress off the bed in the bedroom and put it on the floor.

"We'll have to spend most of our time on the floor," he said, "away from the windows." His eyes avoided hers. "And I'm sorry, I don't think we'll get out tonight. We'll have to stay here."

He still could not believe that it was Sarah. When he'd seen her in that mob of people he'd thought he was dreaming, that he'd conjured her up out of a past he thought he'd forgotten. Her face was pale and pinched with fear. When she cried his name and reached her hand out to him the years fell away.

How many times had he told himself that she was a spoiled child, not woman enough to love a man, and that he was better off without her? There had been other women, Mexican women who were more to his liking, he told himself. As soon as he bedded them he

61

knew he lied and hated them for not being Sarah. More and more he threw himself into the battle. He fought hard, and now he was a captain of Villa's chosen troops, the famous—or infamous—the feared *dorados*.

Villa had sent him here to try to talk to President Madero alone. General Huerta was not to know that he was in Mexico City, and he knew that if Huerta found him anywhere near the President he wouldn't hesitate to kill him. Huerta wielded terrible power, and it was to Mexico's detriment that Madero was fool enough to trust him. He had to get to the President to tell him that unless he got rid of Madero and made some of the promised reforms, Carranza, Obregon, and yes, even Villa, would move against him.

It was going to be difficult now because of the fighting. And he knew beyond a doubt that Huerta would use today's rebellion to turn against the President. Huerta and his trained dogs. Like Andres. The special force of Palace guards.

And Sarah was going to marry Andres.

She had changed in the two years since he had seen her. Her pretty young-girl look had found its definition in her growing womanhood, so that now she was strikingly beautiful. And looking at her, he knew his feelings hadn't changed in the years he'd been away from her. But it was too late for him. She belonged to Andres.

His voice was matter-of-fact, almost cool, when he spoke again. "Why don't you try to rest?"

"Do we really have to spend the night here?"

"I think we'd better. There's still shooting coming from the Zocolo. And I imagine the looters are out in full force. We'll wait and see what tomorrow brings."

And when she still hesitated he said, "Relax, Sarah. Even Andres would understand our being here together." He looked away from her. "When is the wedding?"

"Next week."

"I see." He tried to keep a conversational tone. "Will you live here in Mexico City?"

"For a while. Andres is on General Huerta's staff and . . ."

His smile was thin. "Yes, I know."

"He expects to be sent to the North soon. There are rumors that Villa is gathering his men again. Is he, Luis? Are you still with him?"

"Villa's in Texas, Sarah. I haven't seen him in months," he lied. It was better not to involve her, better not to tell her anything, especially now that she was engaged to Andres.

Changing the subject, he said, "I suppose you've finished school. Are you going to teach after you're married? I remember you said you'd like to."

"Andres' mother doesn't think . . . I mean Andres doesn't want me to teach. I'll be busy with, uh, teas and things. When we're married there are certain . . . social things I'll have to do."

"I see. And you'll like that kind of life?"

She avoided his eyes. "Of course. And what about you, Luis? Do you have a wife? A fiancée?"

"I've been too busy."

"With that bandit Villa?"

"They don't let bandits sit in the President's chair in the National Palace, do they? I was here with Villa when he and Zapata and Obregon marched into the city. It was something to see, Sarah, your 'bandit' riding down the Paseo de la Reforma while thousands lined the street to welcome him."

"And then what happened to your glorious revolution, Luis? What happened when Madero had Villa thrown in prison?"

"General Huerta was responsible for that. He was ready to have Villa shot when Madero stepped in to save him."

"Andres said that General Huerta was furious when Villa escaped. He raged for days. Andres said they should have killed him while they had the chance."

"Did he?" His voice was dangerously soft.

"And where is your wonderful President Madero now? Why doesn't he stop this?" She faced him, her eyes angry. "Was all the fighting worth it?"

"I don't know," he said quietly. "After Diaz resigned Mexico needed a strong hand. With Madero she got a soft heart." He shook his head. "We hoped for so much, Sarah. I was here with Villa when Madero made his entrance into the city after all the fighting was done and Diaz was on his way to Europe. It was June. The trees and roofs were crammed with people. Boys climbed on statues and bronze horses. Girls hung over balcony railings and waved colored scarves. And then he came into view, a small man with a funny brown derby in one hand, waving to the crowd with the other. And I thought to myself, can this be Francisco Madero, the glorious redeemer of Mexico?"

He stood up abruptly and went into the bedroom. It was dark in the apartment now, and cold. He came back with two blankets. "These were all I could find," he said, handing them to her. "It's been a long day. You'd better get some rest."

Outside on the street below someone shouted a curse and a shot was fired. The shooting started again, the rifles, the machine guns, and now cannons boomed. Sarah closed her eyes, willing her tired and bruised body to sleep, but she couldn't still the involuntary jump of nerves each time a volley was fired. She looked up at Luis. He sat on the floor beside her, his legs stretched out in front of him, his back resting against the sofa. A grenade exploded, and without thinking, she reached out and touched his leg. And when he turned to her she said, "I just wanted to touch you."

When he lay down beside her she moved toward him and put her head on his arm. And for a reason she could not define, felt hot tears sting her eyes. "When I saw you today . . ." she tried to say. And had to start over. "When I saw your face in that terrible crush of people I thought I only imagined you." She

64

swallowed, trying to ease the pain in her throat. "I thought because I needed you so much my mind was playing tricks."

"I was afraid I wouldn't reach you in time, I was afraid you'd fall."

She shivered against him. "So was I."

"It's over now. Don't think about it."

The firing stopped. They heard the sound of running feet below the window. Luis eased away from her and went to look out. When he crept back to her he whispered, "Soldiers. They've probably cordoned off the street. I doubt they're letting anyone through." He lay down beside her, but not close, not touching.

"Are you in love with Andres?" he said suddenly.

And when she hesitated he said, "Then why are you going to marry him?"

"It's time I got married. All the girls my age . . ." She started over. "I want children. And people say . . . people say that love comes later. Andres is a good man. He . . ."

"Are you so sure?" His voice was bitter.

"I know you don't agree on some things, but you were friends for years. You know him. You . . ."

"That's right." He turned his face to hers. "We were friends when we were boys because our families were friends. We went to the same academy and the same university before he went to Paris and I went to Colorado. But friends? I'm not sure now that we ever were that. We have nothing in common."

"Nothing?" Her voice shook. She heard his indrawn breath and clenched her hands.

"Damn you! You want me to say it, don't you? You want me to tell you that I still care about you. All right! I care. I've never wanted another woman the way I want . . . the way I wanted you. You've spoiled me for every woman I've ever been with."

"And have there been many?"

"Yes," he said, knowing it hurt her. "Many."

She lay for a long time in the cold February night, listening to the sounds of battle, watching the flashes of light through the broken window. Numb now as the reaction of the day faded. Almost unable to believe all that had happened or that she was with Luis. And that it was too late for them.

Finally she slept, to be jolted awake by an explosion of noise that shook the apartment. Her body jerked awake. "What . . . ?"

"Shhh."

"But what happened? Where . . . ?" She was curled tight against him, her hands on his chest, her face against his neck. Now, awake, she tried to ease away from him and felt the pressure of his hand against her back. Pulling her hands away from his chest, she looked up at him, trying to see his face in the darkness.

He kissed her then, tentatively at first, so that the kiss comforted her, warmed her. I'll just stay like this for a moment, she thought. And the moment lengthened. She didn't want it to end. Ever. But at last she pulled away.

"Don't," she whispered. "We have to stop. Andres and I . . ."

"Andres!" His arms tightened, hurting her, frightening her.

She cried out and tried to twist away. "I'm going to marry him. I can't do this. We have to stop."

"No!"

"Luis, please . . ." She struggled with him now, managing for a moment to pull away from him. Then his hands were on her again, and suddenly afraid, she began to fight him. And knew she'd done the wrong thing when she heard the angry hiss of breath in his throat. When his hands reached out, found the top of the already torn shirtwaist, and ripped it apart.

"Let me go!"

But his hands were on her breasts, tightening, caressing, rubbing the hard-peaked nipples. She put her hands on his wrists, trying to stop him. And again, as she had when she let him kiss her, she thought, only for a moment, I'll make him stop soon. Soon. Feeling

66

the heat creep into her body on warm feathered feet as his fingers teased her breasts. Soon.

When his body moved over hers she tried to pull away. She whispered, "We've got to stop. Darling? Please. Let me go. Let me go, Luis."

She tried to move his hands away, but he grabbed her, holding her wrists with one hand as he moved to kiss her breasts, his lips, his tongue burning the taut nipples until she moaned beneath him.

He released her hands, but his legs still held her pinned to the mattress. He tore his shirt off, loosened his belt, and pulled at his trousers.

Afraid again, she cried, "You can't. I'm going to marry Andres."

He looked like his Aztec ancestors now with his strong angry masculine face, his piercing eagle-like eyes, his lips pulled back showing the strong white teeth. "Perhaps you will marry him," he snarled. "But by all that's holy I'll have you first."

And before she could speak he unfastened her skirt and yanked it down. And when she struggled against him, frightened and angry, he flipped her onto her stomach and ripped off her skirt and underclothes.

"Be still," he said, "or I'll . . ."

"I'll kill you," she screamed. "And if I don't, Andres will. We're going to be married. We're . . ."

"Don't say his name!"

"Andres. Andres. Andres," she screamed in rage.

He grabbed his belt off the floor, wound part of it around his fist, and shouting, "Don't say his name!" struck her across her buttocks again and again while she cried out in pain and terror.

When he flung the belt away he rolled her onto her back. His eyes glinted above her. "Now," he said, his voice soft. "Now. I've waited two years for you, Sarah. Every time I took a woman I pretended she was you. I'm done with pretending now."

Every inch of their naked bodies touched. He tangled his fingers in her curls, holding her head while his mouth sought hers. His hand slid down her body, to her belly, her hips, moved to touch the triangle of hair. His voice was hoarse when he said, "I've wanted to touch you like this from the moment I saw you coming down the stairs of the palace. You came down those stairs like a queen, your head high, that glorious hair piled on top of your head, white shoulders gleaming, these breasts, these hard little breasts almost thrusting themselves out of your gown."

She trembled against the hardness of him.

"And that night in the garden. Do you know how close I came to throwing you down on the damp grass and taking you like a peasant. Do you, little *gringa?* Do you?"

His mouth sought hers, hard and hurting, his teeth biting the corners of her mouth in sharp little nips. Then his hands tightened on hers as he thrust himself into her. Hurting her. Oh God, hurting her.

She cried out in pain, and when she did he slowed the terrible thrusts. His mouth found hers, more gently this time, as his hands caressed her, held her, soothed her, pressing her closer still against his body.

He moved against her, slowly, deeply. And she felt her own body arch and reach.

She was frightened and bewildered, hurt and ashamed. She couldn't understand this strange feeling that spread like sweet fierce fire through her loins.

"Luis?" A low cry. A moan cry. "Luis?"

"It's all right, Sarah."

Moving to kiss her, sweet and demanding and strong. Mouth clinging to mouth.

Past all thought now. Only need. Sweet loving need as his arms tightened around her shoulders, as she whispered his name in one beautiful terrible estatic agony of feeling. Clinging to him as his body shuddered over hers. As he whispered her name over and over.

And finally they lay still, eyes closed, hands clasped. Their bodies eased and calmed, and at last they slept.

Chapter 7

She woke to see the sunlight streaming in through the broken window. Her head was on his shoulder, his fingers buried in her hair, his arm around her waist. She lay without moving for a long time, looking at his face, relaxed and softened in sleep. She remembered the way he had looked last night, his terrible anger, how brutally he had taken her. And she remembered her terror and helplessness, her final acquiescence.

He opened his eyes and saw her watching him. *"Buenos días, señorita,"* he said softly.

"Buenos días."

"Are you hungry?"

She nodded.

"There's wood in the stove. I'll put some water on in a minute. Maybe we can have a cup of tea."

"I'll make it," she said, anxious for an excuse to leave him. She threw the blanket back, started to get up, and suddenly remembered she was naked.

He smiled at her shyness, at the funny agony of her indecision, whether to make a run for it or dive back under the blanket.

She turned her back on him, and over a bare shoulder she said, "Hand me your shirt."

"No. I want to see you." He put his hand on her hip, and felt his breath catch in his throat. Her bright hair hung loosely curled down her long silken back. His hand tightened on her hip and he felt her wince.

And he remembered that he had struck her last night. "Lie down," he said, his voice strained.

She darted a frightened glance at him. "No, please . . ."

His hands reached out and touched her shoulders, slowly forcing her down on her stomach. Faint red marks showed against the whiteness of her skin. His throat knotted in pain when he touched her and felt her shudder beneath his fingers. "My God," he said, "I'm sorry. I didn't mean . . ."

She sat up and when she saw the expression on his face she said, "Don't look like that, Luis."

"I've wanted you for so long," he said painfully. "And then suddenly you were here and we were alone, but you couldn't be mine because you belonged to Andres . . . and when I heard you say his name I went crazy." He reached out to touch her face. "I'm sorry," he said, "I didn't mean to hurt you."

She reached for the blanket to cover herself, but he took it from her. His eyes moved down her body to the narrow waist that he could circle with his hands, the flat belly, the triangle of red-gold hair, the long beautiful legs with the delicate ankles.

"Come here," he said.

She could feel the beat of the pulse in her throat.

"Come here," he said again.

She didn't speak when he pushed her back against the mattress and covered her body with his. His eyes looked down at her, as gently he brushed the hair away from her face as though wanting to ease her fear.

She felt her body tremble beneath his as he sought her mouth. Her lips parted beneath his as slowly, carefully, he entered her.

He reached one hand under her hips gently, holding them to meet his every thrust, rocking her body against his as he moved slowly, strongly, against her.

Her hands touched his shoulders, the back of his neck, and moved to the back of his head. Her mouth, eager now, stirred against his, sweet and hot and hungry, as slowly, slowly the feeling inside her began to mount. To rise, to grow. Warm and urgent and primal. She strained against him, lifting her body to meet his every thrust, quivering against him, her body climbing to an edge-of-the-world frenzy as with one final thrust she uttered a small cry of uncontainable joy. Then shattered, she clung to him and felt his body convulse against hers and heard him whisper, "Sarita, Sarita," over and over again.

While she found the tea and tried to start a fire in the wood stove, he went down to the street to see what was happening. There was still sporadic shooting and the sound of cannon fire was increasing.

There were no windows in the small kitchen so she was able to move around freely. She sang with happiness when she found five oranges, and clapped her hands over half a box of oatmeal. Then she saw the ring on her left hand. She slipped it off her finger and put it in the pocket of her torn skirt.

She set the table with two cracked plates, one good cup for him, and a cracked cup without a handle for herself. She beamed at the mustard yellow paint peeling off the kitchen walls, and thought it was the most beautiful kitchen she'd ever seen. She didn't even hear the sound of cannon fire when it started again.

So this is what love is, she thought. This is the completeness that I knew even two years ago I would feel with him. But I never imagined it would be like this—this giving, receiving, unexplainable joy. She felt a swift second of sadness for all the time she had not spent with him. But the sadness was dispelled by the sureness of all the time that lay ahead. The time, the endless time to lie beside him in the night, to touch and be touched, to love and be loved. The sadness was finished. Now there was only the certainty of the life that lay before them.

"The street is cordoned off," he said when he returned. "No one is being permitted to pass. I'm sorry, but we're going to have to stay here a while."

"Oh. Well, I guess we'll just have to make the best of it, won't we?"

"I'm sorry it worked out this way, but . . ." He stopped at the expression on her face. She tried to look serious and concerned but the corners of her mouth kept turning up as though the smile inside her couldn't be stifled. He felt a rush of happiness. She wasn't sorry about what had happened between them. She had forgiven him for his cruelty, and this morning had filled her with as much joy as it had him. But from somewhere inside his head a thought warned him. Be careful, it said. This is all new to her. Will she feel this way tomorrow, next week, next month? Will she rush to Andres to explain what has happened? If only he could trust her. If only she felt about the revolution as he did.

"What are you thinking? Your face looks so serious. Are things worse? What's happening?"

"Yes, things are bad. I talked to the sentry. General Reyes has been killed and Felix Diaz is in command of the Citadel. General Huerta is in command of the National Palace."

"Then Andres . . . Andres is at the Palace with him."

A muscle jumped in his cheek. "The heart of the city is caught in the middle," he went on, "and they're spraying it with shells. This zone is off limits because it's so close to the Zocolo. The sentry said the only way we could leave would be to obtain permission from the colonel—whoever and wherever the colonel is! And of course he would not permit me to leave in order to find the colonel, for my own good he insisted, because bullets are flying everywhere. He told me that over two hundred civilians were killed yesterday."

"My God! Luis . . ." she put her hand out. "My father. He must be half out of his mind with worry. I wish there was some way we could get a message to him."

"I didn't know he was here. Where is he staying?"

"With . . . with Andres' family."

"I see." He avoided her eyes. "I'm sorry, but there's no way we can get word to him."

"If it wasn't for him I wouldn't mind . . . I mean this apartment is rather nice."

"Rather nice!" He looked at the peeling walls and the cracked dishes and laughed. "You'd be sick of it in a week if you had to live here."

"Not if you were with me," she said.

He felt the breath catch in his throat. "Finish your tea," he said.

Her lips parted. The small even white teeth nibbled at the full lower lip.

"Finish your tea," he said again, his voice sounding harsh and strained.

She raised the cracked cup to her lips. He saw her hand tremble.

He picked her up out of the chair and held her to him, lifted her, and carried her into the next room. And all the while her mouth sought him and she whispered his name over and over.

"You want this as much as I do, don't you?" he asked when he laid her on the mattress.

Her arms reached up for him.

"Tell me."

"I want it as much as you do. I always will, Luis. With you. Only with you."

"Never with Andres?"

Her eyes widened. "No! No, never! How could you say . . . ?" She pulled away from him.

"I'm sorry." He held her.

She struck out at him. He caught her fist in his hand. "I said I was sorry."

"Damn you!" She tried to get away from him, but he held her pinned to the mattress.

"But hear me," he said. "If Andres ever lays a hand on you I'll kill him."

"And if you ever lay a hand on another woman I'll kill you."

He chuckled, still holding her. "I believe you would."

73

"Believe," she said, pulling his face down until it was an inch away from hers. "Believe."

When it was dark he went out to try to find food. Down the street he found a partially boarded-up shop. The soldier posted in front of it eyed him suspiciously before he allowed him to enter.

"It's the looters," the nervous shopkeeper said. "They've carried off most of my stock. Ran in here like a bunch of animals, knocking shelves over, grabbing things up. My poor wife will never get over the fright of it. And the shooting! *Madre de Dios!* Will it never stop?"

The man sold him a few sweet potatoes, some rice, and a handful of beans. When he left the shop he looked down the street toward the Zocolo where he could see squads of soldiers. Farther down he caught a glimpse of the National Palace. There was barbed wire all around it and soldiers guarding it. There was no way he could get to the building. And he knew that even if he did he'd never be allowed to see Madero.

"Halt!" The sentry stepped out of a doorway, his rifle aimed at Luis' stomach. "Stand where you are! Don't move!"

"I'm sorry, *amigo*. I came out to find some food. I wanted to see what's happening."

"That damned Diaz who's holed up in the Citadel is what's happening." The sentry's face was strained, his eyes red-rimmed with fatigue. "The goddamned shooting never stops. Jesus! My ears are sick to death of the noise." He eyed Luis. "But I talk too much. What the hell do you want, anyway?"

"I told you, I came out for food. My wife and I live in one of those apartments farther down. We didn't get out in time and now they won't let us leave."

"All right, but don't come out again. You stay in with your wife until this is over. And the way it's going now it'll last forever."

It lasted ten days. For ten tragic days the two opposing generals, Diaz, who commanded the Citadel, and Huerta, who commanded the Palace, sprayed Mexico City with shells. General Felipe Angeles, who had been in Morelos trying to control Zapata, hastened back to the capital to protect President Madero. But he found himself blocked by both General Huerta and United States Ambassador Henry Lane Wilson.

The street near the Zocolo, which housed the apartment where Luis and Sarah were, was deserted except for the sentries and the frightened shopkeeper and his wife. The sounds of battle went on and on. Buildings shook. Rocks and bricks crumbled with the blasts of shells and grenades. Plaster dust filled the air. And still the battle raged.

For Sarah it was a time of an almost desperate happiness. A make-believe kind of happiness. She knew now what it was to live with a man, to lie by his side every night, to wake to find him next to her. Her body responded to his in a way she had never dreamed possible. For eight days they lived in a sensual dream, growing in their knowledge of each other. And each time they were sure they understood all the lovely secrets of their desires, they discovered new delights. Their hungers were deep; their appetites insatiable.

It would be difficult telling Andres, but no matter what he said or what he did, she and Luis would be together.

On the morning of the eighth day he told her he thought they should try to make a break for it that night. "There's no way of knowing how long this will go on," he said. "The sentries are bored and tired now. I went down to the street last night after you were asleep. The guard across from us was dead to the world."

"Where will we go? Dad is with Andres' family . . ."

"We'll go to the hacienda. I'll get word to your father from there."

She looked around her at the mustard-colored walls, the broken windows, the crumbling plaster. "I hate to leave this place. It's been our first home."

"We'll have others."

"Will we, Luis?"

"Of course." But his eyes avoided hers and she felt a small twinge of fear.

They made love for a long time that morning, doing wild wonderful things, sometimes with a savageness that almost frightened her. Sometimes with a strange sweetness that made her weep. I'll never get enough of him, she thought. I want to live to be very very old, and I want him to live to be very very old. I want to love him and care for him until the day I die.

When it was time to leave he put money on one of the cracked plates in the kitchen cabinet. And he put the mattress back on the bed in the bedroom. "That's that," he said. "We'd better get going."

But Sarah lingered, looking around the room for the last time. And then she untied the ribbon that held her hair back and put in on the plate next to the money. "I want to leave a part of me here," she said. "Maybe there's a little girl. Maybe she . . ." Her voice broke.

He put his arm around her shoulders. And when he spoke his voice was husky. "We'll come back some day, Sarita, just to see who lives here. Just to remember."

She leaned against him. "I'll always remember," she said.

Chapter 8

The steady rat-ta-tat of gunfire and the dull boom of cannons staccatoed the night. Bright streaks of rifle fire crisscrossed the Zocolo. But in spite of the noise and the flashes of light, the sentry slumped in the doorway across from them, his rifle at his side, his hands crossed over his stomach, fast asleep.

They pressed tight against the sides of the buildings, made their way down the street, away from the Zocolo. When they reached the end of the block Luis motioned her back while he peered cautiously around the corner.

"There's a guard," he whispered. "But he's facing the other way. I think we can make it, but if he yells, stop. Understand?"

She nodded.

He took her hand and cautiously they started down the street. They'd gone only twenty steps when the soldier swiveled and yelled, "Stop! Right where you are."

They didn't move.

"What the hell you doing out?"

"We're trying to get out of town, friend, like everybody else."

"Everybody who was getting out got out. Get the hell back the way you came. You can't pass here."

"Now look . . ."

"No, you look." The soldier raised his rifle. "Let me see your papers. You got a pass? The word came down two days ago that Diaz has spies sneaking around. And we heard that some of Villa's men are here. By God, I'd like to catch one of them! General Huerta's got a bounty out—two hundred pesos for anybody that's ever been with Villa."

Luis felt Sarah's hand tighten on his arm.

"Lemme see your pass," the soldier said. "You got no pass I'm going to give the alert."

Luis eased away from Sarah. "You're talking so damn much you haven't given me a chance to answer you. I've got a pass, for myself and my wife. If you'll take that damned rifle out of my stomach I'll get it for you."

"Be quick, then."

"All right, but turn the rifle the other way. You're scaring my wife." He held his hands up in front of him. "Take it easy," he said. "Just take it easy." Then, before the man could blink, his hand came down on the soldier's wrist and the other hand came up in a flat-handed movement that caught the man across his throat. Another chop behind the neck, this time with both hands. His rifle clattered against the street stones when he fell.

"Raul," a voice yelled. "*¿Qué pasa?* Is everything all right?"

Luis grabbed her hand and ran. Behind them they heard footsteps and a voice shouting. "Raul! What happened?"

A shot was fired. They heard steps. Shouts. Running feet.

His hand held hers, urging her on, faster and faster. They reached the corner, turned and ran on. Another corner. Steps pounded behind them. Her breath rasped in her throat, her legs shot hot spears of pain. He pulled her through an open courtyard, across a patio, around a stone fountain, under an arched corridor. They flattened themselves against the corridor, trying to still their labored breathing.

Soldiers stormed into the courtyard, lanterns held

78

high. Muffled voices called back and forth. And finally one of them yelled, *"Adelante.* They are not here. Back to the street."

They didn't move. Then slowly, carefully, Luis peered out into the patio. "They're gone," he whispered. "But they might be back when they don't see any sign of us on the street. We've got to get out of here."

Sarah leaned back against the cool stones, trying to catch her breath, trying to ease the pain in her side, while he looked around. The way they'd entered was the only way out. The other end of the patio was protected by a wall. He pointed to it. "That has to be it," he said. "Over the wall."

"I can't," she whispered. "My skirt . . ."

"We'll fix that." He grinned and reached for her. "I ripped it once, señorita, I can do it again. But I promise you, when this is over I'll buy you the best-looking skirt in Mexico City."

"You'd better buy me more than one. The way you go through them . . ."

He chuckled as he reached down and tore her skirt from the hem up. "If I boost you up can you grab hold?"

"I think so."

He cupped his hands, said, "Ready?" and shoved her toward the top of the wall. She pulled herself up, threw one leg over the top, and whispered, "All right, I can make it now."

When they jumped down the other side they saw that they were in a park. The sound of the battle was farther away.

"We've got to walk a long way," he said. "Are you up to it?"

"Of course." She took his hand.

"I've got a friend. We'll go there, get a couple of horses, and ride to the hacienda. But it's a good distance, Sarah. Almost to the Shrine of Guadalupe."

She groaned inwardly, but she forced a smile and

said, "Well, we need the fresh air. We've been cooped up for over a week."

"The best cooped up I've ever experienced." He squeezed her hand. "Now let's go."

It took them almost two hours. The streets were dark, and as they got farther away from the center of town the street gave way to a dirt road. But at least they were far from the battle area. She didn't mind walking, but she wished they could go directly to her father. She could understand that Luis didn't want to go to the Ortiz house; she didn't look forward to facing Andres either. But it had to be done. Telling her father would be easier. He didn't like Andres and he did like Luis. He would be pleased to hear that she was breaking her engagement to Andres. Luis hadn't mentioned marriage, but it was understood. There was nothing to stop them now. Villa was in Texas, his army disbanded. She didn't know, and didn't want to know, what Luis had done these last years. But his Villa days were over.

"We're here," he said at last.

It was more narrow alleyway than street. All of the houses were dark. Only the sharp warning bark of a dog broke the stillness. Luis stopped in front of a dark wall. The top of it was covered with shards of glass that protruded from cement. He found the door and knocked, and a dog barked, sharp and warning. Luis waited a moment and knocked again. The barking grew to an angry frenzy.

The door opened an inch. Sarah heard the scratch of a match. "Who is it?" a voice whispered, and muttered a warning to the dog.

"Vega."

The door opened an inch. A candle was raised. A voice said, *"Madre de Dios,* it is you."

Arms reached out for him, embraced him, and a voice said, "Thank God, oh thank God, Luis. I thought they had you."

Sarah saw the form then, the long dark hair, the
80

hands that touched his face. "Why didn't you get word
to me, you bastard? I was like a crazy woman. I could
kill you!" She hugged him to her. "Ay, Luis, Luis . . ."

He stepped away from her. "Let us in, Marta.
Somebody might see us."

"Us?" Her eyes widened when she saw Sarah.

When she closed the big wooden door she slid a bar
across it. They were in a yard or a patio of some kind,
Sarah thought. She could hear the soft inquiring
whinny of horses nearby. As she took two steps forward a large black dog growled a warning and snapped
at her heels. She cried out in fear and Luis kicked the
dog away from her.

"He's harmless," the woman said carelessly, and
led them through the yard, up two steps, and into a
dimly lighted room. "That's better," she said. "Now
I can see you." She smiled at Luis. "I've been wild,
querido. Where the hell have you been? And who is
this? Why did you bring her here?"

"This is Sarah. Sarah Finch. Marta Sevilla."

The woman stared at her. She was older than Sarah,
thirty perhaps. She was of medium height, and although she wore a long nightgown and had a rebozo
over her shoulders, Sarah could see that her figure,
while full, was extraordinary. She had the slightly
slanted eyes and high cheekbones of some Mexicans
who were living proof that their Asiatic ancestors had
crossed the Bering Straits centuries before.

So this was the friend with the horses!

"Where did you find her? Why in the name of God
did you bring her here?"

"I've known Sarah for a long time, Marta. I was in
the Zocolo that Sunday when the fighting started. We
both got caught in the mob. We couldn't get out because the neighborhood was cordoned off. Now tell
me, what have you heard? What has been happening?"

"You knew that bastard Huerta has arrested Madero and all of his cabinet, didn't you?"

"That's impossible!" Sarah exclaimed. "General Huerta is head of the Palace guard. His job is to *protect* Madero."

"My God!" Luis' face was white. "He'll kill them all."

"He couldn't do that, Luis," Sarah said, her hand on his arm. "The United States would never allow it to . . ."

"Shut up!" The other woman turned on her, her face contorted with anger. "You don't know what you're talking about, *gringa*. The son-of-a-bitch Henry Lane Wilson, your goddamned ambassador, is as much responsible as Huerta is. General Angeles tried to get to Madero and your ambassador stopped him." She turned to Luis. "Word has come from the North that Villa . . ." She caught a warning glance from Luis.

"Marta, why don't you find something for Sarah to wear? I'm afraid her clothes are in pretty bad shape."

"She'd drown in mine. Perhaps my brother's would fit her." She smiled sweetly at Sarah. "He's fourteen."

Sarah bit her lip. Her nails bit into her palms, itching to claw the other woman.

"Come along," Marta said, and took her to a small cluttered room where she grabbed some clothes off a hook and tossed them to her. She left the candle and closed the door without a word.

Sarah looked at the clothes—a pair of boy's knickers, worn and patched. A dark blue shirt. Built like a boy, was she! She threw the clothes on the floor. She'd never been so angry, never disliked anyone as much as she did this woman. What was Luis' relationship with her? The way she'd thrown her arms around him one would think . . . And Luis! Instead of pulling away he'd only patted her back. Patted her back! Sarah wanted to pat her with a club! She'd lied about General Huerta. Everyone knew he was loyal to President Madero. Andres had told her so, and Andres was as close to Huerta as he was to his own father. She

82

frowned, remembering the warning look Luis had given Marta when she mentioned Villa. But why was he afraid to speak in front of her? And what about Villa? He was supposed to be in Texas.

She couldn't wait to get out of there. She glanced down at her torn skirt and knew she couldn't ride in it. Angrily she pulled it off and threw it on the floor. She picked up the patched knickers and pulled them on. Damn! They fit! She picked up the candle and made her way back to the other room.

"But what if something happens to you? That bastard Huerta would like nothing better than to get his hands on Villa's famous Captain Vega." Marta's voice was low and urgent. "He suspects that Villa is ready to call his old troops together, the troops you are . . ." She stopped abruptly and turned to see Sarah standing in the shadows. She whispered something to Luis and he shook his head.

"Come and have a cup of coffee," he said. "We've got a long ride ahead of us. Marta will get you some soup if you like."

"No, thank you. I'm not hungry." Her voice was cold.

"You do know how to ride?" Marta asked.

"Of course I know how to ride."

"Side saddle?"

Sarah took a step forward.

"We have to go," Luis said, his hand on her arm. "I want to get there before it's light."

"I'm going with you. It will only take a moment to change," Marta said.

"You stay here. I'll be back in three days. If there's any news before that, send a message to the hacienda."

"But I want to go with you!"

"No, it's important that you're here."

And when she saw that his mind was made up, she led them to a corral behind the house, selected two horses, and said, "These ought to do. Walk them until you reach the end of the street."

"We will. *Adios,* Marta, and thank you."

"Godspeed, Luis." Her hand touched his leg. *"Vaya con Dios, querido."* And to Sarah she said, "You have a good horse. Try not to hurt his mouth. And try not to slow Luis down. It's dangerous for him now."

"I won't hurt your horse's mouth, I won't slow Luis down." Sarah's voice was cold. "And get your goddamned hand off his leg!"

She heard the other woman's gasp of surprise as Luis said, *"Vámonos,"* and led the way out of the corral.

Chapter 9

They rode for almost thirty minutes before Luis held his hand up and motioned her to stop. They were in the hills, high above the Valley of Mexico where the air was cold and clear. Below them they could see the lights of the city and hear the dull distant boom of cannons.

When he saw that she was shivering he took off his jacket and handed it to her. "Put this on," he said. "Marta should have given you something warmer."

"I don't want it."

"Sarah . . ." For a moment he looked angry and impatient. Then his face softened and he said, "There's no reason for you to be jealous of Marta. She's a *sol-dadera,* a fellow soldier. I've never thought of her as a woman."

"She's certainly thought of you as a man!"

"You're imagining things. We're comrades, that's all. We fight for the same cause." He reached out and put his fingers under her chin. "You're the only woman I'll ever want, Sarah. Especially now, after this last week, this time we've been together. I'll never want a woman the way I want you. I'll never touch a woman the way I've touched you." He leaned forward out of his saddle, and drawing her to him, kissed her. "And just in case I haven't mentioned it," he said when he let her go, "I love you."

When the sky lightened to smoke gray they could see the tall cactus, standing like silent sentinels of the desert. The quiet was as deep as it was beautiful. But as they came closer to the village, life began to stir. An old man, wrapped to his eyes in a serape, waved to them as he munched a dry tortilla while his sharp-eyed dogs snapped at the sheep. And black-shawled women, water jars on their heads, went to the stream for water.

A man ran out to take their horses when they rode through the gates of the hacienda, but before they'd dismounted a short round-faced woman that Sarah remembered from the times she'd been at the hacienda rushed out to the courtyard. "Ay, Don Luis," she cried, "we have been so worried. Your father and mother are beside themselves, and your brother, Father Carlitos, is here. Are you all right?"

"I'm fine, Antonia. Do you remember the Señorita Finch? We're tired and cold and hungry. Do you have some hot coffee on the stove?"

"Of course. Of course." She took her rebozo off and wrapped it around Sarah. *"Pobrecita,* you are freezing. Come and I will give you breakfast and you can warm yourself by the stove."

"Did you say Carlos was here? When did he arrive?"

"Three days ago. Do you want me to wake him? And your father?"

He shook his head. "No, let them sleep. We'll eat and then perhaps you'll show Señorita Sarah to her room and let her rest a bit."

The kitchen was warm. When Luis went to the wood stove to warm his hands, Sarah took his jacket off and handed it to him. He looked at her and started to laugh.

"What's so funny?"

"You," he said in English. "In those damn knickers. Marta was right. You *are* built like a fourteen-year-old boy."

Her lips tightened and her green eyes narrowed to slits. But she didn't answer him.

After they'd eaten Antonia took her to a large bedroom off the patio. "Get into bed," she ordered, handing Sarah a flannel nightgown. When she picked up the knickers she made a face and said, "Such dreadful things for a nice young lady to wear. What shall I do with them?"

"Burn them!" Built like a boy, was she? Damn him! And he hadn't fooled her with all that talk about Marta being a fellow soldier—any fool could see that the woman was in love with him.

"Can I get you anything else?" Antonia's round face was kind.

"No, *gracias*. I'll just rest for an hour or two . . ." But it was late afternoon before she woke.

Carlos rose early to perform mass in the chapel of the hacienda. He was surprised and delighted to find his brother in the kitchen. "Come along to mass with me," he said. "I've done your praying for you long enough. It's time God got a look at you."

As Luis knelt on the hard wooden board his mind wandered from the ritual of the mass to the man who was saying it. It was still difficult for him to realize that this was his brother Carlos dressed in the vestments of a priest. Luis, almost six years older, could remember, and smile now, at the child Carlos had been. He was sweet-faced and obedient until his big brother wanted to go out. And when their mother said, "No, you are too little to play with Luis and his friends," the small face would pinch like a prune and his howls would shake the house. And Luis always ended up with Carlos tagging after him. If Luis rode a wild horse, Carlos rode one too. When Luis and his friends played the forbidden game of Matador with his father's brave bulls, Carlos did the same. No matter how many times he got hurt, no matter how many times a furious Luis slung him over his shoulder and carried him home, he always returned. He had to do what Luis did. He had to be where Luis was.

When Carlos made the decision to go into the priesthood Luis tried to talk him out of it. "There's a whole big world out there, *manito,*" he said. "Places to go, things to see. Women to meet. Surely, Carlos you . . ." He hesitated.

"I like women, Luis." The smile, like the man, was gentle. "I've thought about this for a long time. And yes, I have thought of what it would be like to marry and have children. But I cannot. God has called me and I must follow His dictates. As for women, dear brother, I have a feeling you like them enough for both of us."

He told Carlos about Sarah on their way back from the chapel. "She was engaged to Andres," he said. "But that's finished. I love her and she loves me."

"And you plan to marry her?"

"Yes, yes, of course I do. I should have married her two years ago. If ever two people belong together Sarah and I do. But this is a bad time for love, Carlos. The revolution is going to catch fire again. It will be like it was before when we fought to rid ourselves of Porfirio. Only this time I am afraid it will be rougher."

"This means you will go back to Villa?"

"I'll have to. As soon as I can."

"And what about Sarah?"

"I'll ask her to wait."

"How long, Luis? Until you're ready?" His face was concerned. "You hurt her before when you went away. Don't hurt her again."

"I don't want to hurt her, but I have a job to do. Mexico is going to need every man she has if Huerta takes over the government."

"Don't some of the men take their wives with them when they join the revolution?"

"Yes, but . . . those women are different, Carlos. It's a hard life. Their home is a railroad car or a tent. Sometimes it's only a blanket next to a campfire. Can you imagine Sarah living like that? She's accustomed to nice things, to a real home, to security."

"But why not ask her, Luis? Let the decision be hers."

Luis shook his head. "No, it's out of the question. She'll be better off in San Antonio. We'll get married when this is over."

"Why not marry her now? At least give her the security of your love and your name."

"No. It's out of the question for now." His voice was abrupt, ending the conversation.

Their father and mother were waiting for them when they returned. His mother rushed into his arms, embracing him, saying, "Luis, Luis, how we have worried."

"What's happening in the capital?" his father asked. "Is the fighting still going on?"

Luis nodded. "This is the tenth day. Did you know that Huerta has imprisoned Madero and the cabinet?"

"No! My God, Luis, this means . . ."

"That Huerta has already taken over the government."

"Then God help Mexico."

"God and her people will help her," Luis said.

His mother started to cry. "This means you will go back to Villa," she said.

He put his arms around her and kissed the top of her head.

Sarah woke in time for the afternoon meal, and when she appeared she was dressed in clothes that had once belonged to Luis' mother. When Antonia brought them to her she said, "These used to fit the Señora Vega. They are out of date, but better I think than those boy's clothes. She said you were to wear whatever pleased you."

She chose a long-sleeved soft wool dress in a warm gold color. And when she went out to join the others the Señora Vega clapped her hands and said, "To think I was ever that slim! That is why I keep some of my clothes. I can always take them out and say, 'You see how slim I was, Alberto. It is only because you have made me so happy that I have grown wider.'"

"Wider and lovelier," her husband said as he kissed
89

her hand. "The dress looks well on you, Señorita Sarah. Now come sit next to me. Luis tells me you've had a meager diet these last days."

Sarah's eyes flicked to Luis. And what else had he told them?

"The family we were with shared what they had, father. But there were six of them living in the apartment. Señor and Señora Fernandez, the grandmother, and three children."

"It was kind of them to take you in," Carlos said. "How old were the children, Luis?"

"One, two, and three," Luis answered, and glared at his brother.

"Thank God Luis found you," Señora Vega said. "It must have been terrible. All those poor people on their way to mass. They say over two hundred of them were killed. Were you in Mexico alone, my dear?"

"No, my father was with me. But I went to mass alone."

"And does he know that you are safe?"

"No, señora. I've got to get word to him. Luis said . . ."

"That poor man," Don Alberto said. "You haven't been in contact with him since the fighting started? He must be half out of his mind with worry."

"There was no way we could send a message. The apartment we . . . we stayed in with the . . ." She couldn't remember the name Luis had used. "With the family," she said finally, "was so close to the Zocolo where the fighting was that the block was cordoned off."

"Then I will send word to him immediately," Señor Vega said, and got up.

Luis held him back. "We'll do it later," he said.

"But Luis, surely . . ."

"I'll take care of it, father."

And afterward, when they were alone he said, "Señor Finch is staying with the Ortiz family."

"And that is awkward because you and Andres are on different sides of the fence?"

90

"And because we're in love with the same woman."

His father's eyebrows raised. "I see."

"Until last week Sarah was engaged to him. As far as he knows they're still engaged. He'll have to be told, of course, but unfortunately I can't be the one to tell him. He's one of Huerta's boys, and if Huerta knows I'm here I'm a dead man."

He hitched his chair closer to his father and lowered his voice. "I came to try to see Madero—to tell him if he didn't get rid of Huerta there'd be hell to pay with the rebel troops. But I was too late; Madero's a prisoner. All I can do now is get back to Chihuahua."

"That's a long, dangerous trip, Luis. How will you go?"

"By way of San Luis Potosi and Zacatecas. I'll cut down to Fresnillo and stick to the mountains to avoid the Federales. My men are ready and waiting. And as soon as Villa hears what's happened in the capital he'll cross the Rio Grande."

"And so it begins again." His father's eyes were full of pain. "I am sad for all of us, but especially I think for your mother and Sarah. It's a hard thing for women. What have you told Sarah of this? And why wouldn't you let me send a message to her father?"

"I haven't told Sarah anything, Father. And I couldn't risk sending a message to her father because I was afraid Andres would get his hands on it." He looked uncomfortable. "That's why I don't want Sarah to know too much about what I'm doing. It's not that I don't trust her, it's that she's politically naive and she might inadvertently let something slip. Andres is a tricky bastard; he'd get information out of her without her even knowing she'd told him anything."

"It's hard to believe he's changed so much, Luis."

"He has, father. Believe me. He's Huerta's right arm—his executioner. Madero didn't know half of what was going on in his own government. Most of the time Huerta gave the orders and Andres carried them out. He's destroyed whole villages; killed every

91

man, woman, and child in them because there were rumors the people might support Villa or Zapata. He's so hungry for power he'd kill his own mother if Huerta asked him to."

"And Sarah doesn't know any of this?"

"She lives in a different world. She's not in love with Andres, but she believes he's a decent man. She's young. There are things she just doesn't understand."

"I don't think you're being fair. I think you see her as she was two years ago, not as she is now. Even I can see that she's matured." His face was thoughtful. "I think you should take her into your confidence, Luis. Don't treat her like a child. Tell her what kind of man Andres is. Trust her. If she loves you . . ."

"She loves me, and perhaps she would believe me. But I can't just think of myself, I have to think of the men I'm responsible for." He shook his head. "No, what is between Sarah and me has to be apart from what I do for the revolution."

Dinner that night was a family affair. The flames from the fireplace cast a soft glow over the dining room. Warm dark wood blended with the red velvet chairs. A bowl of poinsettia stood out against the white tablecloth. Polished silver shone alongside gold-rimmed china plates. When Don Alberto raised his glass the light from the tall red candles in the silver candlesticks deepened the color of the wine.

"To my family," he said. "To Maria, Luis, Carlos, and Sarah."

When she raised her glass she felt quick tears sting her eyes. She loved Don Alberto. She loved them all. They were a handsome family. The mother, Maria, wore her black hair pulled off her face into a bun at the back of her neck. She was dressed in a simple black silk dress, and her only jewelry was a long strand of pearls. Luis and his father wore dinner jackets, and Carlos wore his brown Franciscan robe.

Maria Vega smiled across the table at Sarah. "I think you must keep the dress. It's lovely on you, even if it is old-fashioned. It would make me happy if you would accept it as a gift."

"Thank you, Doña Maria. It's beautiful."

The dress was sea-green velvet. The cut was plain, almost severe. The long sleeves fit her slender arms snugly, the waist hugged hers. There were no tucks or pleats or ruffles. But the bodice was cut low so that the whiteness of her shoulders and her neck gleamed in lovely contrast.

As she leaned forward to touch his mother's hand, the light of the candles caught her copper hair, warming it, changing it to the color of flame. Luis' heart leaped in his throat, and he thought again as he had the first time he'd seen her, that he would never again see anything as lovely as she was.

"Sarah . . ."

She turned to look at him, and when she saw the expression in his eyes, her own eyes widened. She set her glass down carefully, and folded her hands in her lap.

"Perhaps what I want to say to you should be said when we are alone, but I think I would like to say it here, in front of my family."

He saw sudden tears glistening in her green eyes.

"These are difficult times, Sarah. In all frankness I didn't plan to ask you until things were not so dangerous for Mexico. But now I feel . . . I feel such a need to say the words." He covered her hand with his. "Will you marry me, Sarah?"

"I'll be proud to marry you," she said softly.

Don Alberto jumped to his feet to hug Sarah and to embrace his son. Carlos whooped and clapped his brother on the back, and Doña Maria began to cry. "I'm so happy," she said finally, wiping her eyes with a white lace handkerchief. "I have always wanted a daughter. I know no one will ever replace your own mother, but I hope you will think of me as a substitute, as someone who loves you for making my son as happy as he is tonight." She took her pearls off. "This is an engagement present," she said.

"No, I couldn't . . ."

"Please. It will make me very happy."

"Thank you," Sarah said, slipping them over her head, feeling their warmth against her skin, "thank you." She kissed Maria Vega's cheek. And reaching for Luis' hand she said, "This is the happiest night of my life."

It was warm the next morning, and they were having breakfast on the patio when Antonia burst in to say that a message had come for Luis. "It is a woman in pants," she said, frowning her disapproval.

"Tell the lady to join us here on the patio," Maria Vega said before Luis could stop her.

Sarah wiped her lips slowly, feeling her stomach knot, knowing even before she saw her that the woman was Marta. But why had she come here? Why . . . ? She glanced at Luis, saw him rise from his chair, and felt a quiver of fear, as Marta crossed the patio, her boots striking the flagstones with staccato harshness.

She had not been able to see the other woman well the other night, but she saw now, with an awful sinking feeling, that Marta was a striking woman. Not beautiful, but handsome. The pants hugged her flat stomach and narrow hips. Her big high breasts pressed against the shirt that was a size too small for her.

"I must speak to you," she said to Luis, ignoring the others at the table.

"You may speak in front of my parents."

Her eyes flicked to Sarah.

"It's all right," Luis said. "What is it?"

"The President's brother has been murdered. Huerta had him arrested and taken to the Citadel. We have a man there. He told us the soldiers slashed his face to ribbons for sport, and while he pleaded for his life for the sake of his wife and children, they murdered him."

94

"Ay, *Dios mio*," Maria Vega said.

"Last night Huerta had a meeting at the United States embassy." She looked at Sarah, and when she spoke again her voice was filled with hate. "Your dear Ambassador Henry Lane Wilson has persuaded your country to accept the provisional presidency of General Huerta. He even had other foreign diplomats there and introduced Huerta to them as the 'savior of Mexico.'"

"Incredible," Señor Vega said. "Absolutely incredible."

"And what of President Madero?" Luis asked.

"Both Madero and Vice-President Pino Suarez have resigned. Huerta has promised that they and their partisans will not be harmed, that they will be allowed to retire in exile." She brushed her dark hair back. "He's lying, Luis. He'll kill them."

He bit his lip. "I know," he said.

"You've got to leave. Now that Huerta's in power he's rounding up all Madero supporters, especially those who fought for him in the revolution."

Don Alberto put his hand on his son's arm. "She is right, Luis. It's not safe for you here."

"When is Madero to go?" Luis asked.

"In a day or two, they say. He'll leave from Veracruz. His family has been notified to wait for him there. This morning his wife went to see Ambassador Wilson to ask him to intercede with Huerta to spare the President's life." Her lip curled. "And of course Wilson told her she had nothing to worry about, that General Huerta is an honorable man."

"And so it begins again," Carlos said. "And you, Luis, you will begin again."

"No!" Sarah's voice cut in. "No, we'll go back to Texas. We'll . . ."

"You know I can't go back to Texas," Luis said. He turned to Antonia. "My saddlebag is partially packed. Put a change of clothes in it and bring it to me. And hurry, please."

95

He took Sarah's arm and led her to one side of the patio. "I'm sorry," he said, lowering his voice so that only she could hear him. "I knew I would have to leave, but I didn't think it would be this soon."

"But you can't. You can't."

"I should have told you last night, *querida*, before I asked you to marry me."

She felt as though her heart had stopped. She took a deep shattering breath and said, "Are you sorry that you did? Is that it?"

He shook his head. "No, of course not! I want to marry you. I want to live with you. But I can't—not for a while."

"I see." Her voice was cold. As cold and frozen as her heart. She wanted to fling herself into his arms and beg him not to leave. Instead she said, in a voice that was not her own, "And what am I to do? Marry Andres?"

His face went white. "Don't talk like that. When this is over . . ."

"When this is over." Her eyes were bitter. "The revolution will never be over. If I meant anything at all to you you wouldn't leave me. You couldn't."

"Sarah. *Por Dios*, Sarah, don't make this harder than it is." He pulled her to him and bent to kiss her.

"Luis!" Marta's voice was sharp.

"All right!" he snapped. And still holding Sarah he said, "Please try to understand."

"That's the problem, Luis. I understand all too well." She pulled away from him.

"Here is your saddlebag, Don Luis," Antonia said.

"Luis, *por favor*," his mother pleaded, "you must not leave like this. You must consider Sarah's feelings. If it's not safe for you here then go back to Texas for a while, and take Sarah with you. You've had enough fighting. Let somebody else do it now."

"I'm sorry, mother. But this is not the business of women."

"If it's not a business for women, why are you going with her?" Sarah challenged him.

"I haven't time for this now. And I will not have you make a scene. I have to leave."

"Then take *me!*" Her voice was a cry as the ice around her heart shattered and broke.

His face was white. "Go back to San Antonio," he said. "I'll come to you when I can."

"You left me once, Luis," she said brokenly. "Don't leave me again."

"I love you," he said. "But I love Mexico too. And she needs me now, more than you do."

"Nobody, nothing . . ." she tried to control her voice, "will ever need you as much as I do." She clutched his arm. "If you leave me now . . ."

He shrugged away from her. His cold Aztec eyes met and held hers. "Don't threaten me," he said, "and don't, for God's sake, make a scene."

He turned to kiss his mother, to embrace his father.

"God go with you," his brother said.

"And with you, Carlos."

And then he was gone, striding across the patio, down the broad stone steps to his horse. And when he mounted he nodded to Marta and said, *"Vámonos."*

"Wait!" Sarah ran down the stairs and out to the yard. She grabbed the horse's bridle. "If you leave me now," she sobbed, "if you leave now I don't know what I'll do." Her voice was on the thin edge of hysteria.

"Let go of that bridle, Sarah."

"I won't let you go," she cried, tightening her hands on the bridle.

"Damn it," he cried. "I won't have a scene like this. Let go!"

"No!"

"Let go, I said!" He struck her hands with his riding crop.

She let go, more in shock than in pain. She looked up at his face, white and hard and angry. And at Marta, her lips pursed in amusement.

"You bastard," she said. "You vicious bastard. I wish I could tell you how much I hate you. I wish I could hurt you like you're hurting me."

He looked down at her, his face void of any expression. And still looking at her he said, *"Vámonos,* Marta, we have far to ride."

Chapter 10

On the twenty-second of February, while the United States embassy celebrated George Washington's birthday, President Francisco Madero and Vice President Pino Suarez were assassinated.

They were killed in the basement of the Palace. Their bodies were then placed in a carriage and taken to a spot near the penitentiary where they were discovered. The story was told that they had been transferred to the penitentiary for their own safety, had tried to escape from the carriage, and been shot.

And so began Victoriano Huerta's seventeen months as President of Mexico. Seventeen months of an uninterrupted orgy of drunkenness, robbery, and murder. Those in the Congress who denounced him were killed. A hundred and ten congressional dissenters were jailed. Huerta and his thugs ruled Mexico.

On the afternoon of Luis' departure Sarah kissed his mother and father goodbye. When she tried to return the green dress and the pearls Maria Vega said, "No, Sarita, keep them. I gave them to you."

"As an engagement present, señora. There's no engagement now. It's over."

"I don't think it will ever be over between you and Luis. He is my son, Sarah. I know his heart and I know he loves you. But he is a willful man. If he has made up his mind to do something he will do it and nothing will stop him—not even if he loves you. He was the same when he was small. I could plead, threaten, and yes, even beat him, but I could never change him from what he wanted to do. When this is finished, Sarah, he will come back to you."

And Carlos said, "He's not an easy man, that brother of mine. Be patient with him, Sarah. When this is over . . ."

When this is over. When this is over.

She was empty inside. She hadn't cried since that moment in the yard when Luis struck her with the riding crop. She would never forgive him for that.

The foreman of the hacienda took her back to Mexico City. Back to her father. And to Andres.

They looked at her as though she were a ghost when she went into the Ortiz house. Her father, white and shaken, looking older than his years, was unable to rise from his chair. The Señora Ortiz looking—or did Sarah only imagine it?—just the least bit disappointed. Andres, incredulous, rushing to grasp her hands, to pull her to him. And then the difficult part, explaining where she had been these last ten days.

"With Luis Vega?" Andres' face was white.

"And a family by the name of . . . Fernandez," she lied, as Luis had lied. "We were with them in their apartment. The neighborhood was cordoned off, Andres. I couldn't get out. I couldn't get word to you or father."

"But—*Vega!*"

"Well, I for one am grateful to him," her father said. "Thank God Luis was there to help her. She's safe, and that's all that matters."

"But Señor Finch, what will we tell people?" Andres' mother asked, her prim face pinched in a frown. "Andres' fiancée spent almost two weeks with another man, an enemy of my son's. How will it sound to our friends?"

"Now, Mother . . ."

"I'm thinking of your career, Andres."

His eyebrows came together, and Sarah saw the flicker of concern.

"These are difficult times," his mother went on.

"General Huerta has so much to do. Andres is important to him. He can't afford a scandal. And he certainly can't be tied to Luis Vega. Everyone knows that Vega is one of Villa's *dorados*."

"No one has to know that Sarah was with Vega, mother. We can fabricate a story and we can re-schedule the wedding."

"About the wedding . . ." Sarah wet her lips.

"Dreadful!" His mother sniffed. "We had to tell all our friends that it was cancelled because of the emergency."

"Not cancelled, mother. Delayed." He smiled at Sarah, but his smile faded as he looked at her hand. "Where is your ring?" His voice was sharp.

"I took it off. I was afraid I'd lose it."

"You still have it?"

"Of course."

"Then put it on."

"It's . . . with the things I brought from the ranch, Andres. Let me get cleaned up, out of these clothes and into something more presentable. We'll talk then."

"Of course, my dear," he said. But his face was tight, his eyes angry.

She had just finished her bath when he knocked at the door of her room. Slipping into a robe, she opened the door a crack and said, "I'm not dressed."

He pushed the door open. "I must speak to you."

"I'll put something on and meet you downstairs."

"No, I don't want to talk to you in front of the others." He came into the room and shut the door.

She frowned, angry at this intrusion, afraid of what she saw in his eyes. She tightened the robe around her. "Well, what is it?"

"I want to know about you and Luis. What happened between you?"

"I've already told you." Her voice was cold.

"Tell me again." He folded his arms across his chest. And when she didn't speak he said, "Tell me again, Sarah, right from the beginning."

Her face was without expression as she said, "I was

caught in the Zocolo on my way to mass when the firing started. When your Palace troops started firing on hundreds of innocent people. You were there that day, weren't you? How could you be part of something . . ."

"Never mind that," he cut in, his voice sharp. "I want to hear what you have to say."

"People were crazy with fear," she said, her voice low and angry. "They were spattered with bullets. Women and children . . ." Her fists were clenched, remembering. "I was caught up in the mob. If Luis hadn't got me out I'd have been trampled. He pulled me into a courtyard that was part of an apartment complex. A grenade hit the building and we ran up to the second floor. That's when . . . the family took us in."

"And where is Luis now?"

"I have no idea."

"Don't try to protect him, Sarah."

"I'm not trying to protect him. I don't know where he is. Really, Andres, you shouldn't be in my room like this. Your mother . . ."

"I can handle my mother. Just tell me where Luis is and I'll leave."

"He left the hacienda this morning with a woman by the name of Marta."

"Marta Solis?"

"I don't know her last name. She was about thirty, medium height, handsome." And I don't give a damn what you do to her, she thought.

"Were they meeting anyone else?"

"I don't know. They just left. He said goodbye to his parents and to Carlos and . . ."

"Why was Carlos there?"

"I suppose because he was worried about Luis. Perhaps his family asked him to come. I don't have any idea, but I don't see anything unusual in his being there. He's a priest. Surely he can travel where he chooses."

102

"Don't be naive. Carlos is up to something. All of them are 'maderistas.' "

"So are half the people in Mexico." She looked at him. "Or they were until your beloved Huerta had him shot."

"You don't understand about Huerta. He has to have a strong hand. He can't be hampered by people who are against him. Or by people who give aid to his enemies."

She bit her lip, suddenly wary.

"These are difficult days," he went on. "Zapata is fighting in the south. Obregon and his Yaqui troops have joined forces with Carranza. Villa is organizing in the north. I've got to get my hands on Luis before he reaches Villa. You've got to tell me where he went when he left the hacienda."

"I've already told you. I don't know."

"You're protecting him, aren't you? And why?" His eyes narrowed, measuring her. "Tell me again, Sarah," he said, his voice dangerously soft, "what was the name of the family you and Luis stayed with?"

"I've already told you."

"Tell me again."

"Hernandez."

"Oh? I thought it was Fernandez."

The palms of her hands were wet. "Well . . . that's what I meant to say. Fernandez. Look, Andres, I . . ."

"There never was a family, was there, Sarah?"

"Andres, I . . ." She tried to move away from him toward the door, but he blocked her way. "Wait for me downstairs," she said, trying to keep her voice firm. "I'll come down as soon as I finish dressing and we'll talk."

He shook his head. "We'll talk now. You were alone with Vega, weren't you?"

"Andres, please . . ."

"Weren't you?"

103

"Yes, but . . ." She took a deep breath, trying to steady her voice. And finally, anxious to get it over with, she said, "Yes, we were alone."

"And you let him make love to you."

"I'm sorry. We didn't plan . . . It was something that happened. We . . ."

His face was white. "You bitch," he whispered. "You rotten little bitch. A week before we were to be married."

"Andres, please . . ." She was suddenly frightened by the fury she saw in his face.

His hands grabbed her shoulders. His fingers bit into her skin, hurting the tender flesh beneath the thin robe. "Bitch," he said again.

She tried to squirm away, but he held her. "Neither of us wanted to hurt you, Andres. We . . ."

He struck her across the face with his open palm, and when she cried out he put his hand over her mouth and knocked her back on the bed. His other hand groped for her robe and ripped it open.

She tried to roll away from him, tried to free her mouth, but he held her in an iron grip, his face twisted with rage. "You wouldn't let me touch you," he whispered hoarsely. " 'No,' you said, 'we have to wait until we're married.' But you didn't wait with him. You let him make love to you."

His fingers tightened on her mouth. He tore the belt off her robe, knotted it around her wrists, and tied the other end to one of the bed posts.

Her body contorted, twisted, trying to jerk away from him, from the hand that reached for her breasts. "I'd like to rip them off of you," he snarled. And then he slapped her again, a dizzying blow to the side of her head. When she lay still, stunned, his hand reached down her body, parting the robe with deliberate slowness until he touched the triangle of hair between her thighs. He thrust her legs apart and probed with rough fingers, laughing at the look of shame and rage on her face.

Her green eyes were wide, the cords in her neck

104

taut with her renewed struggle as she saw him try to unfasten the buttons of his trousers with one hand.

For a fraction of a second he looked away from her, and in that fraction of a second he loosened his grip on her mouth and she sank her teeth into his hand. And when he jerked away she screamed.

"Sarah?" The voice was her father's.

She screamed again.

The door burst open and Charlie Finch exploded into the room. He stopped suddenly, shocked by the scene in front of him. Andres, gripping his bloodied hand, Sarah, sprawled on the bed, her hands tied over her head, her face bruised.

Then with a cry he leaped on Andres, his hands reaching for the younger man's throat, his face scarlet with his rage, eyes narrowed, lips pulled back to show his teeth as he knocked Andres to the floor and closed steel fingers around his throat.

Sarah screamed again, and saw a maid's horrified face, and behind her, pushing her aside, Señor Ortiz and his wife. Then, almost gratefully, she fainted.

They were together in the dining room when the soldiers came. Carlos had just returned from performing a christening and was warming his hands in front of the fire. The servant Antonia poured the hot chocolate and said, "Come, Father Carlitos, this will warm you."

At almost the same moment they heard the sound of the horses, the shouts of the men, and the heavy steps running through the house.

Carlos swung around from the fireplace as the first soldier burst through the door. "What . . . ? What's this? What do you want?"

"Shut up, padre!" a sergeant barked.

"Now see here—" Don Alberto blurted.

"Tie the men."

Antonia screamed and dropped the tray of hot chocolate.

Maria Vega, her face white with shock, said, "There must be some mistake. What are you doing? Why have you come here?" She started across the room to her husband, and when a soldier tried to stop her, she pushed him aside. He grabbed her, and when she struggled he hit her with his fist and knocked her to the floor.

Her husband shouted. He strained helplessly against the men who held him, his face gray with shock. Carlos broke away from his captors, but he had taken only two steps when one of the soldiers hit him on the side of the head with a rifle barrel and knocked him to his knees.

Slowly, painfully, with Antonia's help, Maria Vega sat up. "Why are you doing this?" she whispered.

The door was pushed open. A man, hands on his hips, looked at the scene before him. A thin smile parted his lips.

"Why?" Maria Vega said. "What have we done to you? What . . . ?" She looked up. "Andres? Andres, is that you?"

"Sí, Doña Vega."

"Oh, thank God. Thank God you are here."

He came toward her and reached out a hand to help her to her feet.

"What is the meaning of this, Andres?" her husband cried. "One of those men struck Maria. There's been a mistake. Tell them to release us."

"Of course, Don Alberto." His face was smooth. "Just as soon as you tell us where we can find Luis."

"Luis? What has he to do with this? He isn't here. He left yesterday. But what . . . ?"

"Then perhaps you will tell me where he went."

"I don't know."

"To the north to join Villa?"

Don Alberto bit his lip and didn't answer.

"By what route? Ciudad Valles or San Luis Potosí?"

And when Señor Vega didn't answer he turned to

the son and said, "And you, Carlos, will you tell me where your brother is? What route he took?"

Carlos rubbed his eyes, trying to bring the room into focus. "I don't know," he said. He closed his eyes against the pain in his head.

Andres reached down and, grabbing a handful of hair, forced the young priest to look at him. "And you would not tell me if you did, would you, Carlos? Now let me see, what can I do to persuade you?" He smiled. "Your mother is a handsome woman, padre."

He turned to his men. "Do you think she is too old, *compañeros?*" He rubbed his bandaged hand.

"What about you, Jorge? Do you think she's too old? Or you, Pepe?"

"No, captain," the one called Jorge said. "I love a woman with big *chichis.*"

"She doesn't want a skinny *pendejo* like you," the other one said. "I am more the man for a woman like her."

Andres laughed. He held up his hands and said, "All right. All right. We won't argue. She's woman enough for both of you."

"Andres, for the love of God," Carlos whispered, his eyes on his mother's face.

"Where is your brother, Carlos?"

"I don't know!" The words were a cry from the heart.

"Andres," Alberto Vega pleaded in a trembling voice, "your family has always wanted my ranch. Take it. And the bulls. Only let Maria and Carlos go free. I'll go with you."

"Very touching, Don Alberto. But I don't want your ranch. Not now. I want Luis." He waited a moment. "But it appears none of you will help me find him." He looked from the father to the mother to the son. "You really don't leave me any choice, I'm afraid. Well then . . ."

He snapped his fingers. "Take the woman, and the maid if you like. Do whatever you will with them."

107

"Andres, please . . ." Her eyes were wide with appeal. "Your mother and I were schoolmates. I have known you since you were a child. You mustn't do this."

He turned away from her. "Get her out of here," he said. "Raul, you and Nacho take the men. The rest of you spread out. Burn the house and then set fire to the fields."

"Why?" Don Alberto's voice was choked with disbelief.

"And the bulls, Captain Ortiz?" the sergeant asked.

"Shoot them."

"Why are you doing this to us?" Don Alberto asked again.

"Because I want your son." The voice was low with hate. "And if I can't find him I'm going to kill you and I'm going to kill Carlos. But I'll do you one favor, Don Alberto, I'll let your wife live."

"Do me no favors," she said from the door. "I would prefer to die with my husband and my son."

"But I want you to live, Doña Maria. I want Luis to know who did this to you."

He massaged his bandaged hand again. "I want him to know that I did it." He hesitated. "With Sarah's help, of course."

"Sarah?" Her eyes went wide with shock. "They quarreled, but she wouldn't . . ."

He laughed. "Wouldn't she? Wouldn't she?"

And as the two men dragged her out of the room she could still hear the sound of his laughter.

Part III

July, 1913

CAPTURE!

Chapter 11

On a sweltering July morning Sarah waited on a loading platform in Eagle Pass, Texas, watching payroll money and rifles being loaded under the floorboards of a Reo touring car. She fanned her face with a white handkerchief, wishing she had worn something other than the long-skirted gray suit and the gray velvet plumed hat.

My suit of armor, she thought. What the well-dressed schoolteacher wears when traveling through a revolution-torn country with four strange men. But she'd gladly have done worse than that to get to her father.

The telegram had come two days ago. "Your father hurt in mining accident near Torreon," it read. "Insists do not try to come. Will advise when extent of injuries known."

She packed at once, even before she spoke to Sister Christina, who was the head of St. Mary's Academy for Young Ladies. Sister Christina was sympathetic, but she urged Sarah not to go.

"Wait a bit," she counseled. "Say a Novena for your father. After all, the telegram especially advises you *not* to go."

"I'm sorry, Sister. I know you counted on me for this summer session, but I've got to see for myself that my father is all right. I can't just sit here and *pray*, I've got to go to him. I'd go crazy worrying." She touched the older woman's hand. "I'm truly sorry, but I really must go."

She felt a small twinge of guilt. She was worried about her father, but at the same time a small corner of her mind was alive with excitement at the thought of returning to Mexico.

Five months had passed since that terrible February day when Luis had left her, when she'd returned from the Vega hacienda, sick with grief and rage, and Andres had tried to rape her. She would never forget the terror of being tied and helpless. If there was a touch of bizarre humor to the incident, it was the look on Andres' mother's thin prim face as she peered into the room over the shoulder of the maid to see Sarah's almost nude body, and Charlie Finch, his face mottled with fury, throttling her son.

Her father had taken her to Torreon the next day, and then on to San Antonio.

Aunt Clara, glad that she was away from that "sinful savage country," had introduced her to Sister Christina. When there was an unexpected vacancy in the language department at the Academy, Sarah was hired. She liked teaching. The girls, ages seven through twelve, had become very dear to her. But, St. Mary's Academy for Young Ladies was tame after Mexico! How many nights had she lain on her narrow bed at school remembering those eight days she'd spent with Luis while the battle for Mexico City raged, their flight through the dark streets with the Federales so close behind them, their walk to Marta's. She tried to block that part of it out of her mind and think instead of the ride to the hacienda, the way the cactus stood like sentinels in the pale morning light, the old man and his sheep, the roll of the land, the smell of tortillas.

Mexico. Mexico. How she loved the country. How she missed it. And Luis. Luis who would always and forever be the only man she loved.

She wondered again if she'd been too hasty in her anger. But anger, like any other emotion, was difficult to control. It was easy now, five months later, to think calmly and rationally, but it hadn't been easy then. She would be sorry all her life that Luis had not taken her with him that day.

As soon as she arrived in Eagle Pass she went directly to the head of Penoches Mining Company's Texas office. Mr. Ettles told her a payroll car was leaving the next morning, but that under no circumstances would he allow her to go.

He hadn't counted on her determination to get to her father.

Now, moving toward her in the pale morning light, he said in a no-nonsense voice, "I'm going to ask you again to change your mind. A four-day trip over dirt roads isn't a pleasure trip, especially in July, especially now when northern Mexico is full of Villa's men. I worry every time I send men into the country. Three months ago the payroll car was attacked and a man was killed."

"Then why doesn't the company close the mines until the revolution is over?"

"We can't. Europe and the United States need the metals we ship. Penoches mines produce a third of the world's silver, and millions of tons of iron ore and graphite. We can't close down because of Villa." He put his hand on her shoulder. "I know you're worried about your father, honey, and I wish I had more information for you. But Villa's troops have cut so many telegraph wires that it's almost impossible to get a message through. I wish you wouldn't make the trip. I wish you'd . . ."

"All loaded up," a man called.

"You won't change your mind?" Ettles asked again.

She shook her head. "I've got to get to Dad."

"You're like him," he said, taking her arm and leading her over to the car where four men waited in the hot sun. "This is Charlie Finch's daughter," he said to the driver. "Sarah, this is Sam. Paco Gonzales, who totes his guitar wherever he goes. Young Jed. And this tall old buzzard is Jim Sprague. Three of

113

them will be riding shotgun. You boys take good care of Miss Finch. Keep a lookout all the time and keep your rifles loaded and ready."

They nodded. Jim took her hand. He was a lanky man. His gray hair was as shaggy as his moustache and his eyebrows. The eyes beneath the brows were a clear innocent blue. "I've known your daddy for a long time, Miss Sarah," he said. "You don't need to worry about him none. He's as tough a coot as I am and he's going to be just fine."

"Thank you," she said, warming to his words. "I know he is, but I'll feel better when I see for myself."

"How far you think you'll get by tonight, Sam?" Ettles asked the driver.

"Nueva Rosita, I reckon. Sanchez will be waiting there to pick up their payroll. Should make it to Monclova the second night. Don't know just where we'll be the third night, but I brought an extra bedroll for the young lady just in case we have to camp out. If everything goes all right I reckon we'll be in Torreon late Thursday."

They crossed the Rio Grande at Piedras Negras. The town was almost deserted, and the road, once they left the town, was lonely. Sam struggled to keep the car steady on the narrow rutted road that ran through scattered mesquite and tumbleweeds. It was hot. The sun beat down on the car; dust and sand blew in through the open windows.

Sarah took the white linen handkerchief from her bag and dabbed at her face.

"Would you like a drink from my canteen?" Jed asked. He was young. Eighteen perhaps. He hadn't quite grown into his body. His hair was a rusty color, and his bony face was dotted with freckles. His ears were too large for his face, and his hands were too big for his skinny arms. But he'd grow into himself, Sarah thought, and be a fine-looking man.

"How long have you been with the company?" she asked him as she sipped the water.

114

"Two years."

"You must have been awfully young when you started."

"I was sixteen. My pa, he worked for the company, and he was killed in a cave-in near Guanajuato. The company offered me a job, but my ma said I wasn't going to work in no mine. So Mr. Ettles gave me a job as payroll guard and helping around the plant. Your father been with the company long?"

"Almost ten years. When Porfirio Diaz decided to reopen the old Spanish mines he contacted a lot of U.S. mining companies. My father was an engineer for a company in Ecuador. He'd worked with Mr. Ettles before and when Mr. Ettles went with Penoches Dad decided to go with him."

"I knew your daddy back in Ecuador," Jim said. "And I knew your mama too. Old Charlie musta been in a different section of the mine than Dan was. Dan was my brother, Miss Sarah. The explosion knocked the shoring-up beams plum to hell in the section where he was working. There was no way they could get to him."

"I'm so sorry. I didn't know."

"Yes, ma'am. I know you didn't."

"Your father is one tough *hombre*," Paco said from the front seat. "When we get to Torreon you see yourself that he is all right."

"The rate we're going," Jim put in, "we ain't even going to get to Nueva Rosita. How much farther you reckon it is, Sam?"

"Three or four hours yet. Can't do no more than fifteen miles an hour on this dang road. And if it gets any hotter this-a-here car is going to catch a-fire."

"This stupid revolution!" Sarah said. "Sometimes I don't think Villa or any of them know what they're fighting for anymore. Why didn't he stay in El Paso?"

"Because Mexico needed him," Paco said quietly. "He is the one who will free Mexico from Huerta."

"That's enough politics, Paco. Why don't you sing us one of them nice Mexican songs?" Jim put in.

"Bien. I will sing a song of the revolution—a song of these so-terrible Villistas."

He picked up his guitar and strummed gently for a moment, and then in a slow sad voice he began to sing:

> We are the children of the night
> Who wander aimlessly in the darkness
> The beautiful moon with its golden rays
> Is the companion of our sorrows

The companion of my sorrows. Did Luis have a companion for his sorrows? Was that companion Marta?

She looked out at the sun-parched plains, at the organ cactus and the mesquite that lay endlessly before them. Was he out there somewhere? Did he ride with his men in this vast plain, or in the purple-shadowed Sierra Madre mountains that hovered in the distance? Did he think of her when he lay down beside the campfire each night? As she thought of him. Only of him.

You are the companion of my sorrows, Luis.

At three o'clock they came to the village. They passed a young shepherd first, a boy of seven or eight, who waved as they went by. Then, as they neared the village, women washing in the river. But although they slowed, the women didn't look up from their tasks. Their movements were slow and methodical—bend, beat, scrub. The wet clothes hitting against the rocks, making *plok plok plok* sounds in the quiet afternoon.

They followed the white dusty road into the center of the almost deserted village square and stopped in front of a windowless church. Across the road from the church stood a cantina. In front of the cantina four men sat around a small table playing cards.

When Sam pulled to a stop, Paco leaned out of the car and shouted, *"Hola amigos,* how does it go?"

One of them, an old man, spat. "Bad, my brother, it goes bad." With a skinny hand he indicated the

116

small dry plaza. "Can you not see for yourself? The Federales came through here a week ago. They took all of our horses, our few goats, our grain, and our young men for soldiers." He lowered his voice. "They even took the youngest daughter of Manolo Leal. Grabbed her up on one of their horses and rode off with her. The mother is so wild with grief that she cannot leave her house. And Manolo . . ." he gestured over his shoulder, "he plays cards all day and says not one word to us." He spat again. "Well, it is a hard life, *compadre*. And this revolution makes it harder."

"Any Villistas around now?"

"No, señor. One day they are here, the next day they are gone. But be assured, they are never far away."

Sam looked at Paco uneasily. Paco shrugged. He reached under the seat and pulled out a bottle of tequila. "Let us share a drink together," he said to the old man.

"Gracias, muchas gracias, amigo." He drank deep and handed the bottle back.

"How far do you go, señores?"

"To Torreon."

"Torreon! That is three days from here." The old man took off his wide straw hat and dipped his head toward Sarah. And he said to Paco in a low voice, "It is not wise to travel with a young lady. Troops are everywhere. The Federales of Huerta and the Villistas who chase them. They swirl down on you like a bunch of buzzards and take everything you own." His old eyes flicked toward Sarah again. "They would take this girl."

"We will be careful, *amigo.*"

And they were. After they left the village they kept their eyes on the land, watching toward the mountains. But there was nothing. Only the car, the cactus, the rocks, the sun, endless miles of lonely rutted road ahead and behind, and skinny-necked buzzards flapping down so close to the car that Sarah could see their small red eyes.

By the time they reached Nueva Rosita she felt wilted and worn. Sweat trickled down her arms and between her breasts. Texas was hot in July, but never as hot as this. Her room at the only hotel in town was small. The plain cotton curtains at the one window scarcely moved. But there was a bath at the end of the hall, and after a soak in tepid water and a cup of tea she felt as though she might make it through another day.

The next morning she put on the long gray skirt that was a part of her suit, but in place of the stiff long-sleeved jacket, she put on a short-sleeved white shirtwaist. And then, making a face at herself in the mirror, put on the gray plumed hat.

The second day was worse. The road was rougher. Hotter, drier, dustier. The men perspired freely and along about noon the air inside the car became so heavy that Sarah was afraid she'd be ill.

And perhaps Jed noticed because he said, "Let's start looking for a tree and pull over for a while."

"A tree!" Jim laughed. "Lord, boy, you must be kidding."

"A tall cactus then," Jed said. "I think we ought to rest a spell outside the car while I break out the refreshments."

"Refreshments?" Sam laughed. "You buy a jug of tequila, kid?"

"Better'n that."

Finally, and miraculously, there was a tree. One thin scrawny tree by the side of the road. And even though the air was hot it felt fresher than in the car. Jed took off his shirt and spread it over the ground. "You just set here, Miss Sarah, and I'll fetch the refreshments." He grinned. "I bought us some watermelons."

"Watermelons?" Jim laughed. "Lord, boy, if you don't beat all. I haven't had me any watermelon in a month of Sundays." And when Jed got them out of the car Jim thumped one and said, "It's a good 'un. Can't wait to sink my teeth into a hunk."

Neither could Sarah. When Jim sliced through the melon and the sweet red juice ran out she could feel her mouth water. Never, she thought, would anything taste as good again. The juicy sweetness of it cooled her mouth and her throat. She could close her eyes and forget for a few seconds how hot and dusty and dirty she was.

When he finished eating Paco went back to the car and got out his guitar. He leaned against the trunk of the slim tree and began to play.

"You still in school, ma'am?" Jed asked.

"No, I'm a teacher."

Paco looked up from his guitar. "Teaching is for old maids," he said. "You would do better to find a husband and have children."

"There's more to life than finding a husband," she said. "I want to travel and . . ."

"Riders," Jed said.

"What? Where?" Paco jumped to his feet.

"Yonder, over to the right."

"Let's roll," Jim yelled.

"Maybe just some cowboys," Sam said.

"Cowboys hell!" Jim growled. He grabbed Sarah by the arm and thrust her into the car. "Ma'am," he said, taking his rifle, "I think it would be a right good idea if you was to scrunch down some. Actually, you better get yourself right down on that floor. And if there's any shooting don't raise your head. You stay scrunched until we tell you to unscrunch."

Sarah looked down at her tight, ankle-length skirt. How in the world am I going to do that? she thought.

Then the cloud of dust came closer, and the dust became horses. And Jed, his face very white, said, "Begging your pardon, Miss Sarah," grabbed her roughly by her shoulder, and shoved.

Chapter 12

—Be ready, but don't shoot lessen they do.

—Maybe they really are just a bunch of cowboys.

—Like hell!

—Here, take more ammo. Best to have it right ready.

—Reckon we might try talking to them?

—I wish Ettles had this payroll up his ass.

—They're getting closer.

—How many you count?

—More'n twenty.

—If it comes down to it let's give 'em the goldurned money.

—Right. We got us a woman to think of.

—You reckon they be Villa's men or Federales?

—What the hell's the difference? Guns is guns.

—Maybe they just want . . .

The sharp ping of the first shot split the sound of their voices. Jed's feet jerked convulsively near her head, scrambling, twisting fast. To the right. To the left. Jerking each time he fired. The acrid smell of the shots mixed with the sweaty smell of the men and the smell of the dust. She pressed her face tight against her carpetbag.

—Son-of-a-bitch.

—Goddamned Mexicans.

—*Cabrones.*

Whomp! The sound was just over her head as the

bullet struck somewhere inside the car. A voice cried out, and she felt the weight of a body on top of her. She screamed when she saw that it was Jim, and tried, in her panic, to push him away from her. But when she saw the gaping wound in his chest she raised her head to tell somebody to help him. A bullet winged past her face and Jed pushed her back to the floor. She managed to get Jim's big red kerchief from his shirt pocket, and pulling out from under him, gently eased him to the floor. She pressed the kerchief against the wound in his chest, frantic as the blood drenched it and ran down his body. She heard herself say, "It's all right. You're going to be all right. I promise you. I promise you."

His blue eyes looked at her. Through her. Past her.

The car swayed from side to side, lurching heavily as a tire blew. "I gotta stop," Sam yelled.

The car careened to the side of the road and Sarah heard the squeal of brakes over the sound of the bullets, over the high piercing yells, the curses, and the moans.

Paco was hit. She heard the ping as a bullet hit the guitar. And heard him cry out, *"Hermanos,* brothers, I am with you . . ." and saw the blood running down the back of his head.

"Viva Villa. *Viva* Villa," Sam shouted. "We surrender. Take what you want."

A few sporadic shots, and then the firing ceased.

"Stay down," Jed whispered.

The sound of horses drawing nearer. The smell of them. Of men.

A rough voice: "Where is the money? We know you carry money."

"We have no money." Jed's voice. The soon-to-be-a-man voice.

"Give it to him or he'll kill us," Sam whispered.

A man laughed. "I will probably kill you anyway."

The door was jerked open. "Hey! What is this?"

A man reached in through the open door and yanked her up to the seat. "Look, *hombres,*" he shouted to the men surrounding the car, "I have found a dove. A little gray dove."

He was fat. He had a four-days' growth of beard, and he smelled like stale fish.

She knocked his hand away and reached for Jim. "There's a man here," she cried, her voice frantic with concern. "He's badly hurt. We've got to help him."

"I've got two men dead and three more wounded." He spat out the side of his mouth. He leaned into the car and looked down at Jim. "Anyway, this one is beyond help."

"No, he's only . . ." She touched the top of Jim's head. Only a few minutes ago he'd been eating a great hunk of watermelon and saying, "I swear to goodness, ma'am, this here is the best watermelon I ever tasted." She brushed the white hair back from his forehead, and felt hot bitter tears sting her eyes. She turned away from him and looked directly into the eyes of the fat man.

"You killed him," she said, her voice low and full of hate.

"I? The bullet in his chest has my name on it?" He laughed and slapped his thigh. "Come out here, little dove. I want to get a look at you."

"Keep your hands off her," Jed said.

The men who circled the car shouted with laughter. "Hear the young rooster," the one said. "Does he frighten you, Pedro?"

"*Si,* Ramon. See how I am shaking?" His stomach shook with laughter. "I think I will shoot the little rooster so that he can join his friends in *gringo* heaven." His fat finger tightened on the trigger.

"Wait!" Sarah pushed Jed's restraining hand away and scrambled out of the car. "The money is under the floorboards," she said in Spanish. "And rifles. Take them and let us go."

"Money *and* rifles. The captain will be pleased."

He scratched his chin. "You speak pretty good Spanish. Where did you learn?"

"Here. I lived in Mexico."

"You like my country?"

"I used to like it."

The men on horseback watched her. All of them wore wide straw hats. Some wore boots, others huaraches, and some were barefoot. They all had bandoliers of ammunition crisscrossed over their chests.

So these were the men of Luis' revolution, she thought with bitterness. These are the men he left me for. These dirty ragged men. She felt the stares and saw their grins as they nudged one another. Without thinking, as though to give herself courage, she smoothed her skirt and straightened her hat.

One of the men hooted with laughter. "What is that she wears on her head? Surely it is a wild gray bird. I must take it back for my woman." He motioned his horse forward, leaned down, and reached out his hand.

She struck out at him with one hand and clutched her hat with the other. "Take your filthy hands off my hat," she said in Spanish.

The man yelled in mock terror. "Do not frighten me so, my little dove," he squealed.

"Enough," Pedro, the fat man, said. "Get that dead hulk out of the car, Ramon, and find the money and rifles."

"*Sí, jefe,*" a skinny man with a large drooping moustache said.

He brushed past Sarah, rubbing his arm across her body as he moved to the car. He handed her her carpetbag, and then he grabbed Jim's body under his armpits and tried to drag him out of the car. When he got him halfway out he grabbed the neck of the dead man and thrust him out of the car.

"Don't do that," Sarah cried. "Don't handle him that way."

"Miss Finch, for the love of God, keep your mouth shut," Sam said.

"He was a *person*. Not a thing, not a thing to be dragged and dumped."

Jed put his hand on her arm. "Don't, Miss Sarah," he pleaded. "Making a fuss now won't do any of us a bit of good."

The fat man hooked his finger under his belt. *"Gringas* with red hair," he said. "What I have heard about them is true. You are brave, señorita. I admire bravery." He dusted his hands off on his dirty pants. "I am Sergeant Pedro Garcia of the famous troops of Pancho Villa."

Sarah took a deep breath and drew herself up to her full five feet, seven inches. She stood eye to eye with him, and although her heart beat hard and her legs felt as though they would not support her, her voice was cool when she said, "I am Sarah Finch. I am on my way to Torreon."

"We are all on our way to Torreon, Señorita Finch. But I am sure the reason for our visits is vastly different. I will take the city from the Federal *cabrones*. What will you do?"

"I am going to see my father. He's been hurt in a mining accident."

He scratched his four-day beard while he looked her up and down. Finally he shook his head. "I do not think you will see your poor papa for a while. I think instead you will come with me and keep my belly warm at night."

She looked at him, at the heavy jowls, the thick lips, smiling now to show the space where a lower tooth was missing, the small close-set eyes, reddened from dust and fatigue.

Taking a deep steadying breath she said, "You'll have to shoot me first."

He shook his head. He scratched himself under his arm. "No, I don't want to shoot you, señorita. So I will shoot your friend, the little rooster." He lifted one arm and made a motion to his men. "Lalo, you want to shoot this little *gringo* for me?"

"*Si*, Sergeant. Or if you like we can go back to the

124

tree and I will hang him for you." He slid down off his horse and went to stand in front of Jed. He reached out a dirty finger and poked it at the boy's chest. "You ever hear of Villa's fruit trees, kid? No? I tell you, then. We hang so many men from so many trees that they are called Villa's fruit trees." He doubled over with laughter. "Some fruit," he cackled. "Some fruit, eh, *gringo?*"

"Jesus," Jed said softly. His eyes met Sarah's.

They'll do it, she thought, not taking her eyes from Jed's. They'll take this eighteen-year-old boy and hang him. He'll die before he's lived. "Don't . . ." she said to Garcia. "Don't hurt him. Take the money. But please, leave him alone."

Garcia snapped his fingers and two of his men hurried to the car. "It is for the revolution, you know," one short fellow said apologetically.

"Put the money in the saddlebags," Garcia ordered. "And divide the rifles." He turned back to Jed. "You, boy, get in the car. And you, señorita, are you ready for a little adventure?" He chuckled. "Are you ready to have Pedro Garcia show you what a real man is like? Believe me when I tell you that in three days you will be whimpering for joy. You will be cooking my tortillas and polishing my boots, and telling me what a man I am." He jerked his thumb toward Jed. "I can do more for you in one hour than this little rooster can do for you in a year." His small tired eyes bored into hers. "And so, Miss Finch, do I have my men hang this rooster from that tree back there or do you come with me?"

"*Jefe,*" the short fellow put in, "pardon, *jefe,* but the captain said we should not bother women."

"But the captain is not here, Nicasio. I will have this red-haired *gringa* as a prize of the revolution and nothing will stop me."

"You're not going with him, Miss Sarah," Jed said. His voice quavered. She saw the fright in his eyes.

She turned to Pedro. "If you let him go . . ."

He laughed and scratched his huge belly. "Well,

125

why the hell not? It is not every day I find myself a woman like you."

He turned to one of his men. "Alfredo, drain the gasoline from the car and take their water. They'll be food for the buzzards by tomorrow, but today I let them live."

"Sarah?" Jed held his hands out to her.

"Tell my father," she said, feeling sudden tears sting her eyes. "Tell him . . ."

"Move!" the man Ramon said, prodding Jed back into the car with the butt of his rifle.

Pedro gazed down at her. "How are you going to get on a horse in that skirt?" he said. "Holy Mother, I solve one problem and I am visited with another." He shook his head, and then before Sarah could speak he reached down and pulled a knife from his boot.

A small man with a big sombrero said nervously, "What are you going to do?"

"This," Pedro answered. He grasped Sarah by her waist, and with the knife cut down the center of her skirt from her thighs to the hem before she could move. Then he swung himself up in his saddle, reached a hand down to her, and hauled her up in front of him.

The animal reared. Sarah grasped the horse's mane with one hand and her gray plumed hat with the other. And by the time she was able to look back the car was far behind.

Chapter 13

She didn't know how long they rode. The air was hot on her face and the heat from the sun burned her skin. The fat man's arm was tight around her waist, and once when they slowed his hand moved up to fondle her breasts. When she tried to jerk away from him he laughed and moved his hand down to squeeze her thigh.

She couldn't believe all that had happened this day. That two men were dead; Paco, who had been killed by his own people, and Jim, whose blue eyes had looked so innocent, even in death. She felt her throat constrict with the need to cry; for the men who were dead, for Jed and Sam who might die without water, and for her father who needed her. And yes, from fear. Fear of this awful man whose arm circled her waist.

What could she do? What did other women do when they were faced with a man like this? With any man they didn't want?

In late afternoon they began to climb up into the mountains. The horses slowed to a walk, picking their way carefully over the rocks. Now there was a snatch of song, a muttered curse, a whispered consultation. She was so tired that from time to time she dozed and would have fallen if the fat arm had not held her. Once she heard a voice quite close to her and she recognized it as the voice of the skinny man with the big drooping moustache. "What makes her your girl?" His voice was a whine. "We were all in this together. We fought as well as you did. Why should you have her?"

"Because I am the boss. She is mine and that is final."

"And who made her yours? I have as much right to her as you."

"Shut your mouth, Ramon, or I will shut it permanently."

"But I haven't had a woman in months."

"What woman would have you, you skinny bastard?"

She kept her eyes closed and held herself so tight that every muscle in her body tensed. She'd never known such crawling clutching fear, such *hopeless* fear.

But later, in spite of her fear, she dozed again. It was dark when she woke. The air was cool, and ahead, through the darkness, she saw the light of campfires and smelled food cooking. Figures ran toward them and there were cries of greeting. A black-shawled woman called, "Venancio? Venancio, are you there?"

"I am here, old woman. Do not make such a scandal."

Other women surrounded them. Searching each face.

"Don't stand gaping," one of the men said. "Take the horses and feed them and then see to our dinner."

"But who is missing?"

"Tonio Sanchez and Jose Vasquez. Three others are hurt."

"Mother of God." Several of the women crossed themselves.

"The fortunes of war," Pedro said. He dismounted, reached up and hauled Sarah down, and when she would have fallen, he held her upright with a strong hand on her arm. He turned to one of the women and said, "Take this *gringa* and give her something to eat and drink."

The women looked at her silently. And then one of them, a tall girl with wild black gypsy hair and a tight

128

dress, said, "Where did you find her? And what is that silly hat she wears? It will look nicer on me." She reached out her hand to snatch Sarah's hat.

"Leave her alone, you little whore," Pedro said, slapping her hand away. "If you don't behave yourself I'll send you back to that cantina in Nogales where Francisco found you."

A short squat man with a dark Indian face jumped off his horse and ran to Pedro. He glared at him, legs apart, hands curled into fists, and he said, "Don't you call Conchita a whore."

"Why not?" Pedro laughed. "That's what she is."

"She is my woman. She is respectable."

"Respectable, is she? She would leave you in a minute for any man who had fifty centavos more than you."

"Liar!" Conchita shouted. "I wouldn't go with a *cabrón* like you for fifty million pesos." She looked at Sarah. "I pity you, *gringa*. When this hippopotamus climbs on you he will squash you like a tomato."

The men laughed. One of the women said, "What do you want with this girl, Pedro?"

"What do you think I want with her, Josefina? The same thing your man Filimon wants with you."

"Filimon is so old he has forgotten what it is he used to want. Now he wants me only to make his tortillas."

"Well, I am not as old as Filimon and there are tastier things in this life than tortillas."

"And what will the captain say when he returns?" The woman who spoke was large, tall and broad and sturdy.

"He is not here, Silvia. He will not be back until tomorrow and by then she will belong to me."

"She won't be well enough to belong to anybody if you do not feed her." She took Sarah's arm. "Come with me, girl," she said. Her voice was not unkind.

She pushed her way through the other women and led Sarah to the campfire. "Sit here a moment," she said, "and I will bring you some coffee." She had

129

large black eyes and the jutting nose of an eagle. "What is your name, girl, and how did you come to be in this fix?"

"My name is Sarah. Sarah Finch." It took great effort to keep her voice steady. "I was riding in the payroll car from El Paso, trying to get to my father in Torreon."

"And Pedro and his bunch stopped the car?"

"And killed two of the men. Then he said he'd kill the other two if I didn't go with him."

"You speak good Spanish. That will help you here."

"But I can't stay here. I can't let that man . . . Surely you can see that I can't let him . . ."

Silvia looked away from her. "I will get you some food." She glared at the other women. "Do not stand there gawking like a bunch of birds," she snapped. "Teresa, you sit with the *gringa* while I prepare her food."

"Señora, please . . ." But Silvia had already turned her back and moved away from the campfire.

She couldn't help it then, she put her head on her knees and wept. It was several minutes before she heard the voice, "Señorita, señorita, please. . . . It will be all right. Please do not weep so."

Sarah raised her head and looked at the girl who had spoken, a girl about her own age, but smaller and thinner. Her skin was a rich cocoa brown, and her hair was combed into two skinny scraggly braids. She wore a long black skirt, as did all of the other women except the one with the wild gypsy hair, and she clenched a dirty gray rebozo to her body.

"Please do not cry," the girl repeated.

Sarah scrubbed her eyes with her fist. "I don't know what to do," she said brokenly.

"There is nothing you *can* do, señorita. You must accept what has happened and make the best of it."

"Accept?" Sarah shook her head. "But you don't understand. That man, that fat man . . ."

"Pedro Garcia."

130

"He brought me here. He kidnapped me. He . . ."

"But there is nothing you can do about it. That is how I came to be here too. After a while it will not be so bad and you will accept . . ."

Sarah stared at her with horror. "Accept? I'll never do that."

"You will," the girl said kindly. "Garcia is too fat, but as a man he is no worse than the others. I felt the same when Lorenzo brought me here, but there was nothing I could do."

Sarah bit her lip. "Well, *I'll* do something. I won't stay here. I won't let that awful fat man touch me."

"How are you called, señorita?"

"Sarah. What is your name?"

"Teresa. Teresa Maria Algundes Morelos. How is it that you are in Mexico? Did you not know there was a revolution?"

"Yes, I knew, but . . . my father was hurt. I was trying to get to him."

"And how did you travel? By horse or by railroad?"

"Automobile."

"Ay, an automobile. How wonderful. What did it feel like? Was it better than a horse? Didn't it smell? What makes it run?"

In spite of herself, Sarah smiled. "It was a bit better than a horse. Yes, it did smell. And it runs by gasoline."

"Imagine." Her small cocoa brown face was full of wonder. And of innocence. "Imagine," she said again.

Silvia came to the fire and handed Sarah an earthenware plate filled with rice and meat and tortillas. "You will feel better when you eat," she said.

"I don't think I can."

"You can. And you must." And to Teresa she said, "You'd better start Lorenzo's dinner or he will thrash you again. Ay, Señorita Sarah, her man is a devil when he drinks. And that's what all of them are doing now. Drinking tequila and telling lies, raising all kinds of hell because the captain is not here to stop them." She

131

hesitated, looking down at Sarah's exposed legs. "What has happened to your skirt?"

"He cut it."

"But you cannot go around like that. Tomorrow we will find you some clothes."

"I had a carpetbag."

"Then later I will look for it."

"It is a shame the skirt is cut," Teresa said. "The material is so fine. And your hat. May I touch it?"

Sarah took the gray plumed hat off and handed it to the girl.

"How soft the feathers are. Truly, they are like the feathers of a bird." In her excitement she forgot to hold her rebozo. It slipped off one shoulder and Sarah saw that the one arm was off just below the elbow.

Teresa gave her an agonized look and grabbed at the rebozo. She thrust the gray hat at Sarah, not meeting her eyes.

"Go now and tend to your man," Silvia said.

And when Teresa had gone she shook her head and said, "Poor girl. Poor girl."

It seemed to Sarah that she could not stand the sight of any more of the pain this day had brought.

She shivered in the chill night mountain air. Shivered with cold and with fear. She tried to pull her skirt together to cover her legs, but there was not enough material. The other women watched her, and suddenly one of them took off her rebozo and handed it to her. "Cover yourself," she said.

The tears came again. And then suddenly she heard his voice.

"Where is my little gray dove?" he yelled, pushing his way into the circle of women. *"Ay, mujeres,* see how she weeps for me. See how she shivers from the cold, knowing all the while that soon I will warm her."

He shoved a bottle of tequila under her nose. "Drink, this will warm you."

She pushed the bottle away, almost retching at the smell of it.

The man Ramon said, "Perhaps she will take it from

132

me. Perhaps she doesn't like fat men. I lived in Texas. I know the ways of a *gringa* better than you do. She will be happier with me."

"Let her rest tonight," Silvia said. "Let her become used to us."

"Shut up!" Ramon snarled. He reached out and tilted Sarah's chin so that she was forced to look at him. "Wouldn't you rather have me than an old hippopotamus like Garcia?"

She slapped his hand away.

"Aha! You see? She cannot stand you." Garcia grabbed Sarah's hand and hauled her to her feet. "She comes with me," he said, and began to drag her after him.

The women scattered.

"Please, Pedro," Silvia pleaded, "let her rest tonight. There is time enough for this. Can't you see how tired she is?"

"She will be more tired when I am through with her, woman. Now get out of my way."

Ramon trotted along on the other side of Garcia. "I have had no woman for a month," he whined. "You had one in the village for a week. Why didn't you keep her? Go back and get her. She was crazy about you. Leave this one for me."

"Shut up, you bastard," Garcia roared, "or I'll shoot you between your skinny legs and you will never have a woman again. You don't have enough now and you will have two inches less when I finish with you."

"All right, all right. I don't want to fight you, but why be such a pig? Why can't we share her?"

"She is mine and you will not touch her."

"But what difference will it make? She is just a *gringa*."

"But she is my *gringa*."

The two men stopped, toe to toe, glaring at each other. Garcia's hand held so tight to her wrist that hot spears of pain ran up her arm. She jerked suddenly, trying to free herself, and at the same time struck his face with her fist.

133

"Goddamnit," he shouted, "stop it. When I finish with this skinny bastard I will take care of you."

"You see? You see? She does not want you." Ramon grabbed her other wrist.

"Stop it! Let me go!" Sarah sobbed, almost hysterical with fear and pain.

They were farther from the camp, moving in the direction of the trees.

She tried to see back to the camp, back to the dark circle of the women who huddled together beside the fire. "Help me," she called. "Please help me."

"Look," Ramon said. "She will be hard to handle. I'll hold her while you do it and then you hold her while I do it." The hand that held Sarah's arm shook. His breath was fast and noisy in his throat. He released her wrist and ran his hands over her bare thighs where the skirt was ripped.

She kicked out, catching him on the shin bone.

"Aha! She almost got you that time." Pedro laughed. "Kick a little higher next time, my little dove. My little dove who is after all not a dove but a wild hawk that needs taming. Come here to me and let me start to tame you."

He pulled her to him. He put his hand on the top of her shirtwaist and ripped, and when she cried out one fat hand cupped her breast. She reached up and raked his face with her nails.

He let go of her breast and struck her across her face. "Perhaps you are right," he growled to Ramon. "Perhaps it will take the two of us to tame her. But I am the sergeant, I will be first."

"Yes, *mi jefe,* yes, you go first. But hurry."

"Please . . ." She screamed again, calling to the women to help her. She felt Ramon's hands on her shoulders, pushing her down onto the cold grass, moving to grab her, squeezing frantically in his excitement. In a frenzy of fear and rage she tried to twist away from his hands, and then from the other hands, the fat hands that pulled her legs apart.

The sound of a gun penetrated her hearing. The

134

hands released her. She turned her head to see Ramon clutch his shoulder, and heard him scream. "It was Garcia, Captain. He made me help him."

"Lying dog," Garcia shouted. He scrambled to his feet, pulling his loosened pants together.

Sarah rolled to her side away from them, sobbing, trying to pull her torn clothes together, unable to believe the sudden reprieve, if it was a reprieve and not just one more of them to fight over her.

"Quiet! Both of you." The voice was cold and angry.

And . . . familiar.

She raised her head to try to see the tall figure who stood with his back to her, facing his men.

"Look, Captain Vega . . ."

Vega? Luis? She pushed herself to a sitting position.

". . . the *gringa* is my woman," the fat man continued. "When you see the money and rifles we got today you will not be so angry. I know you told us about women and I am sorry, but when you see her you will know why I had to have her. I'm sorry she raised so much hell, but I promise that hereafter I will keep her quiet."

The dark figure turned towards her now.

"Luis?" Her voice was a small cry of hope.

She heard the soft intake of his breath as he bent down to look at her. "My God!" he said. "Is it you?"

She gave a cry and reached out for him, waiting for him to pull her into his arms.

He made no move toward her. He stared down at her, his hands clenched as he said, "What in the hell are you doing here?"

"Father . . ." She swallowed. "He was hurt in a mining accident near Torreon. I was trying to get to him."

He drew his brows together sharply. "I'm sorry to hear that. I have great regard for your father."

"I didn't know she was a friend of yours, Captain," Garcia said. "Never would I touch the woman of a *compañero*."

135

"She's not my woman." His voice was as cold as ice. He reached down and when he pulled her to her feet he saw the torn clothes, the roundness of the white breasts, and the slender white legs. He took his jacket off and flung it at her. "Cover yourself," he said.

And turning to his men he snarled, "All right, tell me how she came to be here."

Garcia cleared his throat and started nervously. "We were riding near Nueva Rosita when we saw the car, Captain. I thought, what the hell, let's chase it. And when we caught it we found payroll money and rifles and the *muchacha*." He licked his fat lips. "Thirty thousand dollars, Luis. And more than three dozen rifles."

"We lost two men," Ramon said. "Tonio Perez and Jose Vasquez." He swayed. "Mother of God, Captain, why did you have to shoot me?"

"Because I have given you orders about kidnapping women, and by God I will not be disobeyed. Go and tell Silvia to take care of you and if you ever do this again I'll kill the both of you. I have enough problems without having to worry about a prisoner."

Prisoner? She couldn't believe what was happening. That it was Luis who spoke as though she were a stranger. She couldn't believe the hate she heard in his voice and saw in his eyes.

He looked at her now and she could see the stiffness of it on his face and in the way he held his body. But why? Why? He'd been angry when he left her almost five months ago. She could understand anger. But hate? He had no reason to hate her.

"She is our prisoner then?" Garcia said slowly. He scratched his belly. "Well, Captain, if you regard her as a prisoner and not as your woman perhaps . . . What I am trying to say, Luis, is that since I was in charge of the day's operation it seems to me that I should have her."

Vega's eyes flicked to Sarah. "A captain has some rights," he said at last. "She sleeps in my tent. Now get out of my sight, Garcia, and if you ever kidnap a woman again without my consent I'll have your hide."

He grasped her arm, jerking her so that she stumbled and almost fell, pulling her after him until they were in front of one of the tents at the far side of the campfire.

"Let me go," she cried, trying to free her arm. "Why are you acting like this? Luis, please, I don't understand."

"Shut up!" His voice was a snarl. "If you say a word, one word, Sarah, I swear I'll give you to Garcia. I'll give you to him and pity the poor bastard for the curse you'll bring with you."

"What are you talking about?" she whispered.

His hand reached out and grasped her hair. He pulled her face around to his. "I could kill you," he said, his voice low and filled with hate. "You'd be better off with Garcia than with me. When I get through with you you'll wish I'd let you go with him."

And before she could speak, he shoved her roughly into his tent.

Chapter 14

"Stay where you are. I'll light a lamp."

She heard him strike a match and in a moment the oil lamp was lit and she looked around her. The tent was small, seven by seven feet perhaps. "I'll be back," he said, not looking at her.

When he returned he spread the straw mat on the ground, next to the one already there. Tossing a blanket to her, he said, "I'll try to find your carpetbag tomorrow. You can't go around camp like that."

"What is it?" she whispered, sinking to her knees on the mat. "I know we said hard things that day at the hacienda. I said I hated you, and I guess I did. But that passed, Luis. What happened that afternoon isn't reason enough for you to . . . to be like this." She reached out to him, and in a tremulous voice she said, "No matter what we say to each other, nothing can change the love we feel."

"Love!" His voice choked. "How in the name of all that's holy can you speak to me of love?" He stood over her, his hands clenching and unclenching. "I could kill you," he whispered. "I've dreamed of killing you. Dreamed of you begging me for mercy, dreamed of you writhing in agony."

Her face blanched. "But why?" she said brokenly. "Why?"

Her face was scratched and dirty and streaked with tears. Her hair was tangled, her clothes were torn. He could see the whiteness of her skin, the shape of one bare shoulder, the roundness of breast. And suddenly, hating himself for his weakness, he felt the slow insidious itch of desire.

He dropped to the mat beside her, gripping her arms until she cried out in pain.

"Why are you like this?" she cried. "Is it because of Marta? Is that it? Is she your woman now? Your damned *Mexican* woman?"

"You bitch!" he snarled, striking her across the face with his open palm. And when she tried to get away from him he yanked her around and raised his hand again.

"Don't!" she pleaded. "Don't."

His hand closed to a fist, the knuckles white, his face hard and hate-filled. And then he shoved her away from him.

When he was able to speak he said, "While you're here we'll share this tent. It's either that or give you to Garcia. And if I don't it's only because of your father. I don't know when I'll be able to send you to him. There are Federal troops all around us and I'm not going to risk my men for your sake. We should be in Torreon in a month or two if the fighting goes well. I'll see you get to your father then. While you're here you'll work with the other women and you'll behave yourself. I won't listen to complaints and I won't be moved by tears. If you disobey me or try to escape I'll have you beaten. Is that clear?"

Her face was white. Her green eyes were wide with shock. But when she spoke her voice was steady. "I don't know why you're doing this," she said. "We quarreled five months ago, but I've never wanted to hurt you like you're hurting me."

"Not even when you sent Andres after me?"

Her eyes went wide with shock. "Andres? What . . . ?"

"Shut up, Sarah," he said. "I've had enough of your lies to last me a lifetime." He blew out the lamp and lay down only a few feet away from her.

She turned on her side, away from him, and stared

139

into the darkness. Outside she could hear the men and women around the campfire; a shout, a laugh, a warning to be quiet. And once, quite near, she heard a man say, *"Caramba,* that Captain Vega is a smart man. He takes the best for himself."

"Shhh, *compadre,* do not disturb him at his work."

"Work! Be assured, *hombre,* he is enjoying himself."

"Shut up!" another voice shouted. "How can anyone sleep with so much ruckus? Leave the lovebirds alone and go to bed."

The sound of a guitar and a soft voice singing a song about war and an adobe home and love.

He was gone when she woke the next morning. She lay on the straw mat and looked around her. At one side of the tent a mat and blanket were neatly rolled and tied. His shaving things, a scarf, and a hat were on a small stool.

She was cold, and her body was stiff and sore. The skin on her face and arms felt stretched and tender to the touch, and when she looked at her arms she saw they were badly sunburned, and that there were purple bruises on both her wrists. She remembered Pedro Garcia and the man Ramon, the way they'd tugged at her like two dogs over a scrap of meat. The feel of the damp grass against her back when they'd thrown her to the ground. And Luis.

The sun shone in through the canvas tent. She could hear the soft murmur of voices, smell coffee brewing and bacon frying. Suddenly she heard a faint scratching on the canvas. "Who is it?" she asked, hating the sound of her own fear.

"It is no one. It is only me, Teresa. May I enter?"

"Yes, come in."

"Here is your carpetbag. Lupe Gomez found it this morning and Silvia said I was to take you down to the river so that you could bathe and then you will be more comfortable and happy." She paused for breath. "Will you not?"

And when Sarah didn't answer, she said, "I tried to come to you last night when you screamed but Lorenzo would not let me. He held me so that I could not move and for the first time since I have been with him I fought him, and he gave me a terrible clout. Then Captain Vega rode into the camp and Silvia ran to him and told him what was happening, what Pedro and Ramon were doing with you, and he went very fast." She paused to catch her breath. "Did they . . . did they hurt you?"

"No, Teresa." She touched the other girl's hand. "Thank you for trying to help me. I hope Lorenzo didn't hurt you."

The girl shrugged. "One gets used to it."

Sarah tried not to look at the curious faces, at the eyes that followed her when she made her way through the camp with Teresa. She held her back straight and kept her eyes lowered to the path in front of her. But she looked up when she heard a sharp biting laugh and saw that the girl Conchita blocked her way. Conchita was as tall as Sarah, and her figure, in the low-cut blouse and bright skirt, was full and ripe. Her feet were bare. She stood with her legs apart, hands on her hips.

"Hey," she said, "you don't look so good this morning. Was Captain Vega too much of a man for you?"

"Get out of my way," Sarah said between her teeth.

"*Ay yi yi, gringa,* don't scare me."

"Leave her alone," a woman said.

"What did he do to you, eh? Did you like it? Did it feel good to have a Mexican instead of one of those white-livered *gringos?*"

"Shut up, *puta,*" another woman said.

"Ay, she makes me sick, pretending to be such a little virgin. Who does she think she's fooling? Making the men fight among themselves, causing poor Ramon to get a bullet in his shoulder." She poked Sarah in her chest. "You're like all the *gringos,* think you're

141

better than the rest of us. Well, to me you're nothing. Nothing but a royal pain in the ass." She gave Sarah a shove that sent her stumbling backwards.

Suddenly all the rage that had bottled up in her, rage at the needless killings, at the two men who had attacked her last night, at Luis, and yes, rage at her own fear, exploded. And she struck out at Conchita. Struck as hard as she could with both fists, knocking the girl to the ground, following her down, striking her again and again. The girl struck back, biting and scratching, calling her names, and each time she said the word *"gringa,"* Sarah lashed out. She didn't feel the blows or the scratches of the other girl, she only knew that this was her enemy. She was blind to pain or reason.

And she screamed with new rage when somebody yanked her away from Conchita. Yanked her to her feet and held her thrashing body in such an iron grip that she finally felt the pain and was still.

When she tried to free herself she saw that it was Luis who held her.

His face was white with anger. "I told you last night that if you didn't behave yourself I'd have you whipped. And by God, that's what I'm going to do."

"It wasn't her fault, Luis." Silvia came to stand in front of him, hands on her broad hips, fire in her eye. "It was this devil Conchita who started it."

"I don't care who started it. I will not have the women in this camp fighting with each other like she-cats." He let go of Sarah and yanked Conchita to her feet. "Is that clear to both of you?" And when they didn't answer he said to Sarah, "Now you, get down to the river and clean yourself up. Then come back here and help Silvia. You're not a guest. You're one of the women now and you'll work just like the rest of them or . . ."

"Or what?" Sarah screamed at him. "I won't be treated this way. I'm not one of your women, one of your camp followers. You can't tell me what to do."

"Be quiet, girl," Silvia ordered. Her voice was as

142

stern as her face. "Do what Captain Vega tells you, and when you return we will talk."

And when Sarah hesitated she said again, "Go!"

The two girls didn't speak on the way to the river, until finally, in a timid frightened voice Teresa said, "Are you angry with me also?"

"Everybody else, Teresa, but not you."

The anger had been good for her. She wasn't as frightened as she'd been before. The sudden lashing out, the physical violence had made her feel better. And the sight of the river cheered her spirits even more. The water sparkled clean and green in the sunlight. Big pirule trees and graceful willows rimmed the banks and seemed to make the river an almost private place. She took off her ruined skirt and shirtwaist and waded into the water. The coolness of it stung her sunburned arms and made her shiver, but she kept on until the water reached her breasts. Then she dipped down under it and removed her underclothes. She washed them with the brown soap Teresa had given her, and then, wading to the bank, threw them to the girl. "Come in," she urged.

Teresa shook her head and clutched her rebozo.

Sarah shrugged and waded out again. She scrubbed her body and her hair, and then she swam until she felt all the tired muscles relax, and the pain of yesterday's terror ooze from her body. Even the new bruises and scratches she'd gotten when she fought with Conchita this morning felt better.

It's all a dream, she thought, looking around her. Surely there is nothing that can harm me on this hot summer morning.

The willows dipped into the clean clear water of the river, bees hovered on the scarlet bougainvillea vines, and in the distance the sun glowed on a field of yellow daisies. Birds sang in the huisache trees, and the smell of July was everywhere around her. For a few moments she could forget that she was a prisoner, and that Luis no longer loved her.

Teresa handed her a large rough towel when she

came out of the water. She wrapped it around herself, and taking some clothes out of her carpetbag, went behind a tree to dress. And when she had finished she came to sit beside Teresa.

"You should have come in. There's no one to see us." She smiled. "And I couldn't have gotten away from you. I wouldn't have been able to escape without my clothes on. Why wouldn't you come in?"

Teresa hung her head. "I would have been ashamed of my arm."

She was a small girl, barely five feet, and she was very thin. Her braids were scraggly today. And no wonder, Sarah thought suddenly, how can she braid them? She probably has to wait for somebody to help her.

"You don't have to be ashamed of your arm," Sarah said.

"That's what my mother used to say. She said I should not be ashamed because it was the will of God that I am as I am. But in truth, I do not know what God had to do with it. Surely He did not intend for my father to be a drunk."

"I'm sorry. I don't understand."

"I meant that God did not make me this way. I had two arms when I was born. I lost the one when I was five days old. My mother had to go back to work and she left me with my father and he said he would take care of me. But he drank and then he went to sleep and the pigs came into the house."

Sarah's hands felt clammy. She knew she did not want to hear any more.

"A pig ate the part of my arm that is missing. They thought I would die but my mother and Señora Melendez, the midwife, cured me with herbs and poultices. My father was sorry and he swore in front of the priest that he would never drink again. But he did, of course."

Her eyes met Sarah's. Strangely beautiful eyes, as soft and brown and trusting as a fawn's. Sarah felt her

144

throat knot, felt quick tears. And she said, almost abruptly, "Turn around. I'll braid your hair."

She undid the braids, and taking a hairbrush from her carpetbag, began to brush the long black hair, trying to see what she was doing through the tears that were streaming down her face.

"I went to school for almost three years," Teresa continued, "but it was hard and I was not so smart, and the other children said bad things to me because of my arm. So I did not mind when I left school because I liked being home with my mother. I liked taking care of my brothers and they didn't mind that I had only one arm." She sighed, and when she spoke again, her voice was sad. "A year ago the Villistas came to our village. They were there for a week, and when they left Lorenzo asked my father for me."

"Did you want to go with him?"

"No, I was afraid. I did not want to leave my home. I . . . I did not know about men, and Lorenzo had never smiled at me even. I knew that he watched me, but I did not think . . ."

"Did you tell your father that you didn't want to go with Lorenzo?"

"Yes, but he said I had to because no other man would want me."

The loveliness of the July morning had vanished as Sarah wept silently for this gentle girl. She divided the black hair into three sections, and when she was able to speak she said, "I'm going to make one thick braid. It will be easier to keep and it will look nicer, I think. I'll do it for you every day if you like—while I'm here." She scrubbed her tears away with her fist. "It must be a hard life for you, living like this, your home a camp in the mountains."

"My father says it is better to be with your man, wherever he is, whatever he is. We have a saying, 'She who stands under a good tree is sheltered by a good shade.' "

"And is Lorenzo a good shade?"

145

"He is no better or worse than any of the others. I belong to him and there is nothing I can do."

"But you shouldn't have to be here, forced to live with a man you don't love." She turned Teresa around to face her. "You're as much of a prisoner as I am. Don't you see that? The world is changing, Teresa. Women are becoming stronger. There are women in the United States now who call themselves Suffragettes. They're fighting for all of us. One of these days we'll be able to make our own decisions. We'll be our own bosses and own property and even vote."

She took the other girl's hand. "I'm going to get away from here. I don't know how yet, but I *am* going to get away. And when I do, if you want to, you can come with me. If we can get to Torreon my father will take care of us. He can arrange papers for you so you can go back to Texas with me."

"Ay, señorita, that would be wonderful, but we could never get away from here. How could we do it? What would we do?"

"I don't know yet. Take two of the horses some night when most of the men are away from the camp."

"I'd be so afraid . . ."

"Just think about it. Promise me you'll think about it."

"I will think, but I do not see how we can escape . . ." Suddenly her voice changed. "It is Captain Vega," she whispered. "Do you think he heard us? Do you think . . . ?" Her brown eyes were wide with fright.

"I don't know." She clutched Teresa's hand. "Don't say anything. Don't tell him, please."

He reached them in three strides. He didn't look at Sarah. To Teresa he said, "Get back to camp."

And with one fleeting look at Sarah, the girl scrambled to her feet and fled.

"What have you been telling her?" His voice was hard.

"Nothing. We were just talking. I braided her hair."

"You might try braiding your own."

146

She turned her back on him.

He whirled her around to face him. "I heard what you said to Teresa. I don't want you to put a lot of silly notions in her head. She belongs to Lorenzo and you're not to interfere."

"She doesn't belong to Lorenzo. She belongs to herself. I'm going to . . ."

"You're not going to do anything." His hand tightened on her arm. "You're not going to leave here until I tell you you can. If you have any plan to escape you can forget it. You think my men are bad? You should thank God they stopped you yesterday instead of the Federales or the Colorados."

She glared at him, hands on her hips, bronze-colored hair streaming down her back, curling in ringlets around her face. The shock and sorrow she'd felt last night had disappeared. She didn't know why Luis was treating her this way, but she'd be damned if she'd cry one more tear.

"Braid your hair," he said abruptly. "You're no longer Miss Sarah Finch of San Antonio. Until I say otherwise you're a *soldadera* in the Army of the Revolution. You will cook with the other women. You will clean my tent and polish my boots and do whatever else I ask of you. And you will do it cheerfully and well. Because if you don't I'll let Pedro and Ramon fight over you and pity the poor bastard that gets you."

She hit him across the face, whirled away from him, and ran. Ran away from the camp, through the field of yellow daisies, blinded with anger, her bare feet skimming the ground, the daisies whipping her legs, her mouth open, gasping for air, running, running . . .

His hand reached out and grabbed her shoulder. She spun away from him, stumbled, and fell when he caught her again, bringing him to the ground with her. She cried out in anger, twisting away from him, and scrambled to her hands and knees, trying to get to her feet. But he pulled her down again. And still she fought, rolling from side to side, her fingers curled into

147

claws, reaching out for his face. Until he grabbed her hands and pinned them above her head and straddled her with legs as strong as iron.

She felt as though her heart would burst out of her body, and finally, almost fainting, she lay still. She heard the rasp of his breath, and was glad that she'd made him fight. "Let me go," she said.

"When I'm ready." His eyes shot dangerous sparks. His hands tightened on her wrists. "How does it feel to be helpless, Sarah?" And when she didn't answer he said, "I could take you now. Here in this field, like a peasant. And there's nothing you could do about it."

"Let me go!" she cried, trying to thrust her body away from him.

"But my tastes have changed, Sarah. Actually you're too tall. We Mexicans like our women shorter. And rounder. We like to feel something when we put our arms around a woman." He ran his hands over her body. "You're too lean for my taste, *gringa*. Marta was right, you've got haunches like a boy, and your breasts are too small."

"You bastard!"

She tried to pull away, but he held her wrists in an iron grip. His eyes narrowed, his nostrils flared. He put his hand at the top of her shirtwaist. His eyes looked into hers as his fingers tightened on the cloth and ripped the shirtwaist down the front. He reached for her breast, his fingers tightening, so that in spite of herself she cried out.

"Am I hurting you?" he taunted. "You used to like me to touch your breasts."

"Luis, please. Please don't do this to me."

"I'll do anything I please to you, Sarah."

He slid his body down on hers. His tongue flicked against her breast, and when she tried to twist away, she felt his teeth against her nipple and lay still.

"That's it," he said, his eyes dangerous and threatening, as his lips went back to her breast, first one and then the other, while she cried out in fear and rage.

148

He reached down and pulled her skirt up, paying no attention to her cries. She wanted to kill him for doing this to her. She wanted to beg him to stop. She wanted the Luis she'd known, not this hard-faced man who hurt and frightened her.

He ripped his pants open and she felt him reach between her thighs and thrust himself into her. His hands gripped her shoulders, holding her pinned to the ground. When she struggled, trying to escape the terrible hardness of him, he struck her across the face, and exploded with a shattering terribleness inside her.

When he rolled away from her she turned on her side, hurt and shocked and ashamed. And more frightened than she'd ever been in her life. This man was a stranger. She could expect no kindness from him.

"I didn't mean that to happen," he said. "But if I want you I'll take you. And don't get any foolish notion about escaping because you're going to stay here until I decide to let you go. And if you try to escape I'll find you and I'll bring you back. And I'll beat you until you beg for mercy." He reached out and grabbed her chin and forced her to look at him. "Is that clear, Sarah?"

She pushed her damp hair back from her face. "Why?" she whispered. "Why?"

His fingers tightened on her chin.

"Is that clear?"

"Yes, Luis. That's quite clear."

But she knew, even as she said the words, that she would escape. Somehow, some way, she would get away from him.

Chapter 15

Plok. Plok. Plok. She scrubbed with the other women, kneeling with bare knees on the bank of the river, the ends of her long black skirt pulled up to her thighs. Sloshing the clothes into the water, then scrubbing them with strong brown soap, putting her back into it as the other women did, feeling sweat trickling down between her breasts. Then rinsing in the water again and again. Scrambling to her feet to spread the clothes on the nearby bushes to dry in the midmorning sun. Returning to wash another batch.

She thought suddenly of the women washing clothes at the entrance of the village where they had stopped to eat. She hadn't thought then, hadn't even dreamed, that soon she too would be at the side of a riverbank scrubbing clothes.

She thought of Jim, of his old-world courtliness. Of Paco Gonzales and his song . . . 'We are the children of the night . . .' And of Jed and Sam. Had another car come along? Were they all right? And her father? Dear Lord, what of her father?

And with the thought of him quick tears stung her eyes. She bent her head so the other women would not notice, and pretending to wipe the perspiration from her face, dried her tears.

"Put her to work," Luis had said to Silvia. "For as long as she is here, Miss Finch is not a guest. She is one of the women, and she will work like one of the women."

Her legs ached. Her knees hurt. She stopped for a moment to straighten her back, pressing the lower part of it with the heel of her hand.

"What's the matter, *gringa?*" Conchita asked. "You too good for work like this?"

Sarah ignored her and bent again to her task. She glanced sideways at the other women. They talked and laughed, seemingly unconscious of any discomfort. Even Conchita, who surely had not spent too many months like this, didn't seem to mind the work.

The two women had avoided each other since their fight. Sarah knew the other girl watched her, waiting for her to make a mistake so she could make fun of her. But she had not openly challenged Sarah since that first morning.

"You ever wash clothes before?" The voice mocked her. "Or you always have some poor Mexican *pendeja* do it for you?"

"It is unkind of you to speak to Señorita Sarah like that," Teresa said. "You should not do it."

"Mind your own business, little one-arm, or I'll throw you in the river."

"If you do, you'd better know how to swim," Sarah said.

"Ya, ya, ya. And you are the one who will throw me in? I'd like to see you try it." She sat back on her haunches. "I see how the little sparrow follows you around. Well, who knows, *gringa,* maybe you can teach her some spunk. Some day I'd like to hear her tell that bastard Lorenzo to go to hell." She grinned at Sarah. "The captain's been gone three days. You missing him? He'll be good and hungry for a woman when he comes back. You need any help, just holler. I'll show him what a real woman is like."

"You'd better shut up that talk," old Josefina said. "Your man Francisco hears you talking like that, he'll beat the hell out of you."

"I can handle Francisco. He lifts a finger to hit me I cut it off. I'm not like Teresa—no man is ever going to beat me and live to talk about it. Why don't you get

151

smart, little sparrow? Kick that *pendejo* where he lives and tell him to lay off you?"

"It's a man's right to beat his woman," Lupe said.

"His right!" Sarah looked at her incredulously.

"His God-given right." Lupe's voice was pious.

"Enough," Silvia put in. "Let's get on with our work. I want the clothes washed and the camp clean as a pin before the men return."

"Where did they go?" a woman asked.

"To meet Doroteo." She looked at Sarah and laughed. "Did you know Villa's real name was Doroteo? Doroteo Arango?"

"But why did he change it?"

"Can you imagine someone shouting, 'Viva Doroteo'?"

The other women laughed, and even Sarah found herself smiling.

"When he crossed the Rio Grande he had eight men, Sarah. Now he has thousands, and he has chased most of the Federales out of Chihuahua."

"Do you think Captain Vega's going to see Villa means another battle?" Lupe asked. "Will we leave camp?"

"Only Vega knows what is going on. He will tell us what we should know when he and the other men return."

"Will he bring that woman Marta with him?" old Josefina asked.

"Why should he when he has the *gringa?*" Conchita said. "And I hope to hell he doesn't bring her. She acts too high and mighty for me. You'd think she was the boss instead of Luis, strutting around the camp in those damn tight pants, acting like she was better than the rest of us. But I'd enjoy seeing her face when she finds out the *gringa* is sharing the captain's tent."

Sarah bent low over the shirt she was scrubbing, rubbing it again and again against the slick-wet rock, not even aware that the shirt was in shreds until Silvia stopped her. "What are you doing?" she said, more surprised than angry. "What is the matter with you?"

"Nothing. I'm sorry. Nothing." When she handed the ruined shirt to Silvia her hands were shaking.

"Why didn't he take Ramon? Is the arm still bad?" Lupe asked.

"It is not too good." Silvia bent over her work.

"Perhaps I could look at him," Sarah said. "I know first aid. I could . . ."

"You could do nothing," Conchita said with a snarl. "It's your fault he is this way. If it hadn't been for you he'd be all right."

"But . . ."

"It's better that you don't see him," Silvia said. "If he got worse after you attended him the others would say it was your fault. No, it's better that you do not try to help."

That afternoon, at the hour when the birds flew in to roost in the laurel trees, Luis Vega and his men rode back to camp. Their faces were drawn and tired. They gave the horses to their women and went to the river to wash away the sweat and dust of the trip. All but Vega. When he started for the river, Silvia held him back, saying, "It would be better, Luis, if you saw Ramon first."

The camp was unusually quiet that night. A few of the men played cards. Others lay with their heads on the laps of their women. One or two strummed guitars and sang:

> The bugle of battle plays to war,
> The brave knight leaves to fight,
> Though streams of blood shall flow,
> We will never let a tyrant rule.

> And if perchance I die in battle,
> And my body lies in the sierra,
> Adelita, Adelita, for God's sake I beg
> That you weep for me with your eyes.
> Weep for me with your eyes.

153

In the dark of the tent Sarah put on her long cotton nightgown and tried to sleep. She slept—only to be wakened by loud voices. The men no longer murmured softly to their women or to each other. They no longer sang the sad songs of war. Now their voices were loud with pulque, and the songs they sang were bawdy. There were shouts, a gunshot, a curse. It was a long time before the voices quieted.

And to Sarah the quiet was more shattering than the noise. She pulled the straw mat as far to the side of the tent as it would go. When she heard the stumbling steps approaching she pulled the blanket up to her chin and closed her eyes.

He smelled of pulque. He sat down heavily on the straw mat next to her and grunted with the effort to take his boots off. She heard the sound of his other clothes when he threw them into a corner. She didn't move. She was afraid to breathe.

"Are you awake?" His voice was slurred.

She didn't answer him.

"I asked you if you were awake," he said more loudly.

"How can I *not* be? All that drunken shouting, you coming in here smelling like you've crawled out of a tequila bottle. A fine example for your men!"

"Ah, my men. You don't think much of them, do you? They're dirty and ragged and yes, sometimes *they* smell bad too. But they're my men, and they're brave men."

She heard him pull the cork out of a bottle. Heard him drink deep.

"My men. My brothers." He was silent for a time, and then he said, "Ramon is dead."

Under the blanket she balled her hands into fists. "I'm sorry," she whispered. And was.

"I killed him."

She swallowed hard, trying to control her sudden shaking.

He reached out and found her shoulder. He shook

154

her roughly and said, "Why don't you say something?"

She tried to pull away from him. "I said I was sorry."

"Sorry!" His voice choked. "Sorry! It is your fault that he is dead."

"No it isn't. Don't say that. I tried to see him this morning. I thought I could help . . ."

"Help? Holy Mother! The only place you could help him was to his grave."

"That isn't fair. I . . ."

He grabbed both of her shoulders now. "He's dead, Sarah. Ramon is dead and it's your fault." His voice shook with anger.

"Let me go!" She tried to push him away, but his hands tightened on her shoulders.

"You're hurting me," she said, hitting him on his chest.

"Be still." He let go of one shoulder and reached for her, fumbling at the front of her gown.

"No," she screamed, hitting him in the face with her fist.

"You bitch!" He grabbed her, fastened one hand around her wrists while his other hand found the top of her gown and ripped it down the front, pulling it away from her body, forcing her back on the mat. "Bitch," he said again. "Ramon is dead because of you."

When she cried out, he said, "Have you no pride, Sarah? Do you want everyone in the camp to know what I'm doing to you?"

She fought him silently then, twisting her body from side to side until he grasped her wrists with one hand and held them above her head so she couldn't fight him. He groped for her with his other hand, moving down her body, forcing her legs apart with rough fingers, straining in his effort to hold her still.

He was on top of her, holding her with the length of his body, his legs pinning her tight to the straw mat.

She wanted to beg him to stop. But if she couldn't ask anyone else for help, then she couldn't ask him for mercy. She could only fight, try to twist free of the weight of his body on hers, of the hand that forced her legs apart, of the terrible hardness of him.

Not like this, she wanted to scream at him. Not like this.

"You're hurting me," she gasped.

"Good. That's good. I want to hurt you. Oh God, how I want to hurt you."

"Luis, please . . ."

But he was beyond hearing as he held her closer, and still closer. And thrust himself deeper, and still deeper. Until at last his body jerked and arched and his mouth sought hers while his body shuddered over her.

When at last he shifted his body from hers she moved as far away from him as the tent would allow, turning her back, curling herself into a small ball of misery.

He reached for her, pulling her back tight against him, his arm around her waist, holding her so that she couldn't move.

And when she began to cry he said, "Cry, Sarah. Cry for yourself. Cry for Ramon. Cry for all of us. Cry, for we are all lost bastards on our way to hell."

Chapter 16

He was gone when she awoke the next morning. She put her clothes on and when she left the tent she went directly to the river, not caring what any of them thought, only wanting to be away from all of them. To be alone. To be clean.

She felt empty. Nothing that happened to her now would hurt her as much as what he had done to her last night. Nothing would make her feel as ashamed or humiliated.

When she came out of the water she saw Silvia on the bank waiting for her. She handed Sarah her towel and said, "Go and dress yourself. Then come back and we will talk." She hesitated a moment. "Are the sleeves of your shirtwaist long?"

"To cover these marks?" Her voice was angry. "Yes, they're long. Do you wish they weren't so that everybody could see how *macho* your Captain Vega is?" She turned her back, hoping she had angered the other woman. Hoping she would go away.

But Silvia was waiting for her when she returned, her broad back against a rock, her legs outstretched in front of her. "Come, sit in the sun," she said, "and we will talk."

And when Sarah didn't answer her, she said, "I will tell you about my village, the village of La Cruz. Both Jacinto and I are from there. We were married by the village priest when I was fifteen and Jacinto was seventeen." She smiled. "He is a skinny bent fellow now, but ah, you should have seen him then, Sarah. So tall and straight. And what a worker. Even at that age. We were poor, so we had to move in with his parents. They gave us their room and slept in the parlor. But, when we had a little money, we built another room and gave theirs back to them.

"Jacinto and his father worked in the fields. His mother and I spent our days taking care of the vegetable garden, grinding corn for tortillas, and tending the chickens and the pigs. Life was hard, but it was good. Especially after our child was born."

For the first time since Silvia had started talking, Sarah looked at her. "I didn't know you had a child."

"Federico. He was a beautiful boy. So good. So smart. How his grandparents loved him." She smiled. And when she did her face changed, softened, became almost beautiful. "How they spoiled and petted him, Sarah. But that only sweetened his nature. When he was old enough he took care of the animals in the pasture. He went to school. He even became an altar boy."

She sighed deeply. Her face darkened and lost its momentary beauty. "One day the Colorados, the most hated, the most feared of the Federal troops, rode into the village. Jacinto and his father were in the fields that day. I was in the kitchen preparing the noon meal when Federico came running into the yard screaming, 'Mama, Mama, the Colorados.' He was ten years old."

" 'Run to the woods,' I told him. 'Hide the stock if you can.' "

Silvia's face suddenly looked pinched and old. "All of us, all the women, tried to shoo the chickens and the pigs into the woods to save them from the Colorados, but they were too fast for us. They galloped into the town, roiling up great clouds of gray dust, shouting, shooting, stopping their horses hard so that the animals reared on their back legs, whinnying, nostrils flaring, as excited as the bastards who rode them.

"Old Pepe Macias ran out shouting that we were *pacíficos,* peaceful people who had nothing to do with the revolution or with the rebels. One of them kicked the old man in the face with his boot.

"They jumped off their horses and ran up and down the street, into the houses, taking whatever they could carry. Some of the women were screaming, children were crying with fright, pigs were squealing. They took vases, statues, Señora Guzman's sewing machine, jewelry, whatever they could put their hands on. And one of them took Marguerita Guzman, who was thirteen years old. Her mother flung herself on the man, clawing at his face with her nails. He took his gun and jammed it against the Señora Guzman's stomach and shot her. When she dropped he kicked her out of the way and dragged the girl into the tall weeds behind the house."

Silvia's face was beaded with sweat.

"Don't talk any more," Sarah said. "Please, this is causing you such pain."

"I want you to understand. I want you to know why we fight this revolution. Why we are as we are." Her strong hands balled into fists. "A man, a dirty man with a beard, grabbed me and pulled me into the house. Jacinto's mother was old and she was sick, but she rushed at the man with a knife from the kitchen, shouting, 'Let her go or I will kill you.'

"He picked up the statue of the Virgin Mary from the mantel of the fireplace and he struck her with one hand while he held me with the other." Her voice was hoarse. "It was as though the Virgin bled, Sarah. For she was covered with the blood of Jacinto's mother. And as she lay dying he pulled me down to the floor and raped me. I can remember thinking: when he has finished I will kill him. And if I cannot then I will join Villa and kill others who are like him. I will survive this because I will carry the hate of what this man is doing to me, and my hate will make me strong."

She closed her eyes. Her voice was so low now that

Sarah could barely hear her. "Federico, my little boy, I heard him cry out. I opened my eyes while this man was still raping me and I looked up into the eyes of my ten-year-old son. He held his father's axe in his hand and he struck the man with the axe."

Sarah gripped Silvia's hands in hers.

"They held me while they beat him. And they dragged me out into the yard while they threw a rope over a branch of the cypress tree and hanged him."

"Oh Christ," Sarah said. "Oh Christ. Oh Christ." She pulled Silvia's hands to her lips and kissed them.

"I could not speak for more than two months, but when I spoke my first words to Jacinto were, 'We will join Villa.' "

Her eyes were anguished. "We have all suffered from these men, Sarah. Now we are not the kind of people we would choose to be. We all would like to be kinder, but we do not have the time to be kind." She hesitated. "Captain Vega is not a bad man. He is a good soldier, but he should not be a soldier. This is not the life for him. Nevertheless he is a fine leader and his men respect him. He felt responsible for Ramon's death."

"He said it was my fault."

"But he did not mean it. He has a bad temper and sometimes he is hard. But he is a good man."

"Silvia . . ." She hesitated, feeling a sudden need to confide in the other woman. And finally she said, "Captain Vega and I have known each other before."

"That is what Pedro said, but I didn't believe him. If that is true, Sarah, why does he treat you so harshly now?"

"I don't know." She leaned back against a large rock, hugging her knees to her chest. "We met and fell in love when I was eighteen. My father said I was too young to consider marriage and so I went back to Texas. Luis joined Villa. Two years later we saw each other again, in Mexico City, during those tragic ten days when the opposing troops were at war. When we escaped from Mexico City we went to his parents' hacienda and he asked me to marry him. That was five months ago, Silvia.

"The next morning a woman by the name of Marta came and he went away with her."

"Marta Solis." Silvia's eyes narrowed. "She is a good *soldadera* and I should not say this, but I do not like her. I can't understand why Luis . . ."

"Why Luis what?"

And when Silvia didn't answer she said, "Are they lovers?"

The other woman avoided her eyes. "She shares his tent when she is here."

"I see."

What did you expect? she asked herself. That's the way the world is, Sarah. He's finished with you. He has another woman now.

But not Marta, her heart cried. Not Marta.

She looked away from Silvia, trying to hide her anguish. "We quarreled the day he left," she said, "and I made a scene. He hated that. But I can't believe he hated me. And even if . . . if there's someone else in his life that's no reason for him to treat me the way he does."

"He has changed since his father and brother were killed. Perhaps that . . ."

"What?" Sarah's eyes went wide with shock. Her face became so deadly white that Silvia thought she would faint.

"You didn't know?"

"No!" Her voice was hoarse with the shock of it. "Killed? His father? Carlos? Oh my God. Oh my God. What happened to them?"

"Soldiers of Huerta came to the hacienda. They wanted to know where Luis was, what route he had taken, and when his family would not say they took his father and brother to the Citadel and killed them."

She put her head down on her knees. Sobs racked her body. And when she was able to speak she said, "So that's it. He thinks I informed on him. He blames me for what happened." She closed her eyes against

161

the horror of it. "Silvia, Silvia, what am I going to do?"

He didn't speak to her when he came to the tent that night. She had put on a clean flannel nightgown, and because the air was cool, a shawl over her shoulders. Her hair was pulled back from her face and lay in a thick braid down her back.

"I have to speak to you," she said.

And when he didn't answer her, she said, "Silvia told me about your father and Carlos."

He looked at her then, his eyes flat and cold, his lips drawn to a thin line.

She tried to keep her voice steady. "I didn't know they were dead, Luis. I'm sorry. I loved them both. I've never known a man as gentle as your father."

His hands were clenched. Tte knuckles of his hands were white.

She swallowed. "I don't know why, but I think . . . I think you blame me for their deaths. Did someone tell you I had something to do with it? Is that it? Because whoever told you lied."

"My mother told me." His voice was as cold as death.

"Your mother!" She stared at him in horror.

"Andres told her how you had helped him—just before he let two of his men rape her."

"Oh my God," she said softly, turning away from the pain in his eyes.

"You said that day at the hacienda that you'd get even with me. Well, you did, Sarah. You did. Perhaps you didn't think Andres would actually kill my father and Carlos, or give my mother to his men, or burn our fields and shoot our bulls. Perhaps you thought they'd tell him what route I'd taken. Perhaps it was me you wanted killed."

"No!" She put her hands to her ears as though to ward off the onslaught on his words.

"For five long months I've thought of what I'd do

to you and Andres if I ever got my hands on you. I've got you, and some day I'll get him. I hate him, Sarah, but not the way I hate you. I hate you because, God help me, I loved you."

He dropped to the ground beside her. "And because I want you. I see you look at me with your great green eyes, and in spite of everything you've done to me and mine I want you. And that makes me hate myself as much as I hate you."

"Luis, please." She put her hand out and touched his face. "Please, darling . . ."

He took her hand, and as though it were an object of distaste, flung it away from him. "No, Sarah. No tender words for us. If I want you I'll take you the same way I'd take a prostitute. I'll have my fill of you and then, please God, I'll be done with you forever. Now, will you take your gown off or shall I rip it off you?"

She turned her back on him. She took the shawl off, and then she pulled the gown over her head. And did not turn around when she heard him remove his clothes and lie down beside her.

I won't fight him, she told herself. I'll lie still and let him do what he wants to me. I won't cry and I won't beg. But when he put his hands on her she cried out without thinking, and tried to pull away from him. He grabbed her wrists and before she knew what was happening he bound them together with his kerchief.

"I'm tired of fighting you," he said, shoving her back against the mat. "From now on this is the way it's going to be. You'll lie here and submit to whatever I do to you. You're just a . . . a *thing* to me, Sarah, just something to appease this sick hunger I get whenever I look at you."

And then his mouth was on hers, devouring, demanding, hard and unforgiving. His hands sought her breasts, making no effort to be gentle.

"God damn you," he whispered into her throat, "God damn you to hell for making me want you."

He pulled her legs apart, loving the sound of her

163

gasp of pain as he plunged into her, hurting himself as much as he hurt her, riding her hard, lunishing her with his flesh while she moaned beneath him.

And suddenly it was over in one quick disappointing moment. He rolled away from her and lay on his back, feeling lonelier and sadder than he had ever felt in his life.

Chapter 17

The shot split the stillness of the night. It was followed by a whole explosion of shots, screams, the high whinnying cry of horses, of riders, of shouts, and of curses.

Luis rolled away from her, and in one continuing motion pulled his pants on and grabbed his rifle.

Outside in the night a woman screamed.

Rifle fire cracked.

"What is it?" Sarah said. "What's happening?"

"The Colorados. Stay down." And then he was gone.

Frightened, not knowing quite what to do, she crept to the opening of the tent and looked out. Riders, screaming curses and firing as they rode, streamed through the camp. Vega's men, taken by surprise, fired where they stood, easy targets for the night raiders.

One man went down, another, and another. Silvia darted from the bushes and grabbed the gun of one of the men who had fallen, firing at a rider as he passed her. The rider tried to hit her with the butt of his rifle. She rolled, shot from the ground, and saw the man grab his stomach and fall.

A stray bullet made a zzzzzing sound near Sarah. One of Vega's men—she thought his name was Pepe—fell almost in front of her. She reached out, grabbed his shoulders, and pulled him inside the tent.

"*Cabrones*," he yelled, clutching his leg. "Rotten

bastards, coming in the night like devils of death." He tried to pull away from her. "Let me go, señorita, let me go." He tried to stand, cried out in pain, and fell to the ground. Blood poured from his leg.

She looked around for something to bind him with, saw the scarf that Luis had tied her with, and reached for it. She straightened the leg, trying to see in the dark. She tried to rip his pants leg, and when she couldn't, bent down to tear it with her teeth. She ripped it to the ankle and bound the leg as well and as fast as she could.

The noise and confusion outside the tent was a frightening thing to hear. She picked up the fallen man's rifle, wondering what to do. She stepped cautiously outside the tent and just as she did one of the riders raised his rifle and shot Francisco. Conchita, her gypsy face dark with rage, ran toward the rider and grabbed his leg, trying to pull him off his horse, hanging onto his leg as the horse reared. The rider kicked at the girl, but she clung to his leg like a madwoman, shrieking, striking at him, hitting at the arm that was raised to strike her. He shook away from her and raised his rifle.

Sarah ran screaming from the tent, swinging the rifle by the barrel, running, shouting as she ran, pushing Conchita aside as she swung at the rider and hit him with the butt end of the rifle before he could shoot the girl.

He fell from his horse and hit the ground with a whomp. He rolled fast and Sarah saw him reach for his holster. She saw a spurt of flame and saw him grab his chest, and when she whirled around Pedro Garcia raised his rifle over his head and yelled, *"Viva la Gringa!"*

"You women, run for the trees," someone shouted. The voice was lost in the sound of rifle fire. The smell of dust and sweat and blood filled the air.

She felt someone grab her shoulder and whirled to see Luis. "Go to the trees," he shouted. "Try to get the other women."

But before she could answer she heard a sharp zzzzing close to her face and felt herself being dragged roughly down to the dust. His body was on hers as he half-rolled, half-dragged her behind an overturned barrel.

"Are you all right?"

"I think so."

"Do you know how to load a rifle?"

"A hunting rifle."

"That's good enough." He slung a bandolier at her.

A bullet zinged to the ground near where they lay, throwing the dirt into her face. She had no idea how long the fight lasted. Her hands moved fast as she loaded, handed a rifle to him, took the other to be loaded. The smell of gunpowder, bright flashes of flame, the screamed curses, all became a part of the terrible night.

When at last the sky lightened the camp lay in ruins. Fallen horses lay with fallen men. And still the fighting went on. The women had not gone to the river, or to the trees. They'd stayed by their men, fighting beside them.

As suddenly as it had started it was over. All but five of the Colorados were dead. Four of Vega's men were dead; six were wounded. Two of the wounded lay where they had fallen. One gripped his bleeding arm, another a leg, another a shoulder. All of the men looked stunned with fatigue, their faces covered with sweaty dirt. They sat cross-legged on the ground, shoulders hunched, rifles at their feet, cigarettes dangling from their lips. The five captives, hands tied behind their backs, were shoved roughly to one side of the dead campfire.

The women began to move first, picking up rifles, cooking pots, overturned braziers, trying to make order of disorder. Vega had his wounded men carried to a shaded clearing under the trees, while Pedro Garcia rebuilt the campfire, and Lupe set pots of water to boil.

Some of the men wore their pants, others only long

167

underwear. A few of the women had thrown rebozos over their nightgowns, some had put on skirts. Sarah, who was still in her gown, seemed unaware of what she wore. And when Luis called to her, when he said, "Do you know anything about medicine?" she came out of the shock of the night and answered, "I taught a Red Cross first aid course last spring."

She looked very young standing there in her nightgown, her feet bare, her face smudged with dirt, her dark red hair tangled and loose about her shoulders. Shadows of fatigue showed under her wide green eyes.

"Antonio Gomez is the nearest thing we have to a doctor," Luis said. "His father was a pharmacist and he claims to know everything. Go and put something on and help him with the wounded."

"I just remembered," she said, "there's a wounded man in our . . . in your tent. He has a leg wound. I bandaged it as well as I could last night."

He hurried to the tent with her and knelt on the ground beside the man. "*¿Qué pasó, Pepe?*" he said.

"It is nothing, Luis. Those bastards only nicked me. I went to sleep for a while, but I am fine now." His face was yellow in the pale morning light.

"Don't worry, *hombre*. We'll fix you up as good as new." He stepped out of the tent and yelled, "Pedro, Pepe is in here, help me move him."

Luis was right. Antonio Gomez knew almost nothing about medicine. When he started to touch the men without washing his hands Sarah stopped him.

"Wash your hands," she said. "You'll infect their wounds."

He wiped his hands on his dirty pants.

"No," she insisted. "Wash them. Take some of this hot water and wash them with soap. They're full of germs."

He looked indignant. "Full of what?"

"Germs, bacteria that cause disease. You must be clean and the men's wounds must be clean or they'll become infected."

"I have never heard such nonsense." He reached

168

for Francisco, grasping him by the shoulder. Francisco groaned and swore. Conchita held tight to one hand. She looked at Sarah. "Is what you say true? Will he sicken and die if Antonio is not clean, or is this some fairy tale you are telling?"

"It's no fairy tale."

The other girl measured her, and then she turned to Antonio and snarled, "Wash your hands, you pig, like the *gringa* says. And then *do* whatever she says.

"I will help," she told Sarah. "You tell me what you want me to do and I will do it."

"Is there any antiseptic?"

"Tequila," Antonio put in. "Will that do?"

"It will have to."

Luis and Pedro carried the rest of the wounded men and laid them on blankets under the trees. Pedro stopped for a moment to wipe the sweat from his face. "You are doing pretty good today, little dove," he said. "We'll make a *soldadera* out of you yet."

They took care of Francisco first. Sarah had never seen a bullet wound before, and this was a bad one. When they touched him, Francisco screamed with pain. Pedro and Conchita held him while Antonio made a cut in the wound and probed for the bullet. It was easier after Francisco fainted. Antonio found the bullet at last, poured some tequila into the gaping hole, drank from the bottle, and left Sarah to bind the wound.

When he bent over Pepe's leg he shook his head and called to Sarah. "I do not know what to do with this," he whispered. "It is very bad, I think."

Dark blood oozed from the wound. The man's color was worse. He was semi-conscious, and he called, "Maria, Maria, where is my Maria? Get my clothes, woman. The day is late and I have far to ride. Where are you? Why do you not light a lamp?"

His leg was shattered. The flesh around the gaping wound was torn, part of the bone sticking up.

Sarah could have wept with frustration. She knew so little; how to make a sling for a broken arm, to

169

bandage a simple wound, how to care for a head injury. The Denton branch of the Red Cross had not prepared her for this.

Pepe's breathing was shallow. "Turn the light on," he pleaded. "Turn it on, turn it on. Ay, Mother of God, but it is dark here."

"I don't think we can help him, señorita," Antonio said.

Sarah knew that he was right. "Get one of the other women," she said to Conchita. "Tell her to stay with him."

He died an hour later. She knew after it happened because two men came and took his body away. She wiped the sweat from her face and turned back to help the men who were alive. The sun grew hotter as the day went on. Once she heard shots and she raised her head from what she was doing and asked Conchita what the shots were.

"They are probably shooting the prisoners," Conchita said.

So this is what happens in a revolution, Sarah thought. This is what men do to each other.

Finally the last man had been moved to his tent and they were finished. She didn't know whether she had done a good job or not. She only knew she had done the best she could, and she wished it had been more. She leaned her back against a tree and closed her eyes. When she felt a hand on her arm she opened them and saw Teresa.

"Come down to the river," the girl said. "The other women are there now. When you have bathed and had some food you will feel better."

When she knelt beside the water as the other women were doing, scrubbing her hands and face when the soap was passed to her, she thought that she would have liked to take her clothes off and scrub all over. But the other women would not have approved. And suddenly it occurred to her that she unconsciously wanted their approval. And that was ridiculous. These people were nothing to her. They were her captors, not her friends.

Then why had she fought alongside them? Why had she stayed next to Luis during the battle?

How different these women were from the women and girls she was accustomed to. There was no pretense to them. They were helpmates in the truest sense of the word. They fought beside their men, and cooked their meals, and slept with them. This was where they wanted to be, in spite of the hardship, in spite of the danger.

"How do you feel?" Conchita asked, breaking in on her thoughts.

"Tired."

"I have to tell you, *gringa,* you did one hell of a job today. I think maybe you saved my life. That bastard would have killed me if you hadn't hit him when you did. Sometime maybe I do something for you."

"You can do something for me right now. You can stop calling me '*gringa.*' "

The other girl laughed. "Then I call you Sarah. We gonna be friends or we gonna keep fighting?"

"I think we'd better be friends." She put her hand out.

"*Sí, gringa.*" She laughed. "No, I won't say that again. Sarah, you betcha we gonna be friends."

Chapter 18

Conchita did not sleep for a long time. Every few minutes she raised herself on her elbow to look at Francisco, to listen to his breathing. Mother of God, she prayed silently, let him be all right. Don't let him die. I promise as soon as we are near a church I will make a Novena. I will do anything you ask of me, only please let him live.

"Why do you fret?" His voice was weak.

"How do you feel? Would you like something?"

"A sip of water."

She reached over to the earthen pot and poured him a cup. She raised his head and held the cup to his lips. "Are you better then?" she asked when he finished.

"Yes, *mujer,* yes. Do not worry so."

"It does not pain you?"

"Not so much now." He raised his hand and pushed her hair back from her face. "I saw you try to pull that man off his horse. I was almost unconscious but I could hear you screaming like a wild thing. You could have been killed."

"If he had killed you I would not have lived anyway."

"Don't say that."

"I mean it. Life was nothing before you. It would be nothing now without you."

"Give me your hand," he said, "and let us not talk of such things."

172

She lay beside him and held his hand. After a little while he slept. But she lay for a long time listening to each breath he took.

Lorenzo was drunk. It was late when he finally left the other men at the campfire and staggered to the tent he shared with Teresa.

"Woman," he said, "help me with my boots."

She scrambled to her feet, stumbling in her anxiety to do what he said, and turned her back to him so he could put one leg between hers. And when he did she began to pull on the boot with her one hand. It didn't budge.

"Pull," he shouted. "Damn it, woman, pull."

"I am trying."

"Try harder." His other boot pushed against her back and she sprawled headlong.

"Damn clumsy one-armed woman," he snarled. "I'll do it myself."

"You said you'd never say that."

"I never do say it."

"But you said it now."

"Only because it's the truth."

"I will . . ." She swallowed. "I will no longer allow you to say such things to me."

"Allow? What allow? You are my woman. I can say whatever I choose to say. I can do whatever I choose to do. And I choose to say that you are a stupid one-armed woman."

Teresa was never to know how she came to do it, but suddenly she picked up the boot and swung it at his head, hitting him, sending him sprawling. "I will not let you speak to me like that. I am not your slave. I am a free woman. Sarah said women do not have to let men do this to them. She said . . ."

"You hit me!"

Terrified of what she had done, she shrank back to the side of the tent.

"You hit me!" he said again. "I am your man and you hit me."

"I am sorry. I will not . . ."

"You will be sorrier, I promise you." He unbuckled his belt, pulled it through the loops, and reached for her.

"No, please."

He pushed her down on the mat and began to strike her with the belt. When she tried to roll away from him he grabbed her shoulder. He ripped the gown down her back, and holding her with one hand, beat her with the other.

"I promise you," he muttered each time he struck her. "Treat me like some piece of dirt. Ever since I took you from that pigsty you lived in. Every time I touch you. Every time I make love to you, you shrink away from me. By God, I'll beat you until you treat me like something. Like I am your man."

The blows continued to fall, on her shoulders and her back. And when at last he threw the belt down, he turned her on her back and entered her. He cried aloud when he finished, cried as though he had been wounded. And he said, "Damn you. Damn you to hell for shrinking from me."

Silvia massaged Jacinto's bony shoulders. "You must eat more," she said. "You are too thin."

"I am a tired old man."

"What old? You are fifty-one."

"Tonight I am a hundred and fifty-one, and not enough of a man for a woman like you." He raised his head and smiled at her. "What a woman you are! Today you fought like a man."

"All of the women did well today, even the *gringa*. I know it is not my business, Jacinto, but Luis treats her badly. It is not like him to treat anyone as he does her."

174

"When this is over he will return her to her father. She will be all right."

"Ay, you men. And suppose he does return her? What then? The Northamericans will know she has been with us, has lived with us. With him. Do you think she can just return to Texas and make a fine marriage?" She shook her head. "No, *hombre,* the world does not work that way. I am sad for her because he has taken her by force."

"I took you, Silvia."

She smiled into the darkness. "We were children. What did we know?"

"But you did not want to do it."

"Of course I did. I only pretended to you that I did not." She stroked his bony chest. "Was I convincing?"

"Such talk! Ay, woman, I wish I could be like that now. I am not enough man for you. When the Colorados killed our son and my mother they killed me too."

"Don't talk like that." Her voice was rough. "You are the only man I want. The other . . . well, we have had that. And if it is over we have something else instead. You are . . . how can I explain it, Jacinto? You are the balance that steadies me. Without you, without the memory of our home, my hate would eat me up. When I am at my worst I see your gentleness and it makes me ashamed of the savage in me."

"I wish that I had this savage in me. I wish I had your fine passion. But I do not. I am only a farmer, and that is all that I want to be." His long melancholy face was sad. "I do not like to fight. Killing sickens me. I want to go home. I want to leave here and return to our village. Perhaps we can . . ."

"We cannot. So long as there are Federal soldiers we will fight." She lay down and pulled him to her. She cradled his head in her strong arms and said, "We will go back some day. You will farm again and things will be as they were before."

And when he tried to speak she stilled him and said,

"Some day, but not now. Not until the revolution is finished. Not until every Colorado is dead."

His hair was still wet from the river when he came back to the tent that night. The lamp was lighted, Sarah was asleep on her side, the blanket pulled to her chin, one hand under the side of her face. Her smooth cheeks were rosy from sleep, her strawberry mouth as soft and as vulnerable as a child's. He felt a quiver from somewhere deep inside him, and without thinking he reached out his hand and smoothed the hair back from her face.

She opened her eyes that were as wide and as innocent as a child's. "I didn't betray you," she said.

He was caught in the depths of her eyes.

"I'd have let Andres kill me before I'd have done anything to hurt you or your family."

"Did you tell him we'd been at the hacienda?"

"Yes, but . . ."

"And you told him I'd left with Marta?"

"I was angry and I . . ."

"Whether you did what you did in anger, or spite, or in sheer ignorance doesn't really matter, does it? The results are the same."

"Luis, please listen to me."

"No. I'm tired, Sarah. Tired to the bone. I've got to ride out of here early in the morning." He reached for the lamp and blew it out.

He lay for a long time in the darkness of the tent, listening to her quiet breathing, feeling the need for her growing in him. "I executed five men today," he said. "I need a woman to take the taste of them out of my mouth." He knew, even as he said the words, how much he hurt her.

When he reached for her, meaning to tie her as he had the night before, she said, "Don't tie me. Please don't tie me."

He could hear the terror in her voice.

176

"Somebody else did that to me. I can't stand it. I can't . . ."

He let her go. "Somebody tied you? Who?"

"Andres. My father broke the door in. He almost killed Andres. Please, Luis. please. You wouldn't treat a prostitute this way, would you?"

He felt his stomach tighten, felt his face burn with shame.

"I'll be anything you want me to be, but please don't tie me."

She moved close to him and put her arms on his shoulders, and for a moment, just for a moment, he wanted to tell her that he was sorry. But he said nothing. He pulled her to him, crushing her body to his, searching her mouth, feeling her skin as soft as satin under his hands.

He thought of how she'd been today, how she'd run screaming from the tent like an avenging angel, barefoot, her long nightgown trailing in the dust, swinging a rifle at the man on horseback.

And again he wanted to tell her he was sorry, but couldn't.

She responded to him now, her body arching against his when his mouth moved to kiss her breasts. Her hands caressed his shoulders, and she gave a small gasp of pleasure when he entered her.

When his hands tightened on her hips and his fingers bruised her skin, she knew he thought she was only pretending to feel this passion that ran through her like fire, this burning heat that made her want to scream his name. *Listen to my body, Luis, and know what I can't tell you with words,* she wanted to shout. *Listen, my love, and believe in me again.*

She felt her body tremble against him, heard the rasp of her breath. She reached for him with hungry body and hungry mouth, trying to tell him. Trying to tell him . . . knowing a strange kind of pride and heightened excitement when she heard his quickened breath and felt his hungers match her own.

Her hand pressed against the smooth skin at the small of his back, urging him closer, deeper. Her lips brushed the line of his jaw, her teeth nipped his shoulder. She heard without shame her own quick cry of delighted anguish.

And a matching cry as he shuddered and spent. And still it came, wave after wave of warmth as she cried against him, and he took her cry into his mouth. And quieted her with his hands.

At last, his body still on hers, she slept.

Chapter 19

She woke in the first faint light of dawn. The air was cool. She pulled the blanket up to her chin and moved closer to the warmth next to her. Then, on the edge of sleep, she came suddenly awake and moved away from him.

His breathing was deep and slow, his full lips parted a bit with each breath. Blue-gray smudges of fatigue shone beneath his eyes, small lines marked the corners.

I'm becoming one of them, she thought. I fight beside them and tend their wounded. I bathe in the river with their women. I grind the corn and make their tortillas. I sleep with their leader.

She felt hot tears sting her eyes. Tears of sorrow. Tears of shame because she'd tried to reach him last night. Tried and failed. If he had said one word to her, one word of kindness, one word of remembered love, she would have forgiven all the cruelties he'd inflicted on her because she understood his pain. But it was too late. Nothing would change him now. And if she stayed with him what would happen to her? What kind of woman would she become?

She closed her eyes remembering the terrible urgency of her body, the whispered words, the final cry of fulfillment—to a man who despised her.

He was going away today. If he took most of the men with him as he sometimes did, the camp would be almost deserted except for the women. Today was the day, then. No, tonight. Tonight she would make her escape.

She took a deep breath, feeling strengthened and good. She'd need food and water, as much water as she could manage because she'd be crossing part of the desert and she had no idea how far she'd have to ride before she reached a village.

A pot of coffee boiled on one of the braziers near the campfire. She poured some into one of the earthenware mugs, warming her hands, enjoying the smell of the clay as she raised it to her lips. She'd had only two sips when Conchita came out of the tent she shared with Francisco.

"How is he this morning?" Sarah asked. "I'll see him as soon as I finish this."

"He's better, I think. He slept a little."

"Did you? You look worn out."

"I'm all right." She poured a cup of coffee. "Ay, *Dios mío*, Sarah, if anything happens to him I will kill myself."

"He's going to be all right, Conchita. The wound was clean. He's strong. Please don't look like that. Please don't worry so." She studied the girl over the rim of her cup and thought, she really loves him. And found it strange that a girl as vibrantly alive as Conchita could love a man as dark and silent and somber as Francisco. She said, "How long have you been together?"

"Two years." Her smile was sardonic. "You're wondering how we came to be together, aren't you?"

"No." She felt the color creep to her cheeks, because of course she *was* curious.

"Well, I think I will tell you. Yesterday you said we would be friends. Perhaps after what I'm going to tell you you'll change your mind." She pulled two of the campstools closer to the fire and sat down. "I was working in a whorehouse in Nogales when I met Francisco." Her voice was deliberately casual.

Coffee spilled over the edge of Sarah's cup. She felt her face grow hot. She wasn't sure where to look.

180

"I went to Nogales to try to find work after my mother died because my stepfather tried to rape me. He came after me one night and I hit him with an iron pot. He was still unconscious when I grabbed the few things I had and left. He may be dead for all I know.

"Nogales is a wild town. I was from a village and I didn't know where to go or what to do. I tried to find work as a maid but with the revolution everything was so crazy and people had no jobs and nobody wanted a maid. I was so tired and hungry by the time one of Rosa's girls found me that I didn't care what I did." Her eyes were defiant. "Are you shocked, *gringa?*"

"You said if we were friends you wouldn't call me that again."

Conchita took a deep breath and some of the defiance went out of her voice. "It wasn't so bad, Sarah. The other girls were nice enough. Sometimes it just seemed like one long party, drinking and dancing and laughing. But the rest of it? No, I didn't like that. Then one night Francisco came to Rosa's. He sat alone in a corner drinking tequila. He wouldn't talk to any of the girls. Finally Rosa sent me over. I asked him if he'd like some company and he said, *'Bueno. Upstairs.'*

"I thought to myself, this one is going to be even worse than the others. He'll probably throw me on the bed, finish one, two, three, and tomorrow I'll have new bruises on my arms and he'll tell his friends what a man he was."

She leaned forward, her face intent, but strangely softened. "But it wasn't like that. He was so . . . so solemn, and *nice*. He treated me as though I was someone special. And when it was over he told me that he was a soldier of the revolution. He said his life was hard. He asked me if I would share it with him. And without a thought I said, 'Yes, I will.' "

She finished her coffee. She looked at Sarah and said, "I've shocked you, haven't I? Well, what the hell. I can always go back to calling you *'gringa.'* "

181

"You do and I'll knock you flat." She scrubbed the tears off her cheeks. "We're friends, damn it, and you'll call me by my name."

Conchita looked at her long and hard. She put her hand out and touched Sarah's shoulder. "Friends," she said at last.

It was then that Sarah almost told her of her plan to escape. But, after all, she said nothing.

They washed the cups, filled one with hot water and herb tea, and took it to Francisco.

Sarah knelt beside him. "Can you drink some tea?"

"Yes, thank you."

"Let me look at that shoulder."

She unwrapped the bandage. The wound was still sore and swollen, but it was not red, and it had closed well. When Conchita brought hot water and soap, Sarah cleaned the area of the wound and bound it in a clean white cloth.

"You're going to be all right," she said. "But rest for a few days. Your arm will be stiff but that will pass."

"Thank God you are with us, señorita." His brooding black eyes looked into hers.

She looked away. "I must see to the other men," she said.

The others were not so bad. She changed their bandages, warned them about keeping their wounds clean, and told them to rest another day or two. And when they said, "Ah, but you will be here to help us, señorita," she did not answer them.

When at last she had finished she went down to the river to wash. The sun was hot. Was it still July? She'd left Eagle Pass on the twentieth. The next day she'd been captured. She'd been here . . . what? Two weeks? Three? So much had happened to her that the days all ran together.

She was almost to the river when she heard the sound. At first she thought it was an animal, but as she drew near the sound become more distinct and she knew that it was a woman. Now the sound was

182

closer; it came from the river, from behind the branches of the willow that dipped low to the water. And as she drew closer she could see the form of a woman, could hear small animal sounds of pain.

She rolled her skirt up, and gathering the ends of it together, tied it around her waist and waded into the water. When she parted the branches of the willow she saw Teresa standing naked, trying to splash water on her back.

She didn't realize she'd cried out until the girl turned her face to look behind her, terror and pain widening her eyes.

Sarah couldn't speak. She could only stare at Teresa. The girl's back, her buttocks, and legs, were covered with angry red welts. The skin had broken and bled in several places.

"Do not look at me," Teresa pleaded. "Do not look at my shame."

And still Sarah stood, too horrified to speak. Then she moved to the other girl and put her arms around her. And when she did, Teresa began to sob.

"It's all right," Sarah said. "It's going to be all right. He'll never do this to you again. I'm going away. You're coming with me."

"I can never get away," Teresa gasped between sobs. "Lorenzo will kill me if I try to escape."

"No, he won't. I won't let him. He's going away with Luis and the other men. They'll be gone for two or three days." She held the girl away from her. "We'll be far away from here by the time they return."

"No, no, I am afraid. He'll find me, I know he will."

"Shhh. It's going to be all right. I'm going to take care of you. Nothing like this will ever happen to you again."

She took the soap from Teresa then and gently bathed the wounds, trying to be as careful as she could, trying with words to still the quivering of pain each time she touched a wound, feeling her own body

183

grow wet with perspiration, and her stomach grab with horror at the other girl's pain, the involuntary whimpers, the small cries of anguish.

She took Teresa's hand to lead her farther out into the river so that the cool water could soothe the hurt. And as they moved from shadow to sun she saw the slight roundness of Teresa's belly, the fullness of the breasts. She stopped, clenching the other girl's hand. "Teresa, you're going to have a child."

The girl began to weep again. "I think so, I am not sure."

"How far along are you?"

"Five months, I think."

Sarah's hand tightened. "And Lorenzo would beat you like this, knowing you're with child?"

"He doesn't know, Sarah. I didn't know what he would do to me if he found out. It is just now that I am beginning to show. You would not have known if you had not found me like this, standing here in my shame."

"There is no shame, Teresa. At least not for you. Now lie back in the water. There, doesn't the coolness feel good? Close your eyes. I'll hold your shoulders."

She talked on and on, soothing the other girl, soothing herself. "I'll check the horses this afternoon to see whether or not there is a guard."

"No, it is better if I check the horses, Sarah. If anyone sees me they will not be suspicious as they would be if they saw you."

She had stopped weeping. Her dark fawn's eyes held a glimmer of hope. "Perhaps we can do it after all," she said.

The sky was heavy with clouds that night, but now and again the moon shone through. The two girls moved cautiously through the trees, each with a canteen slung over her shoulder. They had not been able to take as much food and water as Sarah would have

184

liked, but she told herself that with any luck at all what they had would last them until they came to a village. She had money with her, the money that had been in her carpetbag. They could buy whatever they needed and even pay someone to take them to Torreon.

She and Teresa would stay in Torreon with her father until Teresa was well enough to travel. And she hoped that would be soon. If the Villa forces were gathering that might mean they were getting ready to march on the Federal stronghold in Torreon. In that case, they'd have to get out fast. And take Teresa with them of course. Her father would arrange the papers and Teresa would have her baby in Texas.

She stopped her musing when she heard the low whinny sound of the horses.

"The two on the end," Teresa said. "They will be the easiest."

"I'll get them," Sarah whispered. "Give me your canteen, I'll . . ." She stopped.

"What is it?"

"Shhh."

A twig snapped.

Sarah's heart thudded against her ribs. If they were discovered now . . . It wasn't herself she was afraid for, it was Teresa. What would Lorenzo do to her when he found she'd tried to escape?

She pulled Teresa behind a tree, scarcely daring to breathe.

"Is someone there?" The voice belonged to Conchita.

Teresa's hand clutched Sarah's shoulder.

"Who is it?" Conchita stepped out of the trees. "Who is wandering around here? If you don't answer I'm going to yell like hell!" She waited a moment.

"Don't! Please!" Sarah stepped out from behind the tree.

"What are you doing here, Sarah?"

"Nothing. Walking. Just . . . walking."

"And who is that with you? Teresa?"

185

Teresa slumped against the tree and began to cry. "Ay, I knew we'd never be able to do it. Now Lorenzo will find out. You know what he'll do to me. You know. You know. Ay, Mother of God, what am I going to do?"

"Stop crying, you silly girl," Conchita hissed. She took Teresa by the shoulder and shook her. Teresa cried out in pain, and Conchita released her. "What is it? I didn't hurt you. Why are you such a damned baby?"

"She's been beaten," Sarah said. "Her back and shoulders are cut and bruised."

Hijo, that son-of-a-bitch Lorenzo. What a bastard he is! What . . ." She stopped. "You are escaping!"

"Yes, we are. Unless you give the alarm."

Conchita looked at them for a long moment. "It is dangerous out there, you know. There is desert and heat and . . ."

"And villages," Sarah said.

"Ya, and Colorados too. Colorados like the ones who came the other day." Her eyes narrowed. "You do not like us. Perhaps you would . . ."

Sarah's level gaze met the other girl's eyes. "Do you honestly think I would betray you?" And when she said the words she knew that no matter what happened to her she would never betray them.

"You will take Teresa with you?"

Sarah nodded. "She's pregnant, Conchita. I'll take her to my father in Torreon, and then to Texas."

"Torreon is a Federal stronghold."

"That has nothing to do with me. I'm an American, traveling to see my father."

"Go, then. It's none of my concern."

"Thank you."

"Ya, ya."

"I'll never forget you."

She helped Teresa onto her horse and quickly mounted her own. When she was ready she leaned down and whispered, "Tell Silvia . . ." She paused.

What message could she leave to Silvia, after all? "Tell her that I will remember her." She smiled in the darkness. "And you. I left the gray hat in the tent. It's yours if you still want it."

And before Conchita could answer she spurred her horse on and said softly to Teresa, *"Vámonos."*

Chapter 20

They moved slowly and silently, letting the horses pick the way, holding their blankets around their shoulders, shivering in the cold mountain air. The harsh beauty of the mountains shone stark when the moon slipped from behind the dark clouds. The narrow path twisted and turned as they crossed the backbone of the jagged mountain range. At times there was barely room for the horses, times when they felt the brush of rock against their shoulders as the horses made their way on the narrow trail. Other times they headed almost straight down between giant gray rocks, over rough stones, the horses skidding once or twice so that both of them cried out in fear.

When the sky lightened from black to gray to pink, Sarah reined in her horse. "Let's rest for a minute," she said. "I'm thirsty."

"It is better to save the water until later. When we are in the desert we will need it more than we do now."

"Just a sip. And a bite of meat. With any luck we'll find a village this morning and we won't have to worry about water."

Teresa's cocoa-brown face was pinched with fatigue, and Sarah felt a twinge of guilt because she'd insisted the girl come with her. She thought of Lorenzo, with his dark Indian face, and knew how viciously angry he would be when he returned to the camp and found Teresa had fled.

And Luis? What would he think? His *macho* pride would sting a bit, but perhaps, after all, he'd be glad to be rid of her. And when Marta returned she would once again share his tent.

When they had rested they followed the course of a dry riverbed that ran steeply down the side of the mountain. Desert flowers bloomed bright in the sun. The tall green cactus were filled with blossoms. Blue and yellow field flowers grew as high as the horses' bellies.

But all too soon the signs of vegetation were behind them and they were in the frightening arid waste of the desert.

As the day wore on Sarah's fair skin burned and her lips grew dry and parched.

"Cover yourself with your shawl," Teresa said. "Your skin is so white and it is burning cruelly."

"But I'm so warm. I'll roast with the shawl."

"It will help keep the sun off you, Sarah. You must cover yourself."

By midday the temperature rose to a terrible high over the desperately dry plains. All they could see now was desert from horizon to horizon. A frightening wilderness of stones and boulders and rocks, and finally the stones turned to sand. The sun shimmered, blinding them, dizzying them with its awful brightness. They were beyond thought now, squinting their eyes in the sun, hanging on to the reins, stopping too often to sip from the canteens they carried. Sarah's body ached from the hours they'd spent riding, and knowing how Teresa's body was marked from the beating she'd taken, she felt sick with compassion for the girl. But Teresa said nothing. She bore this as she had always borne whatever happened to her.

"It will be dark soon," Teresa said. "Will we rest then?"

"We'll have to. At least for a while. We'll sleep for a few hours, but we should travel as much as we can by night." And to herself she thought, I don't think we can stand another day.

189

When dusk came, when the sun finally sank behind a distant mountain, they stopped beside a large grouping of boulders. Sarah slid wearily off her horse, and then went to help Teresa. The girl clung to her for support.

"Let me spread the blankets," Sarah said, "and then we can rest."

Teresa lay down and closed her eyes, too weary to speak. Her brown face looked parched and dry, her lips were cracked. Sarah sat beside her, hugging her knees, thinking, God, oh God, what have I gotten us into? Where are we? How far from a village or a town? As far as she could see there was only a vast emptiness of sand and rocks and gray-shadowed mountains.

I shouldn't have insisted she come. I didn't think the trip would be this hard. What if she loses the baby?

She touched Teresa's shoulder. The girl's eyelids fluttered and she looked at Sarah with her sad fawn's eyes.

"I want you to drink some water," Sarah said gently.

"We should save it for tomorrow."

"You'll feel worse tomorrow if you don't have some now. We can't be far from a village. I know we'll find one soon."

She helped the girl to a sitting position. "We'll each have a drink and then we'll rest."

When Teresa took only a sip, Sarah urged her to drink more, saying with a smile, "More than that. Remember, you're drinking for two."

But when it was her turn to drink she barely wet her lips and tongue. And before she rested she poured some of the precious water into the palm of her hand and held it to the horses' mouths.

She woke once to hear strange rustlings in the dark, and was afraid, thinking of scorpions, snakes, kangaroo rats, and lizards. All of the creatures that hid during the day and came out at night to search for food. But in a moment her head began to nod and she went back to sleep. We'll have to leave soon, she thought. It's better to ride at night. Better than in the heat of the day, the awful enervating heat. I'll just rest a few minutes more and . . .

And later, frightened by a sound, she reached out her hand and said, "Luis? Luis?"

Dawn pinked the sky when Teresa shook her awake. Her body was sore and tired, her fair skin burned from the sun, her lips cracked and caked with dryness. And when she said, "Is there any water left?" her voice sounded strange and weak.

"A little." Black circles lined Teresa's eyes. "Your skin is burned. Does it pain you?"

"Every inch of me pains me," Sarah said, trying to smile. "What about you?"

"I think if that river was here I would not be so shy today. I would take my clothes off and run into the water. Imagine, Sarah, just imagine what it would feel like."

Sarah licked her dry lips. "We'll find another river," she said.

But there wasn't any river. There wasn't any anything. Only the desert and the sun, and the hard stones under the horses' feet. They moved slowly, trying to save the animals as much as they could. If they fall, Sarah thought, if they fall . . .

The desert floor shimmered in the sun. She swayed in the saddle, caught herself just in time, and tried to will herself to sit straight. Teresa's eyes were closed, her cracked lips were parted. When Sarah put her hand on the girl's shoulder and said, "We've got to stop for a while," she knew that Teresa was almost at the point of unconsciousness. She reined in her own horse and dismounted, but Teresa was so weak that she was afraid if the other girl got off her horse she'd never be able to get back on. And she was so weak herself she doubted that she could help Teresa.

"We'll find a village soon," she said through her parched lips. "So we might as well have a drink."

Teresa shook her head.

"You must."

"You first."

"Very well." Sarah tipped the canteen to her mouth, feeling her heart sink at the small slosh of sound. She touched the water to her lips, allowed a few drops to trickle down her throat, and handed the canteen to Teresa.

"There is almost nothing," the girl said. "I am sure you didn't drink. I think you are trying to save the water for me."

"For your baby. Now drink."

How many more hours did they travel? Sarah's eyes were swollen almost shut. Her tongue felt too large for her mouth, her throat so painful that she could no longer swallow. Everything around her was a bright orange ball of flame. She saw Teresa as though through a haze, and she almost did not see when the other girl began to slip from the saddle. But just in time she put her hand out and stopped her from falling.

"Teresa!" Her voice sounded strange. "Teresa!"

The other girl didn't answer.

Sarah reached for Teresa's hand and put it on the saddle horn. "Hold on," she said.

She slipped from her own horse, fell to the ground, and thought, I'll just lie here and rest for a minute. But when she looked up she saw that Teresa's hand was off the saddle horn and that her head had fallen forward onto her chest. She got to Teresa just as the other girl began to slide, managed to catch hold of her and support her as they both slid to the ground.

She put her arm under Teresa's shoulders, supporting her, trying to hold her. I've done this to her, she thought. This is my fault.

The sun burned down on them. She tried to pull Teresa under the small shade of the horse, but each time she did, the animal moved a fraction of an inch and they were in the sun again. Finally she reached up and pulled the blanket from her saddle and draped it over their heads. The heat was suffocating.

"I'm sorry," she said to Teresa. "I'm sorry, sorry, sorry . . ."

She dreamed of the river, of the willows that touched their tender green leaves into the coolness of it. She dreamed that she still wore her gray gabardine suit and her velvet plumed hat, and that she waded into the river, feeling the long skirt drag around her legs. Waded deeper and deeper, wondering why the water didn't cool her. She leaned to drink, but each time she did the water vanished.

Luis was suddenly beside her and he said, "The water won't cool you, but the earth will," and he led her out of the water into the field of daisies.

"I'm so hot," she complained. "I've never been so hot."

"Then take your clothes off."

"I can't do that. You don't love me any more."

"No, but I still want you."

She could smell the richness of the earth, see the daisy stems and the underside of the yellow petals. "Love me, love me not, love me . . ."

"Be still," he said.

"May I have a drink of water?"

"Afterwards."

"But I'm so thirsty, so thirsty, so . . ."

"Drink!"

"Thirsty."

"Drink, señorita."

"No, it's only a dream." But miraculously, even though it was a dream, she felt the water on her lips, in her mouth, running down her chin. She clutched at the hand that held the water, afraid she'd wake up before she drank her fill.

"That's enough for now, *muchacha*. If you drink more you will be ill."

She opened her eyes, trying to see through the orange haze. "Teresa?"

"Worse than you, but she will live."

"Who are you?"

"José Alfredo Antonio O'Brien. At your service, señorita."

"O'Brien?" She tried to laugh but her throat hurt so that she couldn't.

She reached for the water, and cried out when he took it from her hands after allowing her only one sip.

"Can you stand?"

He took her arm and helped her to her feet.

"Of course I . . ." She started to say. But then the orange haze exploded into a million lights, and finally into blackness, and she fainted.

Part IV
ANDRES

Chapter 21

A woman with a dark Indian face smoothed the juice from an aloe leaf on her face and hands. When she tried to sit up the room tilted and she fell back against the pillow, swallowing hard to fight weakness and nausea. The woman gave her a reassuring pat, hurried away, and returned with a cup of clear broth which she spooned into Sarah's mouth.

The following day the woman helped her out of bed and into the adjoining room so that she could see Teresa. The girl's face was thin and drawn, her lips blistered. Sarah sat on the side of the bed and took the small thin hand in hers. "Teresa," she whispered. "Teresa."

The eyelids fluttered. "Sarah?" The voice sounded weak and strange. "Where are we?"

"In a Federal garrison near the town of Frontera. How do you feel, dear?"

"Tired. And you? Are you all right? Your skin is so red, Sarah. Doesn't it hurt?"

"Not any more. There's a doctor here at the garrison, he took care of both of us. You're going to be fine. You have to rest for a few days, but you'll be out of bed soon."

"How did we get here?"

"A small troop of Federal soldiers, led by a very nice man by the name of Sergeant José Alfredo Antonio O'Brien, found us."

She smiled, remembering the first time she'd seen Sergeant O'Brien. He looked like an angel—an angel with a shock of bright red hair and a bushy red beard.

"My mother was Mexican," he told her when she was well enough for a visit. "My father was Irish. He was part of Winfield Scott's Irish battalion when your country invaded Mexico in 1846. Begging your pardon, Miss Sarah, but when the Irish got here and saw what an unjust war it was, most of them deserted and joined up with Mexico. Some of them were caught and hanged, but my dad escaped. He met and married my mother and spent the rest of his life in Mexico."

"And have you spent all your life here too?"

"I went back to school in the States for a while. But I high-tailed it back to Mexico as soon as I could."

"I'm glad you did. I'd have been buzzard meat if it hadn't been for you."

The garrison was under the command of Major Hernando Valverde, a short spic-and-span man with a receding hairline and long thin sideburns. He questioned Sarah as soon as she was able to talk. Where had she come from? Why was she, a Northamerican, traveling in Mexico? What were two girls doing alone on the desert?

"I was taken captive by a group of Villa's men," she told him.

"Who was in command?"

"In command? Well . . . the name of the man who captured me was Garcia, I think. Yes, Pedro Garcia."

"Was he their leader?"

"Major, I don't know much about military things," she hedged.

"But who was in command? This Garcia or who?" His voice had a dangerous edge to it.

And finally, because she thought—there are hundreds of rebel bands in Mexico, surely Valverde doesn't know one from another—she said, "A man by the name of Vega."

And knew she'd made a mistake when Valverde

clapped his hands and said, "Luis Vega! One of the *dorados* of Villa."

He smoothed his long thin sideburns with a flat finger. "You must tell me where I can find his camp, Señorita Finch. President Huerta would pay a small fortune to find this man."

"I'm afraid I can't do that, Major. I was hopelessly lost when your men found me."

"Where were you captured?"

"Near Nueva Rosita."

"In what direction did you ride?"

"I don't know." Her expression was polite, regretful.

"Come now, señorita, was it east or west? North or south?"

"I've always been bad at directions. I really have no idea."

He paced up and down the room, shooting angry glances at her. "And when you made your escape? What direction did you ride then?"

"It was dark."

"But it was light when you reached the desert floor," he shouted.

"Yes, but . . ."

"Then you'd recognize the mountain you came down." His voice left no room for argument.

His questions continued each night at dinner. How high in the mountains was the camp? Were they near a river? How many men did Vega have? How many arms? How much ammunition?

And to every question she shrugged her shoulders helplessly and tried to keep her answers as vague as possible.

On the fifth day he said, "Another officer will join us tomorrow. It's the first time he's been to my garrison and I want to make it a special occasion. He's high in the government. Very close to President Huerta." He stroked his long thin sideburns. "He won't expect to see such charming company in a remote garrison like this."

That night she wore the only dinner dress she had, a pale green chiffon that she'd brought with her when she left San Antonio because it was easy to pack. She pulled her long hair back from her face, holding it in place with tortoise-shell combs, letting it cascade down her back.

"You look beautiful," Teresa said from her bed.

"I'm sorry you can't get up yet. I know having to stay in bed must be a bore."

Teresa grinned at her. "Ay, no, it's a luxury. Never in my life have I been able to lie in bed and have someone bring me my food."

"When we get to Texas we'll take turns bringing each other breakfast in bed." She sat down next to the other girl and took her hand. "You know, Teresa, sometimes I think I'm being selfish. I'm just taking it for granted that you're going back to Texas with me. I forget that you've got a family here and that maybe you don't *want* to go away."

"I couldn't go back to my family, Sarah. Not now, now that I am with child."

"But your father made you go with Lorenzo."

"I know. He saw no shame in that, but he would see shame in my returning to the family in this condition."

"Well then," she patted Teresa's hand, "I won't feel guilty about taking you to Texas. I've never had a sister. Now I'll have a sister—and a nephew or a niece."

"If it's a girl I will name her after you. Sarita, little Sarah. Is that all right?"

"All right!" Sarah hugged her. "It's wonderful!"

She was still smiling when she went into the officers' dining room, but her smile faded when the two men stood. Her face went white with shock. "Andres," she whispered.

"How nice to see you again. Imagine my delighted surprise when Comandante Valverde told me who his guest was." His smile was spurious as he came forward to greet her, and his eyes held a cold reptilian

200

warning. "The Comandante has told me that you were kidnapped and held in the camp of Luis Vega. I must say I find that surprising." His chuckle was soft and unpleasant. "Considering how close you and Luis once were it's—forgive me—a bit hard to believe that you were held against your will."

"Is it?" Her chin came up and she forced herself to speak calmly. "Luis has changed a great deal since the death of his father and Carlos."

"Ah yes. I heard about that."

"He seemed to think I had something to do with their deaths."

"Did he?" His eyes were amused. "Then I suppose his feelings toward you *were* changed." He took her hand and led her to the table. And while the Indian servant poured the wine he said, "Why did you return to Mexico, Sarah?"

"Father was hurt in a mine explosion near Torreon. I was trying to get to him."

"Ah . . ." His eyes narrowed. "Your father. Ah yes. Well, it's a lucky thing that after all that has happened to you Sergeant O'Brien found you."

"He's a good man," Valverde put in.

"Yes, he is. Now." He took a sip of his wine. "He was in my company, you know. I had the devil of a time with him at first. He hadn't wanted to be conscripted, you see. He was teaching history at a military school when he got called up."

He smiled at Sarah over his glass. "It took a lot of hours in the sweat box and having the skin beat almost off his back before he decided to do things my way." He wiped his mouth with the white linen napkin, straightening the hairs of his moustache as he did. "But then, there are always ways to bring people around."

Sarah tried to swallow the sickness that rose in her throat. If she'd doubted before that he was capable of killing Luis' father and brother she didn't doubt it now. He was capable of anything. It sickened her to be in the same room with him.

"Drink your wine, Señorita Finch," Major Valverde said. "You look quite pale. Perhaps you are still not fully recuperated. I will have dinner served at once."

"Thank you." Her hand trembled when she picked up the wineglass.

Andres said, "Comandante Valverde tells me that you are going to lead us to Luis."

The wine spilled onto the white starched tablecloth.

"You're a bundle of nerves, my dear," the major said. "What you need is some fresh air and exercise."

"She'll get plenty of that when we set out for Vega's camp."

"I don't know where the camp is, Andres. I wouldn't be able to find it. I know I wouldn't."

"I think you can. You and the other girl came down the mountains at night, but you reached the valley floor by daylight. I'm sure if you retrace your steps you'll find your way back."

"I can't go back with you!" She clasped her hands together under the table, digging her nails into her palms, trying to still her rising panic. "I can't."

"Oh?" Andres raised one black winged brow. "Then perhaps your companion can."

"No! She couldn't, Andres. She's not well. She . . ."

"But my dear Sarah, we have no choice. Surely you can see that. If you won't go with us I'm afraid I'll have to insist that the other young lady . . ."

"Andres . . . honestly, I don't think I'd be able to find the camp."

"But you will try?"

"Yes, all right, I'll try."

"And don't worry, Sarah. You'll have a platoon of Huerta's soldiers at your service. We won't let anything happen to you."

"There are women in the camp. If you attack . . ."

"You don't think I'd kill women, do you? What kind of a barbarian do you think I am?"

I *know* what kind of a barbarian you are, she

202

thought. Oh yes, Andres, I know. "The Colorados attacked the camp while I was there," she said. "I saw what they did."

"But the Colorados are savages," Valverde said.

"Oh? I thought they were Federal troops, Major."

His face flushed. "Yes, yes, but not *regular* Federal troops. Even we admit they are scum. Our regular troops are gentlemen, I assure you. Like Captain Ortiz. And I assure you that you'll be perfectly safe when you leave here tomorrow."

"Tomorrow? But I . . ."

"Oh, it's quite all right, Señorita Finch. I checked with the doctor before I made the arrangements. He told me it was all right for you to travel."

"We'll be saddled up and ready to go at five-thirty," Andres said. "I know you hate going back into the desert, Sarah, but I'll be there to take care of you." His eyes, as cold and hard and black as the night, bored into hers. "You know I'll take care of you, don't you?" He reached across the table and took her hand in his. "Don't you, Sarah?"

Chapter 22

The sun was just as hot. The earth was just as dry. She wore a man's straw hat to shade her face, a long-sleeved shirtwaist to cover her arms, and gloves to protect her hands. And she had Andres and one hundred and forty of his men to protect her.

One hundred and forty men who would try to find and to attack Luis and his men.

His ragtag men who wore patched shirts and trousers and huaraches—if they were lucky. Men who complained and laughed and sang ribald songs as they rode along. Not like these silent men in their polished boots and neat blue uniforms who sat so ramrod straight in their saddles.

She'd lain awake most of the night worrying about today, not sure how she would handle it, only certain that she would never tell Andres where Luis' camp was. She'd meant it when she told Conchita she wouldn't betray them. And anyway, she really didn't have a clear idea of the location of the camp.

When Andres rode up beside her he said, "Sarah, about that day at the house when you returned from the Vega hacienda—I have thought of it often. I was wild with anger, *querida,* but I should not have blamed you. What passed between you and Luis was his fault. I realized that later. But when I knew you'd let him make love to you, Sarah, I went crazy."

"I'd rather not discuss it, Andres."

204

"No, no, what I did was barbarous. I hope you'll forgive me. Just as I forgive you."

"You forgive *me?*"

"Yes, my dear, I do. And while I'm not sure I still want to marry you—after Luis, you understand—I could set you up very nicely. A small house in Mexico City, a servant or two . . ."

"Andres . . ." She was so choked with rage she couldn't speak.

"We'll talk about it later, Sarah, when this is over, when you've proved your good intentions by helping me." And before she could answer he snapped his fingers, motioning Sergeant O'Brien to join them. "I'm going up ahead," he said. "You stay with Señorita Finch."

"Yes, Major."

Her face was white and set. Her hands were shaking. She had never been as sick with rage as she was in this moment.

"Is anything wrong, ma'am?"

She took a deep breath, and still unable to speak. she shook her head.

"I didn't know you were a friend of his," O'Brien said.

"We are not friends," she said between clenched teeth. "I've known him for a long time but we—are—not—friends."

"Then why are you helping him?"

"I'm not . . ." She stopped. She'd almost forgotten he was a Federal soldier.

"Tell me about the camp," he said, ignoring her slip. "What were the people like? I know their women travel with them and I've often wondered what type of woman would follow a man to war. Did you get along with them?"

"Yes. I had a fight with one of them the day after I was captured. She's a wild gypsy kind of girl. She shoved me and I shoved back and suddenly we were flying at each other. Now we're friends, good friends.

205

And there's another woman. Silvia. Her ten-year-old son was hanged by the Colorados. That's why she joined the revolution. You should have seen her when the camp was attacked, Sergeant O'Brien. She fought as well as any of the men.''

"And what about you?" His eyes were curious. "What did you do when the camp was attacked?"

"I loaded rifles."

"For Luis Vega?"

When she looked away from him he said, "But if you like these people, ma'am, how can you . . . ? Well, it's none of my business, is it? I apologize. I shouldn't have said anything."

"I didn't choose to come along today. I had no choice. Major Ortiz threatened to take Teresa if I didn't. Can you imagine what this trip would have done to her?"

"But if you were friends . . ."

"Sergeant O'Brien . . ." She felt such a need to tell him everything. She was sure he didn't like Andres any better than she did, but he was a Federal soldier. She had to be careful. "The Major and I *used* to be friends. Just as he and Luis Vega used to be friends."

"Friends! I'll be damned, ma'am! That's mighty strange."

"It's a mighty strange story."

"We have a long ride ahead of us. Why don't you tell me?"

And so she told him; how Luis and Andres had once been friends, about her engagement to Andres, and her love for Luis. "That's over now," she said sadly. "We can never go back to the way we were. But I won't hurt him and I won't hurt his people. I'll never tell Andres where the camp is."

"And why are you telling me this, Miss Sarah?"

"I don't think you like the major any more than I do. He told me last night that he had to . . . to take certain measures . . . to bring you in line when you were conscripted."

"Certain measures? Yes, I suppose you could say

206

that. If you call being held in a four-by-five tin shed for five days when the temperature was a hundred and ten, or being beaten until your back was raw meat 'certain measures.' "

"I'm sorry," she said, ashamed that she had tested him.

The arid wasteland seemed as endless and as bleak as the far side of the moon. She must have been unconscious during this part of the trip, she thought, because she didn't remember any of it. It was late afternoon when they reached the canyon. She took the straw hat off and fanned her face, looking around her at the blue and yellow flowers that grew as high as the horses' bellies. And suddenly and clearly she knew exactly where she was and where the camp was.

Andres spurred his horse forward. "Do you see anything familiar?"

"No. No, nothing." She turned her face away, trying to look unconcerned.

"Are you sure?"

"Quite sure."

He eyed her, his face clouded with doubt. "We'll rest here a bit. Look around, Sarah. Take your time. I'm sure you'd remember this canyon if you'd ever seen it before."

"Andres, look . . ." She wiped her face with a handkerchief. "I'm sorry, but I just don't feel well. I don't think I can go on. I'd forgotten how terrible the sun can be. The doctor was wrong—I'm *not* well yet. You shouldn't have insisted I come." She felt tears sting her eyes and was grateful for them.

"Damn!" he snarled, his eyes narrowing as he studied her. His hand moved to his holster, his fingers rested on the cold steel of his gun.

She was aware of the sudden stillness of the other men. Aware of O'Brien's hands moving away from his reins. And finally, with a forced chuckle Andres said, "You're spoiling my plans, *querida*. I wanted you with me when I killed Vega. Now I'll have to bring him back alive. But don't worry, I'll be sure you get a front-row seat to watch the hanging.''

Before she could answer him he leaned forward out of his saddle and pulled her towards him. His kiss was strong and hurting, and when she wrenched away from him he said, ''O'Brien will take you back to the garrison. My men and I will have a look around. Perhaps ride up into the mountains.'' He saw her face change. ''Yes,'' he said softly, ''we'll ride up into the mountains and see if we can find . . . anything.''

''Son-of-a-bitch,'' Nicasio said. ''There must be more than a hundred and thirty of the bastards.''

He adjusted his field glasses and looked again at the scene far below him. Then he was off and running, jumping on his horse, galloping through the trees. When he reached the camp he jerked the horse to a stop, slid off the broad back, and ran as fast as his skinny legs could carry him.

''Luis! Luis!'' he shouted. ''It's the damned Federales, Luis.''

''What?'' Silvia turned from her cooking. ''What did you say, Nicasio?''

''The Federales, damn it. Where's Luis?''

''Here, Nicasio. What is it, *hombre?*''

''The Federales. Below in the canyon. More than a hundred and thirty of them. The *gringa* brought them here.''

''I don't believe you,'' Silvia said.

''I swear to God, woman. I could see her plain enough through the glasses. I'd recognize that hair no matter how far away I was.''

''You're sure?'' Luis' face was ashen.

''Si, *mano*. I saw an officer kiss her. Then she rode away with another man. I didn't wait to see more. I jumped on my horse and rode like hell back here.''

''I'll get the men,'' Silvia said. And still Luis stood, his face white and sick, and she put her hand on his arm and said, "Luis, I cannot believe that she would betray us."

His eyes were veiled with hate. He remembered his anger and frustration, and yes, his sorrow, when he'd returned a week ago to find that she'd escaped. He'd organized a search party and gone looking for her, so afraid that she had perished in the desert that he'd been sick with it. I should have listened to her, he'd told himself over and over again. I should have known she wouldn't betray me. My God, how could I have treated her the way I did?

He searched for three days, praying that she'd been rescued. Praying that she hadn't died on the desert.

Now his fists clenched. She hadn't died. And he hadn't been wrong before. She'd betrayed him once, and now she was betraying him again.

"Give the alarm," he said to Silvia. "Nicasio, tell the men to get all the rifles and every bit of ammunition we have." He turned away, running, yelling as he ran, *"A las armas! A las armas!"*

Pedro Garcia ran up to him. "What in the hell is going on, Luis?"

"Federales. In the canyon. Get the stash of dynamite."

"Holy Mother!"

They came then, all of them, grabbing rifles, slinging bandoliers of ammunition across their chests.

"The crest of the hill," Luis shouted. "Scatter yourselves behind the rocks. We'll have the advantage of height, but don't shoot until I give the word."

"Bastards!" Nicasio said, spitting against a rock. "Planning a surprise, are they? They're the ones who'll get the surprise. Eh, Luis?"

"Let's hope so, *hombre.*"

He took the field glasses and watched the horses picking their way up the face of the mountain. So many of them. Good Christ! So many! He looked at them, searching for the officer in charge. His glasses swung to a face, to the single star on the cap, and back to the face. He drew his breath in sharply. Painfully. Andres! Good God, Andres!

And Sarah had led him here.

"Come on," he said between his teeth. "Come on, you bastard. I'm waiting for you. I've been waiting for you for a long time."

"The dynamite is ready," Garcia said. "Behind the biggest goddamn boulders on the goddamn mountain. You want to check it?"

"Yes. We've got to get it right the first time." He hurried over to inspect the rocks, jumping from one to another. "Careful here," he cautioned. "A half a stick should do it. Two here, I think. Pile some dirt around the sticks. Not too long a fuse. When I give the word I want them to blow."

The men and women were scattered and spaced behind rocks, bushes, an occasional tree. Flat on their bellies, elbows braced, rifles poised and ready.

"They say it was the *gringa* who betrayed us," Francisco whispered to Conchita.

"I don't believe it, but if it's true I'll tear the gizzard out of her with my own hands," she whispered back.

Garcia lighted a cigarette and shielded it with his hand. "I'll tell you when the captain gives the signal," he whispered to Jacinto. "Then you light the fuses and give the signal to Venancio."

Luis watched the progress up the mountain. They were closer now; he could hear the faint whinny of horses and the murmur of voices. "Closer," he whispered, feeling the cool rifle butt against his cheek. "Closer, you bastards."

When they reached a wide part of the pass and the single file became a group, he raised his hand. Garcia touched his cigarette to the fuse. So did Jacinto and Venancio. A sudden glare reddened the sky, and then came the shocking detonations of the dynamite. The detonations were followed by a volley of rifles. And from below came the screams of the Federales and the sharp whinnying of wounded horses as rocks and boulders shot down the hill, knocking both men and animals aside with terrible force. Dying men and wounded men cried out in pain as they skittered down the mountain, caught in the crush of stone.

At the crest of the mountain a steady flame of rifle fire pounded the men still on their feet. In desperation they tried to regroup, tried to return the fire from above. One of Vega's men took a bullet in the head. Another in the chest. Venancio, about to set off another charge of dynamite, raised himself from behind the giant boulder to check what was just below. Vega turned in time to see him grab his throat and slump to the ground. And before anyone could stop her, Lupe ran toward him, screaming, "Venancio! Venancio!"

Bullets from a machine gun caught her as she raced toward her man, caught her waist high, cutting her almost in half.

"Light the fuses," Vega shouted to Garcia.

And again came the terrible detonation as the thunder of rocks shot down the mountainside. Impenetrable dust almost hid the blue line of men reeling down the mountain, caught in the monstrous avalanche of stone.

The stab of machine-gun fire was sporadic. The Federales who had not been swept down the mountain by the last plunge of rocks began to slip and slide their way down, frantic to escape. Above the screams and the confusion Vega heard Andres shouting curses at his men, urging them back up the mountain. But the steady stream of rifle fire from above went almost unanswered as the men stumbled down, rushing past their wounded, eager only for their own escape.

Vega's men stayed at the crest of the mountain all through the night, afraid that the Federal soldiers might have the power to regroup. And when at last morning came and there was no sign of Ortiz or his men, they returned to their camp. They had won the battle, but Andres Ortiz was still alive.

Chapter 23

In the late afternoon of the second day sixty-five of them straggled back to the garrison. The ones who were able to help themselves clung to their mounts, eyes half-closed, red kerchiefs tied to heads and limbs, lips caked and dry.

Sarah and Teresa stood in the shadow of one of the stone arches in the long corridor, watching the men pass through the wooden doors of the garrison. Sarah's face was white. "They found the camp," she whispered to Teresa. And thought, Oh God, what has happened to them? To Luis? Silvia, Conchita, Francisco, the wounded men she'd taken care of, Lupe, Pedro Garcia?

She took Teresa's hand, and when the girl looked at her she saw that her face was frozen with apprehension.

"It's so strange," Teresa said, almost to herself. "You live with a man and you think there is nothing good about him. And then suddenly you remember one good thing, and then that's all you think about— that one good thing. I fell from my horse once and hurt my arm—my half of arm. Lorenzo carried me to a stream. He washed away the blood and then he tore a strip off his shirt to bandage me. It hurt so much, and though I tried not to, I cried out. And he said, 'Don't cry, little bird. Please don't cry.' And there were tears in his eyes. And that is what I remember now. Not the drunkenness, not the beatings, only that one small tenderness."

They watched the men dismount, heard a corporal shout for the doctor, saw the stronger men trying to help the wounded. Andres shouted orders, glancing around him, his face dark with anger. And suddenly he saw her, and for a moment forgot his men. He wheeled his horse around, stopping in front of her.

"We found the camp," he said. "No thanks to you." His hand tightened around his riding crop. "You recognized the canyon, didn't you? You knew where we were, but you decided not to tell me. I could see it in your eyes, Sarah, I knew you were lying."

She felt the pressure of Teresa's hand. "What happened?" she managed to say in spite of her sudden fear.

"They had a lookout posted. They were waiting for us when we started up the mountain. They set charges of dynamite and exploded the rocks down on us. We didn't have a chance." He slapped the side of his boots with the riding crop. His knuckles were white. "They killed seventy of my men. Seventy men, Sarah!

"I saw him up there among the rocks, but I couldn't get him. I had him in my sights, but I couldn't get him." He looked down at her, his face stiff with rage. "I'm leaving for Torreon tomorrow. I'll get more men. I'll get an army if I have to, but by God I'm going to hang Luis or die doing it."

She made herself say, "You said you'd take us to Torreon, Andres. Teresa's able to travel now. We'll be ready to leave in the morning."

His eyes narrowed.

"You promised to take us to Torreon. I rely on your honor as an officer to do what you said."

His mouth worked. Finally he said, "Be ready at dawn." His glance moved to Teresa. "I hope you're able to travel," he said, "because if you're not I'll leave you along the way. I have no time for cripples."

"I will manage, señor." Teresa's voice held a dignity that Sarah had never heard before.

* * *

213

Sergeant O'Brien was not with the men assigned to accompany Andres to Torreon. When Sarah spotted him standing at one side of the barracks, she pulled her horse out of line and went to him. Leaning down, she held her hand out to shake his.

"Thank you for your kindness," she said. "I wish you were riding with us."

"So do I, ma'am. I requested permission to go. It was denied." He lowered his voice. "You watch out for yourself and your friend. Don't do anything to annoy the major. He's got the devil inside him today."

"I'll be careful," she whispered. "We'll be all right once we're in Torreon—even if it is a Federal stronghold—because my father is there."

"Thank God for that, Miss Sarah."

"Miss Finch!" Andres' voice snapped like a whip across the compound. "Are you coming with us or have you decided to remain here?"

O'Brien squeezed her hand. "Go along," he said. "Don't make him mad. I'll say a prayer to Saint Patrick."

They were at the end of the column of twenty-two men. Andres did not speak to her all that day. When they stopped to rest for the night, she and Teresa fixed a place for themselves, and when it was time to eat they took their plates and sat alone.

The next morning they were awakened early by one of the men who said, "There's coffee and biscuits. We'll be leaving in fifteen minutes."

He pushed harder. The pace was faster; the day was hotter. His commands were brusque, and once, when one of his men said, "My God, Major, this heat is killing. Can't we stop for a minute?" he struck the man across the face with his riding crop.

When it seemed to Sarah that she and Teresa would have to fall back, she saw the spires of a church. "Thank God," she whispered to her friend. "There's a village ahead. Surely he'll stop for a while."

There were no women washing clothes in the

stream, no shepherds tending sheep, no children playing. But there was noise, noise that grew louder as they approached. And shouts and laughter and curses.

Warning shots sounded as they grew closer. Dirty unkempt men ran out into the street, firing their guns in the air, shouting at them. A few women scurried into adobe houses, slamming the doors behind them.

"Holy Mother," Teresa murmured, crossing herself. "I think it's the Colorados."

Andres held up his hand. "I am Major Andres Ortiz of President Huerta's Federal Army," he said in a cold voice. "I'm ordering you to put your guns away."

The men hooted with laughter. "Hey, *cabrón*," one of them shouted, "look at the fine man on the fine horse."

"It seems to me the horse is finer than the man," someone said. "By God, I'd love to have a horse like that."

"Then take him, *compadre*, if you're not afraid of the major."

"Afraid! Afraid of that silly bastard?"

Andres drew his revolver. "Be ready," he ordered his men. And to the rough men surrounding them he said, "Who is in charge here?"

A tall heavy-bodied man elbowed his way through the throng. His black hair hung shaggy over his ears. A red bandana was tied across his forehead to keep the hair from his wide black eyes. His shirt was open at the neck so that a thatch of black hair showed on his chest. The sleeves of the shirt were rolled up to show muscular arms. He wore his pants low and tight across his hips.

"Who the bloody hell are you?" he snarled at Andres.

"I'm a major of the Federal Army of Huerta."

The man spat out of the side of his mouth. "What are you doing in my village?"

"I didn't know it was *your* village." Andres' voice

215

was heavy with irony. "It wasn't the last time I was through. What did you do with the inhabitants?"

"Threw them the hell out. Except for the women who were lucky enough to be chosen to stay with us." He rubbed his face with his big broad hand. "I am Diego Navarete. Since we're on the same side I guess we will not kill you."

"Nor we you," Ortiz said.

"We are two hundred to your . . . what? Twenty, twenty-one men. I hardly think . . ." His eyes swept over the men. He whistled softly and said, "Well, well, I was mistaken. Twenty-two men and two women. *Por Dios*, Major, I didn't know the Federales traveled with their women."

"We're returning the women to Torreon."

"Are you?" He moved toward the back of the column. He stopped in front of Sarah and said, *"Buenos días, señorita."*

"Buenos días, señor." The hand that held the reins trembled.

"Is that the limit of your Spanish?"

"No." She felt a small whisper of recognition. She had seen this man before. And that man who wanted Andres' horse, she'd seen him before too.

"You are a *gringa?"*

She nodded.

"How did you come to be riding with these *cabrones?"*

"My friend and I were lost in the desert. We were picked up by Major Ortiz's men. They're taking us to Torreon."

"And what will you do there?"

"My father is with the Penoches Mining Company. We're going to Torreon to be with him."

"A rich *gringo* working for a rich *gringo* company, eh? I'm sure he's worried about you, señorita, anxious to have you back. I bet he's so anxious to have you back that he'd be happy to pay a lot of money to whoever had you." He slapped her thigh with his big hand. "Very happy," he said.

He turned away from her. "You are free to go, Major. The sooner the better."

"I thought to rest the horses awhile."

"The horses can rest in Torreon."

"Very well." Andres' face was tight with anger.

"But the young ladies will stay here," Navarete said.

"I can't allow that."

"You can't allow?" Diego's smile was sardonic. His men hooted with laughter.

"I'll report this to the garrison in Torreon," Andres said.

"You do that, Major. And when we collect a million pesos ransom for her, will you say that Diego Navarete collected the money for the Federal Army? That the Federal Army would not stand a chance in hell of beating Villa if it were not for the Colorados? Eh, Major?"

A muscle twitched in Andres' face. "Very well, you may have the women."

Diego bowed elaborately from the waist. "Thank you, Major. And now I bid you *adiós*."

Ortiz raised his hand and shouted, "Forward, march!" And to Diego he said, "Take the damned women and welcome to them!"

"No!" Sarah pulled her horse alongside his and grasped the rein of his horse. "You can't do this, Andres. You know what these men are. You can't leave us here."

"Can't I?" He shook her hand off the rein.

"You're a gentleman," she cried. "Doesn't that mean anything?"

"Only when it's expedient, Sarah."

"You bastard!" And then, swallowing hard, she said, "Andres, at least take Teresa with you. You've got no quarrel with her. Take her to my father. She's going to have a baby, she . . ."

"Get out of my way," he said, pushing his horse away from her. And without a backward glance he led his men out of the village.

Chapter 24

Diego Navarete, with five of his men at his heels, led them into one of the adobe houses. Half of the one-room house had the appearance of an untidy office. There was a desk, an over-stuffed chair with the arm broken off it, and two straight-backed chairs. The other end of the room held an unmade bed, a long carved bench, and a stool.

"Sit down," Diego ordered the two girls. "I will write a letter to your father, señorita, and you will help me."

"Any letter will include my friend as well as me."

"Bueno. But in that case I'll add a few thousand more pesos to the ransom."

Sarah gave Teresa a reassuring look, and then she said to Navarete, "You can hold us for ransom, of course, but if you do you stand the chance of being captured by the Federal police."

"There are few Federal police any more, señorita. Only Federal soldiers." He grinned at her. "And I am a Federal soldier."

"But you're still breaking the law, señor. And some day, after the revolution, the law might catch up with you." She smiled, trying to hide her nervousness. "I have a better idea. Take us to Torreon and my father will give you whatever you ask. You can have the money and be a hero instead of a criminal."

His black eyes measured her. At last he said, "Perhaps you believe what you say, or perhaps you

218

take me for a fool. Either way, *gringa*, I could wind up with a rope around my neck. So we will do this my way. We will write a letter and one of my men will deliver it to your father in Torreon."

"But I promise you . . ."

"You're in no position to promise anything. Now, señorita, what is your father's name?"

"Charlie Finch." Her voice was cool. She'd be damned if she'd let him know how afraid she was.

"Where is the main office of the Penoches company?"

"Alvarado Street. But I doubt that he's working. He was hurt in a mining accident. He'll still be at home recuperating. That's number ten Monte Alegre."

"Number ten Monte Alegre. Mr. Finch." He wrote slowly. "We have your daughter . . . ?"

"Sarah."

". . . Sarah Finch and a friend and we want . . ." He tapped the yellow pencil against his teeth. "We want a million and a half pesos . . ."

One of the men at his side gave a low whistle.

"How will we get the money?" a short skinny man asked.

"On the edge of town, just on the outskirts of Gomez Palacio, there are some grain silos. The one nearest the road is falling apart and hasn't been used for grain for over a year. I'll tell him to have the money there . . . what is today?"

"Friday, *jefe.*"

"*Bueno*, let's see. It may be difficult to get that much together. I will instruct him to bring it there next Thursday night. When he gives us the money we give him the *muchachas*." He finished the letter and handed it to a short dark man. "Juan Carlos, you make sure no one but Señor Finch receives this. You yourself will put it in his hands."

"And then what, Diego?"

"Then you run like hell!"

The men laughed. More of them stood in the doorway now, trying to push into the already crowded

219

room. They stood so close that Sarah could smell them. Her eyes darted to Teresa. The girl cowered in her chair, clutching the rebozo to her, her dark eyes wide with fear.

Diego pushed back his chair. "Now we wait," he said.

"Is that all we do?" a man asked.

A couple of men sniggered.

"What do you mean?"

"What the hell you think we mean, Diego?" The man who spoke was as tall and skinny and mean-looking as a buzzard.

And suddenly Sarah knew where she had seen Diego—and this man. They were with the Colorados who had raided camp.

"Some of us haven't had a woman in weeks," the man who looked like a buzzard said. "Twelve village girls, who do nothing but squall every time we take them, among sixty or more of us. I haven't had a good piece in months." He reached out a skinny hand and grabbed Teresa's shoulder. "You give me this one, Diego. I don't give a damn what you do with the *gringa*."

Teresa huddled back against the chair and began to cry.

"Let her go, Tano. You're not the only one here who hasn't had a woman in a long time."

"All right, damn it. Let me keep her tonight and I'll give her to the *compañeros* tomorrow." His hand moved up to touch the back of Teresa's neck.

"My friend is with child," Sarah said to Diego, trying to keep her voice steady. "And she's been ill. If your men . . . if your men pass her around they'll kill her. And the baby she's carrying."

"And what is that to you?" Diego's black eyes bored into hers. "You're a *gringa* with a rich father. What does this poor Mexican *pendeja* matter to you?"

"She's a friend. She matters a great deal to me."

"And the major? Was he your friend also?"

"No, he was not. He was a no-good son-of-a-bitch." Her gaze was level. "I think you're a better man than he is."

"Don't let her talk you out of this," Tano said. "What the hell do we care if this little one is pregnant? A few good screws won't hurt her. That's what women were made for."

"You bastard!" Sarah said, knocking his hand away from Teresa.

"You going to let her get away with that, Diego?"

"Shut up, Tano." He sounded amused.

"Listen, *jefe*," a nervous little man with a drooping moustache said. "Give the girl to Tano for tonight. You take the *gringa*. Tomorrow you pass them on to us. We're your men and we fight good for you, don't we? We deserve a little fun, *jefe*. Come on, what do you say?"

Diego sat on the edge of the desk, his fingers pulling at the black hairs on his eyebrows. His forehead wrinkled as he looked at his men.

Sarah felt her stomach knot with fear, a thin film of perspiration dampen her face. She straightened her shoulders and sat up straighter in her chair. "I'll make you a bargain," she said.

"You are in no position to bargain, señorita."

"Am I not?" It took every ounce of will she had to keep her face calm and her voice steady. She even managed a dry chuckle as she said, "You've got a million and a half pesos riding on me, Señor Navarete."

He frowned.

"And I promise you that if you pass us around to your men I won't be alive when it comes time for you to collect the ransom. I'll find a way to kill myself and there won't be a damn thing you can do about it. If you show up in Gomez Palacio and try to collect that ransom without me you won't get a centavo. Charlie Finch will chase you all over Mexico until he finds you and cuts your heart out."

"I think you mean what you say."

"She's only talking," Tano said.

"Shut up!" He looked at Sarah. "You haven't told

221

me what your bargain is, señorita. Let me hear what you offer as an alternative.''

"Myself." Her eyes didn't waver from his.

"But I already have you."

"Do you?" She smiled. "I saw the girls peeping out of the doors when we rode in. It's like Tano said, isn't it? They're terrified of you. But you can make them sleep with you—just as you can make me sleep with you. It only takes a little more effort to hold a girl while you rape her. But how long has it been since a woman has come to you willingly?"

She made her voice deliberately soft, ignoring the other men in the room, speaking only to Diego. "How long?" she whispered. "How long has it been since a woman has come to you willing and eager, a woman who holds her arms out to you, who welcomes you to her body?"

"Por Dios," a man behind her whispered in a hoarse voice.

"I'll do that to you, Diego. But only to you. I'll be anything you want me to be. I'll do anything you want me to do."

"You're a witch," he said. But his voice trembled.

"A live witch and a million and a half pesos, or a dead *gringa* and not one damn cent." She smiled. "That's my bargain, señor."

In the silence of the room a man coughed.

"Get out," Diego said to his men.

"You son-of-a-bitch!" Tano yelled. "I'm not going to let you get away with this. I'll . . ." He pulled a gun from his holster. "It's all right with me if you want the *gringa*. I don't give a fat shit what you do with her. But I'm taking this one." He yanked Teresa to her feet.

"Sarah, don't let him," Teresa cried.

"Let go of the girl," Diego said softly.

"Go to hell, you . . ."

Suddenly, so swiftly that Sarah barely saw the motion of his arm, Diego drew his gun and fired. The hand that grasped Teresa slowly opened. He stayed

222

on his feet for the second of a heartbeat while the blood from the hole in his bony forehead gushed down his face. And then he fell.

"Is there anyone else who wishes to argue with me?"

No one spoke.

"Then get out. All of you."

When they were gone the only sound in the room was the sound of Teresa sobbing.

He put an arm around her shoulders. "Don't make such a fuss, girl," he said roughly. "No one is going to hurt you."

He put a mattress in the small kitchen that adjoined the main room. "You sleep in here," he said to Teresa.

"*Gracias, señor, muchas gracias*. But Sarah, I cannot . . ."

"Don't worry about me. I'll be all right," Sarah said. "Now help me clean up this pigsty. I won't live in a room as filthy as this."

Diego's eyes swept the room. "It's *my* room," he shouted. "I like it this way."

"I don't!" she shouted back. "Now bring me some soap and water and a broom."

He put his hands on his hips and laughed. "You know," he said at last, "I think maybe after all you are one hell of a woman."

And that night, when the house smelled of soap, she bathed herself, washed her hair, and dried it in front of the fire. And when her hair was dry she got into bed.

Diego stood above her. She took a deep breath. "Come to bed, Diego," she said softly. "Come to bed."

Chapter 25

"Take our lives but not our honor," a Greek chorus chanted from the shadows of the room. Ghosts of Mrs. Baumgartner and Mrs. Zambeck peered over the edge of the bed. A pox on the lot of you, she thought. I'm not going to be sorry or ashamed; I made a good bargain and I'm going to stick to it.

Her hands caressed his back, fingers moving up to the back of his neck, touching the tender skin behind the ears, finger-walking the earlobes. Moving slowly down the spine now, smoothing hard back muscles.

When he moved to enter her she closed her eyes, willing herself not to shrink from him. What if he takes me tonight and gives me to his men tomorrow? The thought terrified her. What is a bargain to a man like him? He'll use me tonight and laugh at me tomorrow.

Not if I'm good, she thought to herself. Not if I'm very very good.

Her body rose to meet his every thrust. His breathing was a hard rasp of pleasure, and soon it seemed as though he was about to spend. "Shhh. Easy, Diego," she whispered, "Wait, *querido*, wait a bit."

"I can't."

"You can. Be still a moment, Diego." She put her hands on his hips, slowing him, forcing him to wait. And felt him shudder as slowly, slowly, she began to move against him and heard the pleasure of his mumbled words. His hands tightened on her body as he moved against her, unable to wait any longer, faster and faster, crying out as he exploded inside her.

His body was slick with sweat when he rolled away. "You're a witch," he said. "A *gringa* witch."

"And did you want an angel, Diego?"

"I wanted no angel, but I thought you'd come to me like some martyred saint, crossing herself and praying forgiveness for the sacrifice she was about to make. But your hands were too busy to make the sign of the cross." He chuckled. "Now we will sleep," he said.

"If you insist." Her voice was light and teasing. "I didn't realize you tired so easily."

The room vibrated with his silence. She leaned toward him and ran her fingers down his body. "Sleep then, I'll help you relax."

She began to stroke him, running her fingers down the hard belly to his legs, along the inside of his thigh, brushing against his groin, back to his stomach, down to his legs, lingering longer this time as she brushed his groin. "Sleep," she crooned, "sleep." Fingertips caressing, reaching, teasing.

"You *are* a witch," he moaned, arching his body to the quicksilver touch.

When he reached for her she laughed and moved away from him. "Don't be greedy," she admonished, her voice mocking him. And when he stiffened with anger she began to kiss him, her lips soft and sure against his, until with a groan he rolled her onto her back, his big fingers twisted in her hair as he held her. He was trembling now as his mouth moved down to kiss the rounded breasts, the flat smooth belly, the crisp red-gold hair.

She put her hands on his shoulders. "No," she whispered, "don't do that."

"Anything," he said hoarsely. "You said you'd be anything I wanted you to be or do anything I wanted you to do. I want you to lie here while I do this." He grasped her thighs and forced them apart. His mouth sought the hidden softness of her. And when at last she cried out he moved up and thrust himself into her, his fingers bruising her shoulders, his face against her throat, shuddering against her as he tried to hold himself back, then racing blindly on to finish in one great driving rushing thrust.

The smell of coffee woke her. She opened her eyes to see him bending over the bed. "Here is your coffee," he said, his voice gruff.

She sat up in bed, trying to pull the sheet up to hide her nakedness.

"Take it. I haven't got all day."

"Thank you."

"You and your friend stay inside today. Is that clear?"

"Yes, Diego."

"I've posted a guard outside the door. No one will bother you or your friend."

"I'm grateful."

"A bargain is a bargain, *gringa*. And you make a damn good bargain."

Four days passed, quiet days when she and Teresa rested, talked and came to know each other better. They did not speak of Diego or of the nights Sarah spent with him. But as soon as he entered the house Teresa went out of the room and closed the door. If she wondered about Sarah's quiet acceptance of the situation she did not speak of it.

Early in the morning of the fourth day Diego rode out of the village, taking only a dozen men with him. "No one will touch you, *gringa*," he told her. "But stay inside." He pulled her close to him. "You get in a man's blood," he said. "Every time I'm away from you I begin to think about you, about what I'm going to do to you when I'm with you. And I feel such an itch of need that I swear at my men and roar with impatience until I return." He kissed her hard, his hands tightening against her back.

And when he stepped away from her and started out the door she said, "Diego! Diego, wait!"

"What is it?"

"I don't know. Nothing." She blushed. "Just . . . be careful."

He grinned at her. "I'm always careful."

She smiled back. "Well, then . . . *vaya con Dios*."

The shooting started just as she and Teresa began their afternoon meal. They looked at each other, then rushed to the window to see men on horses galloping into town, shooting as they rode.

"It's an attack," Sarah cried. "Get down."

"Pedro!" Teresa shouted. "Sarah, I'm sure I saw Pedro."

"It's them! It must be!" Her face was wild with joy as she hugged the other girl.

The fight lasted more than an hour. The two girls huddled together on the floor, listening with mounting alarm to the sounds of battle. When finally the shooting stopped they crept cautiously to the door and looked out. Men lay dead or wounded all around them. Across the narrow street a short stocky man came out of a house. "No one here," he shouted. "I'll check the other houses." He turned toward them and stopped, his mouth slack with surprise.

"Francisco!" Sarah cried, rushing down the steps toward him. "Are you all right? Is Luis all right?"

He jerked away from her. "We're all right, no thanks to you." He turned away from her and yelled, "Luis!"

He was herding a group of prisoners into the corral at the end of the street, his back to them.

Sarah started to run, everything forgotten in her eagerness to see him.

"Luis!" Francisco yelled again.

He turned, angry at the interruption, and then his face froze with shock at the sight of her running toward him. She reached him, reached out to touch him, and she was laughing and tears were running down her face as she called his name again and again.

And before he could stop himself his arm came up

and he hit her across the face, sending her reeling backwards as she fell.

She and Teresa rode horses their men had taken from the Colorados. Teresa, riding silently alongside Lorenzo, was free. Sarah's hands were tied.

Her face still stung from the blow. As long as she lived, she would never forget the hate in Luis' eyes as he'd looked down at her lying in the dust at his feet. "What is it?" she whispered, tears blinding her eyes. But he'd already turned his back on her. "Tie her up and throw her on a horse," he'd shouted at Pedro. "Then you and the others kill every goddamned one of the Colorados."

He hadn't looked at her again. Garcia yanked her to her feet, tied her wrists together, and helped her on a horse. When they camped that night he brought her a cup of coffee and some tortillas.

"What is it?" she begged. "Why is Luis treating me like this?"

"Don't play innocent with me, *gringa*. You know what you did."

"I *don't*."

"The lookout saw you. We know you led your Federal friend to us. Nicasio saw you. He even saw the major kiss you before he sent you back to safety. If you had any sense you'd be with him now. If I didn't hate you so much I might even feel sorry for you."

She stared at him. So that was it. But Teresa would tell them. Teresa would . . . But no, Teresa hadn't been with her. There was no one to back her up. And the other girl had enough to worry about—she couldn't ask her for help.

She sat beside Lorenzo, eyes downcast, face forlorn and fearful. I wanted to help her, Sarah thought. But I've only made things worse. What will Lorenzo do to her now? What have I done to her? What have I done to myself?

Chapter 26

Marta Solis was the first person she saw when they rode into camp. The man's pants, the too-tight shirt, broad-brimmed straw hat pushed back off her face. Rushing out to greet Luis, throwing her arms around him. Eyes going wide with surprise when she saw Sarah.

"Where in the hell did you find her?"

"In the village where the Colorados were." He reached up and pulled Sarah off the horse.

"Why did you bring her here?"

"Take the horses," he said to the women who had gathered to welcome their men.

"Answer me!" Marta's face was red with anger. "Answer me, damn it."

"Because she's still my prisoner."

"She's a traitor. Why in hell didn't you just shoot her?"

"I have other plans for her."

"Luis, please . . ." Sarah tried to pull away from him. "You're hurting me."

"Hurting you! You don't even know what hurting is!"

"I swear I didn't betray you. I don't know what your lookout saw, but I didn't tell Andres anything. I knew where I was. Maybe he saw it in my face. But I didn't tell him."

"Don't believe her, Luis," Marta said. "She's only trying to talk her way out of this. Don't listen to her."

"I have no intention of listening to her. Get me a whip."

"No!" Sarah struggled in his grasp, her eyes wide with shock. "Don't destroy us like this."

His hand tightened on her wrist. Hot sparks of pain shot up her arm. "Us was a million years ago, Sarah."

The men and women trailed behind them. Teresa cried out and ran forward, but Lorenzo held her back.

He found the tree he wanted, took her hands and tied them to a branch so high above her head that she had to stand on her tiptoes. This isn't happening to me, she thought. He wouldn't . . . Luis wouldn't do this. Not to me. Not to anybody. She tried to turn her head to see the men and women who watched her. They were silent, all of them. The men shuffled their feet, looking uncomfortable. The women bit their lips and looked at the ground.

"Here," Marta said, not even trying to hide the excitement in her voice. She handed Luis a five-foot leather whip. "She has it coming, *querido*. If it weren't for her Venancio and Lupe would be alive. She killed them, Luis. She would have killed all of you if Nicasio hadn't spotted the Federales."

She'd been ready to cry out, ready to beg, but the voice stopped her. She took a deep breath, trying to still the frantic beating of her heart, trying to straighten her shoulders. "I didn't betray you." She screamed the words at him. At all of them.

"Don't listen to her," Marta said. She reached out and ripped Sarah's shirtwaist down the back. "Do it!"

Sarah pressed her face against the trunk of the tree when she heard the whip whistle through the air. The leather struck her bare back. She bit down hard on her bottom lip. But even so, the sound of her cry rose in her throat, trembled on her lips. Her whole body writhed and jerked at the sudden blinding pain. Her mouth was against the tree now. She wouldn't scream. She wouldn't. She . . . The whip slashed across her back. She tried to brace herself. Tried not to scream.

230

Knew she was shuddering and writhing against the pain of it. Again. And yet again.

She heard a cry. An arm was around her shoulders, a body was pressed against her back. "If you strike her again you'll strike me also," Teresa cried.

Then Marta's voice, wild with anger. "Get out of the way, you one-armed Indian, or I'll thrash you myself."

"You're not gonna thrash her," Conchita snarled. She rushed forward, a stick in her hands. "Back off, Marta, back off or I'll split your head open." And to Luis she said, "You want to beat Sarah you gotta beat me too."

"Get out of the way," he said, his voice shaking with anger.

"And me." Silvia pushed her way through the crowd. She stood beside Teresa and Conchita.

"And me," another woman said.

And another. And another.

Conchita flung the stick aside. She took a knife out of the top of her stocking and cut the bonds that held Sarah's wrists. "Are you all right?" She put her arm around Sarah's waist.

Now that it was over she was unable to speak. She leaned against Conchita and nodded. Silvia put her arm around her and together they led her away from the tree.

"All right," Luis said, blocking their way. He reached out for Sarah. "I won't whip her. But by God, I'm still in command here." His eyes were as cold as a hawk's as his hand tightened on Sarah's wrist.

"You tell me first that you will not hurt her again." Silvia's eyes were as cold as his.

"I will not hurt her."

"Let me take care of her back."

"I'll take care of it."

"I didn't . . ." She wanted to tell them, but her voice trembled so that she could barely speak. "I swear . . ." she started again. "On the grave of my

231

mother." Her wide green eyes were filled with pain. "I didn't betray you."

"Don't listen to that lying bitch," Marta said, shoving the other women aside. She glared at Luis. "Where in hell do you think you're taking her?"

"Get out of my way," he said.

"You will *not* take her to your tent. Tie her up and let her sleep outside. Give her to your men. Do anything you want to do with her, but she's *not* going into your tent."

"I'm in no mood for this now," he warned.

"Damn it, *querido*. You take her in your tent and it's going to start all over again. Give her to me and tell those other witches to stay away. When I get through with her she'll be so docile she'll lick your boots and thank you for kicking her."

Sarah tried to jerk away from Luis. "Let me go," she cried, afraid of Marta, afraid that Luis might turn her over to the other woman.

"It takes a lot to make you learn, doesn't it?" Marta slapped her hard across her face. And was suddenly propelled backwards, Conchita's hands against her shoulders, pushing her until she tripped and fell. Conchita grabbed a stick and brought it down hard on her head before any of them could stop her.

Marta rolled over on her stomach, her hands holding her head. "I'll get you, you gypsy *puta*," she moaned.

"I think she will live," Silvia said dryly.

"Get her out of here," Luis ordered. "I'm sick to the teeth of her—of all of you." He whirled around, pulling Sarah after him.

When they were inside he pulled the torn shirtwaist off. He looked at the scarlet marks that criss-crossed her back and felt no emotion.

She slumped down on the mat, her body shuddering with reaction.

He took a jar of ointment from a box on the stool. "Turn around," he said.

She saw the ointment. "No, please. Don't touch me."

232

"Turn around," he said again.

She looked up at him. His face was as hard and as devoid of emotion as a stone. Without another word she did what he said.

And suddenly it was as though he'd received a blow to his stomach. The bare back, the glorious hair, the profile of her half-turned face. It was just as it had been before. They were in the apartment near the Zocolo and it was the morning after they'd first made love. She had started to get up and suddenly remembered that she was naked. She clutched the sheet to her then, as she clutched her shirtwaist to her now. He had thought he would never again see anything quite so beautiful as she was on that cool February morning.

He felt his throat tighten with the need to pull her into his arms. He put his hand on her shoulder and felt her tremble. He dipped his fingers into the ointment and touched it to the wounds on her back. Heard her indrawn breath, felt her cringe beneath his hands.

"Lift your hair."

She raised one arm and tried to gather the long tumbled hair into a fist.

He reached out, and pushing her hand away he gathered the hair in both of his hands. And when he did all the old desire came rushing back. He wanted her. He still wanted her. A cry tore out of his throat and he thrust her away from him.

She turned, her eyes wide. A cry escaped her lips when she saw him reach for his razor.

His hands captured her wrists, and before she could struggle he tied them with his scarf. He thrust her down on the straw mat and gathered her hair in his hands. And when she saw what he was going to do she tried to squirm away from him. "Don't," she pleaded. Her voice broke. "Oh, Luis, please. Please don't."

But he pulled her back, and forcing her face down to the mat, began to slash at her hair.

Chapter 27

Early the next morning she covered her head with a rebozo and went to Silvia. After the first shocked silence Silvia had her sit down and placed a cloth around her neck. "I used to cut Federico's hair," she said. "When I finish it will not be so bad."

So this was how he had decided to punish her, Silvia thought, appalled by the way he'd hacked Sarah's hair to dozens of different lengths. She sighed, and touched the girl's shoulder. "How is your back?" she asked.

Sarah bit her lip and shook her head, unable to speak.

Afraid now that sympathy would bring the tears that the girl was trying so desperately to hold back, she said, "Federico's hair curled as softly as yours does. It was brown, not black like mine. He would always say, 'Cut it shorter so that I will look like Papa.' But I never did. I loved the feel of it curling around my fingers." And when Sarah didn't answer she put her finger under the girl's chin and lifted her face. "Your hair will grow again. And truly, when I finish with it you will look fine and . . ." But no, it did no good to chatter as though nothing had happened.

When she finished she handed a mirror to Sarah and said, "This is the best I have ever done."

Sarah looked at herself in the mirror. She put her hand to the back of her bare neck. Then she put her head down on her knees and wept. "Why?" she said over and over again. "Why?"

"He is possessed by his hate, *muchacha*. But the hate is for Major Ortiz, not for you. He doesn't understand that yet. He doesn't understand that what he thinks is hate for you is so mixed up with love . . ."

"Love! I don't think he even understands the meaning of the word. When Andres killed his father and his brother he blamed me. When Andres raided the camp he blamed me again. He . . ." She stopped suddenly. Grasping Silvia's hand she said, "I just remembered. Andres was going back to Torreon for more men. That was four—no, five days ago. They'll be coming back, Silvia, you've got to tell Luis. You've got to get away from here."

"Yes, I'll tell him." She whirled and ran from the tent.

"Well?" she said when she told him. "Do you still think she's a traitor?"

"Of course she's a traitor," Marta said. She had an angry purple bruise on her forehead. "She's trying to cause more trouble. She's already got us fighting among ourselves. She's a hex—a poison. Don't listen to her, Luis."

"Well?" Silvia ignored Marta. Her eyes bored into Luis. "Well?" she said again.

"I can't take a chance. We'll move on up higher into the mountains, then down toward Sabinas and try to rendezvous with Villa."

"You're being a fool," Marta said.

"Perhaps. But I'm responsible for my people. I can't risk their lives. You're probably right, she probably is lying, but I can't chance it."

Two hours later they broke camp; the tents were down, the kitchen disassembled. All that remained to show they had lived there was the charred stones of the campfire and the flattened grass where they had walked and slept. It was the women who looked back. This camp had been their home for almost four months. They didn't know where they were going nor how long it would be before they found another place they could—for a while—call home.

Again, as on the day before, her hands were tied. The other women looked at her, at her short cropped hair, and then, embarrassed, looked quickly away. Only Marta laughed at her. *"Hijole!"* she said in a loud voice, "you look like a plucked chicken."

"You don't," Teresa whispered. "You look nice, like a young girl. I think it's pretty. But I am so sorry for the way the captain has treated you. When I saw that whip cut into your skin it was as though it cut into my heart. Is it bad? Does it pain you?"

"Not so much. And what about you? I was so afraid Lorenzo would hurt you."

"So was I! From that first minute he saw that I was with child. His face had been so dark, so brooding. 'Why didn't you tell me?' he said."

"I thought you would be angry."

"Why should I be angry? Did those Colorados hurt you?"

"No. One of them . . . one of them wanted me but the Señorita Sarah made a bargain with their leader and he promised to protect me."

"I will not ask you to tell me what she bargained. But I am glad you protected her tonight." He blew out the lamp and lay down beside her. "You are my woman," he said. "You had no right to leave me."

"I am your woman only because my father gave me to you."

"But I have taken care of you. I have fed you and clothed you." And when she did not answer he cleared his throat and said, "Sometimes maybe I drank too much. But I did not mean to hurt you. That last night, before you ran away, I did not mean that." He reached over and put his hand on her belly. "I would not have done it if I had known you were with child."

"You should not have done it anyway. Ever."

"But my father beat my mother when she did not please him. He told me that it is up to the man to see that a woman does what she is told and to beat her if she does not. But perhaps after all he was wrong."

236

And when she did not answer he said, "Does the baby hurt you?"

"No. A day ago I felt him move, but it did not hurt me."

"Would you tell me if he moves again?"

"Yes, I will tell you."

He moved closer, lifting his arm so that her head was on his shoulder. And with his other hand he stroked her hair.

"Sleep," he said. "Sleep, Teresa."

Marta rode at the head of the column with Luis. They rode for four hours before he let them rest, and when they stopped he walked among them to make sure everything was all right. Their pace had been slow but difficult as they'd climbed higher into the mountains, the horses picking their way over loose stones, straining hard as the air grew thinner.

Sarah had ridden close to Teresa and Lorenzo all morning, and now, when they stopped, Lorenzo lifted her from her horse and untied her hands, rubbing her wrists to ease the pain. Marta, sliding easily off her own mount, saw him and hurried over.

"And how is the little red hen?" she jibed. She reached out, as though to grab a strand of the short cropped hair. Sarah's hand shot out and grabbed her wrist. "Don't you ever lay a hand on me again," she said, so low the others could barely hear her. "I'll kill you if you do."

The two women stared at each other. Marta jerked her hand away. "Tie her!" she said to Lorenzo.

"Let her alone," Luis said, suddenly beside them. "We've a hard ride this afternoon. She'll need both hands to hang on."

He had not spoken to Sarah that morning. He did not speak to her or look at her now. She had been asleep when he awoke, the rough blanket pulled up to her neck as though to hide her ruined hair. Handfuls of it scattered the ground. She lay on her side to protect her back. Her face was swollen from crying. He reached out and pulled the blanket away from her shoulders, and covered them when he saw what he had done. He put his face on his knees and closed his eyes. And tried to close his mind. What if she had been telling the truth?

When they were ready to continue he motioned Pedro Garcia to his side, and he said, "I am going to send you and the Señorita Marta to Saltillo to see if Villa is there."

"*Bueno.*" Garcia scratched his belly and looked towards Marta. Lowering his voice he said, "She's going to yell like hell."

"Let her. I want her out of here. And if Villa isn't in Saltillo you can bring back whatever relief troops you can find and send her on to wherever Villa is."

Garcia was right. She hadn't liked it. But she'd gone, and he was glad to be rid of her for a while. She was a good soldier, as smart and as brave as a man. At times she had shared his tent, but he felt no responsibility for that. He had not asked her to—she had simply moved in with him when she arrived the day after the attack, as she had other times during these past three years. And now she felt as though she owned him. That was his mistake and he intended to set it to right.

The moon was full when they found the clearing in the middle of a clump of trees. "We'll camp here," Luis said. "But no tents and no fires."

They didn't grumble. The men brought out bedrolls and blankets, while the women went to the stream for water, and returned to fix plates of cold beans and dry tortillas. When they finished eating they looked for quiet places to sleep among the trees.

Teresa's face was drawn and pale, and when Sarah saw that she was shivering with cold, she got a shawl out of her saddlebag and put it around the girl. "I wish we could have a fire," she said. "It's not good for you to have a chill like this. Where is Lorenzo?"

"With some of the other men, probably. Someone

has a bottle of tequila. I thought last night he had changed but . . ." She glanced beyond Sarah suddenly, and before she could say anything else Lorenzo was beside her. He carried an armful of tall grass.

"Buenas noches," he said to Sarah. "Will you spread this under the tree while I get more? Teresa's back hurts and the ground is hard. Perhaps this will help."

"Hijole!" Teresa whispered, her eyes wide with surprise.

And when he came back Sarah helped him spread the bunches of tall grass and cover it with a blanket for Teresa to lie upon.

"Stay here with us," Teresa said. "I don't want you to be alone. I don't want you to be cold."

"I won't be, dear. I have a serape." She kissed the girl's cheek. And then, touching Lorenzo lightly on his arm, she said, "Sleep well."

When she had gone a few steps she turned back. She saw Lorenzo lie down beside Teresa and cover her carefully with a serape. And suddenly, without warning, tears welled in her eyes.

She went down to the stream, as far from the others as she could get. She sat on the grassy bank, her knees hunched to her chin, the serape over her shoulders. I could just walk away, she thought. Follow the stream to wherever it goes. A village, a town, or nowhere.

"Sarah?"

She didn't answer.

"Sarah, is that you?" He knelt beside her on the grass. "Let me have a look at your back."

And when she didn't move he slipped the serape off her shoulders and turned her away from him. "Take your shirtwaist off," he said.

"No. I don't want you to touch me."

"I'm going to put ointment on your back. Now take your shirtwaist off or I'll do it for you."

The moon was bright and her back gleamed pale in the soft light. He rubbed the ointment into the marks.

239

And when he had finished he turned her around. She reached for her shirtwaist, but he held it away from her, wanting to look at her, wanting to see the moonlight on her skin. He reached out and touched one of her breasts, and felt her shiver. His hand trembled.

"Don't," she whispered.

He pushed her back on the grassy bank. His fingers fumbled with the fastening of her skirt, pulled it down, tossed it aside. He leaned over her, as though daring her to move, while he unfastened his own clothes. Then he knelt beside her and touched her, his tanned hands dark against the whiteness of her skin. His lips moved down to her breasts, then to her mouth. When hot tears trickled down her face he caught them with his tongue and gave them back to her mouth.

"I hate you so," she whispered.

His fingers grasped her short hair. His legs imprisoned her, held her when she tried to struggle against him.

She fought him with her hands, until he grabbed her wrists. "Be still!" he whispered, his voice angry. "I don't want to hurt you. Be still, I say!"

"Let me go!"

"Be quiet."

His hands held her. His knee pushed her legs apart. She felt his heart's frantic movement against her chest.

"No!" she cried when he entered her. Her arms came up to push him away. And lingered on his shoulders.

She heard his breath quicken as his hands tightened on her. And then, God help her, she felt her own body answering his, wanting to touch every inch of his skin to hers, wanted him deeper and deeper inside her.

When it was over he covered her with the serape. And after a while, not daring to look at him, she slept.

Chapter 28

The weather turned bad the next day as they made their torturous trip down the mountains. A driving rain dripped off the straw hats of the men and the faces of the women. The ones lucky enough to have rubber ponchos hunched inside them, the others did without, trying not to think of the wet cold clothes that clung to their bodies.

Teresa's face was drawn. From time to time she pressed her hand against the small of her back and closed her eyes. But when she glanced at Sarah, riding beside her, she managed to smile and say, "Don't look so worried. I am not so sweet that I will melt in this rain. But *hijole,* I wish my hair was short like yours. This braid hangs down my back like a long clumsy lump."

And when Sarah smiled, Teresa said, "I know you hate your hair, but truly, it is sweet with your face. Ay, Sarah, Captain Vega is a strange man. I could have died that day he beat you. Now whenever you are with him I worry. I worried last night. Were you all right? Where did you sleep?"

"Near the stream. The grass was softer there."

"I wish you had stayed near us. Were you not cold?"

"No, no, I wasn't cold." Sarah felt her face grow hot with shame. She had wakened when the first gray light streaked the sky, wakened to find herself huddled close to Luis, her face against his throat, her hands against his chest, her head covered by the serape. When she looked at him she saw that he was watching her. His hair, damp from the light mist that was falling, looked like wet silver in the early morning light.

"Let me go," she whispered. "There is nothing left for us now except hate. Give me a horse and let me ride out of here. I'll follow the stream. Please, Luis, please let me go."

He looked down at her and shook his head. "You're right, Sarah, I do hate you. And I hate myself for wanting you the way I do. I told you once I'd release you when we got to Torreon. I hope to God that by the time we get there I'll have had my fill of you."

His hands moved and tightened on her body. "You're like a devil, Sarah. There's a part of me that could kill you. A part of me that could beat you until you scream for mercy."

"And the other part?" she whispered.

"Will never get enough of you."

The rain worsened as the day wore on. They'd had nothing hot to eat or drink since the morning before. Now the strain of the trip began to take its toll. When they rode into a canyon and the rain eased off, Luis raised his hand for them to stop. "We'll camp under those cliffs," he said to Francisco. "It's dry there. I think we'll chance a fire."

"You think somebody is following us?"

"I'm not sure, Francisco. If they are, we may have lost them in the mountains."

Teresa almost fell when Lorenzo helped her from her horse. He carried her to an overhang of rocks and helped her to lie down beneath them. He built a fire and rigged a canvas to protect her from the cold, while Sarah took the wet clothes off the girl and helped her into a flannel nightgown. How strange it was, she thought. It was Teresa she'd been worried about when Luis and his men found them, worried that Lorenzo would treat her even worse than he had before. But he hadn't. Perhaps it was her pregnancy. Perhaps, after all, he really did love Teresa. Whatever it was, she thanked God for it. Her own problem was bad enough; she couldn't have borne it if Teresa had suffered too.

"You are very good to Teresa," Lorenzo said in a low voice when Teresa dozed. "I am grateful." He bit his lip, looking embarrassed. "This is a strange life we live. If anything should happen to me will you take care of her? And the baby also?"

She looked into his serious brooding eyes. "You have my word," she said.

"I was bad to her before. I knew she did not want me, that her father made her come with me. I thought I could change her by force and I drank too much to give myself courage to beat her because my father said that was the way you managed a woman, and it was for her own good. That is what he had done with my mother and since I had always seen it I thought it was what a man should do." He ran his hand over his shaggy hair. "But when she went away with you it was as though somebody had torn my heart from my body. Now I want her to forgive me for all I did to her before, but I do not know how to say the words I feel."

"Maybe you don't have to, Lorenzo. Maybe if you just told her you love her . . ." She felt her throat tighten. "That's all a woman wants to hear. And then the rest of it, the pain and the sadness and the quarrels, don't seem so important any more."

"Is she all right?" Silvia asked when Sarah went to help the other women.

"She's awfully tired. I don't know about pregnancies, Silvia. Will it hurt her to ride for such a long time?"

"Not after the first few months. But she is not strong and God knows she would be better off in bed. This is too hard a life for her."

"For all of you."

"But it is what we have chosen. All of us."

"All of us?" Her eyes were bitter.

"Yes, Sarah." She looked over to where Luis stood

with his men. "I don't think you would leave him if you could," she said.

"I would and I will."

He turned and saw her looking at him. Their eyes held for a long moment and then he came toward her. "Get out of those wet clothes," he said.

"In a minute. I was just . . ."

Suddenly the canyon erupted in a terrible explosion of sound as bullets hit the earth, pinged off the side of the overhanging cliffs, and machine-gun fire beat in staccatoed frenzy.

"Up there!" Silvia shouted, pointing to the cliffs above them. "The bastards are up there!"

They tried to regroup, tried to defend themselves against the merciless barrage. The men shoved the women down, grabbed their rifles, flopped on their bellies behind whatever cover they could find, and returned the fire.

"Bandoliers," some of them shouted.

Jacinto sprinted across the open ground to grab a bandolier off one of the horses. Machine-gun bullets spattered the ground around him. Suddenly his right leg doubled and he sank to one knee as bullets rained down on him, jerking his body with their terrible force. He screamed in rage, shaking his fist at the cliffs before he slumped to the ground.

"Jacinto!" The cry tore from Silvia's throat as she started to run toward her fallen husband. Francisco grabbed her. She swung on him, screaming at him to let her go. And finally, because he knew he couldn't hold her, he gave her a clout on the side of her head and held her as she slumped to the ground.

"Stay down!" Luis shouted. "They'll chop us to pieces." He shoved Sarah under an overhanging rock, slung one of his rifles and a bandolier at her. "Shoot anything that moves up there," he ordered.

"We're trapped," Lorenzo yelled. "The bastards have us pinned down. What in the hell are we going to do?"

244

"Try to hold them off until dark. Then go back the way we came and lose them in the mountains."

The shooting went on so long it seemed a part of the unnatural world of that terrible afternoon. Some of their men lay wounded and bleeding. When they could, one of the others would try to reach them, to pull them back to the shelter of the rocks where Antonio Gomez, the son of the pharmacist, tied makeshift bandages around the wounds and tried to stem the flow of blood.

Luis, flat on his belly, the stock of his rifle against his chin, squinted through the gunsight. He didn't think they could hold out until dark. There were less than fifty of them now, against a hundred or more Federales. Sarah had been telling the truth, Andres had gone to Torreon for more troops. Because he knew as surely as his name was Luis Vega that somewhere at the top of the cliffs it was Andres who gave the orders.

Sarah saw his face tighten. He doesn't think we're going to make it, she thought. He thinks we're going to die here. Her lips were dry, her heart beat in frantic thuds. She moved closer to him.

Suddenly, above them, the firing stopped. And started, but not down into the canyon, not at them.

"What the hell?" Francisco said.

"Holy Mother," one of the men near them screamed, pointing to the end of the canyon. "Horses! The bastards are coming in after us."

"What are they trying to pull?" Lorenzo said. "They've got a white flag."

"They want to surrender to *us?* Who the hell do they think they're kidding?" Francisco raised his rifle.

"Wait!" Luis yelled. "Maybe it's Pedro."

The men, more than thirty of them, rode headlong into the canyon, waving their hats above their heads.

"It's not Pedro," Lorenzo said, fingering his gun.

"Then shoot!" Luis ordered.

"No!" The voice was Sarah's. She scrambled to

245

her feet and before Luis could stop her she ran from the cover of the cliffs. "Don't shoot! Don't shoot!" she screamed. And yes, yes, it was him. She could see the red hair, the red beard blowing in the wind. José Alfredo Antonio O'Brien.

He saw her, spurred his horse forward, drew him to a quick stop, and jumped off his horse. "Where's Vega?" he shouted.

She pointed.

"Part of the troops have revolted," he called to Luis. "They'll hold the others off while we get you out of the canyon."

"It's a trap," Francisco said.

"You know this man?" Luis asked Sarah.

"It's a trap, I tell you," Francisco repeated.

"He was at the Federal garrison," Sarah said. "Believe me, Luis, he hates Andres as much as you do."

A muscle jumped in his cheek.

"Believe me," she said. "Believe me."

He looked at her. He raised his arm. *"Vámonos!"* he yelled. "Let's get the hell out of here."

There were only a few sporadic shots as they made their way out of the canyon to the shelter of the trees. And when they were there, Luis jerked his horse around. "Ten of you men stay here with the women. O'Brien, you and your men can stay or you can go back up there with us."

"Leave your own men to guard your women, señor. I've waited a long time for this moment." And before Luis could answer he turned and galloped up the side of the mountain.

They were sixty against the Federales. Sixty plus the rest of O'Brien's men who were at the crest of the mountain.

Luis felt the blood race, felt his hands tighten on the reins. Wait for me, Andres, he thought. Wait for me, old friend. I'm on my way to kill you.

Now it was Andres and his men who were cornered, caught in their own trap, betrayed by their own men.

He screamed in fury at the ones who had remained loyal, sending them forward to their deaths. His face distorted with rage when he saw O'Brien riding toward him. He raised his rifle, but the man next to him fired first, shooting the horse from beneath O'Brien.

And right behind O'Brien he saw Vega, racing toward him like a demon from hell, yelling as he rode.

Andres snapped off a shot, and felt a surge of triumph when he saw Luis grab his shoulder. But the bastard didn't fall, he kept coming. Andres' finger tightened on the trigger just as Luis lunged off his horse on top of him, knocking him to the ground.

The two men rolled over and over in the dirt. The blood from Luis' wound smeared Andres' uniform.

Luis didn't feel the pain; he was like a man possessed. Here at last was his enemy, the man who had murdered his father and brother, the man who had had his mother violated. The man Sarah had betrayed him for. He could have had a dozen wounds and nothing would have stopped him. At last his hands were on Andres' throat.

Andres, his eyes wild with fear, struck out with his fists and heaved his body from side to side, trying to break the iron grip of the hands and legs that held him. He found a rock, and with the last of his strength smashed it against Luis' wounded shoulder. The face above him didn't change, didn't show shock or pain. The fingers tightened relentlessly.

Andres saw his enemy through a gray mist as his tongue bulged from his mouth and his legs jerked convulsively. He looked up into the hard Aztec-like face, the pitiless eagle eyes. He tried to lift the rock again, but it fell from his lifeless fingers.

It was Lorenzo who said to him, "Let him go, Luis. Loosen your fingers, *mano,* he is dead now. Let him go, my friend."

Part V
SOLDADERA

Chapter 29

Francisco held him down while a man he had never seen before probed for the bullet. He remembered that he'd screamed at them to let him go just before he was swallowed up by the darkness.

And later. Sarah's face above him. Sarah's voice soothing him. Sarah's hands bathing him.

"Take that cat out of here," he said once. "And close the door behind him."

"Shhh. Shhh," she whispered. And the cat vanished.

Days merged into nights, nights into days. And finally he opened his eyes and saw Sarah and knew that it was not a dream.

"How long have we been here?" he asked in a voice that did not sound like his voice.

"Four days."

"The others?"

"We'll talk about it later."

"Tell me now. How many did we lose?"

"Twelve men and three women."

"Christ!"

"I'm going to get you some soup. I'll be right back."

"Tell Francisco I want to see him. And that man with the red beard."

"After you've eaten."

The soup was thick with small bits of fish, rice, and herbs. After he'd eaten she summoned the two men.

251

"Ten minutes," she said, and retreated to a corner of the tent where she could keep an eye on him.

"Tell me," he said to Francisco. "Who did we lose?"

"Jacinto . . ."

"How is Silvia?"

"Tougher. Angrier."

"Who else?"

"Nazario, Pepe, Felipe, Filimon, Rosa Carmen, Gomez . . ." He shook his head. "Too many, Luis. Too many good *compañeros*."

"What about the Federales?" he said to O'Brien.

"As soon as they saw that Ortiz was dead they scattered and ran."

"How did you come to go against him?"

"I've been waiting a long time. So have the others." He scratched his beard. "I was a history teacher, Captain. My only interest in politics was in the way it related to history. When I was first conscripted my battalion was under the command of Major Ortiz. He was a captain then. There's no point recounting what he did to me—he did it to others, too. You knew him, you know what kind of man he was." His eyes narrowed. "And if my horse hadn't been shot out from under me I would have killed him. I may never forgive you for reaching him first.

"When I signed on for duty in the north it was to get away from him. But when he saw me at the garrison near Frontera he asked the commander there to transfer me to his outfit." He glanced toward Sarah. "That was when he came back from Torreon and told me he'd turned you and your little friend over to the Colorados." He shook his head. "I could have killed him, Miss Sarah. It must have been a terrible time for you. Were they the ones who cut off your hair?"

"No . . . no, they didn't do it."

He turned back to Luis. "I knew, even when Miss Sarah was at the garrison, that he was a danger to her. That's why I volunteered to go with him the day he went looking for your camp. And I was right. When

252

she wouldn't tell him how to find you I thought for a minute he was going to kill her. He had his hand on his gun."

"That seems strange, Sergeant. My lookout told me he saw the major kiss her."

"That he did. Almost yanked her off her horse as I remember."

"And that doesn't strike you as strange, if what you say is true, that you were afraid for her?"

"Ah, Captain, men have been using sex as punishment for thousands of years. And what does it prove, I wonder? That we're stronger?" He leaned forward. "A case in point, if you'll forgive me, didn't he do the same kind of thing when he told his men to violate your mother?"

"You know about that?" Luis' face had gone white.

"He told me. Even bragged that he told your mother he did it because of Miss Sarah. He should have known you'd never believe that . . ." He stopped suddenly, his eyes narrowed, his face stiff with anger. "By Christ," he said. "I remember now. She told me once that everything was finished between you. So you did believe that she betrayed you!"

There was a terrible stillness in the room.

"That's why she ran away from you, isn't it? And when you got her back . . . You bastard!" His voice shook with anger. "You're the one who cut her hair."

Francisco put his hand on O'Brien's arm. "Easy, *amigo*," he said softly. "Easy."

When they were alone, Luis said, "Francisco will tell the others, Sarah. It's important they know you . . . you didn't betray them."

"The ones who know me already know that, Luis," she said. "There is no need to tell them." She took a folded serape and pulled it over him. "You'd better rest now." Her voice was cool and impersonal. "Sleep if you can. I'll bring your dinner later."

"Perhaps it would be better if Silvia took care of me."

"She has enough to do. Since Jacinto's death and

253

your being hurt she's taken on even more responsibility. As long as I'm here, Luis, I'll take care of your needs. When we get to Torreon it will be finished.''

She left him alone then. More alone than he'd ever been in his life.

Three days later Pedro Garcia rode into camp with twenty of Villa's men. "He's in a village a day's ride from here," he told Luis. "He sent me to find you.''

"What happened to Marta?''

"She's at the village. What in the hell happened here, *mano*? Half of our own men are gone and there's a bunch of strangers in blue uniforms. I saw Silvia and she looked like she's been through hell and back. Where's Jacinto? Nazario? Felipe?''

"Dead.''

"Mother of God.'' Pedro crossed himself. "Who else?''

"Pepe, Filimon, Gomez . . . We were attacked by the Federales. They almost had us, but a group of Andres' man—the ones you saw when you rode in—deserted. Turned against Andres. We'd have all been dead if it hadn't been for them.''

"Ay, Luis, sometimes I wonder if any of us will survive this goddamned revolution. How many years? How many battles? First against Porfirio Diaz, now against Huerta. How long will it go on?'' He sighed and shook his head. And finally he said, "You rest now. If you and the others are able, we will leave in the morning.''

When he left Luis he went to Silvia. She was leaning over the fire stirring a kettle of food.

"Luis told me about the battle.''

"It was bad.''

He scratched his belly. "He told me about Jacinto.''

Her face tightened.

"If I can help you . . . It is hard sometimes for a woman to manage.''

"I will manage.''

254

"Well, in case."

"Would you like some coffee?"

"Yes, that would be good." He took the steaming earthenware cup from her hand. "We leave to join Villa tomorrow."

"Maybe that means we'll be on our way soon to take Torreon."

"Won't you go back to your village now? With Jacinto dead . . ."

She glared at him, her burning eyes and jutting nose giving her face the look of an angry hawk. "I will not go back to my village until this is over. I carried my share of the load when Jacinto was alive, now I will carry both our loads. Nobody has to look out for me, Pedro. I will look after myself."

Because of the injured it took them three days instead of one. Their rations were low, but no one complained.

In spite of the growing heaviness of her body, these were happy days for Teresa. She didn't know if it was her pregnancy that had changed Lorenzo, or her running away. But he *had* changed. And she was grateful.

One night as she lay next to him she felt him grow and press against her leg. When he turned away from her she asked, "Why do you go away from me?"

"I am ashamed to feel so when you are like this. It is not right."

"It is."

"But I might hurt you."

"Not if you are careful."

His hands were trembling as he eased himself into her. She moved against him, feeling a strange pleasure that she'd never felt before as his hands caressed her back and the maleness of him swelled and grew inside her. She strained against him, a little frightened at this feeling, this itch of need, this heat that warmed her.

"Little bird," he whispered, "have I told you I love you? Do you know I do? Do you?"

He had never said the words to her before, and as though she were melting she surrendered her body to his, and felt the most beautiful feeling she had ever known.

Afterward, when he lay beside her, he said, "When our child is born we will go away. We will not go to the village of either of our parents. We will go some place where we can start anew, just the three of us. And our child will never see his father lift his hand to his mother. We will raise him with love so that he will be able to love."

If it was a time of joy for Teresa, it was a time of strangeness for Sarah. She had come to accept the fact that she belonged to Luis whether she chose to or not, whether she loved him or hated him, whether he loved or hated her. They had been bound together, first by their love, then by his hate. Now all that was changed. He had released her, physically and emotionally. And she felt lost and strange.

She spent more and more time with O'Brien. He had asked if he and his men could join forces with Luis, and now he was on the way to Villa's village with them.

"Villa never went to school," he told her when she said she wanted to know more about the famous bandit-turned-general. "But he's taught himself to read and write. He's a fascinating man, Sarah, a military genius. In March of last year he crossed the Rio Grande with only eight men, nine rifles, and five hundred rounds of ammunition. Men who had been with him before, men like Vega, had already started organizing in Chihuahua and they were ready for him when he arrived. He chased every Federal soldier out of the state.

"He's fantastic. He's encountered the twentieth century with the naive simplicity of a savage and he's made it work. He was an outlaw for over twenty-two years, all over southern Chihuahua and northern Durango, all the way down to Coahuila, right across the Republic to the state of Sinaloa.

"He has a passion for schools because he believes that land for the people and schools for the children will settle every question of civilization. And another thing about him, Sarah, he's a strangely moral man. If he wants a woman he doesn't just take her, he marries her." He laughed. "And he's married a lot of them. Twenty or more. He's got wives all over the Republic of Mexico who more than likely will never see him again. But they were married by priests, and so they consider themselves legally married."

"Incredible."

"Ah, he's an incredible man. And no matter what they say about him, not a vicious man. He doesn't like to kill." He paused and looked thoughtful. "Maybe what's why he keeps Fierro around—to do the killing for him. You've heard of Fierro?"

"Silvia told me about him. She said once he killed five hundred prisoners. She said he shot until his gun was too hot to hold, until his hand was burned."

"I've heard that story too. And worse. If he's there with Villa when we get to the village, stay away from him."

They rode into the village at noon the next day amid great shouting, dogs barking, and children scampering around them. Men ran up to take their horses. "There are tents for the single men," they said. "Those of you who have women will have a house. Villa said you were to choose what you wanted, but the best house must go to Captain Vega and his woman."

There was a commotion at the end of the street as a group of men and women, headed by Villa, started towards them. A tall man in a white suit kept pace with Villa.

Pancho Villa. He was bigger than Sarah remembered. His stomach rounder, his moustache fuller.

He pulled Luis to him, embraced him, held him away, looked at him, embraced him again. "You had me worried, *mano*. I thought they had you. Is your wound serious?"

"No, General. A few days' rest and I'll be fine."

"You will have more than a few days, my friend."
He smiled at the others. *"Bienvenidos,* welcome, this
is your village. You will do nothing but eat and sleep
and make love all day. Your women should enjoy
that." His laugh came all the way from his belly.

"Hey," he said to Luis. "You remember Fierro,
don't you?"

"How could I forget him?"

"How indeed?" Fierro said.

"You want anything, you ask Fierro. We have
enough houses for everybody, so take your women
and . . ." He stopped and slapped his forehead.
"Hijole! The red-headed *muchacha* from the train.
The little schoolgirl." He pulled her to him and kissed
her cheek. "So you are Luis' woman. Good! It's
about time this *cabrón* settled down. Keep a tight rein
on him, girl. God knows he needs taming. Is he a good
husband? Does he take good care of you?"

"She's not his wife!" Marta, her face white with
rage, pushed her way through the throng of people.
"She's his prisoner. Her lover is a major in the Federales. Andrés Ortiz. You've heard of him, Pancho.
He's Huerta's righthand man. The one who destroyed
Comonfort and San Vicente. This schoolgirl, as you
call her, led Ortiz to Vega's camp. I don't know why
the hell he keeps her around, but by God, it's time
she was gotten rid of. If Luis isn't man enough to do
it, then let Fierro take care of her."

Villa's hands tightened on Sarah's shoulders. His
small eyes bored into hers. "If this is true, girl . . ."
His voice was low and threatening. His gaze swung
to Luis. "Well, what do you have to say about this?"

"Yes, I thought she'd betrayed us." There was a
white line around his mouth. "I beat her and I cut off
all her hair and then I found out the truth."

Villa whistled softly. "And how do you know this?"

Luis motioned for O'Brien to join him. "This man
served under Ortiz," he said. "He deserted and joined
us. He was with Sarah just before our camp was attacked. He knows she didn't betray us."

"That I do," O'Brien said.

"Well then, you have a great deal to make up for, don't you?" And when Luis did not answer him, he said, "And this girl has shared your tent? She has been your woman?"

"Yes."

"Then, by God, you will make her an honest woman!" He turned to one of his men. "Prudencio, tell the priest there will be a wedding tonight."

"No!" Sarah wet her lips. "Señor Villa, I don't . . ."

"Don't? Don't? Of course you do! What would your papa say? Running all over the country with this man and not married to him. You leave this to me. Tonight when he takes you to his house you will be the Señora Sarah de Vega."

He looked at Luis. "Do you have any objection to this?" His small eyes looked dangerous.

"No, General. I'm willing to marry her. On one condition."

"Condition?" Villa's face darkened with rage.

"That you'll be my best man."

"*Hecho!* It is done! And after the wedding we'll have one hell of a party."

He turned to Sarah and hugged her. "Now go, *muchacha*, go and prepare yourself for the wedding. I promise you this will be a night to remember."

Chapter 30

As the hour of twilight settled over the surrounding hills, Sarah went down the dusty street of the town to the ancient windowless church at the end of the block. Silvia and Conchita were in front of her, Teresa beside her. She was dressed in a clean white shirtwaist and a patched, but pressed, black silk skirt. Silvia's black lace mantilla covered her short cropped hair. Huaraches covered her feet.

This was the day she'd dreamed of since she was a child, the day she would walk down a flower-strewn aisle toward the shadowy face of a man who adored her. She'd be wearing a white lace dress and white satin shoes, and she'd smell of lilacs and rose water. She'd remembered that dream an hour ago when she sat in the round wooden tub and scrubbed herself with strong brown soap.

When the three Spanish bells began to ring, birds flew from the bell tower, their wings pink-tinged in the reflection of the setting sun.

Teresa handed her an armful of daisies.

Villa, wearing a clean khaki uniform, hair slicked down, moustache combed and curled, waited on the steps to take her into the church.

Down the dark center aisle, past the two rows of wooden benches filled with murmuring faces, down toward the front of the church where stark white altar candles, erect and harsh, flickered on either side of the chancel. The smell of incense hung heavy in the musty air.

Wretched saints stood in peeling gold niches, their mouths drawn down. Mary the Mother, whose eyes were sad, whose nose was chipped, holding faded flowers in her arms. Lopsided angels hovering on either side of the sanctuary. And on the right a dusty Jesus on a rusty cross.

Luis averted his face as she came down the aisle on Villa's arm. And still, when her hand was placed in his, and when they knelt together on the worn red carpet while the mass was said, he did not look at her.

"Estamos aquí en la presencia de Dios . . . We are gathered here in the presence of God," the priest intoned.

"Do you, Luis Alfonso, take this woman . . . ?"

"Do you, Sarah Barbara, take this man . . . ?"

His hand was cold on hers.

"With this ring . . ."

"With this ring . . ." Luis repeated.

"I thee wed."

"I thee wed."

"I now pronounce you man and wife, in the name of the Father, the Son, and the Holy Ghost. Amen. You may kiss the bride."

Cold lips brushing her cheek.

She turned from him to place the daisies at the Virgin's feet, looking up past the chipped nose to the sweet sad eyes. Wanting to pray. Unable to pray.

Her fingers trembled on his arm as they went back up the aisle, oblivious to the faces surrounding them, her eyes on the small candles to the right of the door. Penny candles in amber glasses that cast a kinder light than stiff white altar candles.

They stood on the steps of the church in the darkening evening, afraid to look at each other.

The party was held in the schoolhouse. Paper streamers and paper lanterns festooned the walls. A

261

mariachi group, consisting of one violin, a horn, and four guitars, played Mexican waltzes and rancher songs.

"I'm going to be the first to kiss the bride," Villa roared as he grabbed Sarah and smacked her soundly on the lips.

"I am next, General," Fierro said. He still wore the white suit, and just before he took her in his arms Sarah wondered if it was the same white suit or if he had dozens of them. His kiss was not like the good-natured kiss of Villa. It was a man-woman kiss, an offensive kiss.

Then the others—Francisco, Lorenzo, O'Brien, Pedro Garcia—brotherly on-the-cheek kisses. Until Villa said, "That's enough, that's enough. Now we dance. The newlyweds first." He turned to the *mariachis*. "Play *Carmelita*, but make it *Sarita*."

And as they danced he sang with the *mariachis*:

"Sarah, Sarita, luz de mis ojos . . .

Sarah, Sarita, light of my vision,
If failed the sun you still would be there,
The lovely beacon of my good fortune,
Hope's star irradiant, joy past compare."

"I am sorry this was forced upon you," Luis said as they danced. "As soon as we get to Torreon I will see the bishop. When I explain why this happened he'll give you an annulment."

"Of course." Her smile was stiff.

"We'll have to share a house while we're here. I'm sorry about that too, but it's the only way I can protect you. If Fierro suspects this whole thing is a farce he'll make trouble."

It was as though he spoke to a stranger.

They sat together at a long table, surrounded by the men and women of Villa. Ribald jokes were shouted over the music, toasts were made in their honor, wine

262

was poured into their glasses from an endless supply of bottles.

"You're a good girl to put up with all this ruckus," Villa said, leaning close. "And you'll see—it's a good thing to be married. You'll be good for Luis." He lowered his voice. "I sent Marta away this afternoon. I don't like her, but I do like you."

"And I like you," she answered, smiling for the first time that night.

She looked around her at the people sitting at the table, at the people dancing. I didn't know they existed until a few months ago, she thought. Now they're important to me. I care about them. Silvia with her strength and determination, Conchita, wild as a storm. And true as the sky, my dear Teresa. All of them. And she knew suddenly that they were her people now. This was where she belonged.

Luis thought it was too late for them, and perhaps he was right. There had been so much misunderstanding, so much pain. And through it all he had ceased to love her.

She looked at the wide gold ring on her left hand, a symbol of love, a symbol of commitment and trust. That's what it was meant to be. She felt an irrevocable sadness that it was not so.

Luis said, "I got the ring from Villa. He has a bag full. I had my choice; rubies, diamonds, amethysts, pearls, even an emerald or two. Booty from his raids. I thought you'd prefer something plainer. But if you'd rather have something else I'll change it."

"No." She touched the ring. "No, this is fine."

It was late when Villa got to his feet, pounded on the table for attention, and shouted, "It's time for the lovebirds to leave."

"*Viva* Luis. *Viva la Gringa*," someone said, raising his glass.

"Say goodbye to your freedom, Luis."

"Keep a tight rein on him, Sarah."

When they lighted the lamp they saw that the

women had cleaned the adobe house they were to share. The table was set for next morning's breakfast. The sheets were turned down. A white cotton nightgown lay across the bed.

Silence racketed around the room.

Slipping the black mantilla off her shoulders she said, "I think we have to make the best of this, Luis." Her voice was careful. "We're here, and for the time being at least, we're married. If we don't stay together until we leave the village everyone will know this is a farce. I don't think Villa would like that."

"No, I don't suppose he would." His voice was dry. "Very well, what do you suggest?"

"That we pretend." She bit her lip. "To the others, I mean." She turned away from him. "And when we're alone can we at least be kind to each other?"

His laugh was harsh with bitterness. "I've been unkind to you for so long that it's become a habit. I know I've killed every bit of feeling you've ever had for me, Sarah. And I promise that as soon as I can I'll take you back to your father and then . . . you'll never have to see me again. But perhaps you're right, as long as we're here we might as well make the best of it." His smile was sardonic. "Shall I wait outside like an expectant bridegroom while you change?"

"Yes, please."

When he opened the door to go out she could hear the music coming from the schoolhouse.

She folded her clothes over the back of one of the straight chairs and slipped the white cotton gown over her head, wondering which of the women it belonged to. She wanted to curl herself onto her side and draw her feet up under the full white gown, but she made herself lie flat, trying not to recoil when her feet stretched and touched the cold clean sheets. Virginal white sheets. Pillowcase. Gown. Everything but the bride. She wanted to weep, for herself, and for Luis. And she wanted to be held and warmed.

The pillow was an *almohada,* one long pillow that served both sides of the matrimonial bed.

264

He barely glanced at her when he came in. He turned the lamp down and blew it out.

They lay side by side, their heads on the same pillow, not speaking, not touching.

This is my wedding night, she thought. And after a while she slept.

But he lay, listening to the distant strains of music. What have I done to her? he asked himself. How much more can I hurt her? He could still see the whiteness of her back that day Marta ripped her shirtwaist away. Could hear the sting as the rawhide whip struck the tender skin. Could see again the streaks of red that marked her, the quiver of muscle. Could hear the smothered cry.

"Can we at least be kind to each other?" she had said to him tonight.

Yes, we can be kind, he thought. I can never expect her to love me after what I have inflicted upon her. But kindness? Yes, at least that.

He reached over and carefully pulled the blanket up to cover her shoulders.

Chapter 31

The gentle October days were marked by the chill in the air and the rich golden color of the turning leaves. It was a time of rest, a time to prepare for the winter that was to come.

Each day Teresa's belly grew bigger with child. She had never been so happy as she was now in the coming birth of her child and in her new-found love for Lorenzo.

For Luis it was a time of recuperation. His shoulder was stronger, and while he complained to Villa of the inactivity and swore he was good as new, he found that he was settling into the lazy routine of the village. Except for short scouting trips and lookout duty, the men had little to do. Some of them hunted, always managing to bring back enough turkey, quail, or rabbit to keep the village supplied with meat. He spent his days with the men. But each night he returned to the adobe house he shared with Sarah, for although they had little to say to each other, it was good to come down the dusty street at twilight and see the flicker of lamplight through the window.

For Sarah it was a time of make-believe. She bought a heavy round gray rug off an Indian peddler to cover the floor. She put geraniums in the window, and strawflowers on the table. She pretended she had always lived in this village with these people, and that every evening when Luis came back to the house he came because he wanted to.

New men arrived at the village daily. At first their women were like strangers in a new neighborhood, but as the days wore on they became acquainted with the other women. They met at the river when they did their laundry, and sometimes in the afternoon when the men were busy they sat in front of their houses— or their tents—and talked.

Sarah was accustomed to the women in Luis' camp, but these women were strangers. She listened to their stories and little by little began to understand who they were and how they had come to be here. With her understanding came a new knowledge of the revolution and the men and women who were a part of it.

One, a lovely girl, who looked no more than seventeen, was fascinated with Sarah. "I've never known a *gringa* before," she said. "How did you come to be here? How is it that you speak Spanish? Do all *gringos* speak our language? Is your captain good to you? Ernesto, *mi hombre,* he looks very stern too. I remember the first time I saw him. It was in my town of Linares. I was returning from mass when he and some other men rode into town. They rode slowly by me and I heard a voice say, 'You are going to be mine, *muchacha.'* "

She looked at Sarah with her incredibly beautiful eyes. "I was so frightened, señora. I went as fast as I could and when I reached my house I ran in and told my mother and my little brothers what had happened. And even as I was telling them we heard the sound of horses' hoofs approaching. My brothers hid under the bed in a cornr of the room, and my mother told me to go into the other room and hide in the wardrobe. I did as she said, but I left the door open a crack so I could listen.

" *'Buenos días,'* he said to my mother. 'Tell whoever is in this house to come here immediately.' My little brothers were so terrified they crawled out from under the bed and ran crying to my mother. Then Ernesto said, 'I went to the mountains to fight for the revolution because seven months ago some soldiers

267

assaulted my village. They took everything we possessed; all our cows and horses, our chickens and pigs, our harvest of corn. As soon as my brothers and my neighbors and I could get horses we went to the mountains to try to find them. But they were gone, so we joined with others and now we are all with Villa. I don't want to be as bad as those men were. I don't want to take without asking. But I will take what I want.' "

The girl's olive cheeks flushed with color. "Ay, señora, you cannot imagine how frightened I was. Then he said, 'I want the girl who entered this house a few minutes ago. I will treat her well, I promise you that. Now tell her to come here. And pack a small suitcase for her because my *compañeros* and I must continue on our way.' "

"Pobrecita," Conchita said. "Did you ever try to get away from him?"

"Yes, once I tried, but he brought me back. Now I have grown used to him. When this is over I suppose I will stay with him."

"And I will stay with Roberto," another girl said.

"Where are you from?" Silvia asked.

"Juchitlan, near the coast of Jalisco. We are all very fair in that part of the country, and I was terrified of Roberto when he kidnapped me from my family, because he is so dark. At first I hated him, but now, I don't know, we are making a life together. His home is in the Yaqui Mountains. His family raises horses. He has promised me that if I return there with him when the revolution is over he will give me his prize horse that is the color of *flor de durazno.*"

"Flor de durazno," Sarah repeated. "Flower of Peach."

"He says it is the most beautiful horse in the State of Sonora."

"Ay, the horses from Sonora are known all over Mexico," old Josefina said. "Do you think Roberto will marry you when this is over?"

"I think so. But even without marriage he is my man. Our relationship is sacred."

The words hurt Sarah. They stood for love, commitment, and fidelity. Roberto would give his girl a gift from his heart—a horse the color of the flower of peach. This girl belonged to her man in a way that she, Sarah, would never belong to Luis.

Each night when they lay side by side, their heads resting on the same long pillow, she waited for him to reach for her. They were married. She was the Señora Vega. Señora Vega whose husband had not touched her since their marriage. Even his hate, as terrible as it had been, was not so bad as this coldness that was in him now.

One night, when the October wind chilled the house, she turned to look at him, to study his face in the amber glow from the fireplace. And without planning to, she moved closer to him. She reached for his arm and lifted it so she could put her head on his shoulder. She felt his body stiffen, but he said nothing as she turned her face into the hollow of his shoulder. When his other arm came around her she let her breath out slowly.

When his hand moved up to touch her breasts she felt her body stretch and sigh. She tilted her face up, and because it had been so long since he had kissed her, it was like an electric shock going through her body when their lips touched.

She moved closer to him, impatient, her legs tangling in the long gown.

"Wait," he whispered. He helped her to sit up while he pulled the gown over her head. Then she was back in his arms, the whole length of her nakedness touching every part of him, not caring, not stopping to think of what he thought of this new boldness. Her hands tightened on his shoulders when his lips moved to her breast. He kissed her gently. She heard her own quickened breathing, heard herself whisper his name, knew she wanted to cry, "I love you. I don't care what's past. I don't care what you've done to me. Just love me, please love me.''

But she said nothing, trying instead to tell him with her body, with her hands, with her mouth. And heard his breath quicken, felt the tension of his body as she clung to him with frenzied hands and grinding hips. Until she cried, her face against his shoulder, "Darling. Darling. Darling.''

And she waited for him to say her name. But he said nothing. Nothing.

Their days took on a strange pattern. He spent each morning working around the small house, repairing cracks in the adobe, scrubbing smoke-stained walls, trimming the few scraggly bushes outside. He spent the afternoons with his men, but he always returned at dusk. The flicker of light through the window became a symbol for him, a symbol of Sarah. As long as there was the light there was Sarah.

Each night they sat on the steps listening to the sounds of the guitars, smelling the corn roasting on the braziers, hearing the hum of life all around them.

He never spoke to her of his love. They were pleasant to each other, as two new friends might be. And at night, when they held each other, their words were words of passion, not of love.

And so it was until the day he went on a routine scouting party with Francisco, Lorenzo, and Pedro Garcia.

The scouting trips had become so routine that the women no longer worried when their men set out. They knew that soon it would be time to move on, but they were lulled by the indolence of the October days. And that afternoon when the four men did not return they felt no anxiety. But when it grew late they said,

—Perhaps one of the horses went lame.

—They may have decided to hunt for game.

—There's been no trouble for almost a month.

—Surely there is nothing to worry about.

At dawn Villa sent thirty men to look for them. In the late afternoon they returned, their faces covered

270

with sweaty grime, the reins hanging loose upon the necks of their horses as thin dust rose in lazy clouds at every step the animals took. A body, head hanging down, lifeless feet moving with the motion of the horse, was tied over the back of the animal.

"Lorenzo!" The cry tore from Teresa's throat as she ran to touch the body hanging from his horse.

She pulled at the dead arms, smoothed the black hair back from the dead face, tried to pull away when Sarah ran to her.

"We were ambushed," Luis told Sarah later. "Colorados. They came at us in the late afternoon. We held them off till dark, but they had us pinned down. They were at us again at dawn. That's when Lorenzo got it. We were almost out of ammunition when we heard the horses. Another ten minutes and the three of us would have had it."

They buried Lorenzo the next morning in the cemetery next to the church. Sarah stayed by Teresa through all of it, and that night she said to Luis, "I must be with Teresa tonight."

The day after the funeral Villa called a meeting in the schoolhouse to tell them they were leaving.

"We're going to take Camargo," he told them. "Then Mapimi, Bermejillo, Gomez Palacio and Torreon. We've rested on our *nalgas* long enough. Now we move."

So once again the women turned their backs on a place that, for a while at least, they had called home. They packed their belongings on the backs of the mules and closed the doors on the adobe houses without a backward look.

On the morning they were to leave Luis put their saddlebags on their horses. He waited for Sarah, and when she didn't come he went back to the house to find her watering the geraniums. He started toward her impatiently, then stopped as she reached out, frowning with concern, to pluck a dry leaf from one of the plants. What a strange girl she is, he thought. We're about to leave for God-knows-where and she's

271

worried about her geraniums. He remembered the apartment off the Zocolo during the February battle, remembered how she'd left her blue velvet ribbon on the plate beside the money. "I want to leave something of myself," she'd told him then. That's what she was doing now, leaving something of herself.

And it suddenly occurred to him as he watched her that she was his wife. Until this moment the fact that they were married had not been a reality. But it was true. This tall slender girl with her finely molded face, whose short copper curls brushed the nape of her neck, whose pale hands touched the dried leaves of the geraniums, was his wife.

She turned then and saw him, her sea green eyes widening, waiting.

I could drown in her eyes, he thought.

"Captain!"

He turned from her.

"Captain," Pedro Garcia shouted. "We're ready to leave."

And the moment was lost.

Chapter 32

The golden days of October made way for the gray days of November. They traveled for ten days, camping at night beside a stream or under an overhang of rocks. Life became faded blankets, tired horses, chunks of meat on burning coals, and the smell of coffee on bitter nights.

Then they moved to the railroad cars, crowding together with hundreds of other rebel troops. For endless hours they chugged along the track, freight cars filled with horses, coaches filled with soldiers and their women. But most of the men and women rode on top of the train, their bundles and baskets, pots and pans, blankets and straw mats, everything they owned beside them.

When they neared the town of Camargo the men unloaded the horses and rode away. For three days the women heard the distant sounds of rifle fire, the thunderclap of cannon, the shrill whistle of shells.

Their men—some of them—came back the third night. They staggered like drunkards, their faces gray, their eyes empty.

"Water, give us water," they begged as the women hurried to help them.

A young boy reeled along, carrying the body of an older man. Another man led a horse with two bodies flung across the saddle. Another slumped on his horse, screaming every time the animal took a step. Blood dripped on the railroad ties.

"We've routed 'em," somebody said.

"We hold Camargo," another said, staring at the twisted bloody mess where his hand had been.

Sergeant O'Brien, his face covered with sweat and grime, helped carry the wounded to the hospital car where doctors worked frantically over the wounded men. When she saw him, Sarah, her hair bound up in a clean white cloth, hurried to him and asked, "Luis? Is he all right?"

"The last time I saw him he was."

A blood-stained apron covered her dress. She wiped the perspiration from her face. "Was it bad?"

"Bad? Lord, Miss Sarah, it was purgatory-bad. Lesser men than these would have turned tail and run. But not these men. If I ever had a doubt before about who'd win this revolution, it's gone now. These men, these simple men, are going win hands down."

At dawn the alamo trees burst forth with a shower of bird songs. And in the distance they could see dirty smoke rising from the town, and carried on the slow hot wind, the smell of crude oil mingled with the smell of human flesh. When the fire slackened, broad-winged vultures sailed serene and motionless against the smoke-stained sky.

They mounted one of the cannons they'd captured on the first car, an open caisson full of shells behind it. Then came the engine, followed by three boxcars full of soldiers. Now they were ready for Mapimi and Bermejillo.

"The main part of the army will come from the north by train," Villa told his captains. "Raul's men will come from the east, Vega from the west. Good luck and *vaya con Dios*."

It was good to feel their mounts beneath them again. Good to feel the rush of clean air on their faces. But soon the air cooled; the nip of frost was in the air.

Sarah and Luis continued their strange truce. Both knew their time together was drawing to an end, that when they reached Torreon he would turn her over to her father. The pretense would be over, and so would the marriage. Each evening she served him his food and, like the other women, did not eat until he had finished. To all outward appearances their marriage was normal, but cool.

"That is the way of Northamerican women," some of the new men said. "They have no warm blood in their veins. Surely poor Luis must beg for her favors each night."

"He gets no favors," another man said. "It is a forced marriage that neither of them wanted. He will rid himself of her when we get to Torreon and find himself a Mexican woman."

"I have heard that Marta Solis is crazy for him. Perhaps he will take her for his woman."

"Were you there the day Luis beat the *gringa?*"

"*¿Qué?* Beat her, you say? No wonder she is so cool!"

"*Sí, mano.* He thought she had betrayed us. He was blind with rage, but I think he might not have done it if it had not been for the Solis woman. She screamed for the *gringa's* blood."

"And he beat her?"

"*Sí, hombre.*"

"And after all, she had not betrayed you?"

The man shook his head. "And that, I think, is why Vega's face is like stone and why he treats the *gringa* like a stranger."

But if they were strangers during the day, they were lovers at night. They took their bedrolls away from the others, and when they lay down he pulled her against his shoulder. And when it was over they did not separate, but slept, bodies entwined. And sometimes in the night she would wake to feel him swell inside her, and her hands would find his hips, as together they began again the movements of love.

Each day she rode beside Teresa. Her friend's body was big with child now, and while she did not complain, they all knew the journey was difficult for her. Her small face was often pinched with pain. Her soft sad eyes were ringed with dark circles. She rode, huddled in her rebozo, shivering with cold, as the autumn skies turned winter gray and winter rains began.

They tried to talk her into leaving the troop. "Stay in one of the towns until the baby is born," they told her. "You need a doctor. You need to rest."

"I'll come back for you," Sarah said. "My father will be with me then. We'll take you to Texas, just as I promised. But really, Teresa, you shouldn't be traveling like this."

"No." The small face held a look of unsuspected stubbornness. "I want to stay with the group. I want to stay with you. I don't want to be with strangers."

The rain grew worse, beating hard against their bodies, chilling their bones. It was almost impossible to sleep. And the food they ate was cold and soggy.

"Teresa can't go on like this," Sarah said to Luis one late afternoon. "We've been riding since dawn. Can't we stop now?"

"No. I'm sorry. We've got to be in Mapimi by the first of December." He lowered his voice. "I don't want you to tell the other women, but I think we're being followed."

"Followed?" Without thinking she looked behind her through the slanting gray-white rain.

"Since yesterday midday. We've got to keep going. I'm sorry about Teresa, but I have to think of the others."

"If she'd only let us take her to a town."

"She doesn't want to leave you. Now that Lorenzo's gone you're all she has. Are you going to take her back to Texas with you?"

"Yes. I want to make sure she and the baby will both be taken care of. She can't go back to her family. She told me she couldn't because she's pregnant. Damn! I don't understand these people. Her father made her go with Lorenzo. He didn't see anything wrong with that, but if she goes back pregnant that's a sin!"

"Even if her father was different, Sarah, she might not have a home to go back to. There have been so

276

many girls like Teresa, girls from decent families, good Catholic girls who never looked sideways at a boy. Girls who were only allowed in the town to attend church with their parents. Then one day we came, or the Federales came. We rode into their village like madmen, taking what we wanted, and what we wanted most was women. So we carried them off and we raped them and made them our women. And then someone else came behind us and burned their villages and stole their stock. They have nothing to go back to, Sarah. We're all they have. We're . . ."

His words were lost in a sudden high-pitched scream. They turned to see a rushing wall of water knock Teresa's horse off its feet, saw it try to regain its footing on the slithering mud, and then, as if in slow motion, saw it slide off the edge as Teresa tumbled from its back and horse and woman fell down the steep embankment into the *barranca*.

Silvia was the first to reach her, slipping, sliding down the embankment, all of the color drained out of her face. Pedro Garcia was behind her, then Luis and Sarah.

"Oh God!" Sarah moaned, dropping down beside the girl.

"Let's get this horse off her legs," Luis shouted as other men jumped down to the *barranca*. "Is he dead? If he moves an inch he'll kill her."

"He's dead," Pedro said. "Broke his neck when he fell. "Come on, *compañeros*. Manolo, you and Francisco grab his legs. O'Brien, you help at this end. Together now!" Cursing and yelling they pushed the beast away.

"Teresa! Teresa!" Sarah tried to wipe the mud and grime from the girl's face. "Teresa!" she said again. And when Teresa didn't respond she looked at Luis. "What are we going to do? We've got to get her out of this rain."

"Francisco, take some men and see if you can find a cave or an overhang of rocks," Luis said. He picked Teresa up in his arms and started up the embankment.

When he reached the top he laid her down and felt her legs. "They're not broken," he said. "Thank God for that."

"We've found a place," Francisco called. "It's dry. I think we'll be able to get a fire going."

The cave was big enough for them to stand.

"Get her clothes off," Silvia said when they laid Teresa on a blanket. "We've got to dry her off. Bring me tequila, Luis. Perhaps I can get her to take some."

They dried her with cloths from the saddlebags, rubbing her skin until it was red, trying to restore circulation, and covered her with blankets.

"She's so pale," Sarah whispered. She took the thin hand in hers, rubbing warmth back into it. "Teresa. Teresa," she said softly.

And at last the eyelids fluttered and opened. "Sarah?" The voice was weak.

"Yes, dear. You're all right now."

"Take a sip of this," Silvia said. She put a strong arm under the girl's shoulders and raised her. "It will warm you. As soon as there is a fire we will give you some tea. How do you feel, *preciosa?*"

"I don't know. What happened?"

"Your horse lost his footing," Sarah said.

"And I fell. Yes, now I remember." She put her hands on her stomach. "Oh, Sarah," she whispered, "I fell so hard."

"No, no," Silvia said. "The mud was soft. Don't worry, *querida*, you'll be all right."

"But what if I hurt the baby?"

"You didn't, Teresa," Sarah said.

"Don't leave me."

"I won't. We're going to stay here until you feel better." She looked up to see Luis standing over them. "Aren't we?" she said, her voice challenging him.

"We'll stay awhile. A few hours at least. How do you feel now, Teresa?"

"I'm all right, Captain, it was just . . ." Her face pinched. She drew her legs up. "Ay, ay, *Dios mío.* Aiiiii!"

278

"What is it?" Sarah said to Silvia. "Is she . . . ?"

"Yes, yes, I think so. Luis, did they get a fire going?"

He nodded. "What do you want me to do?"

"Get me all the clean dry cloth you can find. And put up some blankets to shield her from the others." She smoothed the hair back from Teresa's face. "You're going to be all right, *niña*. We're going to take care of you."

"Don't let anything happen to my baby."

"We won't. We won't. It's going to be all right. He has decided to venture out into the world, but Sarah and I are here to see that he arrives safely." She looked across the distended belly, into Sarah's frightened eyes. "We'll help you," she said again. "Soon you will hold your child in your arms. Soon, Teresa, soon."

Chapter 33

It can't go on like this, Sarah thought. No one can stand this kind of pain. How long has it been? Five hours? Six? It was night, she knew that, because someone had lighted lanterns. On the other side of the blankets she could hear the low murmur of voices. Twice Conchita brought them coffee and stayed to help. Help? There was no way to help except to wipe the perspiration from the pinched gray face or hold the hand when the pains came.

The moans and muttered cries were weaker now as the contractions came closer together.

"Soon," Silvia said, "it will be soon."

"Tell me about Texas," Teresa whispered through parched lips. "Tell me."

"The hills and the trees are green in the spring," Sarah said, while she stroked Teresa's forehead. "We'll live in a big gray house on a street that's lined with trees. My aunt sleeps in the bedroom downstairs, so you and I and the baby will have the upstairs all to . . ."

"Aiiiii . . ." The sound was weaker as her body contracted with pain. "Tell me," she panted, her hand clutching Sarah's. "Tell me."

"You'll have your own bedroom. We'll decorate another room especially for the baby."

"Ay, no. He must stay with me, where I can watch

280

him. Lorenzo would not have wanted his son to be alone.''

"All right, he'll stay with you.''

"Lorenzo wasn't a bad man, Sarah.''

"I know, dear.''

"I think he loved me a little.''

"He loved you a lot. He told me he did.''

"Really, Sarah? Did he really?''

"Yes, dear. And he asked me if I'd watch out for you and the baby if anything happened to him. He loved you and he was concerned about you.''

"My poor Lorenzo. My . . .'' Her body jerked. "Ay, Jesus Mary Blessed Mother. Sarah, please Sarah, make the pain go please Sarah make it stop oh sweet Mary please . . .''

"Silvia?'' Sarah pleaded. "My God, can't we do something? How much longer?''

"Ohhhhh, no!'' A thin scream tore from Teresa's throat.

"It's coming,'' Silvia said, bending over the girl. "It's coming, Teresa. Help me now. Bear down, push. Teresa, push!''

Sarah bit her lip to keep from crying out.

The cords in Teresa's neck were like taut wire. Her lips were pulled back from her teeth. Her eyes shut, her face wrinkled with effort. Beads of perspiration stood out on her forehead. The hand that held Sarah's squeezed harder and harder.

"I cannot,'' she moaned.

"You must!'' Silvia commanded. "Once more. Push!''

Nails bit into Sarah's palm as Teresa, her body tightening with effort, strained and pushed, and finally, with a great tearing gasp of pain the child was delivered.

"You have a girl,'' Silvia said, striking the child smartly on the buttocks, laughing in relief at the angry wail of sound. She handed the baby to Sarah. "Clean the child,'' she said. "I must take care of Teresa.''

281

"Let me see her," Teresa whispered.

And Sarah held up the child, slippery from the womb, and said, "Here is your daughter."

The men were silent when they heard the cry. And then they began to talk.

—I wish Lorenzo could have been here.

—*Sí. Pobre pendejo.* Sometimes he drank too much, but all in all, he was not a bad sort.

—A good *compañero*.

—What will happen to his woman now? What man would want a one-armed woman and a child?

—The *gringa* will take them to Texas with her.

—But how can she go, *mano*? She is married to the captain.

—That is not a marriage, *hombre*. She will leave him the minute we get to Torreon.

—Well, it will be a better life for little Teresa. She would leave us anyway. A woman cannot stay here without a man.

—And what about Silvia? Her man Jacinto was killed. What about her?

—She will never leave us.

—But she should have a man.

"She will have a man," Pedro Garcia said.

They turned to look at him, their eyes wide with surprise. But before they could speak the blankets were pulled back and Silvia said, "The child is a girl."

"Well, that is the life." Manolo sighed. And the other men shook their heads sadly.

"Where is Luis?"

"Outside with the lookouts," Garcia said. "Do you want me to get him?"

"Yes." She did not look at him.

"How is Teresa?"

"Too weak to travel. I must speak to Luis."

"I will get him."

282

She waited with the men until Luis appeared, and when he said, "How is she?" she said, "She's had a hard time of it. I don't see how she can travel."

"But we can't leave her here."

"Of course not! But can't we stay here for a few days at least?"

He shook his head. "We're being followed, Silvia. We may have lost them in the mountains but I can't be sure. How can I jeopardize all of my men and women?" He hesitated a moment and put his hand on her shoulder. "All right. Today and tomorrow. I can't do any better than that."

"Thank you, Luis. That will help."

"How is the baby?"

"Fine. Come and see her. And then try to make Sarah rest. I don't think she's ever seen anything like this. Teresa has become like a little sister to her, and it was hard for her to watch such pain and not be able to help. But she was very brave, and it helped Teresa to have her with her."

Teresa was asleep when they pushed the blankets aside. Sarah was beside her, holding the child.

"May I see her?" he whispered, kneeling on the ground beside them.

"Yes. Look. Isn't she beautiful?"

She turned back a corner of the blanket and he looked down at the tiny red-brown face. He reached out, meaning to pull the blanket back a bit more, and was startled when Sarah reached out and took his hand.

"See how soft her skin is," she whispered, guiding his fingers to touch the child.

And as his hand, still on Sarah's, touched the child, he looked at her. For a moment that's all there was in the world, he and Sarah and the child. He didn't hear the murmur of voices. He didn't see Silvia standing beside him. There was only Sarah, looking at him with her great green eyes, her hand on his, and the softness of the baby. He saw the mist in her eyes, saw

283

the tears grow and swell and spill. And still he could not look away.

"Sarah?" The weak voice broke the spell as Sarah turned away from him and said, "Yes, dear, I'm here."

"My baby?"

"She's beautiful," Luis said.

"Yes, beautiful. At first I was disappointed because I wanted a boy for Lorenzo. But instead I have a girl for me. And I don't think Lorenzo would mind."

"He'd be proud of her, Teresa."

"Will you and Sarah be the *padrinos,* the godparents?"

"Of course we will. What are you going to name her?"

"Sarah. Sarita, while she is little."

"That makes me very proud, Teresa. Thank you. Now I want you to rest." She put the child in Teresa's arms.

"You and Silvia get some sleep too," Luis said. "It's been a long night."

"I'm all right."

"No, you're not. Two of the other women will stay with her while you and Silvia rest." He took her arm and led her to where the others were sleeping, huddled in their blankets, as close to the small fire as they could get. He fixed a place for her and said, "Now, don't worry. Teresa will be all right."

"Where will you be?"

"Outside. Keeping watch."

"You're going to let us stay here awhile, aren't you?"

He looked away from her. "Awhile."

"You promise?"

"I promise."

Silvia stood at the entrance of the cave looking out at the rain. It had been a long night and her back ached with the strain of bending. Poor girl, she thought.

Thank God she has Sarah. Thank God she will be leaving this—this war that we fight. How many years had she, Silvia, been fighting? Sometimes it seemed all of her life instead of only four years. Too long. Too long. It was not the life for a woman. For that matter it was not the life for a man either. It hadn't been the life for Jacinto. She was the one who made them leave their village to join the revolution. She was the one who insisted they fight year after year. Poor Jacinto, poor gentle man. All he'd wanted to do was till his land, take care of his family, and drink a little pulque every Saturday night. And that's what he would have been doing now if it hadn't been for her.

She reached out her hands and felt the rain. Then she turned them, palms up, and filled her hands with the wet coolness and splashed her face. What am I do do? she asked herself. She'd heard the men talking. Would they let her stay without a man? She clenched her fists. She *had* to stay. The revolution was all she lived for.

"Come out of the rain, *vieja*," someone said, and she turned to see Pedro Garcia.

"I was only getting a breath of air."

"You should rest. Is Teresa all right?"

"I don't know." She shivered in the chill morning air.

"Here, take this." He took the blanket from his shoulders and wrapped it around her before she could protest. It still held the warmth of his body.

"My mat is over there, behind the fire. I'm going on guard duty. Why don't you rest?"

She held the blanket around her, suddenly afraid to look at him.

"Go on," he said. "Sleep. They will call you if the girl needs you. Go on."

"*Gracias*, Pedro."

"*Por nada*, woman. *Por nada*."

Chapter 34

The rain stopped by noon and a pale sun shone through the clouds. There were a dozen lookouts posted, but so far there'd been no sign of whoever had been following them.

"I think we've lost 'em," O'Brien told Luis.

"I hope so. But I'll feel a lot better when we get out of here. What about the men? How do they feel about the delay?"

"Nervous. But they'll do whatever you say, Captain."

There'd been an uneasy truce between the two of them from the day O'Brien learned what Luis had done to Sarah when he suspected her of betraying them. He showed Luis the respect due a commanding officer, but never with the easy comradeship of the other men.

"I don't like it," Luis said. "I've got a feeling in the pit of my stomach that says we ought to get out of here while the getting's good."

"But what about Teresa? Poor small thing. I remember the first time I saw her. Miss Sarah had covered the two of them with a blanket, trying to protect them from the sun. It must have been a hundred and fifteen that day. I saw their horses, then the two of them. Miss Sarah was in bad shape, but Teresa was a lot worse off. I remember I tried to get her to drink some water, but all I could do was dribble a bit on her lips. Then I thought if I wiped her off it would help.

That's when I saw her arm." He sighed. "Ah Lord, I guess she's had a rotten life."

"I guess she has. But it's going to be better. Sarah's going to take her to Texas."

"That's what I heard." He hesitated. "Are you really fool enough to let her go?"

Luis looked at him, his eyes suddenly flat and cold.

"Because if you are, Captain, I'm going to wait the proper time and then I'm going to follow her to Texas and do everything I can to make her forget you." He leaned close to Luis and made no attempt to hide his contempt. "I heard about what you did to her when you got her back from the Colorados, how you strung her up and lashed the skin off her back. Ortiz did that to me and I wanted to kill him for it. And there are times when I'd like to kill you for doing to her what he did to me. And I would, Captain, I would, if it wasn't that the poor foolish girl loves you still."

"That's enough! And by God, O'Brien, if you value that Irish hide of yours you'll never speak of this again. Now see to the guards. And hereafter report to Garcia. You and I have nothing to say to each other. And as soon as we get to Torreon I want you out of my outfit. Now, damn it, get out of here."

But in less than five minutes O'Brien was back. "They've spotted something," he shouted. "Over toward the east. A cloud of dust and I'll bet my Irish boots it's riders. About three hours from here I'd say."

"Give the order, Sergeant, we're moving out."

Pedro Garcia held Teresa in front of him, trying his best to support her and the child. But try as he would, nothing could lessen the terrible jarring each time the horse's hoofs touched the ground. Her face was gray and pinched with pain. He glanced at Sarah, keeping pace beside him. There'd been a terrible scene when Luis told her they had to leave.

"We can't," she stormed at him. "My God, Luis, look at her. She can't even stand, how do you think she can ride? You promised you'd wait another day. You said . . ."

"I know what I said. But whoever has been following us is hot on our trail. I've got to get my men out of here."

"Then leave us."

"I can't do that."

"Yes you can. Please. Leave us two horses and some supplies. When she's able to ride we'll find a village and . . ."

"Don't be a fool! And don't waste any more of my time. Get her things and yours together. I want us out of here in ten minutes."

"No!"

He jerked her around to face him. "I haven't time to argue with you, Sarah. I'm sorry. I know it will be hard on her, but there's nothing I can do. I promise that if we pass a village I'll take the two of you in and see if we can get help for her. Now do as I say."

"I'm not going to let you kill her!" She spat the words at him. "We're going to stay here."

"No you're not! You're going to do just what I tell you to if I have to tie you to your horse. Now move!"

Well, it's strange, Pedro thought. Luis and Sarah. Probably it was because he was Mexican and she was *gringa*, that was why they'd never understand each other. Luis was right, of course. He had no choice. He couldn't leave the two girls behind. If the Federales found them they'd have no chance at all. *Ay caray!* The revolution was all right for men, but it was hell for women. Well, for most women. He looked at Silvia, riding ahead of him. A blue kerchief covered her black hair. The long black skirt was hiked to mid-calf, strong muscled legs gripped the horse's sides. Her hands were strong too, brown and hard as a man's. Ay, she was one hell of a woman. Not beautiful, but handsome in her way with her deep-set black eyes that could bore through a man's skull. Not soft and pretty like some, but a woman a man could count on.

Teresa moaned and moved against him.

"Easy, little one, easy. Lean on me."

As they climbed higher into the mountains the cold bit into them, stinging their eyes to wetness, hurting their ears, freezing their hands. Steam came from the horses' nostrils as they labored up steep frosty inclines, hoofs slipping on the frozen earth.

Teresa bent her head over the baby, trying to draw the child close to her body for warmth. Garcia pulled a serape out of his saddlebag and wrapped it around mother and child, barely able to hear Teresa's mumbled words of thanks.

They rode until dark. "We'll rest here for a few hours," Luis said. "But no fires. I want guards posted around the perimeter. I think we've lost them, but let's not take any chances. If we travel most of the night we'll reach Olivares by morning. There are other rebel troops stationed there."

Pedro, with Sarah's help, eased Teresa and the baby off the horse, and then he carried her to a sheltered place behind a giant boulder where Silvia spread blankets. The baby, jolted awake, gave a lusty wail that brought a grin to his face. "She's got a pair of lungs. Letting you know it's time to eat."

Silvia helped Teresa turn on her side and loosen the rebozo and shirtwaist. The baby found the brown nipple and began to suck, one tiny hand resting against her mother's breast.

"See how strong she is," Teresa whispered, her voice weaker than it was before. "She's going to be a strong baby, Sarah."

"And a beautiful one," Sarah said. "And now you've got to eat something, dear."

"Not now, Sarah."

"Please try."

Silvia raised the girl's shoulders and supported her in her arms. "Here is some *atole* from breakfast. It will make you feel better." She spooned it into Teresa's mouth, but after two or three swallows Teresa shook her head and said, "I'm sorry. I can't. I'm so

289

cold, Silvia. All I can think of is how cold I am.''

"We'll warm you," Sarah said. She lay down beside the girl and put her arms around her, the child between them. Silvia sat down on the other side of Teresa, her broad back against the girl.

Two hours later, when it was time to leave, Luis came to get them. "They look like children," he said to Silvia.

Teresa, so pale and thin. Sarah with her arms outstretched, trying to hold both mother and child. Looking like a child herself with her short tousled hair. "Do you think Teresa will be able to travel, Silvia? She's so pale."

"Sabrá Dios, Luis. God knows." Her face was pinched with concern. "The fall. The difficult birth. The ride today. I don't know. I . . ."

Teresa opened her eyes. "Something is wrongn" she whispered. "Sarah? Sarah?"

"What is it?" She was awake instantly. "What is it, dear? Do you feel sick?"

"Ay, Sarah . . ." She turned her head from side to side, her eyes closed now. "Ay, Sarah, *por favor.* Ay, *Dios mío,* I feel so strange."

"Let me have the baby," Silvia said. She picked the child up and handed her to Sarah.

"What is it?" Sarah whispered, her eyes wide with fear.

"I'm bleeding, Sarah. I'm bleeding."

"Let me see, *preciosa,"* Silvia said. She pulled the blanket down. Her face went suddenly, blankly still when she saw the spreading circle of blood. "Get me cloths," she said to Luis. "She's hemorrhaging. We've got to stop it." And to Sarah she said, "Tell some of the other women. We need help."

And when Sarah only stared at her, unable to move, she snapped, "Don't sit there like an idiot. Do what I tell you."

Inocencia, old Josefina, Conchita. All trying to help. Tearing shirts and petticoats, trying to stem the

290

blood that gushed like an angry red river from the frail body.

"My baby," Teresa moaned. "Give me my baby."

"In a minute, *querida,*" Conchita said.

"Where is she?"

"I have her," Sarah said.

"Yes. Yes, you have her."

"I do, dear."

"No. You keep her. I give her to you."

"Teresa . . ." She took the girl's hand. "Don't say that, darling. You're going to be all right. We're all going back to Texas. We're . . ."

"Promise me."

"Anything."

"That you'll take her."

"I will. Of course I will. But please, Teresa, please . . ." She cradled the girl's hand against her cheek.

"Lord Jesus Christ receive this spirit," old Josefina whispered. "Holy Mary pray for her. Oh Holy Mary, Mother of Grace . . ."

"Don't *do* that!" Sarah rasped the words.

". . . Mother of mercy, protect her from the enemy and receive her in the hour of her death."

"Mother of grace, Mother of mercy," Teresa whispered.

"Teresa . . ." Sarah pressed the frail hand. "Teresa, please. Christ . . . please . . ."

"I'm so tired, Sarah."

"We'll go back to Texas. We'll buy her a beautiful baby carriage and you can take her for walks down by the river and . . ."

"Jesus, Mary, and Joseph, I give you my heart and soul," old Josefina intoned.

"Jesus, Mary, and Joseph, I give you . . ." Teresa repeated. And then, as quietly as she lived, she died.

Chapter 35

They buried her there, in the cold unconsecrated earth, their fingers touching the beads of their rosaries as they intoned the litany of the dead.

And when it was done they rode to the village of Olivares to prepare for the battle of Torreon.

Villa left his headquarters in Chihuahua and moved south. He closed the telegraph wires to the north and stopped train service to Juarez.

Three trains, carrying the Gonzales-Ortega brigade, moved out of Chihuahua behind him, followed the next day by Zaragosa. The Northern Army was on the move.

At night, along the miles and miles of troop trains, the fires of the *soldaderas* flared from the tops of the freight cars. Out into the desert, so far away that they were only pinpoints of flame, stretched the campfires of the army. Westward toward the mountains strings of cavalry rode, more than a thousand of them, the jingle of their spurs ringing, crossed bandoliers gleaming dully, straw hats shading their faces.

Behind each company plodded ten or twelve women, carrying cooking pots on their heads and backs.

Each day, more and more men poured into the village of Olivares to fight in the battle for Gomez Palacio and Torreon. They stood, long lines of them, while Vega's men passed along in front of them peering closely at cartridge belts and rifles, handing them out to the men who didn't have them.

Sarah was strangely remote from the signs of the coming battle. She spent every waking moment with Teresa's child—her child now. The baby, who looked more like Teresa every day, thrived on goat's milk, and rarely cried.

As they had before, she and Luis shared a house. She understood now that Luis had to push them on to escape the soldiers that followed them. She knew that wars did not stop for childbirth. Women did not belong in this terrible world of men, but if they were in that world, they had to accept the hardness of the life.

Yes, she understood. But she did not forgive.

She and Luis were careful of each other. Their days together were almost over. And it was time. Too much had happened between them. There was too much to forget; too much to remember.

She would go away, and he would be glad when she was gone.

Her major concern now was for Sarita, and for the safety of her father. The battle of Torreon was imminent. Her father was in that city. What would happen to him when the Northern Army clashed with the Federal Army of President Huerta?

"I've passed the word to all of my men," Luis told her. "We'll get him out, Sarah, I promise you."

"And you'll bring him here, to Olivares?"

"When the battle is done."

When the battle is done. She wished she could feel something. Anything.

"I'll have an escort take you and your father and Sarita to Texas. You feel comfortable with Sergeant O'Brien. I thought I'd send him. He's a good man, Sarah."

She wondered at the question in his eyes.

Pedro Garcia was in charge of the new men. He drilled them twelve hours a day. And when the day was finished all he could think of was a bottle of pulque and a night's sleep. He was unshaven and his clothes were dirty. His eyes red-rimmed with fatigue. Three nights before the battle he returned to the house that

293

had been assigned to him. It was a little before midnight. He was drunk and tired and all he could think about was falling into his unmade bed. When he pushed the door of his house open he stopped, sure for a moment he'd ventured into the wrong house by mistake. The lamp was lighted, and he smelled food.

"What the hell?" he muttered.

"Don't stand there like a great fat fool!" Silvia said.

"What?"

She took a pail of water from the fireplace, a bar of strong brown soap and a towel from the table. "Go out back and scrub yourself," she ordered. "You smell like a goat."

"A goat?" He scratched his belly. "Now listen, woman . . ."

"No, *you* listen. You're a disgrace. You forget to wash, you forget to eat, and you drink too much. A fine example for your men. If you keep on like this you'll be too tired to fight the Federales."

"But . . ."

"Outside!" She thrust the water, towel, and soap at him.

He rubbed his red-rimmed eyes, and without another word took the things and went outside. When he came back she put a plate of meat and sweet potatoes in front of him. He sat down and began to eat, watching her cautiously as she stripped the dirty sheet and ragged blanket off his bed, muttering under her breath as she balled them up and threw them in one corner of the room and made the bed up with a clean sheet and a clean blanket.

And when he finished eating she washed his dishes and swept the floor.

"Well, what are you waiting for?" she said, her voice impatient. "You've been up since daylight. Give me those dirty clothes of yours and get into bed."

The clean sheet felt good against his skin. The wool blanket smelled of winter air. He watched her move about the room, stand over a bucket of water, wash his clothes. She rigged a clothesline in front of the fireplace so they would dry by morning. Then she extinguished the oil lamp.

He closed his eyes, too tired, too drunk, too full to wonder what strange reason had brought her here. She was here, that's all that mattered.

When she got into bed, when he felt the warmth of her body next to his he said, "Silvia . . . ?"

"We'll talk in the morning. Now you must sleep."

Warm and silent, his head against her breast. As contented as he had ever been in his life. He slept.

December now. The short gray days of December. It was time for them to leave.

Still Sarah felt nothing except a great emptiness. Luis would go to fight. And return. And send her away.

But what if he did not return?

Her mind stopped at this point.

It was late when he returned to the house the night before the march on Gomez Palacio and Torreon. He was bone weary, and, like Sarah, filled with a great emptiness of spirit. The sounds of guitars, of a woman's voice calling to her man, a snatch of a song, and the soft glow of light coming from the houses that lined the dirt street filled him with wry melancholy. He hesitated in the cold darkness outside his house, savoring for a moment the smell of meat cooking over coals in the fireplace, the light coming from the narrow window. His home. His and Sarah's home. For one more night.

She sat in their one chair, holding Teresa's baby, her cheek against the black fuzz of the tiny head. And it seemed to him that the girl he had first seen coming down the broad marble stairs of the Chapultepec Castle was a million years removed from this woman in her simple white shirtwaist and patched black skirt. Something inside him cringed into a frenzied knot of anguish because he knew he had to let her go.

She looked up at him. "She's asleep," she said, in her strangely remote voice. "Your dinner is cooking. It will be ready in a moment."

They had not slept together since they had been in this village. She slept in the bed with Sarita, Luis on a pallet in front of the fireplace.

He watched her moving from the fireplace to the table, filling his plate, pouring his coffee, washing the cooking pots while he ate, emptying the water outside the door. Sarah, the girl who had worn a pink lace dress and satin shoes.

He dimmed the lamp.

And still he watched her as she undressed, as she folded her clothes on the bench at the foot of the bed, as she reached for the nightgown, her body silhouetted by the near darkness.

She knew that he watched her.

"Come here." His voice sounded harsh in the quiet room.

She stood poised, naked, her hand on her gown. Holding her breath, afraid to move. Flinching when he said again, "Come here."

Holding the gown in front of her, she went to him. She felt shivers of cold, or of fright, as he pulled the gown out of her arms. When she folded her arms across her breasts he pulled them down to her side.

"Don't," she whispered.

"I want to look at you."

His eagle eyes watched her face while his hands reached for her. Hands that turned bronze by the light from the fire. Hands that touched her, hands that felt her quiver and tremble. He took his shirt off and threw it on the floor. Then he pulled her to him.

How many times had they made love? she wondered. Too many to count. And this was the last time.

She didn't resist when he pulled her down to his mat. She lay quietly while he removed the rest of his clothes, watching the play of the flames on his hard muscled body. And when he leaned over her she lay passive, letting him touch her where he would, letting him kiss her where he would.

But at last, knowing he was ready to possess her, she moved away from him. And when he started to speak she said, "No, not yet," and pressed him down against the mat.

She began to kiss him, slowly, without passion. Sweet butterfly kisses lingering at the corners of his mouth, his lips, the line of his jaw. Moving away to touch him with her hands, engraving every inch of him on the memory of her fingertips. She kissed him and touched him until he trembled as she had trembled. Until he said, "Please, please, please." A warm litany of want and need.

She wanted to weld him to her so he would never be able to leave. And again she longed to say, listen with your body, Luis. Listen to my love.

His arms tightened around her as he thrust himself against her. She knew he was about to peak, as she was, and while a part of her screamed for release from this sweet agony, another part of her wanted it to go on and on. The last time, she thought, the last time. And suddenly she was lost in a frenzy of pain, a frenzy of desire, and she held him closer than she had ever held him before. Wanting to die in his arms. Wanting to live in his arms.

"Sarah. Sarah. Sarah." Her name on his lips. His hands, his strong man hands caressing her flesh, slowing her, holding her. Until at last with one hurting painful cry, one final flash of sorrow, she peaked to the mountaintop and began the slow ecstatic fall to the haven of his arms.

Chapter 36

First there was Bermejillo. They took that easily because the garrison, complacent with recent victories, had not bothered to prepare for an attack. The next day they took Mapimi.

Massed columns of them moved into one long single front of six thousand men at Santa Clara. They spread over frozen fields, past rocks and trees, almost to the base of the mountains.

Thousands of others of them moved by railroad. The track was good most of the way, but eight miles from Gomez Palacio it was destroyed. Villa, burning with impatience, said, "To hell with the train, we attack as we are!"

But here the Federales were ready for them—with cannons, machine guns, and heavy artillery. They were bloodied and almost beaten to their knees, almost stopped by Federal troops that shot at them from a water tank on a hill overlooking the city. The water tank had to be taken before they could go on. And so they sent wave after wave of men up the hill so that the few who made it could stick their rifles into the holes of the tank and shoot the enemy.

The march through Gomez Palacio to Torreon moved forward past piles of dead men, stripped of their arms, shoes, hats, most of their clothing.

The wounded were carried back to Villa's hospital train, forty boxcars manned by both American and Mexican doctors. Every night shuttle trains carried the seriously wounded back to hospitals in Chihuahua and Parral. In four days of fighting over a thousand men had been killed. The smell of death and funeral pyres clung to the nostrils of the living.

As soon as the track was repaired, the train with its famous cannon, *El Niño,* moved toward Torreon. Now all of the big guns pounded the city, while Federal shrapnel, well-fired and timed, burst in answering fire. It seemed as though it would go on and on.

In the village of Olivares, in all the villages of Mexico, the women waited.

Old Josefina spent endless hours on her knees in front of the Virgin of Guadalupe.

Conchita paced. Up and down the one dirt street of Olivares, around the outer edge of the village, up to the hill above the town, dozens of times a day.

Silvia washed and mended all of Pedro Garcia's clothes. And when that was done she cut up her good white petticoat and made him a shirt.

On the seventh day refugees began straggling through the village.

"How does it go?" the people in the village asked. "Are we winning? Have the Federales given up? Has Torreon fallen?"

"Quién sabe, who knows?" They said. "The fighting has been going on for days. Cannon fire, artillery, homemade bombs, machine guns. The Federales burn everything as they retreat. The skies around Torreon are black with smoke. But *quién sabe? ¿Quién sabe?* Gomez Palacio fell to the Villistas, but at a terrible cost of lives. Some say that a thousand of our men were killed."

"And now? What is happening now?"

"They are fighting for their lives."

Finally, on the tenth day, some of their men returned. The women gathered on the edge of town as they came, some on foot, some on horseback. Many of them with bloody bandages around their foreheads, or legs, or arms. Their hands and faces sweat-dirty and powder-stained. Their eyes vacant with fatigue.

There was joy in the faces of some of the women as they rushed forward to help. Sobs of disappointment from others whose men had not returned, who perhaps would never return.

Silvia traded a cooking pot for material and made another shirt for Pedro Garcia.

Conchita raged up the hill twenty times a day, scanning the countryside for some sign of riders.

Old Josefina spent every waking moment in the church. And one night as she struggled to her feet she saw Sarah kneeling in the last pew, her head bent, tears falling on clasped hands.

Sarah was still in the church the next morning, her head resting against her hands on the altar rail, when the bells in the church tower began to ring. She raised her head, wondering for a moment where she was, feeling the pain in her back and legs and knees, hearing the growing sound of voices in the street outside. The sharp barking of the dogs. The whinny of horses. The cries, "They're back. They're back." The sobs of joy. The cries of anguish.

She wanted to rush from the church, to run with the other women to see if he had returned. But she was paralyzed with fear. What if he hadn't come back?

She bent her head, wanting to pray, but unable to form the words in her mind. And at last she got to her feet and went to stand in the door of the church.

More than a hundred people crowded the street, most of them women, a few old men and children, pushing toward the returning men.

She didn't see him. She put her hand against the door of the church, feeling weak and faint as her eyes searched the faces of the men riding into the town. Please let him be all right, please let him be here, please, please . . . The frantic litany ran round and round in her head.

Please . . . She saw him. His face was gray with fatigue, his hands loose on the reins, his body slumped in the saddle. O'Brien and Pedro Garcia rode on either side of him.

"Luis!" Conchita screamed. "Where is Francisco?"

"Behind me. Coming."

"And the battle?" Silvia cried.

"We beat the bastards," Garcia said. "Sent them running like hell towards Mexico City. And that's where we're going."

"You won't be fit to go anywhere if you don't get some rest and some food in your body. Get down off that horse and come inside."

"Hijole, manos, listen to her! I am back one minute and already she is ordering me around." He slid off his horse and went to her. "Well, woman? Did you worry about me?" He grabbed her and kissed her soundly. A few of his *compañeros* cheered him on.

"I worried about all of you," she muttered, pulling away from him. "Now come along."

"I have to help Luis."

"No, Pedro, go with Silvia. You deserve a rest. We all do."

His eyes searched the waiting women, looking from one face to another, feeling a dull stab of disappointment because she wasn't there. And then he saw her, standing in the doorway of the church. A black mantilla covered her burnished hair. Her face so white and still.

When she saw him watching her she descended the three uneven stone steps of the church and came toward him through the throng of waiting women to stand beside his horse, her head bent, waiting.

He wanted to touch her hair, to raise her face to his, to tell her that the thought of her was all that kept him alive. Instead he said, "I have seen your father."

She raised her head. Her green eyes were wide, startled. "Is he all right?"

"Yes, Sarah, he's all right. There are some company things he has to take care of, so he needed to stay a few more days. I'll go back later in the week

301

to get him." His face was expressionless. "I've arranged for an escort. O'Brien's leaving the troop. He'll take you to Texas."

It was as though a veil suddenly covered the green eyes. "Thank you for seeing him," she said. Her voice was formal. "Let me take your horse."

"No, no, I'll take him," O'Brien said. "Luis hasn't slept more than a hour or two for the last four days. Get some food into him and put him to bed."

Luis followed her into the house, almost staggering with fatigue.

"Where is the baby?"

"With Josefina. Sit down. Let me help you with your boots."

She turned her back to him, pulling at first one and then the other, biting her lips when she saw the bloodied socks. "You should soak your feet," she said.

"Later."

"All right. I'll get you something to eat."

He nodded, too weary to speak.

She hurried to the fireplace and spooned a good portion of stew into a bowl. But when she went back to him he was already asleep, the upper half of his body on the bed, his feet on the floor. She put the bowl down, and lifting his legs, eased them up on the bed. And then, careful not to wake him, she opened the top button of his shirt and of his pants, and pulled a serape over him.

She looked down at him, dirty, sweat-stained, unshaven, dark hollows under his eyes, his face lined with fatigue.

She stood beside him for a long time. And then she went and sat in the chair across the room where she could watch him.

Chapter 37

Charlie Finch had never fainted in his life, but he came close to it the morning that Luis Vega walked through the crumbled wall of his living room and told him that Sarah was alive.

"Where is your brandy?" Luis asked, and hurried to get it when Finch indicated the chest in the corner. He held the older man's hand steady while he drank, and then led him to a chair.

And Charlie Finch had never killed a man. He'd come close to it that morning at the Ortiz house when he'd found Andres with Sarah. And he came close to it again when Luis, sitting across from him, told him all that he had done to Sarah these past five months.

"Why?" he asked over and over again. "In God's name, why? You loved her once. You wanted to marry her. I thought later, when she became engaged to Andres, that I'd made a terrible mistake making the two of you wait. I blamed myself when she said she was going to marry that bastard. But I'd stopped her once, I couldn't interfere again."

He poured himself another brandy. "She loved you from the moment she saw you at the President's Ball," he said, his voice hoarse with pain. "Now you tell me she's been your *prisoner*. What kind of man are you?"

"A stupid one," Luis said. "I can't ask you to understand or forgive me. I can never make up to either you or Sarah all the harm I've done you. All I can do now is get out of your lives. I'll come back for you in a few days and take you to her. Then I'll furnish you with an escort to take you to Texas.

"There's one more thing, Señor Finch. Sarah and I are married."

"But I thought . . ."

"We were married by a priest, señor. It was done against her will. As soon as things are back to normal I'll see the bishop and have the marriage annulled."

Now, four days later, Finch rode beside Luis on the way to see his daughter. She was waiting for them, standing on the steps of the adobe house, the child that Luis had told him about in her arms. She's not a girl anymore, he thought suddenly and sadly. She's a woman.

"Sarah, Sarah," he said over and over again, feeling the tears sting his eyes when he held her in his arms. "Are you all right? Is this your friend's baby?" He held her away from him, looked at her, then pulled her to him, hugging her hard, releasing her when the baby gave a wail of protest.

"Five months," he said. "Five awful months. I didn't even know you were in Mexico until I had word that the payroll car didn't get through—and that you'd been with the men. Christ! I almost lost my mind. Then when Sam and young Jed were brought to Torreon . . ."

"Thank God," she said. "Were they all right?"

"Dehydrated. They'd tried to walk to a village, and some *campesinos* found them, and somebody notified us. When we talked to them they told us what happened to you—that you'd been carried off by the Villistas." His glance flicked to Luis. "I even thought of trying to find you, to see if you could find Sarah for me." His face tightened. "There's no way in the world I would ever have guessed that you were the one who . . ."

"Don't, Dad," Sarah said. "Not now."

He tried to relax the hands that he had balled into fists. "There was no news, nothing, until I got a message saying you were being held for ransom. I got the

304

money and went to the silos outside of town, just as I was instructed to do. I waited three days, but nobody came. I thought they'd killed you."

She took his arm and led him into the house. "Sit down," she said. "I'll get you some coffee."

"Has it been bad, Sarah?"

"Some of it has. But it's over now."

"Yes. We're leaving tomorrow. Luis said he'd give us an escort."

"Sergeant O'Brien." She smiled. "Jose Alfredo Antonio O'Brien. You'll like him."

"I won't like anybody who's associated with Vega."

"O'Brien didn't have any part in my capture. He wasn't a member of the troop then. I'd tried to escape—with Teresa. Sergeant O'Brien found us in the desert. He was a Federal soldier. It was later that he joined forces with Luis."

"So damned much has happened since I've seen you. I'll never get caught up."

"We'll have plenty of time for that when we get back home."

Home.

She tried to say goodbye to Silvia and to Conchita, to old Josefina and the others. But how can you say goodbye to people you've slept beside and fought beside and wept beside? People you've grown to love. Her words were awkward and fumbling. There was so much she wanted to say to each of them, but the words wouldn't come. Silvia, her strong face set in a frown as she embraced Sarah. Old Josefina, who wept and wailed. Conchita, who tried to be flippant and burst into tears. Francisco, dark and brooding. Unable to speak. Shaking her hand, squeezing it so hard she bit her lip to keep from wincing.

Pedro Garcia, who planted a moist kiss on her cheek and patted her shoulder.

"Take care of Silvia," she said.

"Take care of Silvia! She is the one who takes care of me! 'Shave your bread, trim your moustache, change your clothes, wipe your feet, don't drink

305

pulque.' My life is no longer my own.'' He winked at
her. ''I tell you a secret, Sarah. I let her order me
around because it makes her happy. She is one hell of
a woman.''

''You're right, Pedro. She's one hell of a woman.''

''We'll miss you, *gringa*.''

''And I'll miss you.''

All of you.

Late that afternoon, when gray clouds scudded
across the December sky, she climbed the hill above
the town. She looked out at the dry plains, the tall
cactus reaching with spiny fingers toward the sky, the
mesquite, the alamos, the purple-shadowed mountains
in the distance. And below at the village of Olivares.
She smelled the smoke coming from the chimneys, the
odor of roasting meat and corn and chilis. She listened
with her heart to the sound of birds as they came to
roost in the cottonwood trees, and the bells calling the
people to evening mass.

She watched the black-shawled women hurrying
down the dusty street toward the church. Olivares had
been their home, for a while. But tomorrow, or the
next day, they would move on, to the desert, or the
mountains. Wherever their men went, like Ruth they
would also go.

Mexico. The land and the people. But not her land,
not her people.

She pulled the rebozo closer, feeling chilled by the
cold December wind.

Luis was waiting for her at the bottom of the hill.
''I have to ride out tonight,'' he said. ''I'll be back
tomorrow, but not before you leave.'' He hesitated,
''There are many things I want to say to you. I have
been cruel and unjust. I used to love to punish you.
And I'm more sorry for that than anything else I have
done to you. Love should be the kindest thing a man
can do, not the cruelest.''

She nodded, unable to answer him, accepting his
words.

''You have a great deal to give to a man, Sarah.

Warmth and charm and passion. I've misused them. I hope no other man ever does."

Another man, she thought. He speaks to me of another man.

"Where will you go from here?" she asked.

"I'm not sure. I'll know tomorrow. We'll leave the day after. There are a lot of towns between here and Mexico City. A lot of battles to be fought and won."

"And when will it end?"

"*¿Quién sabe?* Sarah. *¿Quién sabe?* When Huerta is gone. When Mexico is free again. We've come too far and sacrificed too much to stop now."

"Yes, I know."

She didn't know what else to say, what else to do. She'd waited for this moment for almost six months, and now that it was here she didn't know what to do with it. She'd hated Luis. And she'd loved Luis. He'd been a part of her life for so long that she couldn't imagine her life without him.

"Goodbye," she said, holding her hand out. *"Vaya con Dios."*

"Thank you, Sarah." He took her hand and held it for a moment. Then he let it go and touched her hair. "It will grow," he said.

"Yes." She pulled the rebozo tighter around her shoulders.

"You're cold," he said. "You'd better go in."

"Yes."

"Goodnight, Sarah."

"Goodbye, Luis."

Chapter 38

The moon, butter-yellow big, crested the mountain as he rode into Olivares the next night. The air was cold and clear and clean. And so silent that he could hear the dry stalks of corn rustling in the wind.

"*¿Quién es?*" a sentry called.

"Vega."

"*Buenas noches,* Captain. Does it go well?"

"It goes well, *compañero*. We leave at dawn."

"*Bueno!* It's time we were on the move. My woman is packing. Where will we go, Captain?"

"To the south."

"That's good. Good. Maybe we'll finally get our hands on that devil Huerta. But I talk too long, you are tired. Sleep well. God knows when we will have a roof over our heads again."

The adobe houses gleamed white in the moonlight. He could hear the faint whisper of voices, the sound of a guitar, the laughter of a woman.

He hated going to his house. His and Sarah's house. It was strange, even when he thought he'd hated her he'd found a peculiar comfort in returning to the warmth of her presence each night, to the glow of lamplight through the window of a house, or the canvas of a tent. It was a coming home if she was there.

There'd be no light in his house tonight. It was finished. He'd let her go without a word. *"Vaya con Dios,"* she'd said to him, "Go with God."

His horse moved slowly down the dusty street to the house at the end. And when, through the darkness, he saw an amber light in the window, he thought that Silvia had come to light the lamp.

He tied his horse on the hitching rail and opened the door. Sarah leaned over the bed, packing his saddlebags.

"What are you doing?"

"Packing."

"But you were supposed to leave this morning. What happened? Why didn't O'Brien leave?"

"He did."

"But what . . . ? Where are your father and the baby?"

"With O'Brien. Father and Aunt Clara will take care of Sarita until I . . . until we get her."

He put his hand on the doorjamb. His mouth was dry.

"Come in and close the door," she said crossly. "You're letting the cold in."

"You didn't go."

"I didn't go." Her voice was defiant. She crossed to the fireplace and began to stir a pot of soup.

"Leave that alone!" He crossed the room in three strides, reaching for her, taking the spoon out of her hands. "Why didn't you go?"

"You know."

He shook her. "Tell me!"

"Because I'm your wife." Her eyes were angry. "And I'm going to go on being your wife until the day I die. I'm going to follow you all over Mexico if I have to. I'm going to be your *soldadera* and whatever else you want me to be. And if Marta Solis ever comes near you again I'll shoot her!"

"It would be better for you to wait for me in San Antonio. When this is over . . ."

"No!" Her voice shook with rage. "I won't be sent packing."

309

"It's a hard life."

"It's the life I want." She pulled away from him. "Unless you can tell me that you don't love me. If you can look at me now and tell me that, then I'll leave."

His hands tightened on her arms. "Of course I love you. I've loved you from the first moment I saw you. Even when I didn't show it, Sarah. Even when I thought I hated you there was a part of me that cried out to you."

He pulled her into his arms, holding her quietly, one hand caressing her hair. "Even when I did this to you," he said. "Maybe you can forgive me, Sarah, but I can never forgive myself."

She leaned away from him. "Yes you can. We're not going to think about what's past, we're going to think of what lies ahead. The revolution won't last forever, and when it's over we'll rebuild the hacienda. We'll make a life for ourselves—and for Sarita and Charlie and Luisito and Ann Maria."

His eyes widened. "I know who Sarita is, but who in the hell are Charlie, Luisito, and Ann Maria?"

"The children I decided three years ago that we'd have."

She saw his eyes, that had been cold for so long, warm with life. In a voice husky with feeling he said, "The revolution will end soon. Perhaps if we rehearse now . . ."

Her smile was bold, joyful. "I've heard that practice makes perfect," she said. "Shall we practice then?"

As they lay together afterwards in front of the fire, she remembered the words of the song that Paco Gonzales had sung on that day six months ago:

> We are the children of the night
> Who wander aimlessly in the darkness.
> The beautiful moon with its golden rays
> Is the companion of our sorrows.

But she was not going to be a companion of sorrows. She was going to be a companion of joys.

She turned her head into the hollow of his shoulder and whispered, "Companion of my joys. Companion of my joys."

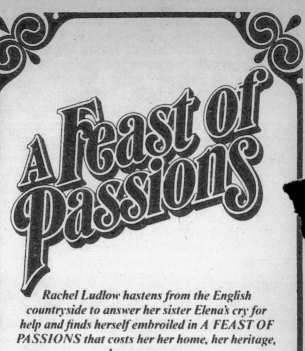

Romance & Adventure

ew and exciting romantic fiction—passionate
strong-willed characters with deep feelings
making crucial decisions in every situation
imaginable—each more thrilling than the last.

**Read these dramatic and colorful novels—from
Pocket Books/Richard Gallen Publications**

___	83164	**ROSEWOOD** Petra Leigh	$2.50
___	83165	**THE ENCHANTRESS** Katherine Yorke	$2.50
___	83233	**REAP THE WILD** **HARVEST** Elizabeth Bright	$2.75
___	83216	**BURNING SECRETS** Susanna Good	$2.75

POCKET BOOKS/RICHARD GALLEN PUBLICATIONS
Department RG
1230 Avenue of the Americas
New York, N.Y. 10020

Please send me the books I have checked above. I am enclosing $_____
(please add 50¢ to cover postage and handling for each order, N.Y.S. and N.Y.C.
residents please add appropriate sales tax). Send check or money order—no
cash or C.O.D.s please. Allow up to six weeks for delivery.

NAME_____

ADDRESS_____

CITY_____ STATE/ZIP_____

RG 10-79